THE
CANNABIS
PREACHER

SERMON ONE

SABINE FRISCH

Publishing Services provided by Paper Raven Books LLC

Printed in the United States of America

First Printing, 2022

Hardcover ISBN: 978-0-9878580-2-3

Paperback ISBN: 978-0-9878580-1-6

PROLOGUE

The congregation, sitting shoulder to shoulder in the pews now.

Smiling, he let the curtain drop, stepping back into the vestibule behind the altar. Gently, he took off his gold watch, placing it into the little cupboard. Not that the congregation would begrudge him it, really, but rubbing their noses in it…that would be a mistake, and he seldom made any of those.

Straightening up, he took a deep breath, feeling the energy of the crowd out there. His people. Eager to hear what he had to say, ready to believe—ready to give. Like a trickle he felt that stream of energy, and he pulled it in closer, seductively, teasingly.

Closing his eyes, he parted the curtains and stepped out.

Big, confident strides. Then, hands on either side of the plain wooden pulpit, he drew in even more of their energy with every breath he took.

Silence—for a moment, he let it just hang there, letting the tension build.

"It's Friday," he finally said in a voice so low that people in the last row would have to strain to hear. "It's Friday." A hitch in his voice and he let the sentence trail off.

The curtain behind him moved ever so slightly, and a pair of dark eyes appeared, watching the preacher, taking in every movement and every single word.

The dark red velvet curtain surrounded him, spilled and pooled over the small bony body, almost swallowing him up as the preacher now slowly raised his hands.

A drumroll slowly built somewhere, like unseen thunder. You didn't know if you actually heard it or just felt it in your bones. The boy knew it came from several high-tech loudspeakers, cleverly concealed in the decorative woodwork of the room, controlled with a minute switch in the side of the pulpit.

"It's Friday. Jesus is praying, Judas is betraying—but Sunday's coming." The preacher's voice rose along with the invisible thunder, and the boy could not take his eyes off him. "The crowd is vilifying, but they don't even know...that Sunday is coming."

The voice rose, trembling on the high pitches. "Sunday is coming." A hoarse breath, all eyes in the room on the preacher whose hands stretched toward the crowd, like he was drawing something from them, taking it and drawing it inside of himself.

"It's Friday—but Sunday is coming," the boy whispered, trying for the same intonation, the same drama, forming his hands into fists.

A hand landed heavily on his shoulder, pulling him back behind the curtain.

"What are you doing back here?"

His mother put her hand over his mouth and pulled him none too gently into the room behind the altar and the great big plush office behind that.

"Now hush. You can watch it from here."

With a flick of her hand, she released the grand television screen, carefully hidden behind an ordinary wooden panel, pushed the boy into one of the plump couches, and pointed her index finger at him. No words were needed; he only nodded and watched the giant screen, where his father appeared once again.

"It's Friday, people, but Sunday, Sunday is coming."

ONE

"Afternoon, Connor, my friend. Fancy meeting you here, at this time of the day."

He slid onto a bar stool beside Connor and clapped him on the back, continuing sarcastically, "Who would think to find you here?"

He grinned broadly and winked at the bartender. "Vodka soda, Brittany, easy on the soda."

"Or you," Connor said, "Rafael, in a bar on a Wednesday at two in the afternoon."

"What bar?" Rafael Covin asked, sweeping his hands around the room. "This is a classy dining establishment. I'm only here to have lunch." He winked at the bartender and took a sip of his drink. "Celebrating another deal done. Aah, it's almost no fun when it's that easy, you know." He nodded after a couple, husband and wife, who were just leaving the dining room. "Million-dollar renovation, which will easily come out at a million and a half when it's all said and done—rising costs, don't you know, and problems we discovered too late—and they'll still think they're getting off easy."

"You're a crook, Rafael."

"And you're not? What's up with you today? Looking like that, you couldn't sell a cold beer on the hottest day of the summer."

"Yeah, I know," Connor growled, taking the rest of his wine in one single swig, nodding when the bartender lifted the bottle in a silent question.

"Let me guess—deal gone south?"

1

Connor nodded. "So far south it's officially off the map."

"Sucks. And you're taking the heat?"

Another nod. "Same ole, same ole."

"Indeed." Rafael twirled the plastic stir stick in his drink. "Things don't work out, everyone's looking for a scapegoat, and you and I, my friend, well, we still make the best ones."

"Drink to that." Connor toasted and took another swig of wine.

"Better times coming, though. I can feel it."

Rafael nodded slowly, signaling the bartender. Knowing Connor Beauregard, he could believe that. *The deal is dead; long live the next deal.* Rafael had seen him pull more rabbits out of more hats when it came to funding oddball projects than was humanly possible. He simply believed him.

Of course, he also knew him well enough not to give him any money—none of his own, anyway. But he'd watched him operate, and he'd been there when Connor was pitching a project, and if there was anyone better than Rafael Covin at separating people from their hard-earned money, it was the man sitting beside him now.

Not when he was in a miserable mood like this, but when he was on...

"Anything interesting on the horizon?"

Connor shook his head and took another gulp of his wine. "Looking for a project—a good one."

"So what exactly happened to the oil, whatever it was?"

"Don't want to talk about that just now. Screw it."

"But I thought..."

He shook his head, turned his barstool just a little so he could see out the panoramic window, and allowed himself a little smile. It never failed, up here in the revolving restaurant on top of The Lighthouse, looking out over the harbor, listening to lowkey jazz over the hidden speakers, drinking their best wine—this was where the best ideas came from. Surrounded by luxury, this was where he built the future. "One deal at a time."

On that note he picked up the little bar menu and looked over the current offerings.

2

"Who's in the kitchen today, Brittany," he asked of the bartender, "Marcel or Jonas?"

"Marcel," the little blonde answered and picked up his empty glass with a questioning look.

Connor nodded, straightening up a bit. "Yes and yes. Have Marcel make up a plate of oysters for us, the way I like them."

"Oysters," Rafael chuckled. "The man is cooking up something, I'd say."

Connor steepled his fingers and put them against his lips.

"What we need now," he said, speaking slowly and enunciating every word as if it were a precious commodity, "is a project. A good, juicy deal nobody can pass up. Something that makes money, lots of it. Something—you just can't say no to."

He smiled a little, and Rafael could almost hear him speak. *Ladies and gentlemen, what we have here is something you just can't say no to.* And his hands would just reach out to them, as if drawing them in.

"Gunrunning," he half joked, to distract himself from the hypnotic image of Connor, "drugs, prostitution."

"No, nothing illegal!"

Connor rolled his eyes to the ceiling and shook his head, but between the two of them, they knew that the very definition of illegal was a malleable concept in the financial world. It had never stopped either one of them. There was always a way to make it happen.

"But I like the way you're thinking."

Marcel brought out the plate of oysters for the two men, with all of the sauces Connor liked, and a smaller portion of the ones Rafael liked. A fact that did not go unnoticed by the smaller man.

"What is it with him? You slip him 100 now and then to get the preferential treatment or what?" Rafael groused, picking up a lemon wedge. "Almost like you're the bloody president or something."

"Always tip the staff." Connor dipped the silver spoon into the sauce and slurped his oyster. "Your life will be that much easier every single day. You, my friend, are just too cheap to realize it."

"Don't believe in throwing money away," Rafael groused and helped himself. "These guys make a decent living as it is."

"These guys..." Another oyster disappeared. "Marcel is a wizard in the kitchen. Matter of fact, the other day we were sitting around just talking, bar mostly empty, and he told me..." The hand holding the oyster lowered, and his eyes narrowed a bit. "Well shit!"

"Something wrong?" Rafael's hand pulled back as quickly as it had reached for the next oyster. "The food?"

"What was it you said earlier? Say it again."

"Say what?"

"I said what we need is a deal, something people can't say no to. And you said... Fuck, Rafael, say it again."

"I don't know. I was just bullshitting. I said gunrunning, drugs, prostitution."

"Drugs."

"Right. I don't think either you or Marcel is going to drive out into the desert in a Winnebago and cook up some meth, no matter how easy it looked on TV."

"Not crystal meth, my friend," Connor said, his gaze narrowing even more. "No, I'm talking about something much better."

"Better?"

"Way better—and legal!"

His breath came a little faster, and his eyes started to get that gloss Rafael had seen many a time before. Always when there was an idea—a monumental one. Something big.

"Cannabis!"

"Great, repeat our misspent youth? You going to go out and sell dime bags, that's your big plan?"

"No dime bags, my friend." Connor's eyes never left the panorama beyond the window, but he did not see any of it. His deal was taking shape inside his head, growing, expanding.

"Marcel told me that his, uh, partner."

"Partner?"

"Friend, partner, don't know if they are a couple or not, but the guy he hangs with. He's also a chef, and he slipped and fell in the kitchen just recently."

"OK, so?"

"Broke his tailbone—he was in excruciating pain."

"Poor bastard, I feel for him. Still don't know where this is going."

"They go to this weird-ass doctor down here in the harbor district somewhere. Guy who will give you anything if you ask for it."

"OK, still with you."

"And he prescribes cannabis to Marcel's buddy."

Rafael stopped for a moment and made a face. "Prescribed it, as in a doctor's note saying you can go smoke a joint? You're joking, right?"

"That's what I thought. But no, it's completely for real—and legal. And you don't smoke the stuff when it's medicinal by the way, not unless you want to. Comes as a pill, comes as a liquid, comes as anything you want. Even mixed into some crazy-ass foods if that's more your style."

"Fascinating story, Connor, but unless you want to serve pot brownies at your next investors' meeting, I still don't quite know where you're going with this one."

Connor nodded and turned away from the fifteenth-floor panorama out there, facing his friend full-on. The wild gleam in his eyes had taken over now, to the point his entire face seemed to glow with an eerie kind of force. Light and shadows, his eyes glowing wildly, it was hard to look away.

"Jason, Marcel's friend, is standing there in the most enviable position of having a doctor's note for cannabis in his hands, and you know what happens?"

"I do not know what happens." Rafael played the game because he knew if he did not, the story would never come to an end. "So?"

"He can't find a place to buy the stuff—anywhere."

"Tough shit. And?"

"And." Connor opened his arms, inviting an invisible crowd that only existed in his head. "And that's where we come in. We are going to be that place."

"That..."

"We are going to grow and package cannabis." He grinned as if he had just invented the stuff.

"Yeah, right. You can't possibly tell me that you, Connor Beauregard, guy who lives in a suit and $500 loafers, are going to go out there and water plants in a greenhouse every day. Come on—let's go back to my office, and we'll work out a couple of construction deals. Matter of fact, there's this tender for the city I'm working on. Road works, could be pretty good."

"No greenhouse, no watering." Connor shook his head. "We're going to go huge. We are going to be the biggest producer in the country. Hydroponics, special grow lights, whatever it takes, we are going to do it. We are going to be the Coca-Cola of cannabis, selling online, to patients like Jason—sick people who need the stuff and can't get it anywhere else."

"Recreational?"

"Some, maybe. Certainly not officially." Connor shook his head. "You know it's only legal for medical purposes, at least for the moment. Shit, we are not going to screw it up, but there might be, well, you know, collateral opportunities, shall we say."

The oysters were gone, and Connor signaled for more wine. "We are going to be huge. You know what the cash potential is here. I mean, the stuff just—grows. You don't have to do anything, you don't have to make anything, you just...I don't know, seed it out or something."

"You don't know."

"No, I don't know how to grow cannabis, Rafael." Connor's voice rose just a touch, and another man at the far end of the bar looked their way. "I don't know...yet. But if I have learned anything in my life, there's always an expert out there on anything you want to know.

And I am going to find him, and I'm going to make him work for me, and then…" He rubbed his thumb and forefinger together.

"Cash city, my brother. You in?"

"I don't know…"

"Does not come any better than this, bro. Matter of fact, look at this." He pulled out his cell phone, ignoring the little red dot that told him 19 messages had been left, and swiped his fingers over the screen madly, "American Cannabis—ACNS—tell me what you think their stock trades at?"

"Cannabis—trading on the stock exchange."

"They do indeed. I told you, it's big business, and we are going to get into it."

"But…"

"40 bucks a share."

"Still."

"Say it with me, slowly this time, *40 bucks a share*, and they just got into this. Dammit, some guy was pitching it to me a couple of months ago, and I said no. I was too deep into oil at that point." Connor put the cell phone away again and frowned. "Matter of fact, I was reading about these guys in the paper the other day. Big public outcry because they had some sort of an infection and had to destroy an entire harvest. Who is watching the people that grow medicine, that kind of thing. Fact is, they have no idea what they're doing. They're just blundering along, trying not to go under. But the thing is they've got so many orders they can't fill 'em. Started this dinky little company with a greenhouse for Christ's sake."

"Again with the greenhouse!"

"A greenhouse! They admit they have no clue. This is not how they should be doing it. And goddammit if they did not issue their shares at a dollar 18 months ago."

"Wait, wait, wait, wait—waaait just one goddamn minute. A dollar, 18 months ago?"

Connor nodded, smiling now. "You are catching on, my friend. One lousy dollar, 18 months ago."

"And now they're at 40."

"Now they're at 40."

"So that's..."

"That's just fucking awesome, my friend," Connor said in a hoarse whisper. "And the best part is we are going to top it."

"Shit."

Rafael drained his wine glass in one single swig, still trying to follow Connor's lead. He used to joke that Connor was the evil sorcerer. If you looked him in the eye while he was spinning a deal, he cast a spell, and you were a goner. He did not want to, but a dollar to 40—in 18 months? He would have to look this one up.

"Don't bother looking it up, my friend." That voice, the one that pulled you in. "Just tell me—are you in or not?"

"In." Rafael nodded without even thinking about it. Drugs, one of the most recession-resistant businesses he knew.

"I know a couple of people," he said after a minute. "People who are going to be ready to drop the big bucks."

"That's the kind of people we like." Connor smiled. "Rule number one?"

"We don't play with our own money," Rafael said and offered his fist.

Bump. "We don't play with our own money."

Connor gathered his stuff, the phone, the iPad he carried everywhere, and his ragged old wallet. He told people it had been his father's, and he had paid for his first deal with cash out of this wallet, always a good story. Made him look like the traditional, family-oriented man, the kind who would have tacked up a dollar bill over his desk, *first dollar ever earned*. In reality, he went down to the Goodwill store every now and then and bought a new ragged one.

Why? Because it made no sense that he would carry a ragged old thing in the pocket of a Brioni suit. Which made people ask. Which gave him an in to start the story and spin the tale.

"Tomorrow," he said, "right here—same time. I'll have a business plan with me. We'll look over it, fine-tune it, then let loose. Let your people know you have something big in the pipeline. Bigger than big."

Rafael nodded. A business plan that made sense and could sell the deal to people? In 24 hours? Couldn't be done, unless you were Connor Beauregard, fired up on a deal, putting everything in to it.

Then it could be done.

Then it was pure gold.

Shit, he would have to work for years to come up with an absolutely prime deal to top this one, which, considering how much money they stood to make, might not even be necessary.

Rafael grinned and shook his head watching Connor basically run to the elevator. He'd hole up in his tenth-floor luxury apartment and write a business plan worth millions of dollars, and that you could bet the farm on.

Brittany discreetly put a little black folder containing the bill on the bar in front of him, and Rafael swore silently.

Of course, the bastard had stiffed him. Typical Connor Beauregard. And you never noticed until it was all over.

TWO

It took two more days before the men met again. Those two days had been studded with phone calls and dozens of emails, going back and forth with segments of the executive summary Connor was creating. With frightening speed, he pulled together facts and figures he had dug up, then pieced together with information from other companies' plans, finally weaving it into a complete and dazzling tapestry.

Every time Rafael read a piece of it, he shook his head. This was the man who had barely known how to roll a joint yesterday. Today, he was putting together something so convincing and seductive Rafael himself had to pause now and then and remind himself who he was dealing with.

Finally, he received the critical phone call. "It's time. You have any luck sourcing potential partners?"

"I have a few in mind."

"Not a few. No more than two or three. We want a core group who understands business and has the money, resources, and connections to make this happen. I thought I was clear about that."

"Perfectly clear—it's just not the kind of business that..."

"It's the kind of business that will make fucking millions. Now do you have the contacts or not?"

"I have the contacts, relax." Rafael nodded, though Connor of course did not see it. Through his construction business and his many government contracts, he knew people in the highest ranks, people who had money that needed an outlet, a target, people who understood that the really big money was only paid out for the really big risk.

"I have three guys who are ready now to hear what you have to say."

"'K. They have the money and the backgrounds? I'm not going to put this together with losers on the payroll, you know that, right? No losers, no leeches."

"Not a loser among them. Businessmen, government contractor—all connected, all know what we are doing. Our kind of people."

"Good man." Connor paused for a minute, and Rafael could almost see him, way up above the town, staring out the picture window, preparing for the moment when he would tell the 'story' to these men. Everything was 'the story' for Connor.

"Tomorrow," he finally said. "Three p.m. at La Cosa. I'll reserve the private dining room, make the presentation—and whoever is in stays for dinner."

Again, typical Connor, nothing too good for the show. The city's most expensive restaurant, the private dining room, and an unspoken agreement. Whoever was in stayed for dinner. Drama! And he would milk it for everything it was worth.

Not for the first time in his life, Rafael felt a twinge of envy—more like a punch to the gut. Yeah, construction had been good to him. And he knew exactly how to wheel and deal the kind of people who made the big decisions. Whose kids were going to college and needed the compact car—Rafael just 'happened to have a spare.' Whose wife had a pet charity that needed support, who owed money. Rafael kept his eyes and ears open and traded in that information. It had always been good to him.

Connor, on the other hand, Connor simply stood up and started spinning a tale. Wove a story out of nothing right in front of everyone's eyes, and when he had them all in tears... the wallets would open.

It didn't really matter if he was collecting money for some charity or other or pitching the latest business project. Rafael yearned for that kind of talent.

But this particular project was shaping up to need both of them. Because, Rafael reasoned, once you got the damn thing off the ground, who would be there with contacts into the government, who would be there who knew the right people, knew what to offer them and what to avoid?

THREE

Saturday night at La Cosa, you pretty much had to be somebody to even see the inside of the place. People had been known to pay obscene amounts of money to book a wedding or some other private function there, but it happened on the rarest of occasions. Usually when a staff member needed money.

Connor Beauregard, on the other hand, was somebody. He had facilitated a share deal a few years ago for the owner when he was renovating and short of cash. He got a number of shares in an exploration company, sold them at the perfect time, made money, everybody was happy, and Connor had a private table for life. Or the private dining room, as the case might have been.

It was really just a small back room, held maybe 20 people, five round tables with plush chairs, plush carpeting, expensive original artwork on the walls, and a state-of-the-art entertainment system. At the push of a button, a 10-by-10-foot screen descended from its hiding place in the ceiling.

Connor had never even looked at the available microphones. But he most certainly appreciated all the little gadgets that allowed him to put his phone on the table next to him, hold a little remote control in his hand, and rise, already speaking to his audience, certain that, behind him, the images on the screen would change, almost by magic, as he spoke. Displaying images, tables, facts, figures, all perfectly synchronized to his voice.

Connor now stood casually leaning against the little bar that served the private dining room exclusively. For the moment, he held a highball glass containing water and ice. He knew enough to take it easy until it was all said and done. Rafael unpacked a few executive presentations out of an envelope, hastily printed down at the local printshop, glossy paper, nice binding.

He straightened his tie, looking down at his own executive summary. He had allowed himself a tiny image of a cannabis leaf on every page, almost subliminal, just where the page number was. Other than that, the entire presentation had the same professional look and feel of the best bank-prepared presentation. He had seen too many other guys making their presentations in baggy jeans and running shoes, long hair and beards. Everything about Connor said class and expertise, the kind of guy you could trust.

The door opened, and a man entered slowly, nodding at Connor, smiling at Rafael.

"Rafael, my man, how are you?"

"Perfect." Rafael moved to stand between the two men. "Simon, Connor Beauregard. Connor, Simon Graff, of Graff Security."

"Pleasure to meet you," Connor said, flashing his sincerest smile. "Graff Securities, best CCTV and electronic surveillance system you could wish for. I hear First National hired you to have a look at their private vault security."

"Well, they might have asked my advice." Simon shook Connor's hand, smiling. "I am impressed by your knowledge. That little fact didn't cover more than three lines in the paper."

"I make it my business to know the people I'm working with," Connor said and gestured to the bar. "Can Brittany start you off with a drink? Please let her know what you'd like."

Two more men were entering the room: Josh Novak, head of a large real estate brokerage, and a man who introduced himself only as Al. For a moment, that abrupt introduction disturbed Connor, although he had learned to trust Rafael's judgment. If the guy was here by invitation, he had something to offer. They exchanged a look, and Rafael nodded almost imperceptibly—*he's worth it.*

OK.

"Al, glad you could join us tonight. We have an interesting presentation prepared for all of you."

"So Rafael tells me," Al said slowly. Connor thought he detected a trace of an accent, but couldn't immediately place it. Damn, what happened to his magic? Usually he could sum up in two minutes in where someone was from, what his social background was, and, usually, what business he worked in. This time—nothing. Al could be the head of a multinational company or Rafael's mailman for all he could read. He wasn't giving anything away, just a bland smile and firm handshake.

"You must have done business with Rafael for a long time then." Assuming that if Rafael had brought him here tonight…

"I have known Rafael's family for a very long time, Mr. Beauregard," Al said, smiling, "and I may even have done business with him at one point or another. But the day-to-day affairs of my various businesses unfortunately pass me by most of the time. I am much more interested in opportunities like this one."

"You won't be disappointed." Connor smiled and silently cussed out Rafael for not preparing him better.

Al turned away as the staff offered drinks and hors d'oeuvres, and Connor took the opportunity to stand behind Rafael.

"What's the deal with that guy?" he asked quietly, casually taking a glass off a waiter's tray. "Al, that's it? Nothing else?"

"And that's all he'll ever give you," Rafael replied just as quietly. "That man right there has enough money to buy this entire city, only nobody knows it, or him. He's got his hands in so many businesses you can't make a move within a 100-mile radius without dealing with one of his people."

"Well, let me know next time. I hate surprises."

Connor smiled despite his sharp tone. It appeared Rafael had chosen well. The three men here represented the things he wanted most at the moment: cash, connections, and reputation. The first two would aid in the getting the business up and running; the last would do nothing but look good on the company profile. So...let the show begin.

"Thank you for coming out here tonight, gentlemen," he said softly. "You all know Rafael, and I am sure he has told you plenty about me. I bring to the table 20 years of experience creating and managing cutting-edge companies."

A small exaggeration, but it sounded good. "I have taken many a business plan like this one," he lifted his executive summary and let it slide to the black marble of the table again, "and made it big, very big. This is what I do. But even I have to tell you—this is one of the most promising I have seen in my entire career. Every now and then, a deal comes along that is so good, so perfect—you're almost in awe of it. This, gentlemen...is it."

Small push of a button and behind him, the screen came to life. Close-up of a green plant, and out of the middle came the words *Perfect Cannabis Products*.

The letters turned, enlarged, and finally settled into a tall red title on the screen.

"As you may know, there are thousands of patients today suffering from chronic pain, cancers, depression, and the like. There is help for all of these patients." Another flick of the fingers, and a small dish of pills appeared superimposed over a handful of green leaves.

"The research is ongoing, but the clinical applications of cannabis and cannabinoids are expanding almost daily. There is a grand need for a product like this, a natural product, yet up until now, there hasn't been a producer capable of high volume, high quality, and consistent production in line with the current health regulations."

He let the images behind him advance once again, this time to the picture of an enormous modern production facility with a small inset of a high-tech laboratory and a young, pleasant woman peering intently at a reactor vial.

"Gentlemen, we have a market opportunity here. The core business of Perfect Cannabis Products will be the cultivation and proliferation of pharmaceutical-grade cannabis. Forget about greenhouses; forget anything you know about putting little plants out in the backyard and watering them. We, gentlemen… we will be playing God."

Another advance of the slides. A number of rooms side by side, opening to a large corridor, almost like cells. Each one of them had enormous shelves of green cannabis plants growing and an enormous blinding light set into the ceiling. Where did he get all his material from, Rafael wondered. He sounded and looked like he had done this a dozen times, just another round of the same ole, same ole.

"Pharmaceutical-grade cannabis, gentlemen, is grown in hydroponic growth media, under light deprivation conditions. We decide how much light and nutrients, how much water and warmth a plant receives at any time. This is how you create perfection. This is how you play God. There will be no waste whatsoever. Everything is planned from the very beginning of the clone. You heard me right, gentlemen, the clone. We will not be bothering with seeds at all. We will be cloning the finest pharmaceutical strains of cannabis. Proprietary strains that are created for the very medical applications we are looking for."

He gave them a moment to take it all in and took a sip of his water.

"But that is not where it ends, gentlemen. Of course we will produce the plant and extract the cannabinoids, the medicinal compounds in our very own laboratories. But we will go further. We will produce extracts. We will produce inhalants and edible products. All designed to treat the very illness it was prescribed for. Furthermore," now he was really picking up speed, "we will create an online cannabis trading platform. No longer will patients in chronic pain have to spend weeks searching for a suitable provider, walking into a dim back alley somewhere, unsure of the quality they are purchasing. Not with

Perfect Cannabis Products. With your medical marijuana permission card and your number, relief will be just as close as your computer terminal. Customers will be able to order what they need, as needed, and have it delivered via courier the very next day. We, gentlemen, we will change lives."

Connor let that statement hang in the air for a moment and rested his steepled fingers against his mouth. Changing lives. He wanted that to soak into their brains for a moment. They were all here to make money and walk away more rich and successful, but they also wanted to stand there as the model citizen. He could feel the perfect moment in their eyes, feel it in the energy of the room, and clicked on to the next slide. Time for the figures. Without turning to the screen, he knew them by heart.

"This company, gentlemen, is focused on building a state-of-the-art cultivation facility. We will harvest 300 pounds of cannabis from every 20,000 square feet dedicated to this technology. What does this mean? It means we are looking at annual gross revenues of over 7 million US dollars in year one, growing to over 70 within three years...then we expand worldwide!"

Another pause. The figures were all there in black and white on the wall behind him.

"That is one hell of a lot of money, gentlemen," he finally said, eliciting a few cautious laughs. "And that is just the start. Conservative estimates figure somewhere short of 50,000 patients with a legal prescription for marijuana in this area alone. I will remind you that most of these patients still source their marijuana illegally, simply because there is no reliable supplier at present. There are statistical records from the Department of Health circulating at present, reporting 100,000 kilograms of cannabis produced legally last year. 100,000 kilograms. With an average price of $5 per gram being used, that equates to almost a billion dollars of revenue at the moment."

He opened his arms and smiled at the group before him. "And we are going to be the biggest producers yet. Gentlemen, you now have the opportunity to be part of something enormous, a monument that will endure through time." He picked up a strategically placed brand-name soda bottle and held it up for all to see. "There exists in the market brand names and logos everyone the world around recognizes. Gentlemen, we will be the next one. There are no limits."

No one reached for their drink or checked their phone; no one shifted in his seat. Their eyes were focused on him and the soda bottle in his hand. Connection...size...potential...no limits. He stood perfectly still until the silence bordered on uncomfortable. The world leader in producing medical cannabis. He had made that connection in their minds once and for all.

Slowly, his hand lowered, and he continued speaking in a low voice, making them lean in to him to hear.

"There are no limits, and right here in this room, we have the knowledge, the experience, and the resources to make this happen."

He advanced the slides behind him again and walked them quickly through capital expenditures and operating budgets, emphasizing his significant experience in capital markets, his abilities to execute on the objective of listing the company on a public stock exchange, creating near- and long-term value for shareholders.

His speech sped up a little then. Time to wrap it up, while the image of the world's largest cannabis producer was still prominent in their minds.

"We, gentlemen, have the ability to make this happen. I leave you with the executive summary in front of you. I envision founders of the company having control over roughly 10 million shares of the company. Please let me know if you have any questions."

The lights in the room brightened a little, as if by magic. The waiters and bartender entered again, having been summoned by a quick press of a button, and Rafael took his cue and rose.

"Well, thanks everyone for coming out tonight. I think we will need a moment to let all of this information settle in, so how about a round of drinks?"

An almost imperceptible nod from Connor. Tag team perfection. Rafael schmoozed, made everyone feel like his best pal; Connor had the information, the deal...the goods.

Josh Novak approached him first with a few cautious questions, no surprise here. The real estate man had made a lot of money in recent years, and not all of it showed up on his company's books, if rumors were to be trusted. Connor gave him solid answers, no wavering, no hesitation. He never used the words *we might* or *we could*. Failure was not an option, not even a possibility.

He could see Rafael working the other men, making them feel they were part of a specially chosen group. Which indeed they were. Rafael...Connor grinned secretly...Rafael's first investment company had been called *The Chosen Investments Ltd.*

One of the waiters had not completely closed the door to the room on their way out, and someone sitting at the main bar caught his eye. Blond, curvy, dressed in enough designer threads to feed a small African village for a year, Kayla Montecito. She looked his way, and Connor quickly winked at her. They kind of moved in the same circles, and he had used her talents once or twice. Kayla owned one of the largest gossip magazines in the area, and if he needed some dirt on someone, well, she was always there to supply it. She wasn't even above plumping up and polishing the smallest detail until it seemed an enormous scandal... just short of making it up, actually. A handy talent to have, and she employed an army of lawyers making sure no one could ever touch her.

Her kind of assistance never came free, but it was usually worth it.

The next waiter slipped through the door and closed it again, and Connor turned back to the businessmen in the room. Now that they were in the drug business, who knew? Kayla's talents might come in handy a lot more often, he thought and planned to go sit with her for a little while after the show in here was over.

"Simon," he said, clapping the other man on the shoulder. "Are there any questions I could answer for you? I have to tell you—I'm glad Rafael brought you in here today because once our facility is built and running, security will be one of our biggest issues. What better solution than to work with a man who is already a shareholder?"

He smiled; he explained facts and figures. He built a world-leading pharmaceutical company right in the air before them, and by the time dinner came around, everyone was ready to put down their money.

Connor looked over the little group with a happy, warm feeling inside. He and Rafael would be founders. Pity he had to share the honors with the little Columbian fella, but Rafael had the connections, the people, and the clout to bring in someone like the elusive Al.

Al stood at the fringes of the little group, the only one who had never touched the document folder to look over the facts and figures Connor had spent days preparing. He raised his hands and smiled very slightly when Connor approached him.

"Don't try to sell me, Mr. Beauregard. I usually make up my mind very quickly, and once it's made up, it stays there."

"I don't think I need to do a big sell on this project, Al. The facts and figures speak for themselves. As a matter of fact, we are..."

Al raised a finger to silence him. "On the brink of something enormous, I know. I have heard it before, Connor. Believe me...I have."

He took a plain black overcoat from a waiter summoned to fetch it and stuffed a generous tip into the man's pocket.

"You will be hearing from me."

"Let me give you my card."

"No need. I will be in touch shortly."

Connor barely blinked, and the man was gone. For the first time in his career, Connor stood there with his mouth agape, unable to grasp what had just happened.

"Who in blazes?" he muttered, only to find Rafael behind him.

"There are a lot of people out there wondering just that—who in blazes is that man? Trust me. It won't do you any good googling him either. Most of us just call him the Shadow."

Connor picked up the leftover executive summary and stuffed it into his own briefcase.

"Guess that one was a waste."

"Don't be so quick," Rafael said, shaking his head. "That's just his way."

"Not taking the material I sweated over, another personality quirk? Like the first name only thing? I thought only movie stars and singers got away with that."

"Nope." Rafael tipped a finger to his forehead. "He memorizes everything, and on the inside of five minutes. Told me once that he never writes a single fact down, so he won't have to worry about it falling into the wrong hands."

"Well shit." Connor turned away and rolled his shoulders, ostensibly to work out a kink, but for a moment a cold shiver trickled down his back.

Don't be paranoid, he scolded himself. Just a guy with too much money and too many personality quirks.

"Interesting new friends you're making." A much be-ringed hand landed on his arm.

"Kayla." Connor laughed and hugged the woman. "I ought to be angry with you for barging in here, disturbing my presentation."

"Your presentation is over. I just saw Al leaving. Things are over when he leaves."

"You know the guy?" Kayla had just climbed a couple of rungs on his people-ranking scale. "So what is it, weirdo or psycho? Just odd? Anything?"

"Aaah, but isn't that what everybody wants to know?" Kayla laughed, firmly attaching herself to Connor's elbow. "You see, the thing is... not even I, or any one of my many, many reporters, know anything, and believe me, I've paid a small fortune to get dirt on him."

"No dirt?"

"Not a speck. Nothing—nada—zero, less than zero actually. Nobody talks about him, drivers, maids, house staff."

"First name Al."

"Exactly, I wonder how much that kind of loyalty costs you. Rumor has it he never writes anything down, does not own a computer that anyone knows of, and only deals face to face. I'm not even sure he uses a cell phone."

"Interesting." That cold shiver trickled down his back again, but then the waiters showed up with their dinner, and Connor knew the job was not over yet.

"Join us for dinner," he said generously, patting Kayla's elbow, "as long as you don't write about it in that rag you call a paper."

"Would I do that, my love? You and I both know the value of information, don't we?"

Kayla's voice told its own story, of too many nights spent partying, too many vodkas, and too many cigarettes. Nowadays, she stayed away from the wild parties, preached moderation in everything, and featured a version of *how to quit anything in 30 days* in her paper on a regular basis, from smoking to overeating, to dating the wrong men.

Clean living, moderation, humility...a carefully crafted public image, although Connor knew that the bartenders at La Cosa counted among her closest friends.

He had a hard time telling how old she actually was. Probably mid-forties, he guessed.

Nevertheless. Kayla and her magazines might add some value to his project just now.

The power of the press, never to be underestimated at any time, anywhere. Could be just what he needed to advance his project at the perfect time.

"Tell me," he asked, turning on the time-tested Connor Beauregard charm smile. "Just how much of my humble little presentation did you actually overhear? I just happen to have one of these executive summaries left."

"Oh, you know I don't invest in anything but my own paper." She took the folder and swatted him lightly with it. "I heard enough to know that you're talking about some very interesting substances."

"Legally produced substances, strictly for medicinal purposes."

"Never try to bullshit a professional bullshitter, Connor."

He squeezed her elbow and led her to the table where the food was being brought in and his guests had already taken their places.

"Gentlemen, Ms. Kayla Montecito. She is helping us through her chain of newspapers to educate the public about the many medicinal benefits of marijuana."

An almost imperceptible lift of an eyebrow and a small squeeze of his knee under the table.

"What an exciting project, gentlemen. Personally, I can't wait to get started. We are going to change so many lives. And people need to know about all the good work we are doing."

Another small squeeze under the table.

Apparently, he had a press speaker now. But it was going to cost him.

FOUR

The remainder of the evening was becoming a distant memory almost as it happened. But blessed with an eidetic memory, Connor studied and remembered the facts and figures of every project he worked on until they became his personal, ingrained truth. Once he had written his executive summary and memorized it, he never had to be careful about what he said. Every word of it became gospel truth, to be recited whenever needed.

The biggest job in this project was done, convincing Connor Beauregard himself. Now all he had to do was project that conviction.

But all the while, his mind spun away at the riddle of Al.

The remaining two couldn't wait to put down their hard-earned money and say they were in the cannabis business. The cool factor of that statement alone would be worth it for them. But what was it about the South American guy?

Or was he even South American? Dammit, it was hard to tell. Everybody had a category Connor could stick them into so he would know how to approach them...every single person. Seemingly except Al.

Al could be Alvaro or Alonzo, could be Alistair, could be Alfredo, Alfred...

"I need you to tell me how you and Al fit," he finally said to Rafael after everyone except Kayla had left. Kayla had gone back to the bar to look after some refills, and as he watched her sashay through the emptying restaurant, he congratulated himself on his quick thinking.

Bringing her in at the last minute had been a sheer stroke of genius. Simon and Josh were both deeply impressed that he had the 'press' on their side already, and Rafael merely grinned from one ear to the other.

She'd be useful all right, though he knew it would cost him.

"As I said, his family and mine have done business."

"What kind of business?"

"Business." Rafael shrugged. "Different things, different times. Does it really matter?"

"Yeah...it does matter, if this guy becomes part of my company...I want to be able to sleep at night. You know, that kind of thing happens, people lose money, things don't work out. It's a fact of life. At the end of the day, you have to work with people who understand that and aren't going to be at your doorstep wanting their money back. Reasonable people."

"Oh, reasonable, is it?" Rafael laughed. "I don't think anyone would describe Al as reasonable, not by any stretch of the imagination. But let me tell you one thing...if he decides to work with you, you won't have to worry about anyone else messing with you—ever again, reasonable or not."

"What's that supposed to mean now?"

"Think about it, man! You're going to grow cannabis, drugs, for god's sake. Now you can stand there all day long and tell me it's medicinal, but I'm the guy who's here to tell you there are 'elements' out there who are...going to want a piece of it."

"Well, we'll have security."

"Screw security. Simon's little electronic boxes full of little blinking lights are window dressing for the government. You're growing tons of drugs, man. You think a public service body, like, oh, let's say the Hell's Angels just to put a name on it, are going to take this lightly? You think they will welcome you into their party, offer you a drink, and discuss how to share the customer base...all friendly and polite like?"

"I hadn't really gone down that road yet. For starters, this company is going to focus only on the medicinal market."

"That's what you tell yourself so you can go to sleep at night and not have any bad dreams, Conn. If it's you and a bottle of wine late at night and no one is listening, you know there's going to be excess product; you know there's going to be stuff going out the back door. Hell, you're probably counting on it. Cash."

That cold trickle was back. He had thought along those lines, for a minute or two, dismissing it almost immediately.

"So what you're saying is—this Al you brought to my table and introduced to my company is the answer to a question nobody has even asked yet?"

"You could put it that way. Sometimes if you're dealing with a scary guy, or a bunch of them—the easiest thing to do is bring in a guy who is scarier than they are, and suddenly, miraculously, everyone gets along."

Connor licked dry lips and put his steepled fingers against his mouth again to keep them still.

OK, change of plans. Obviously, he had not taken this particular problem seriously enough; he had not thought it would be a problem. Since Rafael had brought it up, now was as good a time as any to deal with it. Capitalize it, work it out, and show everyone that he had covered all the bases and thought of a solution to the most offbeat things that might become a problem.

If indeed Al decided to come into the company—and it bothered his professional pride to the point of irritation that he could not even guess at where the man's thoughts were—if Al was in, he potentially could solve a huge problem for them—fabulous. Fabulous, but then… new problem: who on earth was going to control Al? Who was the bigger guy who would scare him, and was there such a person?

He drew his shoulders together and shivered. God, don't think about that just now. That's down the road a bit. For now, the game was just putting the deal together and making the big times happen.

Rafael shrugged as if he wanted to say, *That's the way it is, Conn,* one of his favorite lines, but Kayla's return made him rise briefly, and the moment was gone.

"Celebrate, boys." Kayla held up a large bottle of the most expensive champagne they carried in this restaurant. "Tonight is all on me. Next stop...the big time."

She sat down beside him, close enough so their legs were touching. Oh yes, the support of the press was going to cost him tonight, but then again, he had promised himself to give it his all to make this project happen, just like all the others before.

FIVE

Grey dawn had barely given way to a brilliantly sunny day when he cautiously untangled himself from Kayla, her mass of blonde hair and her silken sheets, and shook his head to clear the cobwebs of the past night.

On tiptoes Connor collected his clothing and shoes from around the room and made his way to the shower. Despite the alcohol and other excesses of the past night, his mind was already churning away at ideas and newly forming task lists, and he needed to get to his pitiful excuse for an office downtown to work them all out.

On his way out, he tripped over two empty champagne bottles, finest vintage, and grinned to himself. Kayla Montecito had excellent taste; he most certainly had to give her that.

Down on the street, hailing a cab, he took the fresh morning air in great gulps, letting it cleanse and recharge his mind as he refined his mental to-do list. It would be a long one today, and his PA, Tessa, had better be prepared to get into the trenches.

Connor hated the thought of being stuck in an office, so he hadn't spent much money on his. With today's technology, he could work anywhere really, but he had come to realize that he needed one central place to keep things organized.

Tessa had become the keeper of all that extraneous stuff, and there were weeks where she did not see him at all, only heard from him if he chose to text or phone her. He really had no idea what she did all day when he wasn't around, but, by any stretch of the imagination, hers was an easy job. As long as she had any given document he needed at any time, ready to email to him.

She surprised him when he walked in at eight a.m., opening the unlocked door and finding her already at her desk, staring intently at her computer screen.

"Morning, boss."

"Morning." He held up his coffee cup apologetically. "Had I known you'd be in this early, I would have brought you one, sorry."

"Not an issue." She nodded across the room towards a coffee machine he did not know they had. "Always ready."

He grinned and unlocked the door to his inner sanctum, his private space. "Well, we're going to need it. From now on, you're going to be busy. We might even have to hire someone to help you."

"Sounds intriguing. Fire away."

She tucked her long black hair into a ponytail, blanked the screen on her computer, and followed him in. Out of the corner of his eye, he saw lines and columns of nonsensical data disappearing before her screen turned into a bland blue background with a sign-on line. Sometimes he suspected her of being some sort of computer hacker; it always seemed she could get any information he was looking for, even confidential that he had no business seeing. It was helpful, to say the least, but in moments like these, he wondered.

"We're going to need to register a new company," he said, tossing a paper pad and pen toward her. "By end of day, I'm going to know who is in it. Get all the paperwork ready. We'll need a bank account; we'll need corporate documents. I need you to handle all the back office nonsense while I'm getting the investors together."

"Got it."

"Set up a website, email addresses, find someone capable to do some design work, and a quick turnaround on corporate branding. It has to look good."

"'K, what's the name you're looking for?"

"Ready? Perfect Cannabis Corporation."

To her credit, Tessa did not even blink. "Cool," was all she said, "on it. The moment you tell me who's in it, you got it. Minute books, corporate records, whatever we need."

They'd worked together for a couple of years by now, and he knew the standard stuff about her: she was single, save for a casual boyfriend, just out of university, tended to dress in some all black, Goth-type fashion, did as told, and got stuff done...quickly. Never asked any questions, never came in late, and didn't complain when he couldn't pay her for a couple of months.

He'd gotten used to the silver jewelry, the skulls and crosses, the long chains on her black outfits, skyscraper heels, and pouffed-out skirts in summer. She didn't give a damn what anybody else thought, and he admired that.

Then there were moments like this morning, when he wondered how long she'd been in the office already and what she did on the computer when he wasn't looking.

"Now then," he said, bringing himself back, "we'll be going public before long, so I'll get us a securities lawyer to catch you up on what you need to know and what you can't know." He winked. "Like I said, we're about to get super busy, you and I, and before..."

The phone interrupted him, and Tessa shrugged. "Mr. Beauregard's in a client meeting just now," she said sweetly. "I'll most certainly ask him to call you back."

"So it starts..." She stuck a yellow post-it on his desk mat. "First ones are calling, wondering who else you may be talking to about a deal."

Connor grinned; she knew the game, all right, and she played on his team, no doubt.

"Shall we see who is the most impatient?" He peeled the note off his desk mat and laughed. "Yup, Mr. Josh Novak, can't wait to come along, in hopes of selling me some enormous warehouse facility he's been trying to get rid of for years. Thanks."

No more than the wave of a hand and she was already back at her desk, the list he'd given her by her side. By tonight, she would have everything done.

If they were going to meet his self-imposed timeline, he needed the kind of people who could make that happen. And that also meant making a few calls and un-ruffling a few feathers from previous deals gone south.

He picked up his phone and thumbed through his contacts, thinking that he really should get himself a new number now that they were starting a new project.

"Want any lunch, C?" Tessa stuck her head into the office, and he looked up from his laptop, confused for a moment.

Alas, she was right; it was well past lunchtime. "No, thanks," he finally said, since, surprisingly, he couldn't even think about food. "I'm right into this. I'll get something later."

"'K, I'm gonna step out then for a bit. Want me to lock the front door?"

"Nope." He leaned back and grinned. "Times people would come around looking for money are gone for good. From now on, we're officially rolling in it."

"Good. I'm really tired of keeping a gun in my desk drawer, you know."

Joking, he asked himself, but she was already out the door. She was joking, he finally decided. Jesus, get a grip.

He leaned back in his comfortable leather chair and spun away from the door to face the picture window behind him. It always had that soothing effect on him to look out over the harbor district, the former dingy area of town, now coming up in value and becoming the trendy spot to live and work. He might only occupy a two-room office, but the address still looked good on the letterhead.

When needed, the guys two floors below would rent him their swanky boardroom, designed by some douche who called himself an artist. Not Connor's taste, but impressive nonetheless.

The activity in the harbor beyond, the constant coming and going, moving of people and goods was exhilarating, reminded him never to stand still, never to rest on his achievements. Keep going, keep moving, always on to something new, always on to something bigger. Routine would bore him to death; a steady diet of same ole, same ole would eventually kill him.

"Mr. Beauregard?"

Connor spun around so fast, he almost turned over his chair.

There, in the door of his office, stood a young man of perhaps 25, neatly dressed, carrying a small black briefcase, all of it plain and nondescript.

He had the kind of bland face witnesses would describe as average, dressed in neatly pressed khakis, a white shirt, grey sweater.

"Yes?"

"I'm so sorry. Your secretary appears to be away from her desk. I saw you through the open door, so I thought..."

"It's fine, although you did startle me. You're just lucky I don't keep a gun in my desk drawer," he joked, and for whatever reason, that neither made the young man smile nor even seemed to rattle him in the slightest. He simply nodded and opened his briefcase.

"I have a delivery for you, from Mr. Al," he said, producing a plain brown manila envelope and a sheet of paper. "If you would kindly sign here."

Connor reached for the envelope and the note neatly clipped to it.

Get the company started—I will be in touch.

I will be in touch. As in don't call me, I'll call you, he wondered.

With an effort, he pulled himself together and reached for his wallet.

"Sure, hang on for a minute."

"You need not tip me, sir; Mr. Al takes care of everything."

"Mr. Al, is it? Tell me again, is that his first or his last name? I get confused, and I don't want to insult him in the middle of a meeting."

"Al will do just fine." The young man smiled. "He understands it can get confusing. Now I just need your signature, saying you received this envelope before I can hand it to you."

"Yeah, sure, give me one second. So, you work for him." Connor pulled the delivery confirmation around and pretended to study it carefully, then pretended to look for a pen, despite the fact that the youngster had taken one out of the briefcase and held it out to him. "Making deliveries, running errands, you're his PA, perhaps?"

He finally reached for the pen and gave the kid his most brilliant *come on, we're all friends here* smile, though he waited in vain for a reaction in kind.

"I do odd jobs for him...amongst other things." The kid might as well have been talking about the color of the rug. He finally understood what Kayla was talking about when she said no one around him talked.

"And what kinda man is he? Good to work for, I mean?"

"Mr. Al is a successful businessman, sir. He is above reproach."

"Above reproach. You are joking, right? I haven't heard anyone say that since...well, actually, I've never heard it used outside a dictionary."

"Mr. Al likes good manners, sir, at all times. Now, your signature if you please."

He had moved in a little closer, and suddenly, Connor noticed it, just below that mild-mannered behavior. The kid actually had a set of muscles on him no nerdy sweater and khakis could hide. He had not gotten those in accounting school unless their methods had changed drastically in the last few years.

Connor held his gaze for a minute and found nothing meek or wimpy there either...rather on the contrary. Steel-grey eyes met his and never blinked or turned away. He read confidence there...and strength, unchallenged strength. This was no delivery boy... and no personal assistant either.

"Here you are." He scrawled his signature and handed the paper back to the man. "Mind if I take a photocopy?"

"Most certainly, Mr. Beauregard. You do want a record of what you have signed after all."

"Yeah...sure."

He got up. "After you," he said and extended his hand to let the man precede him into Tessa's office. Never turn your back on a viper or a man with a weapon. He was now assuming this man was armed in some way.

He struggled with the photocopier for a minute, unused to it, painfully aware of the man's quiet presence behind him. To his credit Al's man never said a word. He simply stood there and waited patiently, his expression carefully neutral and relaxed.

"Then I will thank you," he finally said, taking back the original signature confirmation, nodding, and stepping toward the door. "Mr. Al would like you to know he will be in touch shortly, and he wishes you a wonderful day."

"Yeah...thanks, I think. Tell him, uh, thank you."

Connor watched the man disappear from the office as quietly as he had arrived in the first place. Man, he did not even disturb the air around him. The manila envelope he had brought still rested on the edge of the desk in his office. Now to find out what was so all-important Al had to send a combat-trained delivery man who likely carried a gun in his briefcase to scare the shit out of him.

He slipped his finger under the flap of the envelope when another thought occurred to him. How had this man found him anyway? His business card carried the address of this building, but no suite number. Any and all visitors were expected to register with the doorman downstairs, who would then call up to see if Connor was available. One of the very reasons he had chosen this small suite of offices was the privacy. Just another way for Al to show him who was in charge? Or was he just getting paranoid?

He dropped heavily into his chair again, and, for once, the sunlit view of the harbor failed to soothe him.

He ripped open his envelope and pulled out a sheaf of documents. At first glance, it looked like a standard, boilerplate partnership contract. He would have his lawyer check it later. He would have drafted up something similar, so no surprises here. And another mental note... pay off the lawyer. He would need him.

One final sheet slipped out of the envelope, a plain white piece of paper with—Connor smiled—a cashier's check clipped to it. Son of a gun. Al sure didn't waste any time. He simply sent a check made out in the amount of...

"Holy fucking Jesus. " He dropped the check to the desk as if it had caught on fire and jumped to his feet so quickly this time the chair did topple over and crashed into the glass wall. "Fuck..."

Slowly, he reached for the check again and studied it thoroughly, counting the zeroes this time. Half a million dollars. Dammit, the crazy fuck had sent him a check for half a million dollars with nothing more than an *I'll be in touch*. What if he took the money and disappeared? What if he never signed the agreement?

What if he took off for the Cayman Islands?

OK, maybe not with half a million dollars, but still. Was Al simply trusting Rafael's word that Connor was a standup guy? The man had to be as crazy as a hoot owl.

Or not.

What if he was simply saying, *I am in charge here. I know what is going to happen if you take this money and fuck up... and I know you do too*. Connor straightened up his chair, sat back down, and stared at the check.

Just like that, he had everything to get the company started, no scrounging, no wheedling small-time investors into something they didn't really want to do, just to get everything off the ground and moving. He could sit back, relax, and do it the proper way.

He held the check in both hands, leaned back in his chair, and smiled. He could pay off the lawyers he needed anyway and clear up a couple of other bills left behind from the oil deal. He could use the funds to generate some much-needed goodwill with the people who lost out on said oil deal, bring them in on something bigger and better.

He could travel in style, show up with flair, present the picture he needed to present when he went after the big funds. And for once, it would not have to be so damn difficult.

It would fall into place. Damn, this particular deal would finally show them all what he really could do. On the oil deal he had doubted himself. Barely over 30 and already burned out? That couldn't be it.

He closed his eyes for 30 seconds.

As if on cue, his phone rang. He checked the caller display and grinned. "Well now, Josh Novak, let's see what you got, you greedy bastard."

Before Tessa got back from her extended lunch, Simon too had called to tell him he was in to the tune of a hundred grand. He now had three-quarters of a million dollars, a good plan, and the deal of his lifetime in his hands. Life just did not get any better than this.

He spent the remainder of the day drafting partnership agreements for himself, Rafael, Josh, and Simon, just so none of them could walk away with the goods and leave him in the lurch, and carefully avoided thinking of the agreement still sitting in a plain manila envelope on the edge of his glass desk. He would think about that later.

He might even sign it, eyes closed, not reading what he didn't want to know anyway, and send it back. Wait...send it back? Where?

By five o'clock, he had drawn up a business plan that made sense to him and asked Tessa to make reservations at a nearby basic eatery. Nothing fancy this time. It would be a simple working dinner.

SIX

Connor handed out copies of his plan, explaining the major points. Rafael, his right-hand man on this deal, studied the paperwork he had brought and said very little. According to his general outline, Connor would be president and CEO, handling about the day-to-day running of the newly formed Perfect Cannabis Corporation, or Per-Can as he called it now. Rafael would be secretary treasurer, Josh, vice president in charge of real estate, and Simon, vice president...in charge of nothing, for the moment. If a direct role in the company opened up later, he could choose to take it up. For now, he was an advisor.

Connor had set them all up with nice little monthly salaries, consulting fees, to keep the troops happy and from asking too many questions.

Now the legwork started, he explained, and he needed all of them to do their share. Now that they had a company and a workable plan, they needed senior financing. Fairly soon, they would be trading on a public stock exchange, but for now, all they had was a story...and they had him, Connor Beauregard.

"I can sell the investors," he kept repeating, "any investor, any time. What I need from you, gentlemen, are contacts. I need you to go through your address books and look at each and every single name with the following criteria: Does this man have money to invest, has he done this before, does he understand how the big game is played? If the answer to at least two out of three is yes, I want the person's contact information and an introduction, and I'll go and sell him or her. Not to be discriminatory."

He took a sip from his water glass and paused. Tonight, it looked like plain ice water in a glass, to impress upon his partners how serious he was taking this entire thing, but it actually contained a decent shot of vodka. For the initial presentation, he wanted to be sober. Now, he wanted to be *on*.

"And let's be clear about this one, folks—I have nothing against small-time investors, nothing at all, but let's not waste our time with a guy who is going to put in five grand and then call me up a dozen times to see what's happened to his money. I can't, and I won't, spend time with people like that. If you insist I will bring them in, I will send them a subscription agreement and some documentation, but that's it. I want to talk to the guy who has 100,000 he needs to find a home for, the guy who put all of his money into an offbeat real estate development deal, won big, and now wants to do it again...that is the man you need to put me in front of. The more of them I see, the more money there is going to be. I cannot and I will not lose."

Another pause. "I'm making this company the biggest success there ever was. Somebody will write a book about me, about us. Now, does everybody know what their role is?"

Rafael nodded; Josh and Simon leafed through his business plan, trying to read and listen at the same time. Everything made sense; everything looked fabulous. Damn that Tessa if she hadn't pulled complete business plans and legal forms from *somewhere,* changed a few key items, and presented them to him moments before he left for the meeting. Now that was the real reason why he kept her around.

Her loser boyfriend and part-time artist had even designed a partially usable corporate identity for them. Until he hired one of the top PR firms in the country, which would be soon, this would actually do.

"Coming to the next point," he said.

Kayla all of a sudden stood beside him. "I am so sorry. A meeting ran late. What did I miss?"

"Only the most important part of the meeting," someone muttered, but Connor allowed her to kiss him on the cheek.

"Nothing I can't catch you up on. Gentlemen, meet the lady who will round out our group, Kayla Montecito, from now on vice president in charge of communications."

"I think we need to start by putting out a story about the many benefits of cannabis," she started, "educate people. Take the substance out of the closet, so to speak, and make it socially acceptable. I think that will raise some interest and at the same time aid you," a brief touch on his thigh, "in your fundraising efforts. I've made room in our story lineup for a succession of articles and interviews, the medical benefits of marijuana, along with patient testimonies, important information for doctors, and miraculous success stories. And lastly, information for investors, cleverly clad inside a 'news' item so people will actually read it."

"Hear, hear." Rafael clapped and rapped his knuckles on the table. "Someone has done her homework."

Kayla narrowed her eyes at him and squared her shoulders. "Let's make one thing clear, gentlemen," she said. "I'm here as a partner of yours, and I take this business just as seriously as you do. Whatever you may or may not think of my magazines and their value, let's just put that aside and work on making this company the best it can be, shall we?"

"I second that," Connor stepped in, but Kayla, far from being done, actually took his hand into hers.

"Connor and I have committed to doing everything in our power, to stopping all other...activity in our lives to make this a success. If you cannot say the same, I think you need to reexamine why you are in this room."

"We're all committed around this table, are we not?" Connor said, trying to push back from Kayla a bit, not an easy task with her hand vice-like on his. "We're all in this together."

She held on tight, and, not for the first time, he wondered what he had saddled himself with. He cursed himself for spending the night, for bringing her into the deal in the first place...though that basic idea still had merit. He—they—needed the press. He just didn't relish the thought of a personal involvement at present.

Smiling broadly, he pulled her a little closer. He really could have chosen worse than one of the wealthiest women in the city, he thought. She had a few years on him, true, but she still looked great, she had more money than God and, apparently, she was only too willing to share.

Kayla returned the slight squeeze of his hand, and the unspoken agreement between them was there...for now.

SEVEN

Connor slowed the SUV as he rolled up to the gate and let his window down.

"Private jet to Denver, Colorado," he said, rolling the words *private jet*, as if they were particularly delicious. "With Corporate Jetways."

"Plane is ready to go." The man nodded, stepped out of his gatehouse, and pointed down a long line of aircraft hangars. "Last hangar to the left over there, can't miss it. They're doing their final check right now. Leave the car by the runway. One of us will move it. Have a nice flight."

He checked their license plate number against his records, tipped his hat at Kayla, and stepped back inside to raise the boom.

"Now this," Connor said, grinning broadly, "is how air travel is supposed to be. Believe me, you'll never want to fly commercial again after this."

"Hanson had a private jet for a while," Kayla said, almost blasé, and he had to bite back an angry retort. Exactly why did she have to bring up her dead ex-husband again and again? "He finally gave the thing up again, figured it was too expensive and we might as well fly first class."

"Well, if there's a group involved." Connor pointed toward the end of the roadway, now feeling like he had to justify things! Two other SUVs stood waiting. Another was just being moved into the now-empty hangar. "It's worth it. Looks like Josh and Simon are here, and inside. I bet you Rafael has been crawling all over this place since sunup. He goes nuts over planes."

"Oh, my...now that is a plane."

Two words that made up for every irritating thing she had said this morning, *Oh my*.

"That's right, my dear. Dassault Falcon 2000. Seating for 12, excluding cabin personnel. Rest areas, work areas, twin engine, cruising speed of 530 mph, that's Mach 0.80 to be specific. What more could you ever want?"

He spoke as if he owned the darned thing, which wasn't entirely a bad idea, and not out of his range for long. But in reality, he had just read the darn sales brochure a dozen times before finally renting this beauty of a corporate jet. From now on, he had sworn to himself, he would show up in style, but it was one thing to read about it in a glossy brochure, quite another to stand in front of this snow-white, gleaming miracle of technology.

He felt dwarfed, yet as proud as if it said Beauregard Aviation there on the tail in bright gold lettering instead of Corporate Jetways.

The stairs were extended, and at the bottom stood a uniformed pilot, inviting them inside. If memory served correctly, they'd be flying with two pilots today, one flying the plane with the other one looking after passengers.

Ground personnel still buzzed about the area around the landing gear and the engines, busily reading their checklists, exchanging hand signals. Connor stopped the SUV, reached for his briefcase, and felt the rush of adrenaline and excitement threatening to choke him.

"Sir." Two of the attendants had come around, opening their doors, escorting them from the car to the gangway stairs. In reality, they were likely there to make sure neither one of them took off over the airfield heading somewhere they shouldn't, but Connor wanted to pretend they had been specifically hired to carry his and Kayla's bags and to make sure no harm came to them on their way to the jet.

He heard the SUV start up, knew it was being taken to the hangar for servicing and a wash, just one of the many Corporate Jetways services.

Life behind him on the ground simply fell away as he climbed the stairs one by one. The pilot was there again, taking his overcoat and pointing toward the lushly appointed interior.

They had stepped into another world, an expensive, private gentlemen's club...or so one could have believed. The entire plane had been outfitted in tan leather, chrome, and exotic woods. 11 deep, comfortable club chairs arranged in intimate groups of four, so one could work, relax or recline two of them together to have a nap.

A heavy curtain separated the seating area from what he assumed was the galley, and almost immediately, their pilot stepped out with a tray of champagne flutes in hand. Kayla's favorite brand, one of the many details Connor always paid attention to, and again, it paid off when she squeezed his arm and giggled with delight.

"Better than Hanson's?" he asked in a low voice, and she laughed.

"Oh, dear, so much better, Connor. You are simply amazing."

And that was all he needed to hear.

"Gentlemen." He strode up to Josh and Simon and shook their hands. "How are they treating you in here? Everything OK? You just let me know if there is anything at all they can do for you, please. And tell me, what have you done with Rafael?"

"Up in the cockpit, interviewing our captain," the other pilot said, smiling. "I think he might actually want to fly up there."

"I don't doubt it, but for now, the work is back here. I need him to be with us. Before we reach Colorado, we have a few things to clear up."

"Certainly, sir, I'll let him know. Is there anything else you would like?"

"Not at the moment, Robert." Connor had made a point to study their flight manifest and remember their pilots' names. Looked better that way. "But we will let you know."

"No problem at all."

Connor sank into one of the deep club chairs, closing his eyes for a second.

He pulled out his laptop and signed on, while Kayla beside him was already pecking away at messages on her phone. Whether she was working or simply surfing the web, he did not know. Neither did he care. Either one worked just fine for him.

"Since late 2012, anyone over the age of 21 can legally grow cannabis and possess it in Colorado, as long as it stays where it's grown. There's a provision to possess an ounce while travelling and to give a gift up to an ounce to another person over 21 years of age," he started without bothering to consult any notes. "Consumption is regulated much like alcohol, with equivalent offenses proscribed for driving. Christ, even casual recreational use is legal down there. Consequently, there exists a culture around marijuana from which we can learn a lot. I intend to find and hire the best horticulturists we can locate, gents, and I am hoping you will help me do so by keeping your eyes and ears open."

Champagne appeared as if by magic again, and he briefly tipped his glass to Kayla's, reveling in the pure ring of crystal to crystal.

"While we're in Colorado and Oregon, we'll be visiting several grow operations, and I need everyone to learn and retain as much as you possibly can without being obnoxious in any way. These people know we are there to learn, but we are also there to...acquire, I guess. Information, contacts, anything that might become useful one day. Pick it up, retain it, or give it to me. I will use it. Ours is not just going to be a good operation—I want it to be the best. I want PerCan to be the first place people come to learn how it's done, a state-of-the-art operation like no other in the world."

He leaned back and leveled his gaze at Rafael. "If we walk in with this kind of reputation, it will help us tremendously with the licensing process back home, and from what I've read, we will need all the help we can get. I don't want anyone to think this is going to be easy—we apply for a license and simply...receive it. There are too many quacks out there, running around in jeans and hemp shirts, half-stoned themselves, celebrating Bob Marley's birthday and passing the joints. We are never going to be like that."

He made a point of carefully refilling Kayla's and his crystal champagne flutes and took a sip.

"We are going to come in like businessmen, in our suits, IPO in hand, headed for the stock market. Serious, clean, and trustworthy, got it?"

Josh and Simon nodded; they had expected nothing else. The only one in their midst who was in need of a bit of a makeover, everyone thought, was Rafael. Rafael, the dealmaker and stock promoter who operated on charm and likeability, who really did not care how many designer threads he wore, whose favorite expression was, *I'm an honest guy*. Kayla had already offered to polish his image just a bit, and he'd just shrugged.

"So again, if you see anyone interesting, anyone you think we may want to retain, by all means, point them out to me. I'll get in touch with them and make generous offers."

"How generous?" Josh finally asked, accepting a drink from their pilot and leaning back in his seat. "I mean, Connor, this is all great," he took in the airplane, their attendants and bar with a sweep of his hand and shook his head, "but we are burning through funds like there's no tomorrow, are we not? I mean, Jesus, renting a private jet?"

"It's not really all that extravagant if there's an entire group involved," Kayla said casually and kicked off her high heels. "I mean, there are five of us. First class, come on, at the last minute like this, we would've paid a fortune anyway. And think of all the money you would have to spend on hotel rooms. Instead, we'll all be home tomorrow."

"And the money is not the most important thing at the moment, Josh. The most important thing is to appear serious, well-funded, stable, and confident. Then the money will start rolling in automatically."

Only someone who knew him well would have noticed the slight tightening of his hands on the champagne flute.

Kayla might have; she put her hand on his arm and smiled.

"I think we're about to go."

The Falcon slowly taxied down the runway, and their attendant came to collect empty glasses and to ask them very politely if they would mind terribly putting on their seatbelts until they had reached cruising altitude.

More champagne, some finger foods, and lots of idle conversation later, they landed in Denver, and Connor's sunny mood hit a new high. They were asked to remain seated for just a moment, having more drinks, while customs agents boarded the aircraft, politely checked their passports, and apologized for all the trouble.

"Now this beats standing in line down at the terminal any time," Simon joked. "I could get used to this."

"You're not the only one. Oh, this is exciting." Kayla almost bounced in her seat, and Connor allowed the warm feeling of success to light him up from the inside.

Their visit became a whirlwind of factory tours, introductions, lunches, and dinners with other marijuana producers. Connor found out quickly that he knew next to nothing about growing cannabis, although he'd read enough to throw in the odd intelligent comment here and there and not look like a complete idiot. They showed him grow pods, light-deprivation technology, and grow lights. They explained clones, grow mediums, sterile and sealed environments, and he took it all in.

At the end of the day, they all piled into the Falcon again to sleep on their way to Oregon, where the same scenario awaited them once again.

Connor handed out newly printed business cards like candy and made sure everyone was aware of the size of the operation he was planning. He would need them, and he would need their money. If he saw someone who looked like a seasoned investor, he made an effort to memorize their name and involvement. He spent time with the consulting teams who oversaw the growing, the buildings, the retailing. Like a giant sponge, he took it all in, retained the important facts for future use and discarded the fluff. This trip was his education into the industry. After this, he would be ready to fly solo if necessary. He was the head of this thing after all. He and Rafael, but Rafael had his fingers in so many different pies. He hardly qualified as a serious partner.

While the rest of his entourage had a good time, he suspected at least Josh and Simon took the time to sample some of the product they were shown. Connor flipped open his laptop, made notes, and put his company's foundation together.

He'd met a man by the name of Nick who ran one of the grow operations in Denver, and he knew right away he wanted to hire him. Nick spoke in a very quiet voice and never bragged or exaggerated, but Connor recognized someone who knew his stuff. He needed to make an unbeatable offer to Nick, but not quite yet. They would get started, set the company up, and bring him in. It probably would not be easy to lure him out of Denver, which had its own beauty, but he would find a way. In the meantime, he typed a quick message to Tessa to find out everything she could about Nick Barclay. Who knew what she would dig up that could be of use to them?

"Still working?" Rafael nudged him and swept his hand through the dim aircraft interior. "Everyone else is pretty much passed out from everything we saw yesterday and today. Probably time for you to take it down a gear too."

"Can't. I've got too much on the go. There's this guy we met in Denver, Nick..."

"I know. Man knows what he is doing."

"Big-time. I want him for PerCan."

"Al sent me a message."

"I'm going to see if I can hire him away from the outfit he works for. Just need to find out what it's going to take...What? What do you mean, Al sent you a message?"

"He just did."

"How?"

"Never mind that, C. He likes what you're doing. Nice touch with the plane, his own words."

"Well, I'm so glad Mr. Al agrees with my choice of transportation."

"I wouldn't joke about it if I were you, not even in here. In any case, he wants to have a little meeting when we are back."

"'Kay. He knows where my office is," Connor said with just a touch of bitterness. Not only did the man know where to find him—he had sent a thug to come see him. True, a thug who carried a lot of money, but still.

"Yeah, about that...Al does not come to see you. You go see him."

"Another one of his little personality quirks?"

"Let's just say the attitude of a man who gave you a cashier's check for over half a million dollars, shall we?"

Connor swallowed hard and folded his hands behind his head.

"So you know about that?"

"I'm a little surprised you didn't tell any of the others, but of course I do. I'm the one who brought Al in, remember? And just because it's my nuts too, I would be highly interested in not screwing up this deal too badly."

"What the hell is that supposed to mean?"

Simon, asleep in the seat diagonally across from them, stirred a little, and Connor brought his voice down a bit. "What is that supposed to mean?"

"It's just that I'm the one who introduced him to you and the project, and I'm the one he's ultimately going to hold responsible for the success or failure of whatever we are doing here...just a little reminder."

"Well here's an FYI—I'm busting my ass to make this the greatest grow op ever seen, while you and these two yahoos over there..."

A hard hand clamped around Connor's wrist and held tight. For a moment he wanted to call out, but bit back a curse building inside him and merely glowered at his friend. Normally jovial, Rafael had become completely quiet and tense.

"Let me just say this once, Connor Beauregard. Nobody is denying the fact that you are working hard at this. Just remember that there are people you will have to answer to at the end of the day. And if something goes wrong, that answer had better be a good one. That's all I am going to say on the subject."

Rafael let go of Connor's wrists and looked around.

"Say, I think I'm going to find our attendant here and get us some water. Want some?"

Connor stared down at the red marks on his wrists, slowly fading, and balled his fist tight, slowly counting to ten. Then again.

"Sure," he finally said when he had his voice under control.

He watched Rafael walk away on stocking feet toward the galley of the plane, wondering who the hell this guy thought he was. How dare he?

Rafael handed him a bottle of water and slid into his own seat again. "Next week, we'll set up a meeting next week. I like this plane by the way. What do you think one of these would go for?"

"Buy it used? 15, 20 mil maybe, depending on the age and the shape it's in. It's the maintenance that's going to kill you every time. That and having to keep two of these guys on call for everything." He nodded toward their attendant collecting glasses.

"Two full-time pilots at all times? Jeez, what a waste. Unless of course you'd like to learn how to fly one of these."

"Who says I can't?" Rafael bit into a sandwich he had found somewhere in the galley and leaned back comfortably. "There are some things even you don't know."

"Get off it! You know how to fly one of these things?"

"Well, not quite one of these, but yes, I do have a commercial license."

"Interesting," was all Connor could think to say.

Interesting indeed. He'd never known Rafael knew how to fly.

He finally leaned back in his seat and allowed himself to shut down for a bit.

EIGHT

Two days later, coming in to his office, Tessa was already there, entertaining a clean-cut man in jeans and a flannel shirt he figured to be in his forties.

"Well, here he is," Tessa said brightly. "Mr. Connor Beauregard. Connor, meet TC. Josh sent him our way."

"Thomas Carlyle, actually," he said by way of introduction and offered a firm handshake to Connor. "But your assistant is right—TC will do just fine."

"And what can I do for you, TC? If you're looking to invest in our wonderful company, you need not have made the trip. I could have come to see you at your office...here, have a seat."

Connor pulled out one of his visitor's chairs and sat in his own. "Now then..."

"Well, investing might come a bit later." TC smiled. "What I had in mind is more of a working relationship."

"Intriguing. Please continue."

"I have some...experience in the field of marijuana growing and cultivation, extensive experience, let's just say. When Josh mentioned you went to Denver and Oregon to see a few outfits and learn how it was done, I thought I would come around and offer my services, see if this is something that would interest you and we could strike a deal of some sort."

Connor nodded slowly and took the man in. TC was the kind of man his mother would have called a *likeable fellow*. He looked open and honest. Bright blue eyes, an open, welcoming smile, broad hands that looked accustomed to working hard. TC would be the kind of man who got it done. That kind of likeability could be an enormous asset in the kind of company he was planning.

"There are always possibilities is what my dad would have said. So tell me about your experience. Sounds like you've put a few plants in the ground."

TC laughed and gave the door behind him a little push. "Started growing at fourteen years of age like everybody else. Except I found I had a good knack for it, and I always could get the plants to grow a bit higher or a bit healthier than everybody else. Not that I have an official education or anything."

"Not in growing weed, I would think," Connor said dryly, "which is one of the things that makes putting this business together so… challenging. Every bit of early information has to be sourced in some pretty dark places."

"Well, there's a culture out there as well. You just have to know where to look. We've been growing cannabis for medical purposes as well as recreational for years now, and many of us have a decent reputation. Now the government has decided to legalize some of it, you might find some experts where you thought there weren't any."

"And you?"

"One of the best," TC said simply, and darn it if Connor did not believe him.

"And what kind of operation are we talking about?" he asked, knowing it would be something small, but you had to start somewhere.

"Few hundred plants," TC said slowly. "An old tobacco drying warehouse a couple of hours outside of town. We took it over, refinished everything, put in the grow beds and grow lights, gave the locals some work, and everybody is happy."

"Is that so? I heard those grow lights use energy like nobody's business."

"They do at that. Generate enough heat to be responsible for global warming too, so you've got to air-condition the hell out of everything. But in this kind of climate, you simply can't do without."

"I understand that. We're talking to a few manufacturers from California just now. Not a lot of variety and those things are expensive. Anyway, you grow in regular dirt?"

"Regular old-fashioned dirt in an indoor greenhouse. Hemp plants are actually quite sensitive to any temperature and humidity changes."

"So I heard. I was actually planning to use grow mediums to avoid any soil contamination. You just never know what might be lurking in soil. And for clinical applications, we are going to want the purest and cleanest there is."

He steepled his hands in front of his mouth and studied TC for a long time. The man met his gaze and never flinched or looked down. Confident, knew what he was doing, knew what he brought to the table.

"Well," he finally said. "Sounds like you have a lot more experience than I do, though we are going to have quite a different operation from what you've been used to."

He paused for another moment, and still, TC did not waver

"So, do you think you could get up to speed pretty quickly?"

"Wouldn't hurt to try now, would it?"

"Nope." He stepped around the desk and offered a hand to TC. "Let me roll it around with my partners, and, if they're OK with everything, we'll write up an agreement and see if we can fit you into the company."

TC smiled broadly and took the offered hand. "Thank you, Connor. I'm going to get on the research, and I'm sure we can put this together just right."

After TC had left, Connor stared down at the harbor from his picture window and didn't even try to hide his grin. This deal was just running itself, now wasn't it?

Just a few days ago, he'd been dashing around, worrying about finding the right talent and the knowledge to run the horticultural operation. He had cautiously done some internet research and found that he didn't really know anything about growing cannabis, except for the bits and pieces he'd thrown into the business plan and offering memorandum. And those he had mostly stolen from other companies' offering papers.

He had worried all right. In all honesty that was the reason behind his sudden trip to Denver and Oregon. And then, boom, the door opened, and the answer to his questions waltzed right in asking to be part of this. Damn! He could not lose. This deal really was running itself.

Connor really wanted to light a cigar. Damn smoking laws.

Turning to the practicalities, was he confident that TC had enough of the right experience to run this thing? Not at this point, but that's why God invented the internet, right? You did your reading and research.

On to the next thing.

He still had that Damocles sword of a meeting with Al hanging over his head. If he'd had a choice, he would have marched into the man's office and said...*something*. But he did not have that option, did he? He had no way to get in touch with Al and the little thug or thugs who worked for him. All he could do was sit here and wait. The one thing Connor Beauregard hated more than anything else in his entire life, sitting and waiting!

But nothing to be done about either. So on to the next thing.

He opened his briefcase, and a jumble of assorted papers tumbled to his desk as if it had started snowing in the middle of May.

"Tess."

"You bellowed?"

She appeared behind him as if conjured by magic.

"Dammit, don't scare me like that, would you?" He looked down at her feet and shook his head. "No wonder. Who walks around the office barefoot?"

"It's comfortable?" Tess shrugged. "What do you need?"

He shook his head and looked at her. Black leggings, black, skintight Guns N' Roses t-shirt, silver chains hanging from her neck and waist. He was sure he recognized a few skulls somewhere. And, of course, the black fingerless gloves.

"Remind me to speak to you about fashion sense when we start getting public traffic in here."

"Yeah, yeah. Now what do you need?"

"This..." He swept the pile of papers toward her and made an all-encompassing hand gesture. "This...pile. It's about four subscription agreements for PerCan. They, uh, fell apart somehow."

"Fell apart?"

"Well, you know, I put them in my car, and..."

"Flung them into the back like always, I would suspect."

"Yeah, likely." He grinned. "Put them back together best as you can, file them, wherever and however they need to be. Oh, and be on the lookout—there are a few checks hidden in there too, I think."

Her long fingers and blood-red nails picked one of the checks out from the jumble, and she whistled, clearly impressed. "Wowza. People are giving you money now, aren't they? Big-time, it looks like."

"Yes, well, just make sure you get all of them and take them to the bank. You did get us a bank account, right?"

"Sure did. Bank card is in your desk tray, all the access data on a piece of paper taped to it."

"You're a gem."

"I'll get the paper out of your hair, don't you worry."

She scooped up the lot of it and somehow managed to take it all back to her workstation gracefully without dropping anything. He'd have to eventually sit down with her, make a decent list of all of their subscribers. For now, there were other things needing his attention.

But his phone already showed seven messages again, and he knew one of them was from Bill Grogan, an associate he played golf with on a regular basis. Bill had more money than God and never parted with it unless there was a gun to his head. Connor had come to him many times, but he had never managed to convince him to invest. Until now that was. Now Bill had already left three messages about PerCan, and Connor was making him wait and loving every moment of it.

One more message, Bill, he thought, one more. *Then I'm going to get you to spring for drinks at The Lighthouse, I'm going to get blotted on the finest your money can buy, and then...and then I might take your money. Maybe.*

There were still three men Simon had brought in who were eager to speak to him and give him checks and two more who had come through Rafael and Josh. Shit, life just did not get any better, did it? All he had to do was go in there, tell a story, show around his business plan, and open his hand for the checks. They couldn't wait to sign on the dotted line. Cannabis, seemingly the hottest investment property at the moment. Who would have thought it?

Back in high school, cannabis hadn't seemed like this much work, he thought, and went to freshen up in the little washroom attached to his office. Separating his marks from their money was just that much better if you looked your best.

NINE

The call came a few days later. Among all the other detritus delivered to his office on a daily basis, Tessa had placed a plain rectangular envelope on his desk. White, without any sender information or other imprint. Only his name was written on it in careful black block lettering, 'Connor Beauregard,' nothing else.

Curious, Connor opened it, finding a plain white, rectangular card: 'Would you please come to Jones Family Restaurant at Nassau Street, tomorrow at one p.m. Ask for the original chef. – Al.'

The original chef, Connor wanted to laugh. How truly original. He snipped the card off his desk and watched it sail to the ground.

Satisfied, he checked the time and realized it was well after two-thirty. Time to visit The Lighthouse for a cultured afternoon drink and enjoy the fruits of his labors.

"I'm off, Tess," he called out and took a deep breath for the first time in weeks. Paying Al back might be the best decision he had made yet.

TEN

Jones Family Restaurant seemed an odd place to meet, sounded like a dingy diner.

And, when he turned the corner at Nassau, that's exactly what he found, a plain old, rundown diner, sitting at one end of a weed-infested parking lot.

He had brought the card with him and double-checked, but lord love us, this was the place. Jones Family Restaurant, on Nassau Street. Couldn't be more than one, he figured. But he reversed out of the lot, and a quick look down Nassau Street confirmed it.

"Let's get this over with then," he muttered under his breath, finding a parking spot close to the main window. In a place like this, it might be wise to keep an eye on your car.

He could see no other cars in the lot. So much for getting at least a decent meal out of Al. French fries and gravy anyone? Never mind. After today, it would all be a memory anyway and fodder for the stories he would tell at The Lighthouse or at La Cosa in the not-too-distant future: *There was this crazy dude who wanted to invest in my company. Scary fellow went by the name of The Original Chef, but really, he was just nuts. Crazy fuck gives me a half a million dollars without so much as getting a receipt. In the end I just couldn't keep somebody like that in the company, you know.*

He straightened his cashmere sports jacket and stepped through the door, barely concealing his discomfort at having to touch the worn, grimy door handle. It probably just looked grimy, but still, thousands of hands had pushed it to get in here.

Just as he had suspected, the diner looked deserted. A bored waitress of indeterminate age sat reading a newspaper. Above her, a TV blared in Spanish, or Portuguese, or something, but nobody paid any attention anyway. The coffee in the old-fashioned machine looked as if it had been there for the past few hours, and Connor vowed to stick to bottled water. In a sealed bottle!

He sat in a booth that looked semi-private and waited, but the madam took her time finishing whatever article she was reading. "How to Lose 20 Pounds in Only 10 Days," Connor imagined, before she waddled over and flapped a worn menu card on his table.

"What'll you have, love? I still have mashed potatoes from lunch, you know."

Mashed potatoes. Connor cringed. Nutritional advice apparently had not advanced into these nether regions of town. He looked up, smiling thinly. Her name tag read *Dinah* in neatly hand-lettered script, and her apron at least appeared to be clean. Quite possibly the only thing in the whole place that was.

"Just a Perrier, please," he said. "I'm meeting someone. Is Al here yet?"

"Al?" She shook her head. "Nobody here named Al. Sure you won't have anything to eat?"

"No...thanks, Dinah. Maybe Mr. Al? He asked me to meet him here at one, and I figured he was likely a regular, or at least, uh, familiar with the place."

"Not a clue, honey. Maybe go check your instructions. You might be at the wrong place after all."

She waddled away again, and Connor sat dumbstruck for a second. In the wrong place? No shit he was in the wrong place.

But just the way she said *check your instructions* made him pause for a moment.

Check your...Christ!

He sighed and called out, "Oh, Dinah?"

"Change your mind on the mashed, honey?"

"Not really, no. Do you know when the chef is getting here? The Original Chef, I mean."

Good God, he felt stupid just playing this game of hide-and-seek. Code names, for crying out loud? Really? He would give that little prick Rafael a piece of his mind when he got out of here.

Dinah seemed to be checking him over for a moment, one long look up and down. His irritation with this whole outfit was growing by leaps and bounds, but then, quite suddenly, her entire demeanor changed.

"Wait right here." The drawl was gone; so was the slouching gait. The menu stayed where she had dropped it, on the table beside him, and, as she walked away, he couldn't help but see a similarity with the young man who had come to his office. The nerdy geek and yet...not quite. This quintessential diner waitress, and yet...

Moments later, she was back and inclined her head toward the back area, behind the worn counter and the soda machines.

"Come on. I'll take you to him."

He gathered his overcoat and small briefcase and followed her. Behind the counter, he had a quick glance into the kitchen, where two young line cooks argued about one thing or another. Then Dinah opened a door and motioned him through it.

"Down the hall to the very end, knock on the door that says private, wait for someone to open. See ya."

She gave him a little push, and he walked. Did anyone else even work around here? He saw none of the usual staff that should be bustling around a restaurant, even a greasy spoon like this one, at this time of the day. Instead, each end of the hallway featured one of those small, ball-like internet cameras you could access from any cell phone in the world, to see what was going on. Nice touch to make you feel especially welcome and to protect the immense earnings this place must bring in, of course.

He knocked as instructed and imagined he could hear those cameras whirring and focusing on him. Despite his irritation and inner sarcasm, a bead of sweat rolled down his back, which irritated him even more.

Then there was the silence—more unnerving than anything. No dishes clanging or waitstaff shouting...nothing, just goddamn silence.

Finally, the door opened, and he came face to face with Al.

"Welcome, Mr. Beauregard," he said in the most pleasant manner. "You are right on time. We appreciate that. Come on in and meet everyone."

'Everyone' turned out to be an older, white-haired gentleman with piercing, pure black eyes, two younger versions of him on either side, and Al himself. For a moment, no one spoke. Then Al whispered something into the older man's ear.

"Sit," he said and indicated a seat. "You're on time. I like this in my business partners."

"Sure. I am afraid I don't quite..."

Al put his hand on Connor's arm and shook his head. "In a minute, Connor. Let's just wait until everyone is here. It will make it so much easier for everyone."

Connor sat and folded his hands in front of him on the table, like a damn schoolboy, he thought, but he could feel the sweat rolling down his back again, and any irritation he might have felt out in the parking lot or in the hallways was suddenly gone, to be replaced by a dire need just to get out of here and be done with these people.

Rafael, what the fuck have you got me into, he thought, and not for the first time.

He tried to figure out who these three men in front of him were, with no real success. They might have been brothers, cousins, anything. They looked interchangeable, except for their age. As a matter of fact, even Al fit into that group like an extra chess piece. Same dark eyes, same silent graceful, catlike mannerisms. Connor clenched his fingers and forced himself to remain calm.

He studied the prints on the walls. Scenes from a southern town, maybe Mexico, maybe Italy or South America.

"The artist is a friend of mine," the older man said, startling Connor out of his reverie. "I've always coveted the peace he portrays in those pictures. He is quite successful as a painter as well."

"Very nice. Although I must confess I don't know much about art and its value."

"Not everything has a monetary value, Mr. Beauregard."

There was almost something approaching humor there...almost. And still he couldn't place the accent of the voice. The man spoke with the most cultured, even intonation he had ever heard...as if he had studied it just to make sure no one could place him by the way he spoke.

And what would make someone do a thing like that?

The man pointedly looked up at a large clock behind Connor and frowned.

"Al, I said one p.m., did I not?"

"Yes, you most certainly did."

"It is two minutes after one now. Where are they?"

"I don't know. Maybe..."

"Excuses, Al? Really?"

The words snapped like a whip, and suddenly, Connor thanked his good fortune for always aiming to be a few minutes early for every single meeting. Didn't always work but, as a rule of thumb, he did not tolerate lateness in anyone. Apparently, neither did the man in front of him, although, jeez, two minutes after?

He could feel the physical tension in the room rising. All four men across from him just sat a little straighter, paid a little more attention.

Connor figured he would throw the shirt he was wearing away when he got back to his office. He felt for the checkbook in his pocket and calmed himself mentally. Just pay them back and walk away. He repeated it like a mantra. Just pay them back...

Someone knocked at the door.

Al rose and moved to open it, and three men walked in, casually as you please.

The older man neither rose nor acknowledged them in any way. Instead, he pointedly stared at the clock on the wall.

"You are late."

"Well, you know, man, traffic and all."

"Do not be late when I call you, ever again. Is that understood?"

"Look, like, we're not even late. It's, like, five after."

"Is that understood?"

The words thundered across the room, and for a moment no one dared speak.

"Understood."

Connor sat rooted to his chair and was utterly convinced he would never be able to move or speak another word again.

Now he paid more attention to the three who had just walked in. They looked like about the meanest individuals any motorcycle gang in the area could have produced, walking in casually and self-assured, clad in black leather head to toe, the sleeves of their jackets cut off crudely at the shoulder showing off bulging biceps and a kaleidoscope of tattoos which made your head spin just trying to follow the patterns. At least Connor thought they wore leather vests. For all the patches sewn or stuck to them, they might have been plain old denim.

Their obvious leader, a short, stocky guy who appeared to use a number of chains as a belt, sporting a greasy ponytail that hung to his waist, plunked his enormous body into a chair as if he owned the place and leered at Connor and the other three men.

"So, Chef, you bring the elite troupe today? Got these fellas protecting you or what?"

The generous, filthy fringe on his leather vest danced and flipped while he spoke, mesmerizing Connor's gaze. Some of the fringes had little beads attached to them that now clicked and clacked, sounding like dice...or little bones...rattling.

Connor shivered. The feeling of having stepped out of his life and into an alternate universe became unbearable.

The Chef said nothing at all, merely fixing his opponent in a firm, cold stare.

"You walk into my office late, you take a seat without being offered one, and you insult my sons and business partners? Are those the manners that your mother raised you with, George?"

"Well, uh, you know..."

The sentence trailed off, and a little of the attitude in the man had definitely evaporated. The man they were calling the Original Chef sat ramrod straight, didn't bother to move as much as a finger, and yet he totally commanded the room.

"Stand."

"Chef?"

"Stand, now."

The words thundered across the room, and the two remaining thugs by the door actually took a step back, right into the wall.

George pulled a greasy bandana from around his head and let it fall to the table.

"That what you're doing now, Chef? In front of these fine gentlemen because I was five minutes late and sat down before you said sit? Have it your way then."

He stood, loose, rebellious, obviously not in the slightest inclined to follow the orders he was being given, but somewhere, Connor caught just a little twitch. The bravado slipped a bit, the grin faltered, his feet shuffled, and...

Later on, he couldn't really recall exactly what happened, but one of the two younger men sitting with Al suddenly moved like a flash. One smooth movement from his chair to his feet, pinning George's arms behind him, stomping down on his foot and pulling a knife out from under the stained leather vest.

He held the knife out to the chef and, at his nod, dropped it to the table as if it were hot.

"And if that was not enough, you even dare come into my house armed, George?"

Completely gone now was George's bravado. "Hey, you know, I must've forgotten that was in there. Definitely wasn't on purpose. Chef, you know I would never... I mean, you and I have been doing business for years. You know I would never do anything..."

"What I do know, George, is that you and your ragtag gang have been stealing from me for several years now. Small-time stuff originally, and I let you get away with it because it was too much of a bother to come out and teach you a lesson."

"We're no thieves," he said, voice trembling. "You gotta know we're no thieves. Now, look, there may have been a few, uh, errors in measurements and such...I didn't always have the best help."

"Silence!"

Again, the voice struck like a shot. "Your excuses make everything worse. You must know that my people have kept records about everything. Do not stand there whining."

"I'm, uh, I mean, I'm not..." George stammered now, wiping his palms on his pant legs and running them through his hair, most likely wishing for the bandanna he had so carelessly discarded.

"Tell me how to make this right, Chef," he asked hoarsely and his eyes pleaded. His entire body would have pleaded with the man sitting there, if it could have.

The chef let him stand there, trembling for a while. The two thugs by the door looked down at the floor. Connor did not envy them having to watch their boss being literally taken apart.

Finally, the Chef spoke again.

He motioned quickly, and the man who had moved so quickly taking the knife off George stood and stepped forward.

"This is my bodyguard, Tony. I want you to shake his hand."

George attempted a thin smile and did as he was asked. Again, Al motioned, and the next man stepped forward.

"This is my son, Dan; I want you to shake his hand."

Another handshake and Al stepped forward.

"This is my son, Al; I want you to shake his hand."

Connor was the last one at the long table, and his hands were firmly clasped against the seat of his chair to keep them from shaking. The Chef looked at him with a gentle, if ice-cold, smile and nodded, motioning for him to do as the others had done.

He stood in front of George, not knowing which one of them shook more at that particular moment.

"This is my sons' business partner, Connor. They work with him. He is like a son to me. I want you to shake his hand and seal the bargain."

Connor offered his hand, and the thug shook it. He fought the urge to pull out a handkerchief and sat again. What on earth had he just done? What was the bargain he had just sealed for God's sake? And why were the words *devil's bargain* hammering in his head as if they might never stop?

Connor felt the room tilt around him, and he thought he was going to be sick. Al's mouth moved. He could hear no words spoken, but he felt someone's hand on his elbow. Dan poured water from a glass and put it in front of him, and, thankfully, Connor drank almost half the glass in one deep gulp.

He put the glass back down gently because his hands were still shaking, but at least he could breathe again, and his heart had slowed down to a normal beat. The Original Chef did not appear to have moved at all.

"You have shaken my sons' hands," he said softly. "If any harm befalls them now, it will be considered the worst and lowest of betrayals, you know that, right?"

Connor's eyes locked on George, and time ceased to have any meaning. Every breath, every heartbeat needed to be worked for, deliberately brought forth with effort.

George never flinched or blinked. Almost automatically, his hand went to the concealed pocket under his vest until he remembered the knife was not there any longer. It lay on the table, right before him.

He and the Chef stayed with their eyes locked on one another for what seemed an eternity. Neither of the men was inclined to look away, neither of them ready to concede. Connor felt his fingers clawing around the edge of his chair again with the effort to stay seated and stay still. Finally, George broke the spell.

"No harm will come to you or your sons," he said slowly, and Connor let out the breath he'd been holding.

"Good. We understand one another."

The Chef waited a moment and pushed a document toward George. Connor thought his heart would stop again when he recognized one of his own business plans. Where the hell had this come from? He had purposely only printed enough for the men in his little group, the day they had met at La Cosa. And Al had refused to take one along with him.

He doesn't use any paper. He memorizes everything. Kayla's words. He could not have, could he? A gentle hand pushed on his elbow, and he realized he had half risen from his chair to reach for the business plan. Al shook his head softly.

"My sons and their partner," the Chef said pleasantly, as if nothing at all had happened just a moment ago, "have started this wonderful little business together."

George looked down at the unfamiliar document without touching it, but only a fool would have missed the implications of the headline: Perfect Cannabis Corporation.

"Now, they will mainly be dealing with medical cannabis," the Chef said, his tone still pleasant and jovial. "I want you to keep an eye out."

"Me?"

"You and your boys over there." The Chef nodded toward the two thugs by the door. "I do not want anything to happen to my sons or to their business...nothing at all."

"Well, like I said, uh, no harm."

"That is not entirely what I mean, George. It frustrates me to have to explain things twice. Please listen. I do not want anything to happen to my sons or their business."

"O-kay." George dragged out the word and looked at Connor and the three younger men for help.

"I am making you, George, you personally, responsible for their safety and their ability to run things without any interference...from anybody. Now, do you understand?"

George paled a little, and Connor could all but see the wheels in his head turning over.

"Chef, uh, that is...a bit—"

"That is an entirely normal and polite request. If you would like to say no, of course."

"No, no, it's not that. I'm just saying, uh, all the other crews...I'm not really sure I can control every single..."

"Try, George, just try," the Chef said mildly. "For your own sake. I am sure your mother taught you to at least try before you give up on something, did she not?"

"Well yeah, I mean I will, but, uh."

"Wonderful. Then we are all in agreement."

The Original Chef smiled and actually clapped his hands.

"Why, I think I am going to have Dinah get us some espresso. Who else would like some?"

No one spoke. George and his two henchmen looked uncomfortable, Al looked down at his hands, and Tony and Dan kept a wary eye on their leader.

"Connor, you simply must try the espresso and coffee cake. Dinah makes it herself, simply divine."

"Sure," Connor said cautiously.

"Right you are, my friend. I am sure we are going to get along just fine. Al, why don't you go and get Dinah? George, unless you and your...men are staying for coffee, you may leave at any time."

Coffee and cake. The man's sudden jovial behavior was potentially even more frightening than his earlier anger had been, but none of it was directed toward Connor, and that was all he wanted, for now.

"So, your sons," he said, coming to a point that had bothered him earlier. "They are all looking...to get involved in PerCan somehow?"

"No, my dear Connor, they are already involved," he said mildly. "If you recall, last week, I gave you half a million dollars to get the company started."

"Correct. And I appreciate every dime of this capital. What I wanted to speak to you about was...well, a repayment."

"That money was not a loan, Connor." The steely undertone was back. "That was a proper investment, and as such, I expect to have a small say in the company."

"Yes, but you see—" Connor stopped. The Original Chef's smile unnerved him. "I, uh, I just thought..."

"You have raised a lot of money in the last few days, and you thought you could just come in here, give me a check, and get rid of a man you don't know and who might interfere with the running of your company."

"Well, no. I, uh..."

"Of course. That is exactly what you were thinking, and I certainly don't blame you." Grinning, he continued, "I am not sure I would want to do business with me either, unless I really knew me well. How about you, Tony?"

"Well, I'd really want to know you first, that's for sure," one of the men said and smiled while taking out his cell phone and checking for messages.

"Oh, you know I hate those things, Tony. No one has a proper conversation any longer. Always staring down at those little things as if their life depended on it. Don't you find that annoying, Connor?"

"It can be a bit much," he admitted, though immediately he was dying to check his phone himself. "Now about this deal."

"Yes, let's talk about it. It looks to me like the first thing we all need to do is get to know one another. Then we will all be one happy family."

One big happy family, with an insane man at the head. One who dealt in code names, issued orders to some of the most frightening motorcycle gangs, and held meetings in the back rooms of old diners, all while requiring you to remember a password to actually get in. Right.

His mind was racing now. He had just watched what this man could do to the head of a motorcycle gang without even uttering an actual threat. Did he really want to deal with someone like this? And could he afford not to?

"I have raised a lot of funds in the past few days," he said, not even minding the arrogance shining through his words. "Something tells me that is a skill you are, uh, in need of?"

"Precisely, my dear Connor, precisely. I have watched you operate over the past few days, and I must say I am very impressed. The way you take money from suckers."

"Investors, sir, they are investors. They will receive a piece of the company. They'll receive properly trading shares once we are trading on the stock exchange. This is a very legitimate business. And while we are on that subject, the securities regulators take an interest in the directors of a publicly traded company, if you get my drift."

"Of course I do. And I am far from being offended. We just have to make proper arrangements."

"You need me." The words were out before Connor could bite them back. On the one hand, that was exactly what he was thinking. On the other, though...he could see Tony's hand twitching, as if he wanted to reach for something. And the Chef, well, he simply smiled broadly as if they were having tea and scones together, discussing the latest golf scores.

"Yes...we need each other. I knew you would come around to understanding. Now, of course you will be running the company, the day-to-day operations, the raising of funds, the construction of the building. My God, what an exciting project. I do so envy you for being involved."

"And you?"

"I? Oh, dear Connor, of course I will not be involved...directly. I hardly ever leave this place. This is my home if you will. No, no, after today, you will not meet me again unless there is a dire emergency of some sort, which I most sincerely hope will never happen."

You and I both, Connor thought and nodded. "OK. Then?"

"Al and Dan will be working with you. They will be my eyes and ears so to speak. They are both hardworking men, highly intelligent, universally talented, and I don't just say that because they are my sons, you understand? You will find a place for them in the company, I am sure, and they can let me know how it is going now and then. Don't look so worried now." He actually reached across and patted Connor's arm.

Connor wanted to pull back, but forced himself to sit still. It would not be a career-building move to show revulsion to the man who had just told you as casually as can be he was taking your company over.

"There's nothing to worry about. Unless it turns out you need some serious help somewhere, none of us are actually going to be involved. You will pay the boys a bit of a salary of course. And you will give each of us 2 million shares in the company, but that is it. Nothing else."

"2 million shares?" Connor paled a little. That was also not what he had had in mind. Somewhere in his plan, he had always been the majority shareholder. Well he, Rafael, Josh, and Simon. God, those three would just tear him to shreds when they found out what he was about to agree to.

"And at one point, when we get tired of it or want to move on, we will likely just sell our shares and do something else. You see, it is really not worth losing your head over, Connor."

ELEVEN

"So he sits there," Connor said to Kayla, pouring his third or fourth vodka and tonic of the afternoon. "Just sits there and, calm as can be, tells me either I'm doing this deal or he's going to kill me."

"Jeez, sweetheart, sounds like a scene right out of *The Godfather*."

"It was damn strange sitting in that room with him and his thug sons. I watched a motorcycle gang leader get cut down to about this size." He held his thumb and forefinger two inches apart.

"This guy, this Chef, and for god's sake, why does he not have a name? This guy actually threatened me. This is my business, I raised the funds, I put the structure together. He comes in, wants a piece, and basically tells me if I'm not handing it over, then... Who the fuck does he think he is?"

Connor stood now and paced the length of Kayla's condo.

"I made this company, and I can damn well un-make it if I choose to, and no Al or Dan or Tony or goddamn Chef are going to come in and tell me what to do."

"Just how much of an involvement did he say he wanted, Connor?"

"Officially, none actually. Two of his sons want to work for me, for a *decent little salary*, and he wants shares in the company."

"So? You give him the shares, you hire his two brats, and be done with it. Where's the problem? He could be more useful than you think."

"Kayla, we're working toward getting a license to grow marijuana. We'll be the biggest producer in the country. Part of that licensing process is a very detailed scrutiny of each and every major person in the company... business and private life."

"Even better for you."

"What do you mean better? If we can't get a license because of Al and his family relations, we're done."

"And so is this Chef. That's why he's not going to be involved, or at least be seen to be involved. And did he actually imply his sons were going to be any kind of senior operatives of the company? He knows all of this—he's not stupid. Al and Dan will work for you, in whatever capacity you find for them, and report back to their father, big deal. The actual decisions are going to be made by you and whoever you put on your board of directors."

"Rafael, Simon, and Josh," Connor said, slowing his pacing down a bit. "And you of course."

It had started rather harmlessly, including Kayla in company discussions, using her knowledge about publicity and news, spending time here at her condo. Now he found himself living with her, making her a large part of the operation. Not the worst outcome, but he wasn't really sure it had even really been his choice.

"Thank you. I'm sure I can contribute. But there's your answer: take what you need from Al and Dan and their father. Use them for your own purposes. And when done with them," Kayla grinned like the Cheshire Cat, "when we are done with them, we will find a way. Nothing is permanent."

"Christ, you are cold."

"Maybe, but I don't think I'm wrong, Connor. A few years down the road, the company is going to be so big, nobody will think about messing with us. Nobody would dare. And whether or not that old man owns a few shares then won't really matter."

"2 million shares...each," Connor said bitterly and downed the rest of his drink.

"And you and I both know that's just paper. If you want to have more shares, you just print them."

"Is that what Hanson used to do?" Connor asked and chuckled.

"Hanson used shares for everything and anything, Connor. He had people working for paper, as he called it. Except for the magazine. He never touched the magazine because he knew that was my baby."

Connor stood at the picture window, arms folded behind his back, staring down at the midtown traffic, just getting bad as the afternoon gave way to evening with everyone trying to rush home as quickly as they could.

"So your advice would be to just leave it. Build my company and put up with them for the moment."

"No harm, is there?"

Connor turned around again and grinned, "You know, I never thought it would be possible to find a woman as intelligent and quick as I am myself, but I certainly appear to have done so."

"So you have," Kayla said and took his hand. "And I'd say that is something we need to celebrate."

TWELVE

At the office, Tessa was now making trips to the bank on a daily basis. Connor expected that she would soon be asking for a raise, not that he would mind. She was quick, she was smart, and he knew she had everything in hand.

He stared at the latest designs for his business cards and logos and frowned. "I'm not sure about these, Tessa, although I do appreciate you involving Jay. What I want for this company is, uh, something... classy, yet corporate. Let's just forget about this one with the leaves right away. We want something that screams science and corporate development. Think pharma industry type, think biggest and best, but in a classy way. Right?"

"I'll let Jay know," she said, gathering the designs up. "He was getting pretty excited about the whole cannabis thing."

"Welcome to the club. Every day, seems investors can't wait to throw money the moment I mention cannabis. It's the most interest I've ever gotten out of a deal, and I've been in them all, from oil to beer, to designer clothes. Unreal. But for PerCan's public image, I want something extremely businesslike."

"Boring."

"If you must, but don't forget about the government licensing body. They sure aren't going to hand out licenses to a bunch of stoners partying out back. We are a serious business, producing medicinal substances. And you and Jay are not exactly our primary customers."

"Still boring."

Connor grinned. "OK, make it boring then. Just tell him to get it done. Anything he needs...just make it look good."

"On it. Oh, and I have to go to the bank again. You're just raking it in faster than I can deposit it. And a fellow named Al dropped off a list of contacts for you."

"You met Al? In person?"

"Yes, should I not have?" she asked with a quizzical look on her face. "Nice man. He said he'd be working with us soon. But in the meantime, he had a lot of contacts who would love to hear from you, on an investment basis."

"Is that what he said now," Connor asked, leaning back. Nice of Al to at least tell him before he popped into the office, spoke to his staff, dropped off a list of names. As if he needed help finding investors.

Oh well. At some point, they were all going to have to work together anyway. And in his mind, the words *work together* had huge quotation marks around them.

"So what did you think of him? Of Al, I mean?"

Tessa shrugged. "Seemed OK, a tad weird maybe, but probably no more than most."

"Define weird," Connor said, taking in Tessa and her all-black outfit with multiple silver chains with one long look.

"I can't rightly say, I guess. Just something about him seemed...off? I guess, for starters, the way he talks. Like he studied it. Nobody real speaks like that. And he could have emailed me that list. Instead he makes a trip and hands me this handwritten thing. Who still hand-writes a two-page list? I told him that too, and he just laughed and said email was not really his thing."

"It's not, believe me. And that is just one of his little quirks."

"And I watched him when he left; he had a driver that picked him up. All-black car, tinted windows, like a...I don't know, a movie star?"

"Or worse. Anything else you noticed?"

"No, nothing specific. I can't really tell you why—just that he is kind of, well, odd."

"That he is. Anything else going on today?"

"Yeah, Bill Grogan sent a check, big one too, but there's no paperwork. I need a subscription agreement for each and every one of these guys who gives you money. Remember I told you last week there's a bunch of missing ones."

"Some of them are probably in my car," Connor said, already checking messages on his phone. "I'll get you those sometime. Now I have to run."

"Well, don't forget. And we need to check they are all proper investors."

There were indeed rules about investing in a startup company like his, rules meant to protect people from unscrupulous stock promoters. You had to fit the profile pretty good to fit into the compliance. Connor usually did not care. If you had the money, he figured you should be allowed to spend it as you wished.

"Catherine Egan, the securities lawyer, wants to speak to you," Tessa continued. "There are apparently a few things in the subscription agreements that are not entirely kosher."

"Things?"

"Terms, references. We just copied them from EC Energy, remember. And we were in a rush. It's likely there are some things we missed. Anyway, she thought it would be better to rewrite them properly, make sure everything is checked. And not to forget to get all of them signed."

"Lawyers, always out to make the extra buck." He waved a hand through the air, balled up an invisible piece of paper and tossed it toward the waste basket. "Forget it—it's fine. She's just looking to bill me for making up new subs, and that won't happen. Anything else?"

"Yes, she also said to tell you to look after keeping proper minute books, meeting records, and that kind of thing. She really didn't like it when I said I had nothing yet and would get to it eventually."

"Right." Connor thought of his meeting with the Original Chef and shuddered. There was one meeting he would not write minutes for anytime soon. "I'll make something up...later. Don't worry. I don't need a lawyer for something that mundane. That was it?"

"Not really, but you're not listening to me just now anyway. Your mind is like a thousand miles from nowhere, so I will just email you a list."

"Do that, and I am sorry. I've got at least 15 messages here. So, just tell Catherine I'll take care of everything, you send me your most pressing reminders, and let's just get this done."

"OK." Tessa shrugged and returned to her desk. Contrary to what people assumed from her appearance and her strange boyfriend, she liked to get it right and done right the first time. He'd make it up to her and bring her some of that missing paperwork. At least he would try, later. For now, he had people to see.

He dialed while pacing back and forth in his office, bouncing on his heels.

"Rafael, you got time for a quick lunch?"

"Sure. Where you at?"

"My office. The Lighthouse in half an hour? There are a few things I want to go over with you. And I need the complete story on these gangsters you stuck me with."

"Al's family."

"Al's family...yeah. What the fuck did you get me into?"

"I told you, if you're going to be in this kind of business, well, then you need someone like them for—security, for lack of a better word. To keep you safe...all of us. You remember what happened to Magic Cannabis."

Magic Cannabis, Connor thought, nice little operation, much smaller than the one he was planning, well run and well-funded. One day, they found their entire operation burned to the ground, two security staff killed.

"I read about it," he said tersely. "They said it was some motor-cycle gang?"

"Probably. Didn't like who was moving into their territory. I imagine they might have asked for protection money and been turned down."

"We're just going to have to be smarter than that, Rafael. Talk to your friend Simon. He must be able to help out. He charges enough for his security systems."

"I did. He says he's happy we have Al's family in our back pockets, just in case."

"Change of subject," he said brightly. "Founder's shares. Let's give ourselves founder's shares at $.0001. 2 million for us as startup partners. Al, Dan, and the Original Chef want theirs issued too. Though I'm not sure that's a name I can put on a share certificate."

"He'll let you know what he wants, trust me."

"That's what I did last time. Now, I'll have to find something to do for his two sons."

"Dan and Al, I heard. They are both highly intelligent people, though. I've met them, and I can probably use Al in the property acquisition and construction."

"You can?" Connor was more than a little surprised, having envisioned those two sitting in his front room, idle from now on. "By all means then, takes a load off me."

"And see if TC needs someone to help him. Looks to me like he's struggling putting together a grow op of this size. Don't know for sure, but Dan can probably give him a hand. Make sure it's planned right from the beginning."

"Rafael, you have just earned yourself lunch." Connor grinned again. Once again, his problems were disappearing before his very eyes. "I'm buying. So, get a move on. Half an hour at The Lighthouse. We definitely have things to celebrate."

He ran out, leaving some cash for Tessa, grabbed the list Al had left for him on the way out, and pushed the elevator button before anybody could get to him with anything else. Damn this cannabis business. It just ran itself, did it not?

THIRTEEN

He had it again—the magic, the touch, whatever you wanted to call it—he had it. The ability to paint a picture in front of his marks, his investors. The ability to show them what he was planning and thinking, to build the company right in front of them with nothing but words, concepts, and a few well-placed references to existing businesses. He did not show up with a projector or a briefcase full of paper literature—no, Connor Beauregard had all the facts and figures in his head, and he believed them.

He never let a single bit of doubt or an unanswered question linger in his head, so when he talked, all people could see were convictions, and all they heard was that he was absolutely certain everything would work out just the way he said it would.

He also never came in asking for anything—he showed them what he planned to do; he built it right there in front of them—until they asked him if they would be allowed to be part of this exciting new venture.

Then he would think about it.

He told them he had all of his money tied up in the project, that of his family and his fiancé. And there would be Kayla, smiling, confirming his words, and telling everyone how she had not been this excited about a new project since starting up her publishing empire several years ago. They made the perfect tag team by now. They did not even have to discuss timing or who mentioned which facts—it just happened. They were that good together.

Connor reached across and squeezed her hand gently. Even that bit of a gesture made good publicity—was he not after all a family-oriented man who was trying to do the right thing in the pharma industry and help those afflicted with horrible pain and other problems that hitherto had no other medication? He was their hero, he helped people, and he told himself every day.

And his investors ate it up.

Of course, most of them were committed the moment he mentioned a billion dollars annual revenue. Everyone wanted in on that—and think—they were changing lives in the process…. They were making a difference. Sure, they were growing drugs, but they were the good guys. And everyone definitely wanted in on that.

Connor leaned back in what had become his regular seat at the bar at La Cosa and watched Kayla chat up the gent he had just spoken to. God, the man needed a support system to hold up the wrist with that golden watch. Damn thing must have weighed a ton. His father would have lectured about how that kind of outward display of wealth was nothing but obscene…

For one fleeting moment, he had an image of his father taking the same kind of heavy gold watch off his wrist, and he downed a quick gulp of his drink. He tried not to think about his family if he could avoid it. And anyway—he had Kayla now and the dozens of cousins and other assorted relatives she had introduced him to. Who needed the grief from a life that he did not belong to any longer?

Better to focus on the man in front of him who right now was trying to slide his hand down to Kayla's ass somewhere. Connor covered his giggle with another drink. If the sucker but knew how angry that kind of thing made her. And you did not want Kayla Montecito angry—under no circumstances. Now she'd work three times as hard to get more money out of him and out of all of his friends.

And Connor didn't even have to do anything about it. That kind of talent was rare—one of the things he appreciated about Kayla. She winked at Connor slyly and went back to charming Mr. Small-Car-on-the-Wrist. If he wanted to remember these people's names, he would really have to cut down on the drinking.

He waved to the waitress and signaled her to pick up the check for the entire group. *Never go in light in the wallet, and always be the first guy to reach for the check*—rich people were just cheap bastards. They loved the guy who got the check.

Rafael had taught him well a long time ago when they were just getting started, scrounging for deals. And some things just stayed true forever.

Connor leaned back and let the expensive cognac slide down his throat deliciously. Dammit if he did not own the whole world right now. This was the way things were supposed to be.

Kayla came up to him and took a sip of his cognac.

"I have just separated that ass from a lot of his money," she said pleasantly and took a large sip. "Now let's go do something frivolous with it."

He put his finger across his lips, though he had to grin.

"Psst—it's still investors' money."

"True, but it's your company."

"It is my company, and I'm going to see an investor in Switzerland next week. I think I'm going to need my press department with me, don't you?"

"Damn straight you do, my love." She slid her fingers down his leg and in one smooth motion turned around to his investor, who had just returned from the washrooms.

"Well now, Tom, are you ready to come on board with this exciting opportunity?"

She was almost as good as he himself, Connor thought—almost. Certainly, she had surpassed Rafael by now—Rafael, who was way too careful and had stuck him with the likes of Al.

Al and his crazy relatives. No need to think about them now. He would think about Switzerland instead. He really did know a few people he wanted to see over there—businesspeople who had participated in one or the other of his deals and always had the kind of money he needed—if he was willing to pay their interest rates. More than hitting up investors, he wanted to see about places to put some of his money, though. Now that things were going swimmingly, he needed to think about parking some of the funds. In this kind of business, you never knew what was going to happen, and especially if things took a downturn, people had a nasty habit of standing at your front door wanting their miserable few bucks back.

He'd been there too—and the better part of valor was always claiming poverty himself.

"First class to Frankfurt, and from there, private plane to Zurich," he told her later on. "I know you've been to Zurich before."

"Sure have—lovely city. Where are we staying?"

"Oh—you're going to like this. I've rented a villa in the mountains for us through Essentials."

"Essentials." He had actually made her eyes light up, and she said the name in a whisper, as to give it more meaning. "Really?"

Essentials might well have been the world's most sybaritic private villa rental place. Nothing but million-dollar estates, complete with waitstaff, cooks, drivers if desired, usually exotic cars. Some of them had private planes included. All of it in the most beautiful places on earth, and all of it available to rent if you didn't need to ask about the price.

And that of course was on top of the exclusive annual membership rates which you had to pay just to be allowed to browse the catalogue.

"Essentials—of course. Only the finest for you and me."

Again, her fingers slid up his leg, and Connor's hand tightened around the cognac glass just a bit. Oh, the things money could do for you. He had always known, and finally, he had put it all together, and he could enjoy it all.

FOURTEEN

A few days later, he finally managed to introduce TC and Dan to one another. Dan went by the relatively innocuous name 'Dan Parker'—probably not the name he was born with. Rafael had told him in confidence Dan was actually "Dante," and Dante had taken care of several problems for his father. More to the point—men who had caused problems for his father, who were never going to cause anyone a problem again. So now he wanted him out of the line of fire, in a quiet, unpretentious job where no harm could come to him.

"You're going to like working with Dan," he had told TC. "He's such a talented guy—and knowledgeable in every single way. Unreal, the things he knows about growing cannabis."

Connor did not know if Dan had even the slightest clue about how to grow cannabis—but he figured if TC went in with a good attitude, at least they would avoid killing one another, right? Pun intended.

TC had rented a bit of office space for himself and Dan—somewhere downtown. It seemed to lack light and atmosphere, at the back end of a commercial strip mall right between a dentist and one of those sue-'em-all lawyers' offices, but it was cheap.

He had brought some money for them—to set up shop—but he found the two little rooms were already furnished... sort of.

"What did you do, go to the Salvation Army?" he asked TC, suppressing the urge to brush off a faded visitor's chair before sitting on it.

"Better—the lawyer's outfit next door just got all-new furniture, got rid of all of this stuff."

"I can see why," Connor muttered and tried not to touch too much of the chair.

"Relax. We got it cleaned before we put it in here."

Dan appeared out of nowhere and shook Connor's hand firmly.

"How you doin'? You like what we've done with the place?"

"Just fine." Connor fought down the urge to resent the man for his attitude. It would not do any good, but still, a bit more deference might have been in order. After all, he was talking to the man who owned the company, or at least founded it, OK—but without him, none of them would be here.

"Figured we didn't need much—TC and I. The stuff we have to do doesn't require uncomfortable designer furniture and a gal at reception with half-inch fingernails.

"TC and I have been going by your business plan and started mapping out a facility of approximately 200,000 square feet of growing space, plus additional supply areas."

He led Connor around into the next office, where a huge, beat-up drafting table dominated the room.

"Now, 200,000 square feet sounds huge, I know, and there's no way we are going to need it all starting up, but I figured you're looking at expansion, right, talking about going big. So, I went and started with big and figured we can grow into it."

"I like it," Connor said and looked at the enormous drawing on the table that said nothing to him. "I like it, the way you're getting right into this. I'm glad your father suggested it. Well done."

"I do have a bit of experience," Dan said mildly. "Didn't just step off the immigrant train here, you know what I'm saying."

Connor forced himself to smile. "No offense, Dan. Wasn't aimed at you. It's just not often you get to work with professionals like yourselves who take their work seriously, you know. I've met my share of slackers over the years."

"I'm sure you have."

TC joined them with a few chipped mugs of coffee and set one down in front of each of them.

"Dan's awesome, Connor. I'm glad we're working together. He's the one who reminds me to think big when I'm ready to pull back. So have a look. Tell us what you think."

Connor had no idea what he was actually looking at, but he made himself look down at the drawing and shook his head.

"You've done an incredible amount of work over the last few days. Can't believe all of this." His fingers traced a few words. "Growing room A, growing room B, flowering rooms. Drying rooms…packaging. Jesus, guys, you've built my company."

Dan took a sip of his coffee and sat back in an old chair. He pulled off his glasses and kept his eyes on Connor's for an uncomfortably long time before he finally spoke.

"Yes—we did the solid research behind it all and put together a schedule that might actually work. There's a lot more to be done when it comes to costing, assumptions, estimates, that kind of thing. I am sure you know."

Connor locked eyes with him, making an effort to keep calm.

"You have done excellent work here, and thank you for catching me up. Now I have to run. I have an investor to see. We will talk in a couple of days."

He forced himself to rise slowly and leave the office at a leisurely pace, and only when he had reached his car did he allow himself to floor the accelerator and peel out of the parking lot as if someone was chasing him. Damn that entire brood.

"It's all for my company," he reminded himself and pounded the steering wheel with frustration. "All for my company, goddamn it."

Indeed, he had read some of the literature he had found about growing cannabis, anything he had been able to pull off the internet quickly. There was just such a glut of information out there on the substance. Now this Dante… "Damn them all!"

He pulled into the parking lot at The Lighthouse and took the elevator up to the bar. His earlier good mood was all but gone. He needed a drink now and a conversation where he was not the one lagging behind when it came to knowledge and information.

"Fancy meeting you up here," he said, sliding into his accustomed bar stool, laughing as he recalled they had been sitting in the exact same spots, exactly a month ago, complaining about deals going sour, when the idea had struck.

Rafael raised his head from a spiral-bound document and grinned. "Fancy that. What are you up to? I figured you'd be either sweet-talking investors, taking care of your lovely girlfriend, or packing for Switzerland."

"Screw packing." Connor signaled the bartender for his usual. "Anything I need over there, I am going to buy, Kayla, I am taking with me, and the investors—well, I might have to leave a few for you."

"Don't mind if I do. The list of interested parties Al dropped off is long—and each and every one of them is good for over 100,000. Nice not to fund raise a thousand bucks at a time. But seriously, you look like sh… well, down, let's just say."

"Dante." Connor rolled his eyes. "Smartass. Probably read a couple of books, *Growing Weed for Dummies*, or something. Now he delights in sounding like a professor making sure everyone thinks I know dick."

"You do know dick, at least about growing marijuana."

"That's no reason to act like it and to spread it around. It's not their company—it's mine."

"Technically, it is…"

"Rafael, I swear to you—if you don't quit with the *it's a public company* bullshit."

"Easy, big boy, easy. Man, he really gets to you, doesn't he? Relax. I heard he's like that—really gets into what he's doing, studies it down to the smallest little detail, until he really is a professor about it. But that's not a bad thing. Nobody would expect you to know everything, just as long as you know to hire the right people and get the knowledge you need out of them."

"Right again..." Connor took another deep draught from his drink and nodded at the fat document on the bar. "So what are you studying, how to close the sale?"

"Don't be a smartass." Rafael turned the document around.

"*The Cannabis Growing Bible*," Connor groaned. "Et tu, Brute? Does everybody around here have to make sure they know more than I do?"

"Actually, I'm just reading this thing so I know what to look for in a building when we finally get around to buying or leasing one. All well and good to renovate it to where we want to be, but why do more work than we have to?"

"So, what have you learned thus far?" Connor asked bitterly, giving the book a little snip with his fingers.

"For starters, did you know that the males are actually useless?"

"Couple of girlfriends told me so, yes."

"Male plants flower, but they have very little cannabinoids, the chemical stuff we will make our money from. The female flowers, however," Rafael leafed through the well-thumbed book, "those flowers are what you want because they develop without seeds, and those flower buds will produce resin. And that resin is actually what we are after. Cannabinoids and THC. After a couple of weeks, Bob's your uncle."

"Bob?"

"Well, you know what I mean."

"Rafael?"

"Yes?"

"You are starting to bore me."

Rafael leafed through the book again. "I had no idea how important the exact number of light and dark hours are, or how susceptible these things are to diseases, fungi, bugs, temperature fluctuations, airflow issues..."

"Rafael…"

"Yes, yes. I'm quitting. Don't beat up on me. I just started reading this for the building search. I had no idea how fascinating this was."

"Fascinating." Connor downed the remainder of his drink and looked around. For once there was no one else he knew at The Lighthouse. Strike two. He did not feel like going to see investors at the moment. If he wasn't in the mood, chances were he would not be able to raise any money anyway. He'd go home—hang out with Kayla. She was sure to put him in a better mood.

Grinning, he slipped off his stool and patted Rafael's shoulders.

"Well, you go ahead and study this interesting stuff then. I have a few things to prepare for. Let me know how it's going."

"Will do."

To his dismay, Rafael had already found another spot in the book that appeared utterly fascinating, and he hardly looked up as Connor left.

"See you later."

Much later, Connor thought and took great delight in sticking Rafael with the check.

He already knew what he wanted to do with the suddenly available day, and the anticipation drove him on. Since he had moved in with Kayla, he had not had a lot of opportunities to admire members of the opposite sex. Charming and wealthy as she was, Kayla kept a strict eye on him, never quite saying it, but never letting him forget either what she had done for his company thus far.

They were getting the royal treatment in her magazines, getting all the public exposure he could have wanted, access to Kayla's remarkable contact list in business and politics. He could hardly fault her for any of it. Sometimes, he quietly wondered why she was doing all of it, only to shrug, move on, and enjoy it while it lasted.

But it also meant he could not allow himself one single misstep. She did keep her eye on him, and while it was enjoyable to walk into any black-tie event with a beautiful, successful woman at his arm, he had to check himself regularly to keep from checking out the younger women in attendance.

This afternoon, he found himself in a classy little bar off Decantur Street, known as Señor Paul's. Señor Paul, a wily little old man, owned the entire building. Some rumors said it was the entire block, and he hired only the most beautiful, cultured, and educated women to entertain his guests.

For an afternoon, Connor immersed himself in the pleasure of their entertainment and let it recharge and revitalize him.

FIFTEEN

Dan studied his drawings again, making a few minor adjustments. TC, he found, did not know nearly enough about growing, so he was glad his father had invited him to step in, but in reality, he was having fun with this one.

"You kind of pissed off Connor," TC said, looking over his shoulder. "Why are you putting all those little squares in?"

"I want to separate the plants as much as possible, avoid the risk of contamination. If anything happens, it would be disastrous to wipe out an entire harvest. But if you can contain it... To answer your first question, I enjoy pissing off Connor."

"You sure that's such a smart idea?"

"The man knows nothing, nothing whatsoever. He has no clue about growing cannabis, he only marginally grasps what it takes to run a company of this magnitude, and he is too arrogant to realize any of it. So why would I be polite to him?"

"Well, it is his company," TC said, looking down at his shoes, "and he did hire me, giving me a chance when no one else would."

"He hires good people. You are right there. I don't know if that's by accident or by design, but other than that, I don't have much respect for him."

"Josh told me he is unbeatable as a sales guy."

"Then he should own a used-car dealership." Dan leaned over his drawing again and followed a line with his finger. "We're going to need massive power supply lines through here and here, where the grow rooms are. Each one of these plant pods will have its own grow light, red just before they are flowering, blue thereafter, stimulates growth."

"We used to have a smaller version in the greenhouse—nothing like what you're planning, though," TC said, picking up a drawing Dan had quickly put to paper earlier. "I've never seen a light like this one."

"It's fairly new. Perfect light and temperature to stimulate growth in all the different phases. Unfortunately, they generate a ton of heat, so we're going to have to air condition each and every one of the lights, too, or we're going to burn the plants.

"And over here, I want the mother room," Dan muttered. "That's where we will grow the plants we make clones of, so that should also be connected to this main power supply line."

He drew more lines in red and blue, stepped back, erased again, asked TC's advice, and wandered through the room pulling his hair. At one point he sat heavily in the chair, muttering, but somehow the smile never left his face. He was having a grand time. Who would have guessed that by the time he finally did make a splash in the drug business, it would be the legal way?

"Hey, Dan, can I ask you something?"

"Sure, something I missed on the plan?"

"As if. I feel like a high school kid beside you. That's my point. I mean, I don't know half the stuff you know. If at any time you're not comfortable working with me..."

"Why shouldn't I be, TC? You know your stuff, enough to pick up what you need, you know you have a lot to learn, and you're ready to admit it. Far as I am concerned, I'd rather work with you than your fearless leader Connor."

"What about you, though—how did you get into all of this? It's like you've been doing this all your life, if you don't mind me asking. And I know a lot of the hobby growers out there. I'm thinking your name might have come up before, but..."

Dan grinned broadly, toed open the bar fridge, and pulled out a beer. "You're thinking, huh? No, my family, at least, my father, invested in Connor's outfit. Thought it might be a good idea if one of us were working here."

"To keep a bit of an eye on how things are running?"

"Maybe." Dan shrugged. "It's an interesting business, and I needed a new project anyway, you know."

"But cannabis, how come you know so much about growing? Shoot, those lights? They're, like, right out of Star Wars. I know grow lights, but that stuff..."

"You pick it up, TC. You just pick it up. You'll see. Read a bit of the literature I've put on your desk, and you'll know where to start."

"I saw—thanks, by the way. You have to lend me your library card some day. As far as I can see, none of that stuff is available in a regular bookstore or even on the web."

"Not hardly." Dan grinned and took a big swig of his beer.

Rob's library, his older brother Roberto. He probably wouldn't be impressed to see a lot of it in here, but he wouldn't need any of his reading materials for a few more years.

But he had to admit one thing: when it came to growing, cooking, or mixing drugs of any kind, Roberto had all the knowledge you could ever want. Distribution, well, not so much. Telling an undercover cop from a regular old mark...also not so much. But everything else...

"Here's to you, Rob," he said softly and made a silent toast.

Early parole was always a possibility.

SIXTEEN

Newly energized, Connor returned to his office early evening. Tessa had of course gone home a long time ago, and an empty office was just what he needed at the moment.

All due deference to Kayla, but since he had moved into her posh condo, he had stepped into the role of *Connor Beauregard, Kayla Montecito's boyfriend.* Idle moments spent by himself drinking, shooting the bull on the phone with Rafael, or just doing nothing were hard to come by. Every now and then, he just didn't feel like talking, being *on*, being Connor Beauregard, superstar…it was just too much hard work sometimes.

This was one of these moments. For now, he just wanted to hang out, cuss, be in a miserable mood, complain, and be down on everything and everybody in his way.

That was not a side he willingly showed to his business partners, his investors, or even Kayla. Not if he could help it in any way. He had to be the upbeat, dynamic go-getter for everybody all day long—the self-assured star. God, just now, 10 minutes of absolutely nothing would be heaven.

But work was always there…and one thing kept pressing on him, and he had been putting it off for a few days, simply because he did not quite know how to get a handle on it. He finally had to make a decision on buying a shell, and while he talked like he knew everything there was to know, he also knew he needed to do a bit of serious research on the details, in private, of course.

He had sold a ton of subscriptions just recently, more than ever, as a matter of fact, and the real money would start coming in once they traded on the stock exchange. For this purpose, he needed a little shortcut.

Getting a company listed on the stock exchange, any stock exchange—even the investor-oriented pink sheets bulletin boards or venture exchanges—meant enough scrutiny, paperwork, and legal fees to make his skin crawl, and they'd still be tied up in red tape by the time Connor hit 50.

He needed to be trading now—not 25 years from now.

Fortunately, he knew a few people—OK, so Rafael knew a few people—who had a nice little clean company trading on one of the smaller boards, doing not much of anything, except waiting for someone to take it over.

Once he had picked one, they would amalgamate the two companies, change the name, issue new shares, and bingo, large and in charge, Connor Beauregard's Perfect Cannabis would be trading. Then he could really go out and show them what raising funds was all about. The legitimacy trading on an exchange would give him, the money, the deals...the possibilities were endless.

He knew the basics of buying a shell company and being listed almost instantly. He knew how it was supposed to work on paper, but he still had not nailed all the details into place. And those pesky details could trip him up later on.

He put his feet up on his desk and started flipping through the emails on his phone. Rafael knew a guy who apparently had a shell worth looking at.

Connor looked back down at his phone's screen. This shell he was looking at, it looked great on paper. There was a limited number of existing shareholders and enough of them in the 'inner circle' of the guy offering the shell, so a unanimous shareholder vote would basically be guaranteed. They had actually done some sort of business before, nothing big, nothing earth-shaking, but there were records, a bank account, and a couple of true financial statements. Even better—nobody would be able to accuse them of being a literal 'shell company,' existing solely for the purpose of this takeover.

Although he suspected that's exactly what he was looking at. The name of the company told you nothing, nothing at all, and that was the way he liked it.

But there was still the matter of the kind of people running this shell. The last thing he needed was some yahoo shareholder in this thing going crazy on him because of the whole cannabis thing. He'd learned that one the hard way. Not everybody was as convinced about the future of medical cannabis as he himself was.

Drugs, as if he were going to peddle heroin on the next street corner. He shook his head and forced himself to move on. You could lead a horse to water, but if the sucker had his head up his rear end, nothing was going to happen.

Back to the issue of the shell company. God, this dry technical stuff bored him!

He put his phone on speaker and wandered through the room, watching the sun setting over the harbor.

"Rafael, where you at? What's going on?"

"Looking at some prospects on buildings for lease. What about you?"

"Relaxing at the office. I've had a tough afternoon." He could almost hear Rafael mouthing *poor you* and plowed right on before Rafael could say something rude. "Is Al with you?"

"Not at the moment. Did you need anything from him?"

"Not likely, Rafael. He gives me the creeps. I'm after some privacy for now. But I'm looking at this shell you sent me over."

"Image Group—nice, clean little shell. Good fit for us."

"Everything looks great, I agree, but for one thing."

"And that is?"

"And that is, Rafa, I don't necessarily want Al and the Original Chef and his entire clan in my company, in the position of pulling the strings."

"They will own a certain number of shares in PerCan anyway. You agreed to that, remember?"

"And I am going to live with that. I already said that, but when this deal happens, the amalgamation, the name change, the relisting... I need every single one of the original shareholders to be on board with me, voting the proper way. I don't need some fool standing up at the last minute, going what about this, and what about that, and maybe it would be better... I'd rather shoot myself than deal with them in that kind of situation."

"Well, don't shoot yourself yet. The people who own this thing are all 100 percent trustworthy."

"And you are guaranteeing this?"

"Todd, the guy who is in control of this thing, is one of us. He is not going to let anybody fuck this up. He is CFO on another deal I am working on—he is totally clean, Connor, nothing to worry about."

"I suppose he's going to want a fair bit of cash here, no?"

"Shares—personally, he'll take shares. The way he's thinking is that every one of the original shareholders will keep maybe 100 shares, you're buying the rest of them, roll the original shares back, bring in the PerCan people, and reissue shares forward."

"You are making my ears bleed, Rafa. None of the small stuff. Just tell me it is going to work, and nobody is going to accuse me of buying a shell company or shortchanging them in any way."

"Relax, it's nothing but a mathematical exercise, so everybody gets the same value of shares they had before—old company or new company. Let Catherine handle it, and all you have to do is write a glowing letter to our shareholders about what a wonderful thing you are doing."

"Catherine is a bloodsucker. She'll charge for getting up and breathing in the morning if you let her. Did you see her latest bill? 50 thou, just for doing a few corporate filings because we are selling shares in a company that's not trading yet? Tessa could have done it, if anyone had the patience to sit and teach her. And you would only have to show her once."

"All lawyers are serial billers, my friend. So, what's the deal? You want to talk to Todd in the morning, set something up, have a chat?"

"I am thinking so," Connor said slowly. He had a few other options, but really, if he decided to go with Rafael's deal, he could rightly roll all the paperwork and the small details off on him, which suited him just fine.

So long as all of his conditions were met.

"And Al and his gang are not in this deal?"

"No, Connor, Al and his family have no relation to anybody who owns shares in Image Group. You want me to write that down, or is this good enough?"

"No—if you're sure, set up something for the morning. I will go talk to Todd. Then we can both go see Catherine if necessary, give the bloodsucker a bit more money, let her inflate her bill, and get the takeover started. I promised Kayla we're going to Switzerland."

"Switzerland," Rafael whistled. "Nice. What's going on over there?"

"There is a pharmaceutical manufacturer I want to talk to—get their take on medical marijuana—see a few investors, have a vacation, and make a few contacts in the banking world, hopefully. Soon, we're going to be rolling in the dough, my friend, and it never hurts to be prepared."

"Connor..."

"I know, I know—the government frowns upon that kind of thing. Don't you think I know that? I'm just looking—nothing else, just looking, making a few contacts, getting a few feelers out there, just to see what is possible."

"Grow up, Connor—it's not like in the old days, when they let you do what you wanted. Geez, in the old days you could carry around bearer bonds and shares like cash." Rafael got almost wistful. "Whoever had the damn things could clip the coupons and collect the cash—great way to move money around. Now, now it's hard to find somebody who will take an actual printed share certificate. Everything's got to be digitally traceable and taxable, electronic records—the whole bit. You know."

"Uh-huh, and you are telling me to be careful, Rafael?"

Rafael laughed wistfully. "Old days, my friend, old days. Long gone by. We've all gone legitimate by now, but 20 years ago..."

20 years ago, Connor's mind trailed off. He had heard Rafael's stories many a time at The Lighthouse Bar or La Cosa. If you went by his stories, the man had cut a swath of half-legal deals clear across the country, but Connor was never sure how much of it was bar talk and how much reality. Though if you looked at Al and company...

He realized he had missed the last half of what Rafael was saying and laughed because he heard his friend chuckle.

"Good one, Rafael, really good one. Now, I am beat, so can you set this thing up with Todd tomorrow and get it started in a way that makes sense? I'd really appreciate it."

He hung up the phone and sat staring out at the harbor again. Finally getting to trade—how exciting would that be? There would be more than one bottle of champagne Kayla would open.

Kayla! Shit! He'd completely forgotten to call her in the busy-ness of his afternoon. He quickly called their favorite restaurant, ordered all of her favorites delivered, and hoped she would be only marginally mad. Well—he'd make up for it...

SEVENTEEN

Todd he found to be a likeable guy. They met at a coffee shop midtown, one of the ones that had dozens of lookalike branches, and he took an instant liking to the man. Tall, open, friendly face, but enough corners and edges to him so you could call him a man's man, a guy who knew how to work and was not afraid of it.

He also did not waste a lot of time talking about the weather, sports, the government, or other boring minutiae, but pulled out a folder with a couple of sheets of paper in it and got down to business.

"So you're interested in our little company, Mr. Beauregard, are you?"

"Call me Connor, and yes, I am thinking this looks like a good fit for both of us."

"Medical marijuana." Todd nodded slowly and looked over one of the glossy investor presentations Connor had brought with him. "Looks like we're going to make a bit of money in the near future, does it not?"

"That would be the plan." Connor grinned. "I cannot tell you how excited people get to hand over large sums of money when I mention cannabis."

"Everybody is doing it—medical marijuana, I mean. It's the hot investment property of the day."

"That's why I am coming to you, Todd." Connor leaned across the table a little closer. "I mean—you know where I can take this company, right?" He tapped the folder with his index finger. "This is going to be the best thing to happen to all of your shareholders since they decided to purchase stock in this—this..."

"Dinky little outfit?"

"Small but viable trading company."

"Nice save." Todd's turn to laugh. "Hey, you don't have to convince me here—I know exactly why you are interested in this company and what you want to do. Not my first time at the rodeo either. All I need to know is what you're prepared to offer, how you're planning to roll this out, and we're all going to walk away with a lot of money in our pockets, right?"

"Right." Connor actually had to look at his notes. "You've got, what, 20 shareholders, about 350,000 shares outstanding?"

"Correct, give or take."

"And all of your shareholders are aware of what is going on and are going to vote along with us in the takeover?"

"Leaving 50 or so shares with every original shareholder. Got to leave these people something to make money on, above and beyond what you're paying them for their shares up front, which are trading decently right now as you have seen. Not high value—but decent."

"Understood—and agreed to. Now I, on the other hand, have 20 million outstanding shares."

Todd whistled softly. "You don't do things in half measures, do you, Mr. Beauregard?"

"Connor—please. Now Image Group has no assets to speak of, correct?"

"Correct." Todd shrugged. "We haven't needed to do much business."

Connor took a sip of his coffee. There it was, the thing he'd been afraid of—Todd had put this entire company together to serve as a shell company. They'd never done any significant business, except waiting for the right target to take them over.

Damn—the exchange commissions frowned on that kind of thing. If they decided Image Group had never really existed, as a going concern, except for the purpose of serving as a shell.... No—there were records.

There was a bank account. He remembered seeing them in Rafael's files. He pushed the thought away again and pressed on.

"Perfect Cannabis, on the other hand, does have a few assets," he said and wrote a figure on a piece of paper. "So, we will purchase all of Image Group's shares, or at least most of them, as you say. After the takeover, we change the name, issue PerCan shares. If I am reading this correctly, after the amalgamation, we'd end up with roughly 25,500,000 shares...."

"Give or take."

"Give or take." Rafael had done the math ahead of time, and Connor had merely memorized it. Now, however, he frowned and tapped the paper in front of him with his pen. "Which means we are rolling the shares back by a factor of 19, amalgamating, and then reissuing as full shares in the new company again—sound good to you?"

"Sound good to me."

"I will draft a letter of intent then. We are agreed that current management at PerCan will be in control of the new co, the amalgamated company after the deal, and all of Image Group's directors and officers will resign?"

"Not a big problem on my end—there are only a couple anyway."

Todd still looked cool as a cucumber. "We'll be trading financial statements, of course, do our due diligence—just so everyone can be sure the other guy is not a crook of some sort."

"I am putting the fate of my company at stake here," Connor said, a little miffed, but he knew all of that was just due course, the way it was done. Still, it could take forever. Lawyers would be trading paperwork back and forth; forms would need to be filled out and filled out again, reviewed by more lawyers and accountants. He just wanted to get the deal done.

"We will have to be pens down until the deal is done," Todd said and fixed Connor in a tight gaze. "No material changes in the business—no selling of big assets, et cetera."

"I need this amalgamation and takeover to happen yesterday. We are looking at purchasing a building. We need to get started with the refit the moment it happens…"

"Well cool your heels for a bit—this is going to take time."

Connor's mind was already racing a mile a minute. Free trading shares, in Todd's Image group…. After the amalgamation and reissue, they'd be worth a small fortune. Right at the moment, no matter how much money he raised, all of his shares were restricted for a year—which put off a lot of his people.

Maybe he would have to bring in more investors initially. They'd buy up all of these shares, nice wonderful free trading shares, and keep them for the real owner—Connor Beauregard. Then, when he needed them, transfer a few shares, sell them off in a private agreement. The possibilities were there.

Right now, he needed a lot of people he trusted buying up most of the shell's shares. Original shareholders would make some money—check. The shares they purchased would be worth a small fortune within a very short time—and money would be made again—check. The shell would basically be 'his,' although on the surface he would have nothing to do with it. They'd be trading in no time, and money made again—check. This was good. He could do it; he just needed to install a number of offshore companies to buy those shell company shares—and quick.

"Know who is going to buy all of those shares yet, Connor?" Todd grinned broadly, seemingly knowing what Connor had been thinking. "It's not going to be all you. Don't tell me that. You must have your share of ratholes somewhere."

"Well, if I did, I would have them only because I don't discuss them in public places," Connor said, lowering his voice and looking around. Ratholes, hiding places, or people who would hold shares for him, for a small price—not exactly the kind of thing to be discussed in a coffee shop.

Todd chuckled. "You think the waitresses in this place are making notes? There's a reason I come here, you know."

"Maybe." Connor became more than a bit annoyed. "Maybe so, Todd, but you don't exactly have to be blatant about it."

Matter of fact, Todd was starting to annoy him now, his earlier sense of friendliness and connection all but blown away. The man was just way too blatant about things he should not even have spoken out loud. Why could he not just play the game, say the things he was supposed to say, and walk away? Instead he sat there, acted like the big man on campus, acted like Connor had to do his bidding, and laughed at him in the process.

As a matter of fact, how well did he really know Rafael? Connor had the distinct impression he had seen a printout of Rafael's email to him in Todd's hands. What the fuck was that all about anyway? Was the little man playing both sides or what?

"Relax," Todd said in suddenly hushed tones. "I can see your mind spinning in tight little circles, man. Nobody is out to get you. I've known Rafael for a very long time, and he shoots as straight as they get. Get my drift? I don't screw him, he doesn't screw me, and you are included in this deal."

"It's still my company," Connor said sullenly and slid all of his papers back into the single folder he had brought.

"So it is." Todd rose and offered his hand. "We have a deal then? Do you want me to ask our securities lawyer to call you in the next couple of days?"

Our securities lawyer. Connor suddenly grinned again. Perhaps he could roll off the surely inflated legal fees on this man. Not a bad deal in this case. He shook the man's hand.

"I'll be drafting an LOI the moment I get back to the office."

EIGHTEEN

He rushed back to his office, storming by Tessa without stopping to say hello.

"I need you to drop everything and work on something very special," he called out, as he barreled into his office. "This afternoon—no, right now as a matter of fact."

"'K—right now—good morning by the way, how are you, and did you have a good evening last night?"

"Good morning, I'm fine, and how are you, and did you have a good evening last night? Now—this is what I need from you."

"This is what you need from me—OK, shoot."

Connor frowned and did some math in his head. Rafael knew a few guys with offshore companies—two at least. He was sure Al would come in on the deal—as well as he should because he would need to fund a large portion of it too. That was another two. He'd take care of a couple in Switzerland, and nobody could know they were his. And he needed a couple of real ratholes. People nobody would know—not even Kayla… They would take some of those shares, and only he, God, and the fencepost would know who was really holding them.

"You've got some relatives in Europe right?"

"Yes—distant relatives, but I do."

"I need names and addresses of people in Europe—people you would trust with your lives."

"What is this all about?"

"Nothing. They are just going to hold some shares for me—for a while. They won't have to pay taxes on them. They won't even need to know they are holding these shares. We'll have the certs sent here."

"Is this something illegal?"

"You know we're amalgamating with another company—a company that's already trading on the stock exchange."

"Right—we're taking over, and we'll be trading."

"You are almost right. In reality we're buying most of their shares and amalgamating. Then we change the name later on. But to fund this takeover deal, I need to come up with big bucks to buy most of the other company's shares. I can't own them, or I would be an insider—but I want to keep them."

Tessa furrowed her brow, but said nothing.

"All I need is a few people to hold on to them for me for a little while. They'll all be sold before you know it. Nothing at all illegal about it. I'll be paying for everything."

"OK," Tessa said slowly. She smiled politely, but he could see the wheels turning in her mind.

Dammit, he did not have time to explain the realities of a shell company to her at this stage of the game.

"No big deal, OK. I just need a few people to hold on to some shares for me for a little while, that's all, but like I said, if you don't want to get involved…"

"It's fine," she finally said and smiled again.

Connor gave her the brightest 500-watt Connor Beauregard charmer smile. "Just stick with me. Now get me those names and addresses while I set up the share deal."

The entire deal also hinged on Al providing some much-needed funds because as much as he had raised in the past few weeks, Connor found himself almost broke once again, and he knew he needed funds for this building they were going to purchase. Fortunately, Al seemed to have bottomless pockets and would, according to Rafael, take a promissory note and walk away smiling.

Smiling, and making a ton of dough in the process, Connor reminded himself bitterly. Now he could have used the 30 grand he blew on the private jet to Colorado.

He called Rafael and asked him and Al down for a meeting, after office hours, here in his little office, to discuss how they were going to pull it off.

In the meantime, he drafted a letter of intent for Todd, spelling out what everybody was going to do and what they would refrain from doing. He still did not like the superior attitude of the man, but for the moment he just had to live with him.

After he traded, who the hell cared? He would never have to speak to the little ass again, now would he?

Al sauntered into the office in his usual inconspicuous, friendly manner—just a guy dropping in for a quick chat, nothing serious—but Connor remembered that day at the *Family Restaurant* only too clearly.

"We found ourselves a nice little shell," Rafael began. By mutual agreement, Connor let him take the lead on this meeting. Firstly of course because Rafael knew Al and his family so much better, in reality, though he did not want to deal with the minutiae of the deal at this point in time. He wasn't there to deal with minutiae—he was there to set a general direction and let others follow where he led.

"Todd seems like a good guy," he said, shaking Al's hand. "Honest, decent businessman. Their little company is perfect for us to take over."

"Officially."

"Yes, officially." Rafael reached for a spreadsheet and pushed it across the table to Al. "They've got 350,000 shares outstanding, which we..."

"First things first, Rafael my friend," Al said and sat in Connor's chair, a fact that nagged on Connor more than if the man had walked in here and started typing away on the computers and using his coffee cup.

"Do we have a letter of intent worked out already?"

"Got the redline here," Rafael said and flicked another piece of paper across the table. "Todd wanted a few things inserted. Connor cleaned up the language a little."

"Mmm. Nevertheless." Al picked it up, studied it thoroughly, and put it back into Rafael's folder. Must have an eidetic memory, Connor thought, and Al leaned back in his chair.

"Looks good. Now we can talk. I assume you've called me in here because you want my family and me to fund the purchase of this shell."

"Well, I wouldn't quite say fund the purchase, Al, but—yes—we are in need of funds to make this thing happen," Rafael said cautiously. "But you know, at this point in time, it is exactly what we need. It's in the best interest of the company and its shareholders."

"Of which we are a large part." Al took back Rafael's spreadsheet. "350,000 shares, and we are buying all of them?"

"Not all of them. The existing shareholders want to retain a few for themselves—for their troubles, so to speak."

"No shit. Those will be worth a small fortune after the amalgamation."

"Right—19 times as much to be correct. In order to equalize assets and value of the company, we are going to roll the Image Group shares back by a factor of 19—and then forward again after the amalgamation."

"Interesting way of doing it." Al studied the spreadsheet again. "I can commit the funds to it. That is not a problem—as you knew it would not be."

Oh, here we go, Connor thought, looking up from his phone, where Kayla had just emailed him copies of her latest articles on medical marijuana, its applications and benefits. The woman really was worth her weight in gold.

Al's *but* dangled in the room like a giant Sword of Damocles. Of course he could commit the funds—*but*—he would want something in return. Something big. The fucker always wanted something.

"How about the three of us in this room share in the spoils," Al said, Cheshire Cat grin firmly in place. "Rafael, I know you have a few Panama companies that can take some. My family and I will take some—a lot, as a matter of fact. And you, Connor?"

"I have a few companies on the go—couple of business partners who will kick in to buy directly. I'm good."

"There are a couple of guys I'm going to approach as well," Rafael said. "Connor, how much are you good for?"

How much was he good for? How much was he good for? Were they serious at all? Connor clenched his fists under the table and forced himself to relax them.

"Like Al said, Rafael, why don't we do this by threes. Each one of us comes up with a third of the funds for the share purchase, and we allocate the shares as we see fit—that sounds like a great idea."

"Just make sure you don't end up being an insider."

"That goes without saying," he said and smiled. "So, are we good?"

"We are good." Al offered a cool hand, and Connor had that *deal with the devil feeling* once again. At the moment, however, he could not afford to indulge in it—he needed both of those guys to make his company go. God, and he hadn't even asked Kayla if she was OK kicking in the funds for a good portion of the shell.

"Gentlemen, we have got ourselves a company trading on the pink sheets bulletin board. Next stop, wealth."

He grinned and pulled a bottle of champagne out of his little office fridge, but Al only smiled and shook his head.

"Sorry, Connor, I've got another meeting I have to run to. Don't take it personally."

"At this time of day?"

"Time never stands still for some of us. You know that better than anyone. Rafael."

He shook hands and disappeared from the office again as quickly as he had come in. Connor stood with the champagne in hand, looking dumbfounded.

"Well, I'll be..."

"Don't take it the wrong way, Connor. I assume his father has got him running errands. He owns a couple of private clubs midtown."

"So, he just walks out on me? Shake on the deal and go? Jesus…"

"We need to go raise funds," he said curtly. "350,000 free trading shares, 300,000 of them ours. When they hit the exchange at three or four bucks each, we'll have it made in the shade."

"You can't just go trading willy-nilly…"

"I know that. I am not exactly an idiot, Rafael. I'm talking value. I'm talking raising funds—selling subscriptions into PerCan—collecting the money for ourselves transferring some of the shares we are about to purchase from Image Group. Private share deals—nothing wrong with it. I don't know about you, but I could use a bit of cash. And I certainly wasn't talking about dumping the shares all at once."

He paced his office with the irritation of it all. God, it chafed having to explain everything constantly—as if it were not hard enough getting the investors to see the light, now he had to explain things to Rafael? This wasn't the first deal they had done together. By now, he should know.

"Connor—you're running a mile a minute. Cool it."

"I am going to cool it when we're finally trading, when the building is ours, when the first plants are going in, when the first sales roll around, you get my drift?"

"I get your drift, but you still need to be careful. 100,000 shares—yours—split forward by 19 is enough to make you one hell of an insider. So, no one, absolutely no one, can ever find out you own these shares. You understand that, right? This thing has got to be planned carefully."

Connor sighed and hooked his thumbs into his belt loops. "Yes sir, master. I am having Tessa put together a couple of companies over in Europe—people she knows, people who are trustworthy, who will sign the share sales agreements for us no questions asked. Nobody will know it is either you or me who owns them."

"Tessa's relatives—good, but still a bit thin."

"I also have some contacts in Switzerland. I will see them next week when Kayla and I are over there. Same deal goes. They will own the shares and sell them as I tell them to. Nobody will be the wiser."

"Good." Rafael seemed honestly relieved. "When you get this excited..."

When I get this excited, good things happen, Connor wanted to say. *The magic starts coming out.*

Out loud he merely said, "You know how I get," smiled winningly, and offered his hand. "I just want things to happen, Rafael. It kills me when I get mired down in all of this shit. I need to be moving."

He rushed out of the meeting ready to cut somebody down. Did not matter if it was the valet who took too long to get his car, or the incapable bartender at the corner bar where he stopped to suck down a quick drink. Guy should not be tending bar if he did not know how to make a basic martini, for crying out loud.

An hour and a couple of drinks later, he had himself under control again and called Rafael.

"Sorry, man—Al just has a way of going under my skin. The fucker just acts so goddamn superior..."

"I get it, Connor, and he is doing it on purpose—pushing all of your buttons and watching you launch off into space. I'm telling you. Do yourself a favor and learn to ignore him. The only reason I brought him on is because of the money. We needed him at first, and we are going to need him when we get started on the building. If you absolutely can't live with him..."

"I can live with him," Connor interrupted. "I just need to take off on somebody now and then because I cannot stand..."

"His attitude. Just tell yourself you're using him for the money."

I am using him, Connor thought and found a small bit of comfort in the phrase, growing quite quickly. *Dammit, yes, I am the one who is using Al. It's still my company, and the moment he is no longer of any use to me...*

"It's going to be fine," he said, a lot more cheerful all of a sudden. "Like I said—I just needed to let off steam. Now, we are OK with splitting the free trading shares from Image Group by threes? That's going to be a small fortune shortly, license to print money."

"You got it, man," Rafael said and laughed. "Shares we are buying today for pennies are going to be worth 10, 20 bucks pretty soon, and we're getting 19 times as many after the split."

"Fucking-A." Connor leaned back in the booth at the anonymous corner bar he had chosen and laughed out loud. "Fuck, deal of a lifetime. Todd is a greedy little bastard, though. He handwrote an obscene figure on a piece of paper and slipped it into my stuff on the way out. I'm assuming that's what he wants to facilitate the whole deal."

"Doable?" Rafael asked, and Connor could hear him clicking away on his computer, probably checking bank balances. Doable, yes. Easy, no. Everything he owned would have to go to Todd for making this deal—and, if there were a few pennies left, to Catherine the blood-sucking securities lawyer and whatever lawyers Todd dragged in off the street.

God, he hated lawyers.

Doable...yes. Easy, no. But, he thought, but there was value in pushing this deal through on his own, making Rafael owe him for once.

"Can you come up with your share for the share purchases, Rafa?"

"Barely."

"Then go ahead and do that. I'm going to take care of Todd and the lawyers' fees. Consider it all done."

"What about your shares?"

"Kayla. I mean, there's enough at her condo to keep a guy in liquor for months. Shit, I'm just gonna have to make sure she does it."

Rafael laughed. In his own self-deprecating ways, he often called himself an 'experienced husband,' only because he did everything Josie, his wife of 10 years, asked of him and exactly when she asked it of him. In exchange he enjoyed certain—liberties. Those liberties did not extend themselves to the checkbook. If he wanted to do any crazy financing schemes, he had to figure them out on his own.

"I don't envy you, man—that one is going to be a hard sell. Better buy jewelry to soften her up."

"Hard sell is what I do best, my man—and thanks. The jewelry is not entirely a bad idea."

He pushed end on his phone and thumbed through his contacts. He was going to Switzerland anyway—might as well have a bit of a safety built in here...

Just as he had known, Kayla was not overly excited when he asked her for the funds to buy up 100,000 free trading shares he had committed to from Todd's original shareholders.

But, in the end, she could see the value in the transaction. His superior convincing technique, Connor thought smugly, with a couple of extra measures thrown in. In the end she went down to the bank and dutifully bought a nice clean bank draft to be sent to Todd.

Al and Rafael were buying almost identical bank drafts at their financial institutions, and, by the end of the day, the funds were sent to the trust account of Todd's lawyer. Email messages went back and forth furiously between Catherine, Todd's lawyer, and Connor. His phone just would not stop ringing, but he let it all run off him like water. He was that close to tying it all together.

In time a spreadsheet appeared in his email, showing all the original shareholders and the amounts they held. Along with an extra column of what they wished to retain and a column with a question mark. Who was going to receive the balance of the shares in detail? Todd's lawyer was ready to make up share purchase agreements; all he needed were names and amounts.

Connor pushed it over to Tessa, showed her how many shares everyone was supposed to be owning in the end, and left her to figure out the sales agreements. A hundred thou for Al's people, for him and for Rafael, split six or seven ways in each case. At the end of the day, it looked good, he thought. Everybody would be happy.

NINETEEN

Just as the experienced husband Rafael had prophesied, Kayla, meanwhile, had a hankering to spend her investment. Switzerland held a huge appeal for her aside from mountains, chocolate, and creative high finance. She had been there only once, with her former husband, and this time she intended to really live it up.

Kayla Montecito hits Zurich. Look out, Bahnhofstrasse, Kayla was coming… and the stores had better be stocked with everything, including… everything.

Having pilfered his private account to accommodate Todd, Connor had liberated large amounts of cash from the PerCan account, despite Tessa's near fit at trying to account for all of it. Let's see, he was going to see investors in Zurich, right, and another pharmaceutical company, so it was definitely business travel, and she could surely make it work somehow.

And then there was Essentials, another business expense. *Essentials.* Even the name rolled off the tongue like the finest aged cognac. The uninitiated might superficially read the word *essentials* and think of soap and toothpaste, but those in the know became wistful and sighed with pleasure. Essentials the company owned a good 200 luxury villas around the globe in some of the most beautiful places on earth, and as long as one was a member in good standing—which meant membership fees in excess of 50,000 a year—one was allowed to rent one of these gems and enjoy the vacation of a lifetime. The last remaining fellowship of sybarites, as it were.

Connor had stayed with a friend of his at an Essentials property once, and from then on, there was no going back. No more five-star hotels for Connor Beauregard if he could at all avoid it. He became a member, PerCan paid for his annual dues since he was mostly travelling on business now, and the world became his luxuriously appointed oyster.

The Essentials villa just outside Zurich was considered a particular gem, partly because of its historic appeal for being several hundred years old, partly because careful, extensive renovations had turned its interior into a true oasis.

What had once been a minor nobleman's hunting lodge had turned into a 7000-square-foot original log cabin in the mountains, with both a saltwater pool and a freshwater pool, a spa, three staff to run the fitness center (one of them a licensed massage therapist), skiing equipment, mountaineering equipment, a helicopter, three luxury cars including drivers, a cook, several maids…and a butler. All-inclusive for $7000 a week.

Kayla was in heaven. All through the long flight to Zurich, she kept gushing over the description of the lake house property, read out loud little gems from the printout he had given her, and planned her upcoming shopping and entertainment excursions to the smallest detail.

Connor kept filling her glass with expensive champagne and paid her no mind. Oh, he nodded at the appropriate times and said things like, "Wow, that'll be spectacular," but his mind ran through his own agenda.

The moment they touched down, he needed to get a hold of Dominik and Karl, the two men who had helped him out on other deals before. They were crack hands at setting up Swiss-registered companies within moments, supplying all the paperwork and credentials he would need to be up and running. Problem was neither Dominik nor Karl were exactly easy to get a hold of. People like them did not advertise, and the last Connor had seen of them was in an upscale dancing establishment—better word for a strip club—that one of them owned outside of Zurich.

Adding to his burden, their services did not come cheap. Now why, he fumed, did a man like Connor Beauregard constantly have to deal with the frustration of having to come up with cash?

Here he was, one of the most brilliant minds in business. He stood to earn millions on these original free trading shares—literally millions. He had put together the biggest medical marijuana company in the country, and still he had to worry about a few 100,000 to set up the company that would make it all happen. The company that would make it legal. And tax-free.

For God's sake...

Kayla kept going on about a particular Louis Vuitton handbag she apparently desperately needed to locate the moment they got there, and for a minute, Connor wanted to strangle her. Really, a goddamn purse? Forcing himself to breathe, he filled her champagne glass once more and patted her hand.

"Why don't you ask one of the maids or the butler at the house when we arrive," he said mildly. "After all, that's what they're there for: making sure we have the best possible stay."

"Brilliant." Kayla clapped her hands. "I bet you they know just where to find the best fashion deals. You know, I realize this is first class, but my neck is all tense. This was so much more fun in the private jet. I really don't understand why we're flying commercial again."

"Small jets aren't really equipped for intercontinental flight. Here, let me." Mechanically, Connor massaged her neck while running through the possibilities of finding Dominik, the cash he had hidden in Kayla's little carry-on, and the need to get this all done on the inside of two days.

Two days. He literally did not have the time to worry about a handbag.

Fortunately, they basically flew through customs in Zurich. Connor found out that one of the benefits of bringing a very blonde, slightly inebriated, and bubbling Kayla along was all the male customs officers gave him a mildly envious look, checked their papers with a cursory glance, and let them pass. Another thing that went on his 'mental notes' list—he could easily imagine having to come back here with a bit more cash in his luggage…or a few other, items.

He put Kayla into a car to take her straight to the villa, and he stayed behind on the excuse that he had to meet another investor right inside the terminal, one who needed to catch a flight out of Zurich just after.

Kayla pouted, but he'd filled her up with enough liquor to ensure all she wanted was a hot bath, a massage, and bed.

Meanwhile, he strode back into the terminal, lingered until her car had left, and then hailed a cab.

Not even a raised eyebrow when he mentioned the club Dominik owned. The driver merely nodded and peeled off into traffic. It was barely noon, and Connor knew by dinner time, Kayla would be rested, refreshed, and wanting his attention again.

He could have used a nap himself when he finally arrived back at the log cabin barely scraping past five p.m. Instead, he asked the butler, a huge fella with a sharp buzz cut who went by the name of Jon, for a double espresso, and another one chasing it, then rushed to have a shower, rinsing the smell of Dominik's establishment off himself.

The cost for those privately held Swiss companies was just short of astronomic, and he had promised Dominik a check by noon the next day. Not a problem. All he had to do… all he had to do was convince Kayla. This on the heels of her having to finance the share purchase.

He turned his face into the waterfall cascading from the rain-head shower and put himself into sales mode. Give it to me now, Connor, the spiel. Asking people to invest, to put out money. He had a little insurance in his pocket, though; he grinned to himself when he thought of it. There was not a woman on this planet who could resist diamonds, simple fact of life. And he would make that fact work for himself.

Showered and changed into a fresh suit which had thoughtfully been placed into the room by Jon, he went to find Kayla in the cavernous place.

"Kayla, you look absolutely stunning tonight," he said when he had finally located her in one of the libraries, casually holding a glass of fine champagne, studying the list of shops, nightclubs, and dining establishment so helpfully provided by the Essentials people.

A sheer white dress draped from her shoulders in lovely soft curves down to her ankles, belted at the waist with a narrow gold band. When she leaned forward, it revealed just enough cleavage to be enticing without being trashy. He had never seen it on her, but it was the kind of thing he himself might have chosen at the shops this afternoon, had he not been otherwise occupied.

"Why, thank you, Connor," she said coolly. "How did your meetings go this afternoon?"

"Fine, just fine. Um, is something wrong? You seem…perturbed, somehow."

Bad news, big-time bad news. He'd spent years reading people while he was giving them a pitch. He could tell exactly when somebody was pissed off or simply in a bad mood—and Kayla was boiling just beneath the surface. He could not afford to mess around; he had to make things work right.

"Well, if you must ask…" she said, studying her freshly painted nails. "I'd like to know exactly why we came to Zurich in the first place because it is not to see investors, that's for sure. Unless meeting investors happens in a strip club nowadays."

Jesus Christ, what did she have, surveillance on him? Somebody watching his every move? Fuck, no time to wonder now—think, Connor, think fast.

"Not completely, although it's certainly been done before," he said slowly, buying time, but Kayla's narrowed sharp eyes did not exactly tolerate BS. "Not unless your client owns said strip club. And Dominik, well, he has several of them—or so I am told."

"So you are told. And that means the first thing you have to do is run off the plane into one of his seedy dives to try to do what? Convince him to invest? I would warn you not to come up with another story, Connor—because I am not in the mood. And you lying to me where you were going for the past few hours is not putting me into a better one either."

"Well, OK, if you must know…" he said, fumbling in his pocket for the little silver-wrapped box, "you are right. I wasn't seeing an investor—I was totally lying to you." All or nothing, Beauregard, kill with the truth. Some of it, anyway… "I was going to wait until tonight, for a better setting and better ambience. However."

He dropped the little package on the coffee table between them. "Dominik is the only person in Switzerland I would trust to make a purchase such as this one for me and not cheat me in the bargain. I couldn't exactly bring something like this across the border just casually. Go ahead—open it."

The package sat for a moment on the table between them while Kayla's eyes never left his, searching, trying to catch him in a lie, an excuse—anything.

"Go ahead, Kayla—open it."

She still eyed him warily, but no woman on earth could have resisted the pull of that jewelry box. *Thank you, Rafa.*

Kayla reached for the package, tore off the silver wrap and the little silver cord and bow that held it all together, opened it—and let the most exquisite tennis bracelet fall into her hand.

"Oh…"

Dear God, Dominik had done better than he had expected him to. He'd saved his ass for God's sake. Until that very moment, even Connor had not known what was inside that little wrapped package—only that he had mentioned to Dominik he needed to bring something back for the little woman. Dom had just simply sent somebody to get this. That damn thing had better be real, but it sure looked it.

"Connor, I had no idea," Kayla breathed and held out her wrist for him to fasten the bracelet. "I know I mentioned wanting one of these last week, but I had no idea you would be paying attention."

Paying attention, yes; had any plan to buy this, no. He smiled and fastened the bracelet around her wrist, making a note to have the thing checked first thing when they were back home. For starters, if they were zirconium, he would have to have the darn things replaced PDQ, and if not... if not, he would owe one hell of a lot of money to a man who could screw the deal of a lifetime to hell and back. Not going to happen.

"I'm glad you like it," he whispered and put his arms around her. "I really did have something a lot more romantic in mind. But you see, Dominik is the only man I would trust to make such a purchase for me. I am sorry if his...chosen occupation is a little bit off-putting to you."

"Nonsense, I should be the one to apologize to you." Kayla put her finger across his lips and shook her head. "I should never have doubted you, should have trusted you always. Can you ever forgive me?"

"Always my love, you know that." He pulled her closer, and kissed her as passionately as he could manage. "There's nothing to forgive."

"You are under so much stress with this company and I—I've only added to it."

"Don't waste another thought on this, love, please. Once we are through all of this nonsense, you and I will be at the head of the biggest medical marijuana company in the country, I promise you that. There's no one else I would want to be there when it finally happens. I really want to apologize for being so dreadfully preoccupied the last few weeks. There are just so many problems, people who don't share my vision, people who come to me to solve their problems, and I was hoping..."

"You were hoping?"

"I was hoping this visit to Switzerland would solve all of this, but once again, I've been let down. Forgive me—here I go again. I really should not dump all this on you. Let's forget we ever had this unpleasant conversation and go out to dinner, shall we?" He offered his arm. "You look absolutely radiant, that dress is divine, and it would be a waste to sit here in this house all night and be depressed."

"Oh no, no, no, no." Kayla took his hand and motioned him to sit in one of the wing backed chairs that faced the crackling fireplace. "If you are having a problem with the company, then I want to hear about it. After all, we are in this together, are we not?"

"Yes, but I don't want to burden you with…"

"No burden, just go and tell me."

"Kayla—I might be old-fashioned, but a man has to solve his own problems, be the provider for his family, his woman. If he cannot do that…"

He spoke with downcast eyes, but he could barely catch a glimpse of her features softening when he said the words *his woman*. Bingo.

"Please, let me share in your troubles," she said softly and squeezed his hand, allowing him to pull it free and drag it though his hair.

"I don't know, this is… This is not real easy." He took a deep breath and let it out in one mighty sigh. "I need a holding company—more than one as a matter of fact. Here in Switzerland, to hold some of our shares, just for a little while."

"I don't understand. We own our shares. I've seen the certificates. Why would you need somebody else?"

"You own shares, and I own shares…personally."

"You gave them to me." Kayla smiled broadly. "And it was the most thoughtful gift anyone has ever given me."

"Yes, but, you know what an insider is, right?"

"Of course, anybody who owns more than 10 percent of issued and outstanding… Oh."

"Yes, oh. With the takeover, we need to acquire a lot of shares from the original company, the one we are taking over, and I want to hang on to those for future financing, but if you and I have too many shares, that will severely limit what I can do with them, so I need them in a holding company."

"Which you would like to have in Switzerland because…"

"Because I don't want to pay capital gains taxes every time I move shares around to accommodate one or the other investor, or somebody who needs to work with us for paper rather than money."

"OK, I understand, but that is not a problem, is it? I mean, we are here. It shouldn't take all that long to get it done, no?"

"Well, yes, you are right, but again…we need someone we can trust. It's not like you can walk into a guy's office and say, 'I'm here to get a holding company.' Secondly, there is a cost involved in all of this, and I'm afraid looking at the prices of everything in this country…"

"Jesus, Connor, sometimes…" Kayla jumped up, poured him a glass of champagne, and returned to the fireplace, putting it into his hands. "Sometimes you men can be so stubborn and thick-headed, you know. Did you not just tell me we were in this together—we are at the head of this company?"

"Yes." Connor took a sip of his champagne and forced himself to look down. *Do—not—grin—now, Connor.*

"Well, then, you already know someone you can trust here in Zurich, this Dominik person. No matter what he does for a living if he can purchase something like this." She shook her wrist and made the diamonds sparkle. "If he can do that, then I am sure he has contacts in the business world that can make a holding company happen. Especially in his line of business, he is going to know somebody. And secondly, why would you even worry about asking me for the money? I know you'll pay me back when we get back home, so problem solved. Now can we please go to dinner?"

Connor looked up and smiled. "I don't know what I ever did to deserve you," he said softly, "but it must have been something pretty darn big."

Connor partied like there was no tomorrow. For now, he seemed to have everything he wanted right at his fingertips. He had a project that was taking off, he was collecting investor money like candy at Mardi Gras, he would be trading on a decent stock exchange before long, he held a small fortune in shares which he would be able to sell soon for a very large fortune, and there was just no end in sight.

He was indeed the greatest. He was the king of deals—none better.

"My God," Kayla said as he dragged her into the third nightclub of the night. "You are just full of energy today. "

"Success does that to a man, my love. You better get used to it."

He was too drunk to care at this point. He knew there were two blondes and a redhead eyeing him and Kayla from the sidelines, and if he had been alone and sober. Oh well, some other time. This night belonged to his success and nothing else.

"I could not have done this without you," he whispered into Kayla's ear and found to his surprise that he actually meant it. Without her money and her connections, and her first-rate publicity, things would still have worked—but not this smoothly, not this quickly. So yes, he did owe her a debt. But then again, he lived with her now, he came home to her every night, and he brought her to every public occasion and paraded her out as the woman in his life, so perhaps they were even. Perhaps.

TWENTY

Kayla spent a few whirlwind days shopping in Zurich, spending money as if it were going out of style, and he did not begrudge her one cent.

He went to see Dominik and dropped off a check, disappointed that for all that money all he received in return was a letter saying his companies, WB Capital Schweiz and BM Capital Schweiz, had been registered. That was it. He had expected a little more. Official papers, a seal perhaps—but Dominik told him that was all he needed, and who was he to question the man?

Relieved that everything had gone so smoothly, he dove headfirst into Zurich's shopping and nightlife, indulging, for once not worried that an investor would see him somewhere. Dutifully, he made a brief visit to a Swiss pharmacy concern that was in the business of producing medical marijuana, just so he could say it had been a business trip. But in all honesty, at the time, he was far too hungover to see much more than their enormous lobby and a few offices.

He could barely drag himself out of bed the next morning and dreaded the flight back home. Eight hours in an airplane—even in first class—sounded like sheer torture. Kayla, on the other hand, as if to mock him, already stood in the shower, singing.

When she stepped out, she threw a wet towel at him and laughed so loud his head threatened to explode.

"My, Connor, are you getting old already? Here I thought you were *so much* younger than I am."

"Get lost."

He buried his head in the pillows and tried to ignore the pounding. He knew he had to call Rafael and give him the good news. Knew he needed to check in with Tessa. He also knew he would not get any of it done today. Matter of fact, he knew getting out of this bed would be hard.

"What's making you so damn chipper, anyway?" he asked and eyed Kayla, prancing through the room, humming to herself, sorting through the spoils from her shopping hunt. "I'm pretty sure you had as much champagne as I've had."

"Oh, I might have had more."

"You are disgustingly energetic."

"Connor, Connor. For a guy who's in the drug business, you have a lot to learn, you know that?"

"What are you talking about?"

Connor sat up and immediately regretted it, brought his hands to his head, and shielded his eyes.

"Fuck..."

"World spinning?"

"And then some."

He wanted to fall back into his pillows, but Kayla appeared beside him with a glass of orange juice and three small white pills in the palm of her hand.

"Here. That'll make you feel better."

"Thanks, but I really don't think aspirin is going to cut it."

"Not the way you look, love. That's why this is no aspirin. Just take it; you'll feel better in a few."

"What is it then?"

Suspiciously, he eyed the pills in her hand and took them in his own. White, round...nothing printed on them.

"Oh, my, I didn't think I would have to be the one showing you," she laughed. "Your friend Dominik came up with these last night. They'll keep you going for the next three days if you so choose."

"Drugs?"

"Stuff to make you feel better." She closed his fingers over the pills in his hand and put the juice by the bedside. "That Dominik is one interesting person, you know."

Connor shrugged, washed down the pills, and immediately felt as if he had been punched in the gut. He thought he'd get sick, but a few moments later, his head actually cleared, he could feel the energy shooting through him as if he had just slept for three days straight, and the hangover had no choice but to recede into the background.

"Well, hellfire," he muttered. "The things I've been missing while I've been trying to do one deal after the other."

He pulled Kayla back into the shower and let her explain exactly what these pills were she had just given him and what they did—perhaps not in so many words.

His day just got better and better and better.

This was the life. This was what it was like when you were the king of the world, and all you had to do was call the shots.

He didn't feel like packing and simply decided to leave most of his stuff behind, while Kayla asked one of the maids to ship her purchases back home. Together, they went for one last drink at the airport lounge, which turned into two, three, and four. He should have been dead on his feet, but he wasn't. Jesus, right at the moment, he felt as if he could fly back home without the aid of an airplane.

"And another interesting thing your friend Dominik told me," Kayla prattled on. "For some reason he thought it important that I tell you UBS bank has a deposit and withdrawal terminal around here somewhere, on the other side of the security barrier. Did you ask him or something?"

Connor stopped dead in his tracks and looked at Kayla.

"On the other side of the security barrier—you're sure that's what he said?"

"Yeah, kind of silly, isn't it? I mean…I get the people who have to run and check their phones the moment they get off the plane, but banking? For god's sake, I think that can wait until you are in the country, right?"

"It probably can," he said and took her hand.

The possibilities were more than delicious... Coming to Switzerland and doing his banking without ever having to officially come into the country. Stepping off the airplane, depositing money...or shares perhaps? The ones he was not supposed to have, but that would keep him in vittles when everything else fell apart?

TWENTY-ONE

By the time their plane touched down again, Connor felt as if he had had the last peaceful moment of his life back there in Switzerland.

Pandemonium reigned grandly. Rafa and Al seemed to have found a building they insisted he needed to look at, immediately if not sooner. Simon and Josh called Rafa almost every day wanting to know where their company stood and what the mysterious Al was even contributing, and some newspaper had captured a shot of him and Kayla off on their brief jaunt to Zurich.

Admittedly, it did not really look great, the two of them taking off on a holiday at this particular point in time. But then again, that trip had not really been about vacation time at all—it had been work from one end to the other, and nobody seemed to want to understand that. Instead, they were jealous because he was going to Zurich with a beautiful woman.

"God, people, just leave me alone," he muttered, walking into the office, as his phone rang again, and he tried to balance a coffee, a bag of pastries, and his laptop, all while having his overcoat slung over one arm.

"There you are." Tessa looked up from her computer terminal and glared. "'Bout time we see your face in here again."

"We?"

"I'll tell you about it—in a minute. How was Zurich?"

"Fabulous. Fun, expensive. Everything I expected it to be. Kayla and I needed this, you know. We've been working too hard. What's going on around here? I can't leave town for three days or the place starts falling apart? What the fuck?"

"You don't know the half of it. Coming to the 'we' part of the story. Remember William McDowell?"

"Can't say I do. Who is he?"

"Investor. You sold him shares a few weeks ago. Now he wants to know what's happening to his investment. He's basically been camping out at our doorstep since he saw that picture of you and Kayla in the paper. Wait half an hour. He'll be here."

Connor finally maneuvered everything he carried in his hands into the office and dumped the lot onto his desk. Papers piled high everywhere, in the corner a new file cabinet had taken residence, and his visitor's chair seemed to have disappeared.

"Love what you've done with the place, Tess. How much does this McDowell own?"

"5,000."

"5,000 shares! That's it? You can't be serious?"

"I am very serious. You sold the man 5,000 shares at $2 a couple of weeks ago. Now he thinks it's OK to come around every single day, annoying the heck out of me, sitting there, wanting to know where we are at, what I'm doing, and why and what you are doing, and for how long."

"You have got to be shitting me. For 5,000 shares? Dammit. It's always the guys who put in dick who give you the most trouble. I remember him. Wasn't even going to take him for crying out loud—he had trouble coming up with the money as it is."

"Yeah, well. Now he wants to know what you did with it. The moment he saw the article in the paper about you going to Switzerland he decided you were probably squandering the money, so that did not really please him at all."

"Tell you what, Tessa, I don't really give a fuck if Mr. 5,000 Shares is pleased or not. I have a company to run, and if he doesn't like it, that's too bad. And now that I remember, by the way, the only reason I took his money in the first place is because he seems to be a friend of one of Kayla's friends. Little fucker got in where he had no business being. How the hell does he know where our office is?"

"Your language is in fine shape this morning, Connor," Tessa commented, one eyebrow raised.

"Really? Now tell me how this maggot loser knows where my office is?"

"Don't ask me." Tessa shrugged. "I'm thinking he's retired, probably spends his entire day on the internet cruising around, and if you really want to find someone..."

"As you would well know," Connor muttered. "Next time he shows up, tell him to wait for news releases and investor updates, just like everybody else, and not to show his sorry ass around here again. I will not have him interrupting our work here."

He dumped four sugar packets into his coffee and took the first sip without stirring.

"Now what's this all about?" he asked, nodding toward the piles of paper on his desk.

"Agreements concerning the amalgamation, share purchase agreements I drew up, a couple of names of people in Europe you wanted..."

"Lovely. They'll own companies in Zurich fairly soon. I have the paperwork right here. You will not regret this. I just want you to know."

"Good, I hope. Josh and Simon keep calling me when they're not calling Rafa, and a few guys from Blue Bayou Investments are also looking for you."

"Blue Bayou? Yeah, I've heard of them. That would not be at all bad if they came on board. They represent a lot of high-quality investors." He grabbed the note with the phone message and rolled it into his pocket. "They might take a shitload of shares and sell them on to their people. But this mess here needs to go, you know that right? I can't have all this paper around. Besides," he nodded toward the file cabinet, "you branching out into my office or what?"

"There's a lot of paper being generated here, Connor. Catherine told me..."

"Number one, I need you not to listen to Catherine all the time. The only thing that woman is after is billable hours. She is not your friend, and she is not somebody you want to chat with on a regular basis."

"I know, but she has really been helping me recently..."

"Don't—if you need to know something, come to me. I know everything there is to know about running a company like this one and setting up an amalgamation and share reissue. Stop talking to her."

"OK..."

"Hey, it's not your fault." He softened the blow a bit. "She is good at this game, but this time she has just picked the wrong guy to overcharge, that's all. I'm not blaming you."

"I know that." Tessa looked down at her enormous Doc Marten boots, black of course, like the rest of her outfit. "I'd just feel better if she had a look at this stuff I just finished. Just in case there's something..."

"There is nothing wrong there whatsoever. You took all the templates I gave you from Energy Six?"

"Yes, but..."

"There you go then. They were all drafted by a securities lawyer only a couple of years ago. And I'm telling you I do not need Catherine looking at them once again if they were vetted then. They were fine then; they're still fine now. What's the problem?"

"Nothing—I would just feel better. There are a few areas I'm unsure about..."

"If you're not sure, show it to me and I'll have a look, but I guarantee you. It's all fine."

"OK, well, if you say so..."

Tessa shuffled off to her desk again, shoulders down, a hurt puppy-dog look on her face, but she'd have to learn. In his company, he called the shots, and this friendship between her and the female dragon securities lawyer could only end badly—in bills.

"I do say so," he called after her. "And take all of this paper with you—you're killing me in here."

He pulled a couple of documents off the top and scanned the first two pages. Of course it was fine. It was the stuff he had paid good money for back when Energy Six was still happening. Change a few names and dates, and all would be good again. Lawyers!

He called Michael Mullins from Blue Bayou, and immediately, his mood took a turn for the better. These guys indeed had the cojones and the customers to make big things happen. 5, 10 million: no problem. They would take it and pass the paper on to their customers. That's the way he liked it. No more of this little *one investor at a time* shit; he'd wasted enough of his precious time on it!

Tessa would love it when she saw the wave of paperwork coming her way from them. But so far, she was fighting the good fight, always getting what he needed, just when he needed it.

He would have to give her some shares at some point, he decided. If she would only dump that no-good boyfriend of hers.

None of his business, though, he guessed.

His phone rang again, and he looked at it, saw it was TC, and finally decided to answer it after a ring or two.

He still hadn't done any more research on medical marijuana, figuring that TC and Dan had that end of things in hand. Whatever he had quickly thrown together for his original presentation was it, and Dan and his superior attitude never failed to irritate him and make him feel like a moron.

TC he could handle. He usually expressed himself cautiously, politely, and never forgot who he was speaking to: the owner of the company. OK, founder. Something Al and his double-damned family would do good to remember.

"TC, long time no speak. How's everything coming along at your end?"

"No problems at all, Connor," TC said brightly, and, for a moment, Connor missed his usual deference.

"That's exactly what I want to hear. You have plans for me already for the building refit when we find something suitable to buy?"

"Dan is pretty much done with those, Connor. He drew up a new capital expenditure plan too, and it's a little..."

"A little what, TC?"

Warning bells, warning bells, something had happened while he was in Switzerland, something he would not like whatsoever, and he didn't even have to wonder.

"Well, Dan's new plans are a lot more... let's say inclusive."

"What does that even mean, inclusive, TC? Just give it to me straight up and in 20 words or less—what's the matter with the cap ex tables?"

"Nothing the matter at all, Connor. It just seems—well, it seems that we did not quite take everything into account in our first round of planning."

"So Dan wants to pad the bill a little, is that it? A few extra things here, a couple of bells and whistles there. Is that what you're telling me?"

"Well, we kinda scrapped the plans I had drawn almost immediately, and Dan came up with something that will be workable right off."

"And...?"

"So—well—instead of $13 million worth of renovations it will be—well, it will be a little more."

A little more—had he called it right at the beginning of this conversation? Of course he had, and he could make a damn good guess why. One or more of Al and Dan's other relatives were probably in the construction industry, and jobs were being pushed back and forth. Of course. That's what it had to be. They told him he had to raise $13 million, and that was it, and he had gone out with that goal in mind. So now it would be 13.5, or 14, if they got greedy.

He had a choice to make—make a fuss out of it right here and piss everybody off, or get back at them in one way or another. Usually, he would have made a fuss. That's what everybody was expecting anyway. *Connor is going to blow his stack when he hears this—a million-dollar overrun.* Then, later on, when something went south, they had a scapegoat.

"If there's a bit of an overrun, TC, that should not be too much a problem. I know how these things work, and construction is an unpredictable business. Jeez, you don't have to come ask permission every time plans change."

"Yes, well—this might be a rather big…"

"It's not a problem. I'm telling you—I want this to be done right. I want it to be done perfectly, that's all. I want you two guys to build the best goddamn marijuana-growing facility in the world. I have a guy in mind I'm bringing over from Colorado. He's already chomping at the bit to get going."

"Well, first, we still have to get a license, and…"

"And we have to do all the renovations, and we have to get clones developed for us in another country and import them. I know all that. Look, TC, I don't need you to worry about running this business. That's why I'm here. What I need you and Dan to do is build the best damn facility there is. Everything else, I am taking care of. Got it?"

"I got that, Connor, believe me I do, but there's still another matter. This facility—it will be kind of different from what we thought… You know what, why don't you just come down here to the office? Dan can explain it so much better than I can."

"Look, TC, do you have a workable reno plan and layout for me or not? Al and Rafael tell me they have, uh, a line on the perfect building for us to buy, I've got investors lined up through Blue Bayou Capital—you heard of them?"

"Yes. They're a huge outfit, true, but…"

"But nothing. I have everything lined up, just waiting for you guys to give me a piece of paper that says this is what everything needs to look like, and this is what it is going to cost us. Now can you handle that or not? Because if you can't…"

"We can handle it, Connor. That's not the problem at all."

"Then what is? Because for the last 10 minutes, TC, you've been giving me shit, and…"

"29 million."

"29 million?"

"We ran the costing on the new plans, and the total cap ex on the reno is going to be 29 million."

"29—fuck."

He felt the fury inside him rise, heard an enormous crash, and saw Tessa rushing his office as if he had screamed for help. His fist came crashing down on his desk, and he realized he had thrown his phone against the wall while letting loose a string of curses that did more than turn the air blue. Even Tessa cringed, and she was used to a thing or two.

Connor jumped up from his chair, stormed out the door, and slammed it behind him as hard as he could. $29 fucking million. He'd been counting on 13. All of his plans said 13 because that moron, that goddamn moron TC, had told him 13 was all it would take.

Now what did he look like?

He looked like an ass; that's what he looked like. Every investor who had put money into this thing would ask only one question: *Connor Beauregard, how could you make a $16 million mistake?* Never mind that TC was the moron who had misled him, never mind that Dan was probably the guy in the background who had put it all in motion. Never mind any of that. All people would see was that Connor Beauregard made a $16 million mistake.

Goddammit, he swore, and all but ran the 10 blocks through midtown to Kayla's condo.

TWENTY-TWO

He stabbed the call button on the elevator so hard it almost broke under his fingers. He could hear the plastic crunch and balled his hands to fists in the pockets of his windbreaker.

Goddammit...

Up on the penthouse floor, he rushed through the front door and headed for the built-in bar, pouring a whisky and soda almost in one motion—right past a stunned Kayla, who lounged on the chaise reading a magazine.

"Connor, honey, is something wrong?"

"Not now."

He downed the drink in three big gulps, wiped his mouth with the back of his hand, and poured another.

"Connor, you are scaring me—tell me what's going on so I can help you."

The next whisky went down just as quickly, and, when he had mixed the third, he finally reined his fury in enough to tell her. To his surprise, Kayla took it all in stride, mixed her own drink, and shrugged.

"So, you were a victim of bad advice. It happens, you know. It happened to my ex plenty of times, and usually, the perp got fired."

"TC is so beyond fired..." Connor took another gulp of his drink, still unable to speak clearly. Slowly, the heat of the whisky spread, and he was able to sit heavily in one of Kayla's designer chairs.

"He's gone, so gone he might as well be dead. I'm going to take that little maggot and grind him into the dirt." His hands clenched so hard he was almost afraid he would break the glass.

"Relax," Kayla said, opening the bar again. "This is not even a bad thing."

"Relax? You're telling me to relax?" he roared and just stopped himself from throwing the glass in her direction. Whatever else Connor Beauregard was, he treated women with respect. "I can't relax."

"Yes, you can, and I'll tell you why." Kayla was by his side again and opened her hand. Two innocent white pills lay on the smooth palm, identical to the ones she had offered to him in Zurich. "Go ahead. Take it."

Connor hesitated, and she pushed her hand a little closer.

"Take it. It's going to take the edge off, and right now, you can't make one straight decision. Jesus, Connor..."

Obediently, he took the two pills and could almost immediately feel the calm spread throughout his entire body. Carefully, he set the glass down beside himself and took a deep breath, letting it out in one big sigh.

"That's better. Now listen to me and listen to me good."

He nodded and relaxed back into the chair, letting the big blue wave roll over him and take away the last of the anger.

"TC is obviously not what we needed. A man who knows nothing and started this thing wrong right from the beginning."

"You don't say."

"And you're going to make sure people know that—everybody is going to know that."

"So they know I've been made a fool of. Kayla, I don't think..."

"No, you don't think, Connor. It's not your job to know everything about operations or horticulture. You are the CEO. Your job is to run the overall business, to bring in money, and to set the general direction the company is going."

"OK." The dreamy feeling spread, and Connor felt good again. He hadn't felt this good since Zurich.

"So, you hired a man who obviously doctored his résumé a little." Her mind filled out the PR spin she'd put on it.

"He never showed me a..."

"He pretended to be someone he isn't, and you're going to give him a chance to redeem himself. To learn that is why you brought Dan in. Dan, who obviously has experience through his, umm, slightly shady connections..."

"He does?"

"He does. He has a brother in jail on drug charges for god's sake—you think he's a choirboy? No, you're the victim here. You hired a liar, gave him a chance to learn and the best mentor you could find, and still things went wrong."

"Deniability."

"Exactly, plausible deniability. You did the best you could. Those two screwed up. They presented you with a set of facts that were completely wrong and did what they wanted while your back was turned."

"Oh, you are good."

"Your investors will be outraged, not because of anything you did—you put a great team together and gave them everything they needed—but because they screwed the company. Plain and simple. They did not know what they were doing. And Dan, the guy who was foisted on you by... well, Al's father made you take him into the company, did he not?"

"Yes, but I probably should have kept a better eye on him—on both of them."

"It's not your job babysitting people. A good leader hands out tasks and steps back, letting his people accomplish them. That's what you did. If it works out, you're the star. If it doesn't? Well who says Dan did not set out to sabotage you...or TC? There's no need for you to look foolish here. We can spin anything."

"Damn, you are good," Connor muttered again, even as the combination of whisky and whatever Kayla had given him took hold and gently transported him into La La land. A land where big multinational corporations ran themselves, all advice was good, and Connor Beauregard was God!

Kayla looked down at him and put the little glass vial of white pills away again. Dominik was right; this stuff really was powerful. She'd have to be careful with it.

We can spin it. Damn straight we can. Hanson's favorite line, and he had taught her everything about the perfect spin.

She looked down on Connor again and tucked the white blanket on her chaise just a little tighter around him. He'd have a nap for now, and, when he woke, he'd be ready to take on the world. He'd make more money with this cannabis thing in a few months than she had by running her magazines for years, and she would make damn sure that she ended up with a lot of shares for all of her trouble.

Hanson might have left her a magazine, but Connor, Connor would give her an empire. She'd make sure of that.

Connor only needed half an hour, then woke again, indeed ready to conquer the world—barehanded, if need be.

First thing he did was drive to Dan and TC's office. He parked well away from their little hovel and simply dropped in, as if he were a neighbor coming over for coffee.

TC stood, a little shellshocked, when he saw who had strolled through their door, but Dan barely looked up from his drawing board.

"Come to see the little people, Connor, see what we are doing to your company?"

"It's not quite like that, Dan—but yes, I wanted to see what was going on, see why our original cap ex has suddenly doubled. Not pointing any fingers of blame here, just want to know. Besides I need to be able to explain this increase to our investors."

Dan had expected him to make a scene. Scream, holler, point

fingers, anything. He was prepared for drama—not for a calm and collected Connor coming in for a friendly chat. He could see that and congratulated himself on having taken the time to calm down and look at things rationally.

"You see," Dan started slowly, "cannabis is a fickle plant."

"I know that."

"Sensitive—to temperature changes, bugs, fungi, several different diseases…"

"OK."

He didn't need the lecture—did not need to know any of this. But for the sake of getting to the bottom of things…

"Anybody can just grow pot, if you will. Sink some seeds into the ground, get rid of the male plants, take care of the females, and bingo. In less than a year, you'll have a mother plant you can use for cloning—taking cuttings of for your young plants."

"You make it sound easy, Dan. So, the problem is where?"

"The problem is that we don't want to *just grow pot*. We want a stable product—consistent, medical-grade cannabis—grown as required by law. Which means we can't just dump any old fertilizer on the plants. It means we can't experiment around. We need a facility, an environment that is absolutely perfect. We need to play God—you need to be God."

Connor nodded. "I've heard it, and I am liking it, but I still don't understand…"

"Most marijuana growers out there think greenhouse—growing in dirt. Putting on a few lights, hoping for the best. We can't do that. And I hope you were not planning on it."

"I was not," Connor said, although from the very beginning, he hadn't really had a clear picture in his mind what the grow facility should look like. Not until he had gone to Colorado and Utah had he seen what they were doing.

"We need to be in charge of how much light these plants are getting, how much water, how many nutrients, and exactly when. That means we want to grow them in hermetically sealed pods in an artificial grow medium. Each one of these pods needs its own environmental controls, lights, air conditioning. Every light itself needs its own air conditioning unit, did you know that?"

"I did not," Connor admitted and for the first time studied the drawings on the board with more than a cursory interest. He hated to admit it, but Dan had done more than good work. The entire facility started to take shape right there on his drawing board, and finally, he understood what Dan and TC had been talking about all along.

"Shit, 15 different pods per room? All with individualized controls?"

"Exactly," Dan said nodding. "That way, you have trouble of some sort in one pod, well, you might lose that, but not the entire harvest. Plus, you can grow different strains, different combinations of CBD and other medical substances…"

"CBD?"

"Cannabinol, the 'stuff' that makes this actually medicine."

"Not THC."

"No, not a lot," Dan laughed. "THC is what you wanted in your plants as a teenager. That's the stuff that makes you high. Medical-grade marijuana, you're actually after CBD—that's what helps in medical therapies. Big difference."

Connor only nodded. He could see how much work had gone into the drawings and plans in front of them, and he knew in an instant that TC could never have gotten there on his own. If he ever wanted a license, he needed Dan. Badly.

"Jesus, Dan," he said, "I really appreciate everything you've done on behalf of the company. I know I don't nearly say it often enough, but I can see how thorough you are, and how hard you've worked on this, and I want you to know how thankful I am."

Dan blinked once or twice, like a man who stepped out of the basement into the bright light of day, and actually lost his train of thought for a minute.

"Well—er—thanks, Connor. I didn't know…"

"You didn't think I gave a shit about all of this." Connor swept his hands around the small office. "And I will grant you that I have been way over-occupied just recently. That's not an excuse, just an explanation. I've left you guys with the hard work without acknowledging it."

"Well, you know, it's a big job running a company and all that—I surely wouldn't want to do it."

Connor smiled and clapped Dan and TC on the shoulders.

"I'm glad I managed to get two smart, hardworking guys like you on my team, though. So now, explain the rest of it to me. Cannabinol, consistency. You thought I wasn't paying any attention."

"Well." Dan looked back down at the drawing and ran his finger along one line of little squares. "Growing pods—only a few plants in each one of these. You—when you are a patient, and you have a license to acquire medical marijuana, you rely on the quality being consistent each time you order the stuff. It just can't be that one month your medicine works better and the next month not so much. That's where greenhouses can't compete with us."

"Too many variables?" Connor asked because by now, the picture was forming in his head too.

"Too many variables. The hours of light and temperatures for one. Look at the average greenhouse. Do the plants by the side walls get the same amount of light and heat as the plants in the center? No, of course not. What about the soil they are grown in—is it the exact same chemical consistency from one pot to the next? It is not. This is where we come in. Because in our case, it is."

He ran his finger along the little rows of squares again.

"Each one of these growing pods has the exact same conditions for all the plants. And they are sitting in artificial grow medium, not soil. You decide when the light and heat come on, and when they go off. We are God."

"I like that." Connor grinned. "I am God."

142

Dan nodded. "In a $26 million nutshell. But for the size and scope of operation you're planning, that will be the minimum you need to get started."

"Then I know what I have to do." Connor rose and shook Dan's and TC's hands in turn. "Go back to my investors rattling the tin can. Thank you, gentlemen, for all the fine, hard work you have done on this project in the meantime. I assure you it will not be forgotten."

TC stared at the door, dumbfounded, after it had closed behind Connor.

"Well, I'll be. Who was that? That's not the Connor Beauregard I spoke to earlier."

"Oh, it's the same guy, you know." Dan leaned back in his draftsman's chair and folded his hands behind his head. "He just realized that he is utterly fucked without the two of us, who actually know what we're doing, so he put on a bit of an *I appreciate you two so much* show."

"Well, you know what you are doing here, Dan. If I had gone ahead with my original ideas and setup, I'm pretty sure the whole thing would have crashed and burned on the inside of a couple of months."

"Yeah, maybe. You would have picked it up, TC. Don't give me that. Besides, who's been working on the damned license to grow for the last couple of weeks straight? Hell, I bet you Connor hasn't even thought about that bit yet. But when he does, well, when he does, he's going to thank his lucky stars you looked after it." Dan pointed at a five-inch-high stack of paper at the edge of his desk. "'Cause there's no way in hell I know what all that paper is all about. I don't even want to go near it, never mind deal with it."

"Yeah. The license kind of turned into a full-time job. You're right about that." TC sat heavily in his own chair and gave the stack a little push. "And this stuff is just the start. Pretty soon Connor's gonna have to get involved here, too."

"And he's not going to like it."

"You think? He's going to hate every fucking minute of it!"

Dan laughed and toed open their little office fridge, filled with water, soda, and the occasional beer.

"So, we had better get him while he knows he needs us, 'cause sure as there's an amen at the end of church service, this morning he was going to fire both of us, till he thought better of it. And I can guarantee you that mood won't last long."

TWENTY-THREE

He needed them; he needed both of them to keep doing what they were doing. But both Dan and TC could make a fool of him if they wanted to. That put them in a position of power, and Connor despised the mere thought.

He had made a living reading people, and he knew Dan hadn't fallen for any of his lines. No matter how often he said *I appreciate you* or *thanks for all your hard work,* Dan saw right through him. It did not make the tiniest little impression on him, and Connor wanted to kick his ass just for that. For a lot of other things, sure—but mostly for that.

He would have to read up on this stuff—desperately.

No way he was going to let those two ride roughshod all over him while he stood there, like a rube, mouth agape, not knowing what was going on.

They asked for a $26 million budget to build their little facility—his little facility—and if he was going to spend that kind of money, he would know what for. His ace in the hole was the guy from Colorado. Once he had him in the company, he would demote those two to errand boys in the grow facility. They would well deserve it. *In the meantime, tread lightly, Connor,* he told himself, *tread lightly*: another thing he hated.

Accordingly, he was in a foul mood when he walked into The Lighthouse just after noon and ordered a drink without even looking around. The first sip went down quickly; then he allowed himself to slow down.

"Wow, you look actually pretty miserable there, pal."

"Rafael, of course. Where else would you be?"

"Might ask you the same thing, since you seem to be doing the same thing."

"Do not start in with me. I just had a meeting with TC and your pal Dan and… it didn't exactly end with smiles and handshakes all around."

"I see. That explains the face quite well then. Dan's a bit of an acquired taste, isn't he?"

"Distaste more like it. Jesus, he is an arrogant little…" Connor looked sideways to where the bartender was fussing with glasses and signaled for another drink. "I cannot believe I have to take his bullshit."

"Al calls him… a bit opinionated."

"A bit? He's an arrogant piece of…"

"Remember, though…"

"Yeah, I remember, Rafa. I remember he's the son of the man you saddled me with. The man whose name I don't even know, who seems to have more money than God and connections other men just dream of."

"And he's on your side, so what do you want?"

"I want for these people to remember. Remember that this is my company—that I founded it, that I had the idea."

"We did."

"We did. That's right. We made it all possible. You think a man who calls himself the Original Chef could go to the government, hat in hand, and say, *Hello, can I please have a license to grow marijuana? I promise I will not use it for any kind of nefarious purposes.*"

"Would probably not go over all that well." Rafael nodded. "So what do you want? Just cool your jets a little, remember they need you as much as you need them, and let Dan do his bit. He is an arrogant, annoying son of a bitch, I hear you, but you won't need to deal with him much, and we'll just seat you at another table for the company Christmas party."

Connor looked at him as if his friend had suddenly grown a set of horns and opened his mouth to let loose another string of complaints, but they stuck in his throat. The drink already blunted his anger, and he knew Rafael had a point. Dan was one of those necessary little evils one had to put up with now and then in life, as was Al, as was their triple-damned annoying father the Chef. Use them; let go of them. Didn't mean he had to like them.

"The Original Chef, my ass. The man is a bloody criminal if you ask me. Why he is not in jail I don't know."

"That is why nobody is asking you, Connor. Because one way or another, the answer to that question might be not all that supportive to your general health and wellbeing, nor that of your company."

Connor glared at him and took a generous swig from his drink, signaling for another.

"Shit. Now on to another subject. What about that building you and Al got all excited about? Are we getting close to finalizing something yet?"

"I've got something," Rafael said and unfolded a piece of paper that had been sitting inside his jacket for a while.

"Rafa, can you not afford to buy a decent briefcase?"

"These are just my personal notes." Carefully, Rafael unfolded the paper and smoothed it out on the bar between them. "I think I've been hanging around with Al a bit too long. The thought of carrying a briefcase and regular, old-fashioned files and notes all of a sudden has become a bit, well… repugnant."

"Well, un-repugnant it. I refuse to deal with a guy who carries loose bits and pieces in his pockets. It's disgusting."

"Right, boss." Rafael indicated a lazy salute and pointed at his paper. "Now this here is just about as perfect as it gets."

Connor glanced at the real estate brochure.

"Almost 300,000 square feet," Rafael continued. "Some of it is rented right now. The rest is all empty warehousing space. Great for our purposes. Not much to knock down. All you have to do is put Dan's pretty plans to work."

"Dan's pretty plans. Please don't call it that. I might be sick."

"You've got two major highways basically at your doorstep, a rail line. It's less than 20 minutes to the airport, and the lot itself is huge."

"OK. I get the building. The lot is a bit of a waste, no?"

"Storage, my friend, basic storage. For now, we won't need or use it. We can rent it out for some of these transport companies to use." He flipped the brochure over and pointed to a couple of darker shaded sections of the building. "These four sections over here are rented out, basic warehousing space, nothing spectacular. But they might want to park their trucks somewhere or need some outside storage space. You never know."

"All extra income, I understand," Connor said softly. "Income that is steady while we work on Dan's... on the design specs for the grow areas. Good work, Rafael."

"It's a damned ugly old building, and nobody in their right mind would call it anything but that, but I think it would do quite well as a grow op."

"Location?"

"Well, out of town. Like I said, close to the highway and the rail line, and next-door neighbors are a couple of small time industrial plazas, nobody who would think to complain about that kind of facility. Next residential area is a couple of miles away. It's perfect."

"That whole lot will have to have some serious security fencing around it," Connor said, tracing it with his finger. "Simon can take care of that, the kind of bulwarks that won't even let you drive a truck through it. I bet you it's in the license that we need that kind of thing."

"Probably. Beauty is we can start in stages, Connor. Take this first half over here and put in our grow op, let it go for a while, then kick out whatever tenants remain, and let it go again for a while. And who knows? By that time, we might be the biggest bloody weed growers in the country—we'll expand."

"We will be the biggest bloody weed growers," Connor corrected and picked up the brochure studying the pictures, ignoring for a moment the fact he had thought them disgusting a mere few minutes ago.

"You're right—this is bloody ugly, but darn it, I like it. When you are right, my friend… This would make the perfect cannabis grow op. I want to see the thing. Tour it, put my feet into that warehouse, smell it…"

"OK, I'll tell Al."

"If I'm going to put the biggest grow op in the country into that thing, I want to be the first one over the doorstep. See if it speaks to me."

"Man, you can be one weird dude, Connor. But I have to give it to you—usually, you are right."

"Usually?"

"Most of the time."

Connor opened his mouth to argue and grinned instead.

"OK, let you have that point. Now go talk to whoever you need to talk to. I want to see that building, I want to see appraisals, estimates, et cetera. If I like it, I want to go straight ahead and make an offer."

"I should have known as much." Rafa raised his hands into the air and then drained his drink in one gulp. "When you see something you like, you don't go for the 'take it easy' approach, do you?"

"Nobody who has ever taken it easy has put something this grand and this spectacular together. Remember that one. Now go. Arrange for everything I need for this building, make it happen, and make it happen fast. I'm going to check on Tessa and this damned amalgamation. It's taking forever, and we need to be trading. Tomorrow, Rafael. Tomorrow."

Rafael walked out. He'd have to teach that little man to quit the little fake lazy salute. It wasn't like they were in the military. Just made him look bad. He ordered another drink and called Tessa.

"Tess, my dear, working hard?"

"You got that right. The paperwork on this amalgamation is the worst I've ever seen. And I think we have a small problem in the agreement somewhere."

"Says who?"

"Well, I just..."

"Catherine, am I right or am I right? Catherine had to get her hands in there again and tell you something is wrong with the agreement."

"Well, she was handling it anyway, Connor—it's not like I went out and hired her. I want this to go smoothly and right for you, don't you?"

"I want it to go fast. And if everything is right, and everything goes to plan—and there is no reason it should not—then we are on track. Never mind the agreement. There's nothing wrong with it. I guarantee that. Tell me what we need next."

"We need a shareholder vote agreeing to the amalgamation with Todd's company, and it needs to be unanimous."

"Not a problem. I know pretty much all of the shareholders in there. And Al knows the rest. Then?"

"Then it's just a matter of filing the agreement and a bunch of forms I'm working on and bingo... we are Image Group, at least until you get the name changed."

"No problem. OK, I'm going to sit down right now and draft a letter to the shareholders, something they can't say no to. Can you meet me at The Lighthouse later and bring the contact list for our shareholders? We are going to get this done."

"At The Lighthouse?"

"Why not? They've got wireless here. We can get it all done today."

Connor looked around. A couple of booths at the far end provided just the right amount of privacy. Why the heck even go back to the office? This was the perfect place to work. And his favorite bartender was in attendance.

"Brittany," he signaled her again, "I'll be back there in one of the booths. When my assistant comes in, show her over, please."

"Right-O, Connor, want another one?"

"Is the Pope Catholic?"

He sat down and flipped open his laptop. Now this stuff he was good at. Spinning the story for the shareholders—telling them not what he wanted them to do, but always making them want to do it.

Dear Shareholders:

We are on the verge of an important step in this company's history, the merger transaction into a publicly trading company. This is the moment we have all been waiting for. We have made great strides since the company was founded only a few months ago...

Yada, yada...tell them the wonderful things that had happened, tell them all of the great plans he had, draw a picture in front of them... Not as easy on a piece of paper but doable. For the master of the word, anyway.

You will find in the attachments a special resolution for your consideration. We need a response from all of Perfect Cannabis's shareholders to move forward with this merger by Friday June 15th, noon EST. This is an important step in the company's history, and the PerCan board of directors respectfully requests your prompt attention and response.

The board of directors, what a laugh. Connor himself, Rafael, Simon, and Josh—and really, only he and Rafael—were doing any kind of real work or shouldering any kind of responsibility. The rest of them were perfectly happy to be dragged along. Now, all of that would have to change. They'd have to step up.

Connor drained his beer and prettied up the letter. Always look good, no matter what you were doing. Worked for women, worked in business just the same. If you looked professional, acted professionally, people would believe you. Nothing worse than an important letter like this one going out with a spelling error or without the proper letterhead.

Thankfully, Tessa could make all that happen with a wave of her magic wand, pop in the letterhead picture, his actual signature—the woman was a treasure.

They all needed to sign it. He had less than 100 shareholders at this point, and still it would come down to the last minute, he was sure. This vote had to be unanimous, or it would not happen.

Connor felt the adrenaline making his heart beat faster, his hands shake just a little. God he loved this stuff. Making the deal happen, putting it all together, right down to the wire like this one. Watching it happen…

The only thing that felt even remotely this good were Kayla's little pills.

Suddenly annoyed, he picked up his glass, realized it was empty, and signaled the bartender. Where on the black earth had that come from? Those pills, whatever they were. He really did not want to know what was in them. It could not be good news; that much was certain. Then again, that had been a one-time exception. OK, two-time. He really did not need that kind of stuff to feel great.

This, this right here, was what gave him the kick he needed.

He saw Tessa by the door and waved.

"Back here, Tess."

She sat beside him and flipped open her laptop as well. "Hard at work already?"

"As always. You brought our latest shareholder list?"

"Right here." She nodded to a spreadsheet open on the laptop.

"OK, give me two minutes. I'm going to identify whose people they are."

"Whose people?"

"Who brought them into the company, who knows them best. What I need you to do is send out the shareholder letter to each and every one of them, attach the vote sheet to the email, and a link of some sorts so they can digitally sign it."

"'K, easy enough. I got a few online places."

"I don't need to know that, just make it as easy as possible for them to sign the damn thing and return it, without having to print it, whatever you do. If they can sign it right on their phone, even better, just do it then and there, if possible. Include the fax and the email, prominently. I need this thing to come back fast. Then copy the person I identify in the last column of your spreadsheet. That's the person who brought them in, their handler if you will. I also need you to write an email to all of those 'handlers' making sure they know to get in touch with their shareholders and stay in their face until the resolution is signed."

"To make sure…"

"To make sure everybody signs the damn thing—right away. I don't want any last-minute problems, like our little 5,000 shares guy there. Everybody needs to sign this. Everybody."

"And if somebody has a problem with it? Connor, they may have questions. They may want to talk about it. Not everybody understands reverse mergers and going public like you do. Don't you want a contact in there in case anybody is unsure?"

"We don't have time for questions and handholding. They can't doubt this for one moment. We need this merger to go forward ASAP. We need it, period. Anybody who does not sign this is a complete moron. Moreover, I'll be willing to give him his money back and take his shares away from any such person, do you understand?"

"Yes, but…"

Tessa squirmed a little uncomfortably. To his mind, as much as she was young, and a computer hacker, and dating a complete idiot—she had this annoying irritating sense of *the way things ought to be*. He'd have to drive that out of her, wouldn't he?

Because he, Connor Beauregard, decided the way things ought to be, when, where and how. Period. It was still his company.

"Tessa, focus over here. This is the best thing to happen to this company since we founded it way back. This is what is going to make all of us rich, OK? I can't have anybody doubt this and screw up the deal for everybody else. Now that would not be fair to the shareholders who understand, who know what they are doing and sign the resolution the moment they see it, now would it?"

"Not technically, no, but still..."

"But still... I don't want them to have the time to take it to their lawyers, talk about it with their brothers' wives and cousins. If we do that, we'll still be sitting here when you are of retirement age, with no merger and no public company, understand?"

"Yes, I understand." Tessa finally nodded, reluctantly, but she nodded.

"This is a good thing! Smile. This is the best damned thing that ever happened to us. Let's focus on that and get those letters out, shall we?"

"Yes, OK. It won't take long."

"Good, because I just saw Kayla coming in, and she's going to want a few minutes with me alone."

He rose, leaving Tessa to her laptop and the shareholder letter. On his way he asked a waiter to bring Tessa anything she wanted or needed, more specifically an expensive afternoon lunch and her favorite brand of wine. Anything to keep her happy for the moment. He really needed to get this out.

"Hello, my love." He kissed Kayla on the cheek and ordered for her as well. "Champagne?"

"You know me too well. Things going OK?"

"Things are going better than OK, love. Tessa is preparing the letter to the shareholders so we can get the merger executed, and before you know it, we are going to have a little public company, well, big public company. What about you?"

"Oh, nothing special—some trouble with a few of my journalists. Apparently, they think I've been spending too much time away from my office and in yours."

"You don't spend any time at the office."

"No, but since I've known you, I've devoted a lot of time to Perfect Cannabis. And we were in Denver and Oregon and just recently in Switzerland... It adds up, you know. I guess they think I ought to be doing more of the work."

"Well, my love, they still work for you. They are your employees, and what you do, and what hours you keep, frankly is none of their business. If they don't like it, that's too bad."

"They are still good people, Connor. I want to keep them around."

"If they start criticizing you, you don't want to keep them around. This is the way you run things. Anybody does not like it—well, they can not like it elsewhere. You need their respect, not their friendship."

She ran her hand up and down Connor's leg and took a sip of her champagne. "Why is Tessa working in here? Does she not have a perfectly good office to be in, to do all of this—without watching us?"

"She's not watching us, trust me. I gave a lot of work to her just now. Besides, I don't think she gets out all that often. Let her have a bit of fun, get a taste of the fine food and fine liquor.

"I need her to get this done, and I need to get it done now, understand?" he continued and returned the gesture of running his hand down her leg. "Easiest way is to make her feel like she is special. That'll add more fuel to her enthusiasm and effort than anything else. Now where were we?"

Women! He would have laughed about it, but that would have signed a death warrant for him to be sure. Instead, he concentrated on flirting with Kayla, keeping an eye on Tessa in the corner booth, and thinking of calling all of his main investors. Rafa would have to speak to a lot of guys to make sure they knew how to vote, and did so within the next three days, as would he himself.

And Kayla. She had brought in a lot of investors; even she would have to carry her load. Wasn't that annoying little man one of hers—McDowell, was it? The man with the 5,000 shares? He had an instinctive feeling this guy would cause him a load of trouble he neither needed nor wanted at the moment. He also had a feeling Mr. 5,000 Shares did not know about Kayla and the trouble she'd be causing him.

"Where would you like to go when the company finally hits?" he asked dreamily. "Hawaii, Bali, the North Pole—you name it. We are going to celebrate properly."

"South Pacific maybe," Kayla said dreamily. "I've always wanted to go. Certainly not the North Pole. You can scratch that one right off."

"Good because we are going to go and celebrate."

"Celebrate." Her eyes lit up as if he had said shopping, Christmas, and around-the-world trip all at the same time.

"That's right. Celebrate big-time. Just a couple of things I have to take care of first. Make sure all these shareholders vote with me."

"Well, all the ones I brought in will—I can guarantee you that," she said. "These are all friends of mine, and not one of them will dare vote against you."

"Good." Connor grinned. "I was hoping you would say that—pardon me for assuming." He pulled her list out of his portfolio and slid it over the bar. "I've put together the folks who are definitely yours. Would you mind..."

"Not at all." She looked over and saw that he had his own list. "Oh, we'll both be doing the same thing. How fun!"

"I love it." He blew her a kiss and turned a bit on his bar stool, dialing his phone.

"Rafa, the shareholder vote is about to be let loose. I don't have to tell you what that means, do I? We're all going to be hounding our contacts to make sure they vote with us. I've emailed your list. Can I count on you?"

He swiveled back in his chair took a drink, winking at Kayla. "I know it, you know it—this has to be unanimous, and we need it. So put the pressure on. I don't care what it costs. Anybody does not want to sign, I will personally take his shares back and return his money, got it?"

A minute later, he was on the phone with Al, repeating much the same script, with a bit more politeness in his voice. Give him one thing, he thought, Al knew how the game was played. He agreed to do what needed doing with one or two clipped sentences and hung up the phone. Consider it done. Unlikely anybody would dare to disagree with Al, he figured.

Simon and Josh did not really like the idea of being somebody's handler, but the prospect of 'collective prosperity,' as Connor called it, convinced even those two. Connor stepped away and called a stockbroker friend of his about a little bet they were having, all the while surveying the room. Tessa was furiously working on the shareholder email. Kayla was phoning her contacts, putting on the pressure. Al, Rafael, Josh, and Simon were presumably doing the same. Just as it was supposed to be, just as he liked it.

Connor allowed himself a little smile. The world was back where he wanted it to be.

TWENTY-FOUR

The next morning, he almost beat Tessa to the office. As it was, he dropped in just as she fired up her desktop.

"Good morning, dear Tessa. The moment that thing there tells you, let me know how many shareholder votes we have in. We should be almost done."

"You think?"

"I don't think, and I don't hope, Tessa. Always remember that. I know this is going to happen because it has to happen!"

He almost wanted to whistle while he waited for her update. He'd been following along on his phone as the emails started to come in, one by one. His fellow board members first, of course. They knew what was expected, and almost all of Al's people came in in one single document, scanned and signed all together. He did not even want to know how that had been accomplished, but quietly, when nobody was looking, he had to give the man credit. Shareholders could be an odd breed—especially when they knew you needed something. They could smell it when you needed something, and Connor hated nothing more. To have to be slimy and smarmy just because you needed a signature.

He shook visibly and scanned down the list. Great—all the major shareholders accounted for, just as he knew it would be. The men who knew how to play the game. William McDowell, still outstanding.

"Little fucker. I knew you would make me sweat," he murmured and seriously considered calling the man up and giving him his money back. That whiner did not deserve it. That was the only thing that kept him from doing so right now. That goddamn little nuisance did not deserve the few bucks he had put into the company, and he deserved even less all the money he would make off it.

"Catherine is on line one for you," Tessa called, and he shook his head. Jeez, he carried a cell phone—everybody did. Only losers called on the main office line. And lawyers.

"Good morning, Catherine, and how are you today?" he asked, sweet as pie.

"Good, working on your amalgamation paperwork. Have you reviewed the items of concern with Tessa?"

"Of course I have, and she will work on remediating them all. Thank you for being so thorough."

"And your shareholder vote. How is that coming? You know you need…"

"I need 100 percent of the votes, I am aware of that, and I'm as good as there."

"As good as?"

"Consider it done, Catherine. By tonight, I will be dropping a letter off at your office that I have 100 percent of shareholder votes in hand, supporting the amalgamation and reverse merger between Perfect Cannabis and Image Group."

Catherine said nothing for a moment, and he knew she was thinking. Did he really have all the votes, and, if so, would she call him on it? Likely not. She was, after all, his lawyer.

"You know, if there is anything…not quite 100 percent about this vote, we could have trouble later on. It would make the amalgamation invalid, and it would give us humongous problems. Your entire company…"

"I promise you, Catherine, we are not going to have the slightest problem. Everything about this shareholder vote is 100 percent correct and documented."

"If you say so."

"Of course. My dear Catherine, I hate to hustle you off the phone. It is always a pleasure to talk to you, but I have to jump on this call. So please stand by. I will deliver the certification to you tonight. In the meantime, you may prepare everything else, based on that fact. Bye."

He hung up the phone, wishing he could slam it down like the old-style receivers, and sat there thinking. Of course the vote would be fine. Why was he even worried about it? Right at this minute, all of his people were on the phone, talking to the shareholders, making sure the votes were coming in, just as expected. Lawyers just had this way of making you think something could go wrong; something would screw your plan at the last second. God, he hated lawyers!

"Tess?"

"Yes, boss?" Her head popped in through the door so fast she startled him with her appearance. Almost as if she'd been waiting for him behind the door.

"What's going on with the votes? How far are we?"

"About 85, give or take a few."

"I don't want to give or take a few, Tess. I need all of them. No room for error."

"Well, a few people are out of town."

"Out of town? Out of town, Tess? How could you be out of town without your damned phone or tablet? Who does that? You sent the docs ready to be electronically signed, did you not?"

"Like you asked me to."

"Then there is no excuse. Get me a list of who's missing."

"OK, coming up."

She knew better than to argue with him when he was in that kind of a mood. She drew back a little from the wave of fury he knew rolled off him, but he could feel time literally burning away right under his fingers. He. Had. To. Get. This. Done. Period.

He dialed the phone again. "Rafa, how do I get a hold of Al?"

"With difficulty."

"Don't bullshit me, Rafa, not now. I need to talk to Al. Right this minute or this amalgamation deal may not go down, and he might as well flush his money down the crapper. Do you have a phone number?"

"What's the hurry? This does not have to be rammed through tonight, you know. There is time."

"The hurry is I want it done, Rafa. You know the plan for crying out loud. Every minute we delay is lost forever. Now, Al, do you have his phone number?"

"Yes, private one."

"Then give it to me please."

"No can do, Connor. Al is very specific about who has and does not have his number. I'll find a way to let him know you need him."

"Rafael, goddamn it..."

"Stand by. Won't take long."

Connor sat there staring dumbfounded at the phone in his hand. Rafael had hung up on him.

"Tess, where is that updated list? I need it, like, now."

"Coming."

He paced by the window, raking his fingers through his hair, almost pulling it out. Not happening—this was not happening again.

Tessa stepped in quickly and put a hot cup of coffee on his desk. Maybe not the upper he needed right now, but he appreciated the gesture anyway and forced a tight little smile.

"Rafael just left a message," Tessa said. "He's driving out to pick up the last three of his people so his list is complete. Josh, I don't know what Josh has been doing, but I hardly have any of his, and Simon says he is working on them."

"Thanks. I'll go after Josh."

"Kayla?"

"Kayla is working on her people—never you mind that, Tess. She has one of her personal assistants driving around getting signatures."

Then there was McDowell. The thorn in everyone's eye. And Josh, who apparently did not think it was worth lifting one finger to ensure they would all earn the money they so richly deserved. God, if he did not do everything himself...

The phone interrupted his mental rant, and he almost did not answer, seeing a blocked caller ID, but then he thought of Al. Oh, that would be like him, wouldn't it?

"Beauregard."

"Connor, I heard you need me."

Al, of course it was Al. Blocked caller ID, secret phone number...the whole bit. He was so damned sick of the secret fraternity rituals. Did these people really think playing hide-and-seek would get it done? Seriously?

Taking a breath and forcing himself to sound cheerful, upbeat, and unbelievably friendly, Connor caught Al up on the latest developments in the amalgamation.

"I know I'm sounding like a broken record, Al, but we need to be trading, and we need to be trading fast. If we want to raise more money, this is necessary."

"I understand. Who are the holdouts?"

Time to throw somebody under the bus. Not like the man owed him anything. Not like he had brought in a load of capital.

"From what my assistant tells me, almost none of Josh's contacts have signed the shareholder vote. He appears to be out of town and perhaps a little disinclined..."

"I will take care of it. Have your assistant make up a list. I will send someone to pick it up in a few minutes. When do we need all of this by?"

"Tonight would be ideal. As the president and CEO I'll be required to sign a statement saying I have votes from 100 percent of the shareholders in my hands."

"Anybody going to check up on this?"

"Not right away, but, surely you don't suggest..."

"I'm not suggesting anything, Connor, just covering our asses in case we are not quite ready by tonight. You go ahead and sign that paper. I will make sure all of the votes are in and on file. A couple of them might just take a few extra hours to convince, that's all."

Connor hung up the phone, allowing himself to breathe again.

He could smell it, taste it—see himself pulling up the quotations to check the price of their stock, his own company. It was perfect. Everything would work out just fine.

Al certainly got things done, didn't he? After all, that was why he had let him into the company in the first place. He found himself smiling.

He glanced at Tessa's list of outstanding signatures and quickly balled up the second page and tossed it into the waste bin. Kayla's people would be taken care of by Kayla personally. Not Al. He needed Al to see that he and Kayla were running things just as they should be run. They did not need his help. Simon and Josh, different matter. Not Kayla.

The same young man who had delivered the check what seemed like ages ago showed up at his door a mere 10 minutes later.

"Good morning, Mr. Beauregard," he said in his precise and polite way and nodded at Tessa. "Mr. Al sent me to pick up a list from you. I hope it is ready?"

"Ready to go." Connor folded the piece of paper and handed it to him. "Al knows what this is all about."

Tessa looked at the page changing hands briefly and shook her head. "Connor, should there not be a second..."

"No, this is everything, Tess. Everybody else has been taken care of."

She opened her mouth again, but one look from him convinced her to close it again. Al's assistant took the sheet, glanced at it, and looked from Connor to Tessa.

"You're sure?"

"I am sure. This is everything. Thanks. Tell Al I really appreciate his help on this matter."

"All right then," Connor almost saw the man shrugging his shoulders as he left.

"Connor, the entire second page was missing," Tessa hissed once he was safely out of hearing range. "All of Kayla's people. There had to be at least seven or eight."

"Not going to be a problem, Tess. Kayla has her people in check, and I'm not going to have Al coming in, telling me I need help running my own company. Kayla is doing just fine—don't you worry about it."

"All the best to her, Connor. I don't doubt she can do it. She is a great businesswoman. All I was worried about was that little troublemaker McDowell. I wanted this Al character to take care of him. That would have at least given me a laugh."

"McDowell? The troublemaker—the $5,000 guy? He is on Kayla's list?"

Of course he was. He wasn't sure why that kept slipping his mind. Kayla would just have to do the best she could.

In the meantime, he would just certify the 100 percent, and life would be good. By the time anybody ever checked into it, they would either have gotten the man's vote or given him his money back.

He would take the shares personally if he had to—no, he would take them gladly. McDowell had bought fairly early, he recalled, when the shares were still at a dollar. Now the latest offerings were at three. Oh yes, maybe that would be the best solution after all. Give him his measly few bucks back, take his shares, and sell them for $3 to the next sucker.

Connor was smiling again as he dialed Kayla's number.

"Well, my love, I can smell the stock market from where I'm sitting. How are you doing on those shareholder votes?"

"Dialing as fast as I can, Connor. It's not easy having to explain the same thing a dozen times and then some. Could you not ask Tessa to do a few of these?"

"I could. I just thought you knew these people personally. It might be faster than Tessa explaining to each and every one of them who the hell she is, but if it becomes critical, don't be afraid to ask for help. You know we are all here for you."

"Well, I think I've got it," she said, but he did not hear a lot of conviction in her words. Not any as a matter of fact.

"Look, Simon and Josh gave up on their lists way before now. Matter of fact, I just asked Al to step in and handle it for them because they could not get the job done. So, if you are overwhelmed, let me know."

"No, Connor, I'm perfectly fine doing this. There is just one guy who is giving me a hard time, and I don't know what to tell him."

Good girl. She could read him almost as well as he read her.

"McDowell, that the troublemaker?"

"You know him?"

"Well, enough not to want him anywhere near this. Tell him if he has a problem with it, we will give him his money back and no hard feelings. That's all."

"OK, if you say so."

"I do say so. We don't need this kind of troublemaker. Everybody else you are pretty solid on?"

"Everybody else is going to sign, Connor. Just give me a bit of time. I don't know if I can do this by tonight."

"Take all the time you need, love," Connor said dreamily, smiling at the vista beyond the panorama window. "We're getting it done. No worries."

He flipped open his laptop and pulled up the certification Catherine had emailed him earlier.

'I, Connor Beauregard, President and CEO of Perfect Cannabis Corporation, hereby certify...'

Nothing to it—of course he would have 100 percent of shareholder votes. Not even the slightest doubt. Maybe not right this minute as he was certifying, but in a couple of days—max.

Add electronic signature and dates and hit send. Done.

He pulled up the amalgamation agreement and did the same, sent it on to all of his other directors for signature, and the whole lot to Catherine Egan, securities lawyer and serial biller. Not long now. He couldn't wait.

TWENTY-FIVE

The adrenaline rush of the amalgamation had barely had a chance to wear off when he was ready to dive into the next thing, purchasing a building for Perfect Cannabis Corporation.

The type of building he had in mind would be everything but cheap, but Connor did not do things on a small scale. After all, he was building the biggest and best medical marijuana grow facility in, well, the country, but after that, why not the world? Why not go so big everybody would know the name Perfect Cannabis? And the name Connor Beauregard. Why not indeed?

Why believe in limits in the first place? He could just reach out and touch infinity. Kayla had given him a couple more of her magic pills, and they really took the edge off. The McDowells of this world ceased to matter; the queer look Al gave him every time they spoke ceased to matter; thinking that Al and his rotten family believed him to be a moron, good enough only to be a well-dressed spokesperson—all that ceased to matter. The world had no limits, and it was within his reach.

He had traded up to an enormous SUV, and now he cruised around in style. He seemingly spent all day in this damn car, seeing investors, seeing his business partners, and he didn't want to arrive at his destinations scrunched into a matchbox, hurting through every minute of the meeting.

It did not take him near as long as he thought to get to the lot on the outskirts of town and to find the building he wanted to see.

Rafael had chosen well. The highway took you basically to the front door, and the roaring overhead told him how close the airport was. Two major factors in his general plan taken care of.

The aerial photos had shown the building to be a squat two-story 'T' with the horizontal section of the T housing all sorts of office and administrative spaces, while the long section was nothing but warehousing space, with five busy loading docks on either side.

Cussing softly, he maneuvered his SUV—which suddenly did not seem so big any longer—between giant transport trucks coming and going, zooming in against the open loading docks. Suddenly, the need for such a large lot became quite obvious as well. If you didn't want to waste ages waiting for your trucks to get into position, you had better give them space. They would never need ten loading docks, not in a dozen years, but again, Rafa was right. Why not rent out the space, make a few extra bucks that way?

Connor sat at the edge of the property for a few minutes, pushed his tinted, reflective aviator sunglasses up on his forehead, and watched the traffic coming in and out of the lot.

He almost jumped when someone knocked at his driver side window, only to find it was Rafael.

"Christ, Rafael, you scared the crap out of me!"

"A bit paranoid this morning, are we, Connor? What on earth are you on?"

"Nothing. Is Al coming anytime soon?"

"Touchy, paranoid, and you look like you've been up for 48 hours. Al is going to be here in a few minutes. His driver couldn't find the area right away."

Connor rolled his eyes, ignoring the remark about his appearance. He'd indeed rushed out in jeans, an untucked shirt and flip-flops. He'd been busy trying to find out how many of the 100 percent of shareholder votes he had certified they had actually on file. No doubt Catherine would be on the phone within the next few hours asking exactly that very question.

"Couldn't find the area," he snorted. "What, his driver only delivers in the better area of town? Wouldn't be so snooty with the business they are in."

"Maybe he's new." Rafael shrugged. "What do you care? Anyway, what do you think?"

"First glance, it's the ugliest thing I've ever seen. If we are going to work here, we're going to have to renovate big time. Perfect Cannabis needs to look like the professional group we are. This is…"

His hand swept along the long, faded grey building, the doors with the fading and peeling paint, the unkempt and dirty lot, and the garbage pile in the far corner.

"This is kind of disgusting, you know."

"That's what makes the whole deal affordable at the moment," Rafael said and looked through his notes. "Also, half of the thing is not rented. Motivates the owner even more."

"Needs work, needs new tenants, and needs a whole facelift. Fine by me as long as we get it for a good price."

Connor saw a mid-size black sedan with tinted windows turn into the lot from the road and nodded toward the driveway.

"Looks like the cavalry has arrived. Let's go see what this ramshackle thing looks like from the inside."

They'd better be getting the deal of the century, he thought. Having arrived in flip-flops, he slipped on several patches of slimy, non-identifiable spills. He noticed a definite, disgusting odor in the air wafting over from the garbage pile in the corner and saw the rat traps at the corner of the building. One hell of a deal. But Rafa had a point; much of this would be bulldozer bait anyway.

"Structure is sound," the agent for the seller said and let them into the former admin areas at the end of the building. "If you are thinking of putting a big facility in here, it won't take much to knock out a few walls, renovate this admin area here, and be up and running quickly."

"I'd want to knock out this admin area," Connor said pointedly and looked at doors hanging half off their hinges, holes in the fake wood paneling, and a couple of broken windows. "Define fixer-upper for me, will you?"

"Just means we can configure the whole thing to our specs," Al said, smiling, and scanned the fact sheet. "Long-term tenants?"

"Three. The rest you can get rid of any time you like."

"Won't need all the space right away anyway," Al said, musing over the fact sheet. "At least that's what I hear from Dan. Could take the build out over a couple of years, start relatively small..."

"Nobody is starting small, Al," Connor said and did his best to get a hold of the rising fury. "We are going to start guns blazing and hit the market hard. There are now enough consumers out there to sustain a large-scale grow."

Al gave him a long look from deep dark eyes and finally shrugged lightly with a smile.

"I guess that will also depend on how much money you can raise in the short term, will it not, Connor? I hear the renovations will be extensive and costly if we are to have a high-quality, consistent, and modern grow op."

"Guys, that's not something we have to argue about right this minute." Rafael walked away, breaking the staring contest between the two, and poked his head through a connecting door into the warehouse space beyond.

"The great vast nothing," he called out and giggled like a kid when his voice echoed. "Perfect—ready for us to put in anything. Hey, what shape is the roof in?" He pointed toward a couple of darkish puddles at the end of the warehouse. "That does not look really good."

"Tell you the truth, you are probably going to need roof repairs fairly quickly," the agent said, "but all that is reflected in the price. I have a schedule here, drafted by a civil engineer, shows you all the short-term and long-term work needed."

Connor tuned him out. He already knew he needed money—lots of money. The kind of money you couldn't raise without having shares on a public stock exchange. Was that not what he had been telling them all along? Was that not why he had been pushing for this amalgamation so hard, while everybody else was telling him to take his time and do things by the book?

Screw that. Here they were, and they were doing this. They were standing on sacred ground—the future home of the biggest cannabis grow operation anybody had ever seen. He was making his mark.

He opened the door and stepped out into the warehouse. Skimpy little skylights let in enough light for him to see rows upon rows of supporting pillars. This thing was beyond huge—it was enormous.

"Let's do this," he said, interrupting a conversation between Rafael and the agent. Al had been looking at the cinder-block walls separating this warehouse from the next one. "Guys, let's put a deal together and do this. Rafael, Al—you both agree this thing is perfect from a location and size point of view. We're going to have to renovate and rebuild anywhere we go, so what the heck? Let's just put a deal together, sit down to see what kind of financing we can get, and get moving. No point in sitting on our asses and waiting for heavenly inspiration, is there?"

"We might want to look around a bit more, don't you think?"

"Rafa, look around for what? To get a sore neck? To find something that is sorta like this, needs a bit more of one thing and bit less of another, and is essentially the same kind of deal? I say let's just get moving and do it and worry about everything else when it's actually time to worry about it. Not now."

Rafael gave him a queer look and sidled up close.

"Bit wired, aren't you," he said so low no one else could hear.

"I'm just excited about getting this thing moving, Rafa," Connor said, not feeling the need to whisper. "This is why we do this, for the kick, for the excitement. This is as good as it gets. Nothing better."

"Connor is right, Rafael." Al had finished his tour of the warehouse walls and now stood in the middle of the enormous space. "The differences between this and the next seven objects we look at are going to be minor, at best. Since we like the location, and see nothing that we absolutely can't work with, why not? I'm with Connor. Let's just do this."

God, he wanted to punch him, agreeing with him and still making him look like a loser, *I'm with Connor.* Only Al could manage to make him feel rotten and agreed to in the same sentence.

In the meantime, the agent came over, bouncing like a little kid. The man could smell a deal a mile away, and he obviously had just gotten rid of what he thought of as his biggest lemon.

"15 million gentlemen, and considering the size and the location, that is the best deal you are going to get on an object this size."

"15," Connor choked on the number and coughed to cover his surprise.

$15 goddamn million. Shit! He should have read the damn brochure everybody seemed to have in his hand

"That sounds like a fair deal," he managed to say cheerfully, seeing everybody's eyes on him, and shrugged his eyebrows so the sunglasses would slide down over his face once again. "Yeah, let's go and see about some financing. You," he shook the agent's hand, "may expect an offer fairly shortly…gentlemen…"

He strode out leaving them behind, staring after him. He could all but feel their eyes boring into his back, wondering what the hell was going on with him.

He drove like a man possessed and finally made himself slow down a bit. The last thing he needed was getting caught for speeding right now. Some overly eager cop would be delighted to get him.

His phone kept ringing, but he had no desire to answer it. He stopped at a strip plaza just before getting into the downtown core, bought himself a cup of coffee at a rundown donut shop, and just sat there for a minute, getting his heartbeat and emotions under control again. Why was he the only one who could see the potential they had on the go with this project? Why did he have to drag them kicking and screaming toward their own good? Deep draught of coffee as he continued thinking. Without the people like him, the trailblazers, nothing would happen in the business world; nothing would move.

Was it an Einstein quote? Nothing happened until something moved? Einstein, he was pretty sure. He would just have to be the one that moved—and dragged everybody else with him—because they sure and enough would do nothing without him.

His paper cup emptied, he balled it up and threw it into the nearest waste bin and started his car up again. And Rafa to boot. He and Rafael had always been best buddies and partners—until now.

All of a sudden, Rafael had become strangely hesitant, did not want to take the risks, did not want to make the big moves any longer. In a way, it dragged him down a bit. They had always played well off one another. But what was he going to do if the other man refused to move, refused to blaze the trails with him?

"Screw it," he muttered. "Just gonna have to do it without you, Rafa."

He merged back into traffic and headed for his office, only to change his mind at the last minute. Just now, he had no mind for Catherine and her dozens of forms and questions for the amalgamation, or for Tessa, who would nag him for the same thing.

He turned around again, heading for his old haunt, Señor Paul's on Decantur. The ladies would have to work hard this afternoon to work the disappointment out of him, but they too would manage. He grinned and sped up a little. Oh yeah, that was just exactly what the doctor had ordered.

An afternoon of fun and entertainment, followed by a couple of generous drinks at The Lighthouse. No phone, no emails, just unplug for the next few hours. Recharge the old batteries. Nice—and why not? He deserved every bit of luxury and comfort he could get for the hard work he was doing.

TWENTY-SIX

The next morning found him somewhat bleary-eyed on the couch in the bedroom, with Kayla staring down at him.

"What on earth happened to you last night, Connor? You were out of touch all afternoon, all night. You roll in here in the early morning hours, drunk as a sailor—disoriented. The cabbie had to carry you most of the way for crying out loud. What is the matter with you?"

"Lot of work," he murmured, trying to work his tongue, which felt like an old dishrag in his mouth. The small slit of sun that made it through the blinds cut through his closed eyelids like a knife, and he groaned. "Jesus."

"Jesus is not going to help you just now, Connor. And I doubt he was helping you last night. Where the fuck were you?"

She rarely swore, and her voice became hard and brittle like glass when she did, so Connor blinked and tried his best to sit up.

"We—looked at a building," he began because literally that was the last thing he remembered. "A building..." He frowned and finally gave up on the last attempt at sitting up. Wasn't happening anyway. "We looked—at this huge warehouse out by the airport..."

"Yes, I follow you that far. And what? Somebody abducted you, dragged you to a whorehouse, and force-fed you vodka? I hope that's not the story. Because if it is—don't bother. Just go pack your things."

"Wasn't a whorehouse," he muttered, as his brain gathered bits and pieces of information, assembled them under great pain, and he slowly realized how much trouble he was in. "No, no, I wouldn't. You know I…"

"You what, Connor?"

"Well—you know I wouldn't," he said weakly and looked down at his hands.

"I beg to differ." She pulled up his formerly white shirt, and even in his state, he could smell the smoke and spilled liquor—never mind the obvious lipstick traces.

"Ugh, get rid of that—I don't even want to think about it anymore," he groaned, mind scanning seven different directions for an escape. There had to be an excuse in here somewhere, a way to turn away this impending disaster.

"Oh, I am sure you don't want to think about it, Connor Beauregard. Nevertheless, I want to know what happened and where."

"$15 million," Connor groaned. "The building we want, it's $15 million."

"That's a lot. I agree. Still—what does this have to do with you ending up drunk at a whorehouse?"

"And the buildout, Al's brother, Dan, tells me it's going to be 29 million."

"Still…"

"They're all looking to me to fix things, to make magic happen somehow. I don't know—to draw blood from a stone. Here it is, Connor, we need 45 million. Go out and make it happen. I just couldn't anymore. I must have had a breakdown or something."

"A breakdown?"

OK, she didn't sound convinced yet, more sarcastic, if anything.

"A breakdown? Really, Connor—that is what you're telling me happened?"

"No, what I am telling you is I don't know what happened. I went with Al…"

"Al, your business partner?"

"The one and only. The son of the Original Chef. Jesus, they own dozens of clubs around town. I don't even know how many. We went to one of them. We were going to talk about financing…"

He covered his face with his hands and groaned again, keeping an eye on her through his fingers. Kayla's features had softened a little—not much—but a little.

"Al's family has more money than God—you know that. In the short-term, I'm going to have to come up with at least 4 million to secure the building deal, and we don't have it. Plain as day, we don't have it, even if we strip every last cent out of every bank account, business and personal. So… I thought I'd meet with Al for a while, explain to him, make him see that he would have to help out a little, just in the short-term."

Kayla sat down and waited, eyes narrowed, shoulders tensed. But at least she was not cursing at him any longer.

"OK, so then what happened? This," she kicked at his soiled shirt with a bare toe, "this does not look like a conversation about short-term loan financing."

"You want the truth? The god's honest truth?"

"Isn't that what I'm asking? Yes, Connor, yes, I want the fucking truth."

He flinched and looked back down at his feet. "I don't know what happened. So help me god—I don't remember. We went out to a couple of bars and clubs he owns. Al's father sent him to—whatever—talk to some owners or collect some money or shit. What do I know? We had a few drinks, and the rest is blank until you woke me."

"You really want me to believe that?"

"Believe it or not, Kayla, it's the truth—the only one I've got." He finally managed to stand, gather whatever presence he had left, and run his fingers through his hair. "You ought to know me better than this, Kayla. You ought to know I wouldn't go out and deliberately mess around with whores. I live for this business. I live for the deal. I swear to you I was trying to have a conversation with Al, get some financing, keep this deal from dying. Things must have—gotten out of hand. You want to crucify me for that and throw me out, go ahead."

She watched him for a long tense moment, arms crossed in front of her chest. Clearly, she still had a good amount of anger going, and she wasn't going to let him off that easy. Not at all. Jesus, what a dumbass he was; this was not what he needed at this point in time. Damn stupid move, sleeping around on her and coming back here.

"What do you mean keep this deal from dying?" she finally said, a little less furious, a little less ready to draw and quarter him. "It's not like you're down to your last ten bucks, is it? Because if you are, it would be even stupider to sleep around."

"Jesus, Kayla, stop accusing me of sleeping with whores. You think that's all I have on my mind? Christ—that's the last thing I am thinking of. I need 15 million for a building that's nothing but a big and ugly hole in the wall, I need 29 to build it out into a grow facility, I need some really heavy financing and attractive compensation packages for these growers from Denver, and a promotions company and a web designer, and I haven't even gone into the legal fees yet. Do you seriously think some girls wrapping themselves around a pole are at the forefront of my mind—really? Because if you do, I shouldn't wait for you to pack my things. I should just leave."

He grabbed the shirt off the ground, balled it up, and threw it into the wastebasket by the door. Without another word, he headed into the enormous bathroom and slammed the door. She did have a valid point; he looked like shit. Unshaven, hair dirty and disheveled, bloodshot eyes, and a couple of marks on his neck and shoulders he did not care to identify just now.

Must have been quite a night.

Must remember to tell Al… Never mind. Kayla would never go so far as to check up on him, and Al would just hold it against him. Perfect.

He stood under the rain head shower, blasting hot water onto himself for nearly 10 minutes, until he was truly the color of a lobster and the last of the alcohol and whatnot from the previous night had been good and well boiled out of him.

Kayla was not around when he stepped out of the shower, so he took his time getting dressed and took a little more care with his appearance. He hadn't exactly covered himself in glory the day before, in jeans and flip-flops. After all, he represented something now; he stood for something.

Strangely enough, instead of feeling hungover, tired, and worn out, he felt energized when he strode into the kitchen/dining room in search of something edible. When his head cleared, he realized he was starving. He could hardly remember the last time he had eaten.

He did not find a trace of Kayla in the kitchen either—but she had left him a present. Grinning, he pulled up a chair to an enormous plate of bacon, eggs, toast, hash browns, a glass of orange juice—and a small silver tray with two little innocent little white pills.

He dialed up the strongest brew their built-in coffee center could manage and eyed those pills. Innocent enough—and that time in Zurich, they had worked magic, hadn't they? He'd promised himself to be careful with this stuff, but what the hell? Difficult times demanded difficult decisions and tough measures.

He shrugged and washed the pills down with his orange juice, just before devouring every last bit of food on the server—probably enough for three people. Difficult times and all.

TWENTY-SEVEN

He should have known it! Of course Tessa and Catherine had spent the entire previous day trading paperwork. Tessa buzzed around in a state of frenzy, and he heard Catherine's voice from the speaker phone.

"It's got to be there, Tess. You guys must have a workable minute book. At least some semblance thereof."

"I can't find anything, Catherine, and I've been over his file drawers twice—I swear to you."

Connor put his hand on Tessa's shoulder and shook his head, grinning by way of saying good morning.

"Hello, Catherine," he said into the speakerphone, "don't panic. All of those files are probably on my phone. Just tell me what you need and you'll have it in half an hour."

"Jesus, Connor, where have you been? We're trying to beat this due diligence issue. Image Group's lawyers are asking for everything."

"Everything?"

"And then some. Tessa can't find half those documents—and you knew you would need them before they signed off on the amalgamation. Financial statements, banking records, personal statements from all the directors, minutes from the meetings..."

"All on my phone, Catherine, don't stress. You'll have them in a minute. Bye."

He hung up the phone and hugged Tessa. "Tessa, you trooper, hanging in there for me. I had a rough day yesterday."

"So I heard," she said. Struggling free, she took a step back. "You really disappeared? Kayla went crazy looking for you."

"I had a few urgent things to deal with, no big deal. Tell me now, what do the lawyers want this time?"

"You heard Catherine. Documents, documents..."

"OK, personal information statements from the directors. Prepare them please. You have most of the information in your files. If not, ask Rafa. Then send them to the directors copying me. Tell them they need to be in within the hour. Financial stuff you mostly have."

"Not all of it."

"Then ask David. He's not my favorite person, but he will walk you through what you need."

Not his favorite person was a mild description of the lanky accountant whom he hated with a passion, but David had a way about him that 'kept you out of jail,' as Rafael would say.

"The rest of it I will make up just now," he said and unlocked his office. Meeting minutes, forms—paper crap. He could make that kind of stuff up on the inside of ten if he had to.

Due diligence! Now there was a concept invented by lawyers and accountants so they could charge more for sitting there with their thumbs up their rear ends doing nothing remotely relevant or important to the project. Who'd ever heard of pushing THAT much paper from here to there and calling it diligent? Right!

"Did you pay David recently? Because I don't want to be the one calling him for advice and then he tells me..."

"Not you too, Tessa! Is it all about money around here? What do you guys do, form a line in the morning, to see who gets to ask me for money next? I work extremely hard every single day to keep the lights on around here, and I really don't appreciate everybody standing there with their hands out! Yes, tell David he will be paid in full for his work on the EC Energy file by the end of the week. I will pay him from my own personal funds if necessary, but I need this one particular thing done, and I need it done today. Can you do that?"

"I can do that."

She disappeared like a shadow.

He really needed to get out there and talk to a few investors, make money, instead of sitting at his desk staring at paper, making up a minute book. A minute book—really? Did any of these paper tigers know what it took to get a company like this one off the ground? And, if they knew, did they have the guts and the balls to do it? No and no!

The EC Energy mess, yes, he needed to clean that up too, sometime soon. The past was the past, and he would deal with it. He'd get to it—eventually.

For an hour or so, he worked like a man possessed making up meeting minutes and directors' resolutions as needed. Really, this stuff was readily available on the internet for download—insert a few names, a few minor details, and bingo. If he wanted to pay $9.95 and input a credit card here, he could even download the template for posterity, including his company logo. What a steal!

For now, though, he didn't bother with the template or the logo—he knew what Tessa could do given even a bad PDF—but he bookmarked the relevant sections.

"Tess? I know I'm a bear today. You can't imagine the pressure. And Catherine…she's among the worst, pushing until I don't know where my head sits. Hey, I need you to insert the guys' electronic signatures into all of these documents and send them on to her billable nastiness. Mine, Rafa, Josh, and Simon. Any word from David?"

"He will get to it—later on today."

"Brilliant. Thanks for your work on this, really. Couldn't do it without you."

Tessa looked at the meeting minutes and board resolutions in his hands as if they were on fire.

"You just wrote those up, on the spot?"

"Just being efficient. We really did have those meetings, and that's close enough to what came out of them. Anybody wants original signatures, the guys are just going to have to drop by, that's all. For now, this will save them having to drive halfway across town through the worst of traffic. And we do need it tonight, or it won't get done."

Tessa only nodded and took off. He'd really have to get her to stop looking at the securities lawyer like a friend. It didn't, and it couldn't work. Next she'd tell him cutting a few tiny little corners for the sake of efficiency was just wrong or some such nonsense.

Lawyers!

His phone rang, and he rolled his eyes and added accountants to that statement.

"David, great to hear from you again. Did Tessa fill you in on the little project I'm doing here?"

"Cannabis? Really, Connor—cannabis? I don't know if I want to look at another one of your little startups. The stuff you made me sign on the energy deal still gives me nightmares when I think about it, and yet the money you promised..."

"Is right here on my desk, David, in the form of a check. All you have to do is send somebody to pick it up?"

"Really?"

"Of course, really. What, you think I would bullshit you? David, what's going on with you?"

"Nothing. Everything. Those financial statements I signed for EC—only because you insisted, mind you—that was borderline criminal."

"Nonsense, David. We did nothing wrong—just pretty the numbers up a little bit, make people see what they expected to see, that's all."

"You hid half a million dollars in... Never mind, never mind—I don't even want to think about it any longer. What I am saying is I am not so sure I want to work on this cannabis thing with you, if it's going to turn into another fiasco."

"Which it won't. David, this is no EC Energy. Just yesterday, I went out to buy a $15 million building out by the airport. 15 million, David—this is a well-funded company. People are lining up to put money in when I mention cannabis. There is going to be enough money to make all of us wealthy—extremely wealthy."

David hesitated. Yes, another man without the imagination to see where this thing could go and the guts to actually take it there.

"I guess I understand where you are coming from, David. EC burned all of us. So, if you are telling me no, you don't want to get involved, then no hard feelings. I will find someone else, and I will still buy you a beer down at The Lighthouse when I run into you. I understand—totally."

"I am not really saying no outright..."

Gotcha, sucker. Even accountants knew cannabis was an extremely hot investment property.

"I appreciate it, David. I just don't want you to feel... uncomfortable."

"I guess I could take Tessa's stuff and turn into a pro forma financial statement for the purpose of your due diligence only. She said there wasn't much."

"Hardly anything. We've been so busy for the past couple of months we haven't had the time to breathe."

"OK. Everything else we will talk about later. And you do have a check for me."

"Thanks, David, I really appreciate it. You won't regret it, man—seriously."

Another one down. By tonight, he would have every damn piece of paper on this damned due diligence list.

TWENTY-EIGHT

"Al, you are a businessman, and your father is a businessman."

Al leaned back in the bottomless brown leather couch at the Starbucks where Connor had invited him and folded his hands in front of his face, elbows on his knees. His eyes never left Connor's, who thought the stare just a tad irritating.

"I can imagine where this is going, Connor, and I really don't think I much care for that direction."

"I know. But you've seen the building, Al. It's perfect for what we are trying to do. For our type and size of operation. You yourself said let's go and do it."

"I did, and I fully expected you to have put at least some of the money you raised off your investors aside for just such a purchase. Dear god, you've raised a small fortune by now—what happened to it all?"

Private jets, Switzerland, Kayla, bills, a bunch of old stuff from EC Energy hanging over his head which he had to pay off PDQ...

"I don't have to tell you what it takes to start up an operation like this one, Al—you know. You of all people know. Everybody has their hand out. Everybody wants money ahead of time. Before they even form a concrete thought, they want to see money."

"I know that you are short on your down payment, Connor—extremely short—and that is why we are sitting here. Why don't we quit pretending this conversation is about anything else but you wanting me to front a large sum of money to make the building possible?"

Al folded his arms and sighed, just like a school teacher who was about to lecture you, and right at that very moment, Connor wanted nothing but to punch him. Wipe that superior grin right off his face and punch him into next week, where he belonged. With a superhuman effort, he took a deep breath, closed his eyes for a moment, and saw the building in front of him. There it was, all cleaned up, with a nice large sign at the front, Perfect Cannabis, and the lot had been cleaned up too, and a tidy parking lot had been put in, and a few plantings... They needed this building—he needed this. And he needed Al to make it happen.

"Al, you know it, and I know it. This is going to be the biggest damn project either one of us has ever worked on, and it's going to be the most expensive one. That's a fact. To make this kind of money, we have to be willing to take risks."

"Don't give me an economics lesson, Connor—that's beneath you. I would respect a man who would come straight out and say, 'Al, I've wasted the money you gave me. It was a mistake. With just a little more, I want to do over and fix it. I've learned something.' I would respect that. But there you sit, trying to teach me about the startup businesses, not taking any responsibility."

Two more minutes and he really would kill him. He would put his hands around Al's throat and just squeeze. Oh, the beauty of that fantasy.

Finally, Connor smiled and shrugged casually.

"Al, there's really not much to admit. I came to you because it was the easiest way. You don't want to be involved in financing of the building—that's OK. That's perfectly fine. Perfectly OK. I just thought I would ask. No hard feelings."

He got to his feet and actually managed to shake Al's hand, through some veil of self-control that separated his sheer fury and anger at the man from polite, public manners. He reached into his pocket and tossed a folded $10 bill onto the table between them and finally nodded at Al.

"No hard feelings, Al—I will make this happen. I just thought you wanted to be in it, that's all. I didn't mean to make assumptions."

The same self-control allowed him to nod and make his way out of the Starbucks, head held high, smiling at the people who passed him, until he was out in the parking lot, beside his car where nobody could see him.

He kicked the rear tire of his SUV again and again until his toes hurt, shook his fists in his pockets, and barely kept in the scream building inside his throat. Why, oh why, did God strike him with business partners who were better suited to herding sheep than to building a large-scale, once-in-a-lifetime-opportunity business? Why, God, why?

It would have taken Al only five minutes or less to liberate a million or two to make the down payment happen and arrange financing for the rest, done. They would have been able to move on. Instead, the little fucker wanted to hear him say, *I am sorry, and I messed up.*

With some effort, he finally unlocked the car, pulled himself into the driver's seat, and sat there, breathing heavily until he had himself under control again.

"Don't make a mistake now, Connor," he told himself. "Never show your hand. You can do this. Just get this deal done."

All we need is money. Now—where to get it? Al was right about one thing. He had raised a ton in the last couple of months—more than ever before—and yet he was no further ahead than he had been on his other deals. How the fuck had that happened?

Of course, private jets, the trip to Switzerland, wining and dining investors almost every night at La Cosa, his new car, paying off the debts from EC Energy—yes, it did add up. He'd had to front the money for all the Image Group shares—well, more than he would ever admit to anyone—which were now quietly languishing in a Swiss company, waiting to be sold. And so far he had paid in excess of $80,000 to the securities lawyer. You wanted to see the black hole of financing—there it was.

None of it changed the facts: he needed money, and he needed it quickly, or Al and his family would gladly rush in and take this deal away from him. He could see it now. They would say he failed, put in some puppet CEO, and pull the strings—on his deal! His very own deal. That was not going to happen. No matter what, he would die before he let that happen.

His mind clicked through the possibilities. Money—he needed at least $2 million. He did not have it. Who would lend it to him if not investors? He could hit up a few investors. That would make up half a million, maybe three-quarters. Rafa—Rafa was not a rich person, but he had resources. He might be good for half a mil, period. Still not enough. Kayla… Forget Kayla—he had asked her to foot the bill so often in the last few months. It wasn't going to fly.

Then there was the whole prostitutes thing! No, no counting on Kayla. Who else, who else would lend him a million on short notice? Come on. He had made money for so many people, had put them into deals, had made things possible—so now, now when he needed something, nobody was there to give him a hand? How could this happen? How could he let it happen?

This deal was not going to die here, no way. He struck the steering wheel hard and clenched his hands again. No way.

"For god's sake, if somebody gives you a shit sandwich, find some water and wash it down—or, better yet, use wine."

He stopped and rested his hands in his lap. The thought had flashed into his mind so quickly he hadn't even seen it coming. Who said that? The one about the wine and the shit sandwich? Who said that? The image hit him with brutal clarity—the man in the black suit, perfectly starched white shirt, shoes polished to a mirror shine.

People want to do the right thing, boy. They want to believe that inside they are good and Christian citizens, no matter what they might do in their day-to-day lives. All you have to do is show them a simple and easy way to do it.

His father, the reverend Marty "Matthias" Beauregard—standing there bigger than life, with that humble wooden collection plate in his hand.

"This, my son, is the simple piece of wood that turns the sinner back into a saint, my son. All you gotta do is make them believe it, and they will do it every time."

Connor shook his head quickly to clear the picture. God, he had not thought about his father in a good 15 years. He'd walked away from the Holy Church of Redemption swearing he would never set another foot into it or go to another religious service ever again as long as he lived. But, boy, his father sure had the way, didn't he?

He could stand there and preach, and by the end of the sermon, people in the aisles were crying, convinced that giving money to the good Reverend Beauregard would somehow redeem them and save their souls. And he always needed money for one project or another, whether he was saving poor starving children or needed a new roof for the church or simply needed money to 'spread the word of the savior'—he always got it.

Connor wanted to force his thoughts onto another subject, but for some reason, the vision of his father at the pulpit would not let him go. Arms just a little raised, eyes flickering with something akin to madness, and that voice—that voice gravelly as if he had just been raised from the dead himself. *Sunday is coming. Satan does not know it, but Sunday's coming!*

That one had always worked—so simple and so effective, it fascinated the masses.

And somewhere in the Cayman Islands, there existed accounts with millions of dollars, quietly languishing, waiting to be needed…

Connor smiled all of a sudden. "That's right, Al," he said softly. "You don't know it, but Sunday's coming—my Sunday!"

He reached for his phone and dialed Rafael.

"Rafa, bad news. Al won't play ball. He is absolutely refusing to pitch in any more on the down payment for the building."

"This surprises you, Connor? I got a feeling he was not really happy with the books, such as they are."

"You knew about this? Dammit, Rafa, what are you, my enemy, all of a sudden? You knew about this, and you let me walk into a meeting with this character for the second time, not knowing what to expect? And what do you mean he did not like the books? Who the hell showed him anyway?"

"He came to ask Josh, and Josh being a director..."

"Dammit." Connor stuck the steering wheel again. "Dammit. So Josh walks in and asks Tessa for financial statements? What the hell—is everybody trying to make this deal impossible for me? Are you all working against me now? What is this shit?"

"Calm down, Connor. Nobody is against you. As a director, Josh had a right to see the statements, and you know it."

"He did—maybe. Good manners would have been to ask me for them and then to keep them confidential, especially from a character like Al."

"This character, as you call him, has a lot of money in this business. Connor—please. Just come on back into the office. We will sit down..."

"You know what, Rafael—why don't you all just go and fuck yourselves? I mean it. Go. And. Fuck. Yourself. You hear me? I am going to make this deal work. I am going to raise this money. I, Connor Beauregard, all by myself, if I fucking have to, so you can just go and crawl back into your respective holes and do what it is you do. I don't need you. I don't need any of you."

He hung up, and this time, he did fling the phone into the floor area of the passenger seat—which entirely failed to make him feel better. He peeled out of the parking lot like a man possessed and headed down toward the highway.

Damn traitors, all of them. Rafael was the worst. How many deals had they done together, how often had they sat together and got drunk—and he just out and turned on him like that?

Connor reached out and found a hard rock station on the radio and turned it up as high as his eight JBL speakers would allow. Down the access road, he merged into traffic and forced his way into the left-hand lane.

Connor just floored it, as fast as the SUV would go as long as it took for his brain to clear from the red-hot fog that had spread when he heard what Josh and Rafael had done. Later, when he realized how far and how fast he had gone, he thought it was a miracle the cops had not caught him speeding.

He dug around in the glove compartment, until he found the vial with little white pills Kayla had left in there, 'just for emergencies,' and washed two of them down with the last bit of water from an old plastic bottle. Immediately, he felt better and let the warm calm spread throughout him. Of course he would figure it out; of course he would find a way... There was always a way.

He pulled off the highway and tinkered along the service road for a while, wondering just where he was and how he was going to get back home. He should call Kayla—on the heels of last night, he should definitely call Kayla. He pulled over into another littered parking lot of another dinky little coffee shop when his blood suddenly ran cold, reading the sign at the coffee shop. Danville Donuts.

Danville. Christ, he had gone far enough to reach his father's old haunts. Danville, home of the Holy Church of Redemption and the holier-than-thou Reverend Matthias Beauregard.

His hands shook on the steering wheel for a moment. He stepped out of the car and stood there for a moment, instinctively turning to the south where the road took a dip, and he looked down into the tiny little valley, where the early evening lights were slowly starting to come on.

So peaceful, so quaint, so filled with lies, deception, and fraud.

"Damn you, Reverend Matt," he said softly because he had never called his father anything other than Reverend Matthias.

Down into the valley—up and out the other end, he could just make out the grey ribbon of the Hillview Road, the one that would lead into the forest and to the enormous monstrosity that had been the reverend's home.

Wonder if he still lives there—or has he joined his millions on the Caymans?

Connor shuddered, realizing he did not know, had not cared for the last 20 or so years, but if fate had led him here, there had to be a damn good reason for it because Connor Beauregard did not do anything without a reason.

He stared down into the valley and followed the road with narrowed eyes. Really, was he thinking of going there, the ass of the world he had left 20 years ago?

He would have turned around and driven back into his own city, to be among the tall buildings, exhaust fumes, overpriced restaurants, and snobby attitudes, but for one thing: He knew, as well as he knew that there was an amen in his church, Matt Beauregard had more money than God himself.

That pure gold and diamond Rolex he had been taking off his wrist before every single service? The wine cellar in the old house, filled to the brim with invaluable bottles, the art room, the media room, the study wing, the tutors for him, Connor, who came and went? At the time he had not known it, but people's donations paid for all of it. They put their money down in order to atone for their sins, and the good rev took it all in and pronounced them cleansed. Best racket in the universe.

He hadn't seen his father in more than 20 years, and common sense told him to turn his car around and hit the highway before night fell—but desperation whispered he had been led here on purpose.

"Got nothing to lose now, do I," he said softly, put his car into gear, and drove down into the valley.

Serendipity. If it wasn't meant to be, then Marty would not be there. If there was some sort of cosmic plan behind it, he would be, and Connor would walk in, ask for a small loan, and let the chips fall where they may.

Marty had to be of an age now where an investment such as Perfect Cannabis would be a nice little sideline for him, no? Surely he would not want to preach forever.

He laid out all his best arguments in his head as he drove up the familiar road, the one that disappeared up the hill and through the dense forest, right up to the wrought-iron gate, made to look like an old relic from 100 years ago, but strong enough to withstand a tank, or any semi-convinced burglar who wanted to try his luck. Connor was almost tempted to input his old code into the keypad, just to see if it still worked, but reason won out, and he pressed the call button.

"Hello?"

"Connor Beauregard here to see Marty Beauregard," he said and turned his face into the camera. He'd always been told he and the old man looked alike, so if anybody doubted his identity... The gasp through the loudspeaker told him he need not have worried.

"Connor..."

The gate buzzed almost immediately, and he leisurely drove up the long, tree-lined drive. It was almost a mile long, and he remembered there were cameras everywhere. By the time he got to the house, there would be no doubt that everyone—including the last person on earth—would know he was back.

It was a manor in the old-fashioned sense of the word—a squat, two-story building with tall ornamented windows and a wide staircase leading up to an enormous, double-winged wooden door. Pea gravel crunched under his tires, and almost immediately, the front door flew open, and a diminutive grey-haired woman flew out the doors, down the stairs, and threw her arms around him.

"Connor, I never thought I would see the day."

"Mom..." He picked her up and spun her around and then looked up to see the man who had appeared at the top of the stairs behind his mother.

Dad, he failed to say the word, and the man mustered him top to bottom and took in the black SUV with a dismissive look.

"Well now, son, you being here after all these years? That could only mean one thing—you need money."

It took all of the self-control he had not to jump back into the car and reverse the hell out of there the way he had come in. When had this seemed like a good idea? Carefully, he let go of his mother and straightened his jacket.

"Good to see you too—Reverend."

"Well, don't stand out there in the driveway like a salesman—come on in and tell me what this latest emergency is that brings you here."

In for a penny, in for a pound. Connor slowly walked up the stairs, stood in the familiar black-and-white tiled hallway for a moment, gazing at the fake ancestral portraits, and finally squared his shoulders. Game time.

Over drinks in the reverend's study, he made small talk and finally leaned back, crossing his legs and resting his arms on the arms of the chair.

"Indeed, Marty, you are looking at the president and CEO of one the world's leading pharmaceutical companies. Since we have just gone public, I thought I would share my good fortune and offer you and Mother a deal that can take care of you for years to come. Surely you don't want to rely on preaching forever."

"Oh, son, I have not stood in church preaching for many a year. I mostly take care of the financial issues now—licensing rights, the books, the TV shows—that kind of thing. I hire talent to do the preaching."

Talent—that was new. They had gone national, just like he had always suspected. Still...

"Well, that is wonderful for you—surely, then, you understand the value of diversification. I am at liberty to offer shares to you for $3 a share, which you can turn around and sell immediately on the open market for five and more. That is today's course..."

Indeed, if he convinced Marty, he would liberate some of the shares in the Swiss company, the ones he had bought for a dollar. If Marty took three—Jesus, he was saved. He could buy his building, tell Al where to shove his superior attitude, and pay a few people who were breathing down his neck. He could see a spark of interest in Marty's eyes. The old man was arrogant—not stupid.

"PerCan has just completed a reverse merger and takeover..."

"PerCan—that cannabis outfit I read about in the paper almost every weekend edition? The company that peddles drugs to ordinary people?"

"Well—actually, medical marijuana, Marty. But the opportunity..."

"Connor Beauregard, you dare come into my house—the house of a reverend, a man of God, selling shares in a drug company? Have you completely gone out of your mind?"

"Father, it is not..."

"Marijuana? Drugs? Really? It's not so bad. It's all for the betterment of mankind. Is that what you are trying to tell me? I've spent years on the pulpit preaching against the danger of drugs, and you walk into my house, sit in my chair, drink my liquor—" Marty's hand swept across the side table like a sword, dropping the crystal Brandy glass. The glass shattered into a thousand shards against the black marble floor, and the spill of the liquor spread like a bloodstain.

"And you dare peddle drugs in my house. I'm ashamed you carry my name. Leave my house..."

"Father, it's not like that. It's a medicine like any other. If you will just let me explain."

"Get. Out. Of. My. House."

"We are really not selling the kind of drugs you are thinking of. We are helping people, really—just look at the literature. All I need is a small investment to make our building a reality, much as in the days when you wanted to build your church..."

"Out."

Marty jumped to his feet, and a butler summoned by the noise appeared in the doorway, standing undecided between helping his employer and cleaning up the mess at their feet.

"Get out of my house, right now, and I swear to God, if I ever see your face again—ever—I will personally drive you out of this town, no matter what it takes."

Connor got to his feet and gathered his briefcase with shaking hands. It had been a mistake to come here—he should have known right away. A mistake to wander in and offer an investment. But who else was he going to ask? Jesus.

He scrambled for the door even as he heard his father cursing and yelling behind him. His mother was nowhere to be seen, and a servant helpfully held the front door open for him. Out—just out.

He jumped into the SUV and floored it. Somewhere in the rearview mirror, he could see his mother appearing at the top of the stairs waving madly, but he could not stop, could not turn and say anything to her. He had to get out of there as fast as the bloody SUV would go.

Worst mistake of his life to come here—it had not solved a thing. He had reopened all the old wounds he had thought closed a long time ago. Plus, he still had a tremendous problem. He needed a million dollars to make the building deal happen, and he needed them by tomorrow.

Outside of town on top of the hill, he stopped again and fumbled in the glove compartment for the little vial. Two of these pills would be just the thing to take the edge off right now. God, the reverend Marty was stark-raving mad.

He stood and waited for his heart to stop pounding clear out of his chest, then put the car into gear and headed back toward the highway. A million dollars did not fall into his lap, not by any stretch of the imagination. He would just have to keep beating his head into it until he came up with a brilliant idea. He had done it before and would do it again. Connor Beauregard never gave up.

Still on the highway, he remembered to call Kayla, just to avoid a repetition of this morning's fight. Kayla did not say more than a few words. She was still trying to cling to her anger; he knew her. She did not want to give up that easily—but he also had her. She knew too much about his passion for the deal to believe the prostitute story.

Dammit, Connor what a stupid move, he thought. Really. He could have wiped out everything he had worked for. Fortunately, he'd pulled his head out of the noose just in time, but he'd have to be a lot more careful from now on.

He had barely put down the phone when it rang again. Out-of-range problems—Danville still had them, and finally, he was getting back to civilization.

"Connor?"

"Here, Tess, I had—business in Danville."

"Danville? Good God, who lives way out there?"

"Good God is right. What's up?"

"David is here. Says you told him to pick up a check?"

David—fuck—he had forgotten about the accountant. Fuck. He wanted to strike the steering wheel again. Worse yet, he knew he owed close to 10,000 to the accountant, and the money wasn't there. Simply was not there.

"Make one up for him."

"I don't understand. What do you mean?"

"Ask him what we owe him and make a check out to him. You can do my signature well enough."

"You want me to fake..."

"He's not standing there, is he?"

"What am I, an idiot? No, I'm in your private office. He's gone for coffee while I search. Search for something I good and well know is not there. You want me to fake your signature—Christ, Connor."

"Just do it. There won't be any trouble. If the bank asks, just say I was—whatever, drunk or something. It's fine. I will confirm it, and they won't ask anyway—I've done it a dozen times."

"He said it was ten grand."

"That's fine—close enough."

"Not fine, Connor—have you forgotten? There's no money in the account."

"There will be. What's he going to do—stop at the bank on his way home?"

"He might. He is one suspicious bugger."

"Just do it, Tess—trust me. Make a small mistake. Date it for the twenty-first instead of the twelfth. By the time he realizes and comes back, the money will be there. But put it into a sealed envelope. Do it."

"OK."

"I swear to you, it won't be a problem. Seriously. Everything is going to be fine. Please."

He could almost see her pulling out the checkbook, slowly, as if it was going to bite her, and mentally, he willed her to get over it and just write the damn check. He needed David right now. He needed those damned financial statements in a few hours to satisfy the lawyers and their idiotic due diligence. He needed this deal, and he needed to be trading, period. That's why it had to happen. End of story.

For the Nth time, he wondered where all the money had gone.

In a way, Al was right to ask. He had gone through more than a million dollars—just like that—in the last few months, and he hadn't even noticed. The new car, the private jets, the free trading shares he had bought out of Image Group. Maybe he should not have sent as much money to Zurich as he had, but in the end, those shares would save his ass, and the company's, if need be.

He'd sent a courier with a small fortune to Switzerland who had never officially entered the country.

Kayla hearing about the UBS bank terminal at the airport—outside the customs gate—had given him this brilliant idea. Nobody would ever have made it through customs with enough cash on them to buy the amount of shares he was planning to buy, not without ending up on the wrong side of questioning. Before you hit customs, though, on that end, everything was fair game, so he had hired a guy.

It was such a brilliant scenario: A guy flies into Zurich, goes down five floors and around 15 corners, hits the bank terminal, deposits the cash, and turns right around, flying back to Canada. His buddy Dominik goes to the bank in Zurich the next day, takes the money, and waits to buy a huge chunk of free trading shares in the name of Connor's holding company. It was perfect—it couldn't get any more perfect if he tried. They'd buy shares for a dollar and wait a couple of weeks for them to hit eight or nine. Bingo.

Of course, the courier wanted to get paid and take a cut. Dominik wanted to get paid and take a cut. Everybody wanted to get paid and take a cut.

Upfront, no less—no trust among gentlemen any longer. Enter his problem:

How exactly was he supposed to explain any of this to Al—or to Rafael, for that matter? Rafael would not only have had a dozen ways in which this could go wrong; he would have been pissed because Connor did not cut him in for a piece of the action.

A million in shares today, 10 million a couple of weeks from now, just after the amalgamation. Math was so exceedingly simple, and still, he was missing a million dollars right now on the down payment for this goddamn building.

"Back to reality, Connor," he muttered to himself. "Who is going to lend you money? Who?"

He'd gone over his entire contact list on the phone, looking at each and every person with one question in mind—*would this guy lend me a million dollars?* And the answer had been *no* for most of them, *not on your life* for a few, and *get fucking real* for the rest.

He dug through his glove compartment, but the little plastic vial with Kayla's little white pills turned up empty. When had this happened—did the damn thing open in there, and they all rolled around loose by now? Was this the goddamn worst day of his life, officially?

His cell phone rang, and his finger hovered for a moment over the 'fuck off' button. Unknown number—that never meant anything good, never ever. Especially not on the worst day of his life, but theoretically, things could not get any worse, right? At some point, it had to turn around.

"Hello."

"Connor Beauregard?"

"Yes—who is this?"

And what do you want from me, because whatever it is, you are not getting it. Should have hung up in the first place.

"This is Mirko."

"Mirko—good for you."

Connor was getting irritated. The one thing he did not have time for right now was foreigners who had no proper command of the English language, bored him, and did not come to the point. He needed money.

"You need money."

Connor almost swerved into the next lane. What the fuck?

"Who exactly are you, Mirko, and, more to the point, who gave you this number?"

"Does it matter right now? What matters is that you need money—badly. Paul is a mutual friend of ours, no?"

Paul, his club-owning friend! Just what all had he said during that ill-fated night out with the—well, the dancing girls? Not only had it almost cost him his sweet deal with Kayla, Al's respect, and now this joker... God, he really had to stop drinking and screwing around, one day. One day—just not now.

"Well, Mirko, I am running a startup company. Money is always an issue at this stage of a company's development, you know. If we are talking about the same Paul, I might have been a bit—well—frustrated when I was visiting his establishment."

"I have no time for bullshit, Connor. I do have a million dollars to loan, and the money can be in your account almost immediately—for a price."

Connor hit the brakes and pulled over, despite the noisy protests from the drivers behind him. A million dollars to loan, right now. The answer to his prayer. And everything had its price—he already knew that. Everybody knew that. This was where it got interesting.

"I need to close a real estate deal. I'd be looking at needing funds pretty quick."

"Like I said, not a problem. Money is ready."

"So..."

There would be a hook—a big one, he could smell it—but that did not matter as much right now as staying alive and keeping going did. Every deal had a hook in it somewhere. All you needed to do was work it out. He'd make it work; had he not always made it work? Of course, and he would this time. All he needed was time, sweet time.

"You're ready?"

"Yes, how much?"

"500,000 shares..."

"Done," Connor almost laughed. Shares? Really? For a loan shark, this dude was a beginner. What luck! He could issue shares just by signing a piece of paper. Really—that was it? Was this guy insane?

"Also—percentage equity in the building you are buying. You're making a real estate deal?"

"Yes." A little harder, this one. The other directors would want to know who this guy was who would hold a piece of the property, but he would explain it to them. Damn, he would spin some sort of story. Neither Josh nor Simon paid that much attention to what the hell was going on, and Rafael—Rafa owed him for sticking him with Al.

"Doable," he said, not committing himself to anything yet.

Doable, yes, and soon enough, he would have all of the money he needed to get rid of this joker, no matter what—whether or not he actually cut him in. The shares... the shares he could keep as a tip.

"Then you are going to wire $100,000 to an account I am going to specify in a text to you."

In the Cayman Islands, most likely. "100,000," Connor asked, a little dumbfounded. "For..."

"Fees, Mr. Beauregard, fees. Everything has a price, no?"

"I am sure it does, but I can't just wire $100,000 to a voice on the phone and hope for the best. I am sure you know that, right?"

"Oh, ja, I know." The heavily accented voice became almost gay. "You wait at your office. I will send someone. All will be good."

"Yes, but..." Connor wanted to say something, but the line went dead on him, just like that. He sat and stared out the windshield in front of him, wondering whether he had just made another deal with the devil or solved everybody's problem.

Then someone knocked at the passenger side window. He let it down and looked straight at a cop.

"Everything OK, sir? You are standing in a no-parking zone. Do you have a problem of some kind?"

"Yeah, no, I thought the engine was overheating," Connor said and did his best to smile. "Sorry—I guess I didn't pay attention, but I have it solved now. It's fine again. Thanks for checking on me."

"Are you sure? You should probably see a mechanic right away."

"I will, the moment I hit town again. Thanks, Officer—very kind of you."

He pulled himself together and drove back into the city like a saint—partially because the cop was still behind him, watching, and partially because he had an idea the vial with the pills hadn't really broken and spilled its contents all over the messy interior of his glove compartment. Not what he needed right now, to be taken downtown for drug testing, not at all. Not when he was just about to solve all of his problems all at once.

Damn that Paul—for a guy who owned strip joints, he was pretty sharp. What did he have, someone paying attention to who complained about needing money so he could send a suitable lender?

Depending on the severity of the problem, of course, and Connor's problem was pretty severe. Did the girls make notes on this shit? Jesus, if anybody found out—if Kayla found out—he could kiss his ass goodbye if she did.

The shares... the shares were easy. Nobody ever asked. He'd fill out a simple form, put in services to the company in the payments section, and once they were trading, they'd just be issued, no big deal. The equity position in the building was just a tad harder. He'd have to bury it deep inside the contracts somewhere—very deep—which meant any other lawyer but Catherine had to draw them up. Somebody younger, hungrier, somebody not as suspicious as the damn securities lawyer harp.

Note to self: get rid of her as soon as possible and hire somebody else.

Lastly, 100,000. Where was he going to dig up $100,000 on the inside of what sounded like a few hours? Connor almost laughed. See, his problem had improved already. An hour ago, he'd been pondering where to dig up a million—hell, at the rate he was going, he'd borrow a dollar tonight and be just fine. Chuckling to himself, he dialed Rafael's number.

"Hey, Rafa, gangster, what are you up to?"

"'Bout five foot eight—what about you?"

"Joker. Get some new material, will you. I need to see you—quickly."

"What's this all about? Some new disaster you need me to unravel for you? Because I am telling you, you hang up on me again..."

"Nothing like that. I have a short-term funding bottleneck."

"Does this have to do with the building?"

"No. I have some trouble with old EC Energy stuff—but I don't want to screw up the PerCan deal, you understand?"

Two different, unconnected statements, both of them true. Worked every time.

"Don't come around at the last second and tell us the money you have raised has all disappeared into deep dark holes, and all of a sudden, the building is not coming through the way it is supposed to. I met with TC and Dan. They're all fired up and ready to go on the construction and refit plans."

"And they will get going as soon as a horde of lawyers signs the papers. Not a minute of doubt. I just need to clear up a couple of problems, and I need to do it now."

"How much do you need?"

"Hundred thou."

Rafael whistled. "Geez, Connor, you don't have tiny little problems, do you."

"Our business is crazy. Who am I telling this to, Rafa—now can you help me out?"

"I suppose so. When do you need it by?"

"Yesterday."

"Jesus Christ, Connor..." He said nothing and waited for his friend to start feeling guilty—which he would. Rafa's biggest problem was his overly developed sense of guilt, likely beaten into him by a severely Catholic grandmother and mother.

"OK—meet you later at The Lighthouse?"

"Can you wire it to me—like now?"

"Connor—I am really not comfortable."

"Thanks. I knew you would come through for me. You don't know what it means to me to have you in my corner. Some days, when you do our kind of deals, it feels like everybody is just waiting to watch you fall, don't you think?"

"Connor, the way you play the game, it's not waiting to watch you fall. It's knowing you will that worries me."

"Shit, I got Tessa calling me. I bet Catherine has another last-minute lawyer emergency. I gotta take this. Thanks for helping me out, bro—I owe you big-time."

Connor hung up the phone and started breathing normally again. Problem solved.

All of them.

Connor Beauregard was at the top again. Dammit for doubting himself in the first place.

Really, he felt like going to The Lighthouse and having an enormous drink just then—or seven—but at the same time, the niggling doubt about Catherine and her excessive document shuffling kept him on the edge of sheer madness. If that lawyer screwed up this merger...

Quickly, he dialed Tessa again.

"Hey, Tess, any news on the amalgamation?"

"Not really. David was here..."

"Forget about David for a minute—he'll be fine and do his thing. Have you talked to Catherine? Has she said anything about completing this thing?"

"No, but then again, I did not expect it until everything was done..."

"Everything is never done with lawyers, Tess, you know that. There is always one more thing, one more goddamn piece of paper they want. She needs to do this—the woman just needs to finish this one thing."

He hung up the phone again and flung it into the passenger seat with a curse. She would not dare screw this up for him, would she?

Like a man possessed, he reached for his phone again and dialed Catherine this time.

"Catherine, tell me my merger is done," he said without any kind of preamble.

"Well hello to you too, Connor. How are things?"

He wanted to strangle her—right there on the phone. Wanted to wipe that smarmy tone right out of her voice. What the hell, how are things? She knew he was waiting, knew he was desperate—unfortunately.

"Things are just peachy," he said through clenched teeth. "As long as my merger is on track and about to be completed."

"Well, there are just a few things..."

The red haze shadowed his eyes again, and he had to remind himself a couple of times to breathe. Had he not known she would say just that? Had he not called it?

"What 'things,' Catherine? I gave you every little piece of paper you asked for. What else could there possibly be?"

"Well—the financial statements..."

"David is working on those, and I asked him to confirm to you that he is working on them. For crying out loud, there are no more than a handful of transactions..."

"Some of them are a bit—unconventional, I believe."

"It's a startup company. Of course things are a bit unconventional. You have to think on your feet, do what needs to be done. Process and procedure can come later..."

If at all. If he had his way—never mind. If he had his way, securities lawyers would cease to exist, but that little fantasy would have to wait for another day.

"You know how these things work, Catherine—this is not the first startup you've worked on. Why are you putting stones into the road now? You too will make money with this thing once we get going."

"No stones, Connor—just making sure things are done right. If anything gets missed, your entire merger might become invalid. You don't want that to happen, do you?"

God give me strength. One. Two. Three. Breathe, Connor. "No, of course not, I trust you are doing the right thing. I have just a certain—anxiety—about things going off smoothly and without any last-minute crises."

"That makes two of us. David Williams is a good man. If he is working on the financial statements, they will make sense. You ought to think about bringing him into the company full-time."

"Later—maybe. What else?"

"That minute book you sent over is—a bit of mess to say the least."

"That was not at the forefront of our minds, as you might imagine. Nothing unfixable, I am sure."

"Fixing things after the fact is never a good idea, Connor, and I have told you this before. What you should..."

"Let me know what needs fixing, and I will fix it." He could hear his voice getting louder and more aggressive and took another couple of deep breaths. *Don't piss her off now.* Even if he hated the woman with enough passion at this very moment to drive a sharp stake through her heart. "I will personally ensure everything is correct and in order, although I'm sure it's not a big deal. Anything else you see missing?"

"The director's information statements are incomplete."

"I'll have Tess email them right now, get them to move in the next half hour."

"And something about the shareholder consent to the amalgamation."

"The shareholder consent?"

Connor got right quiet then, remembering the little troublemaking ass—what was his name again? McDowell, right, McDowell. He had not and would not send his consent in unless Connor agreed to sitting down with him and explaining things in nauseating detail. Like that was going to happen. The first of never. Except Connor had signed the papers that said he had 100 percent of votes in his hands...

"Really, that's odd."

"There appear to be some—signatures—I'm missing." He heard her shuffling papers in the background somewhere. Signatures? She wouldn't have...

"I asked Tessa to send me all the signed agreements, but it does not look like I have enough here."

"A clerical error, I'm sure," Connor croaked out while his mind skipped ahead ten paces to figure out a solution. "Probably sitting on my desk or in that triple-darned scanner. That thing always drags in multiple pages when it shouldn't, you know?"

"You're sure about that?"

"Absolutely. I have all the signatures. Double-checked them three times before I signed the statements. Wanted to be sure." It rolled off the tongue so easily he believed it. Of course, it was complete. "That's a kinda new regulation—that you have to hand in all the signatures. Never heard it before."

"Not a hard and fast rule, Connor, but PerCan is going to be a huge concern. I wanted to make sure everything was perfect from the beginning."

"As well as you should." Connor chuckled lightly. "Look, I'm half an hour away from the office. I'll send everything to you when I get there."

"Sure thing, Connor."

He hung up and suddenly became aware of his hands clenching the steering wheel hard enough to numb his fingers and turn his knuckles white. That woman—that greedy bitch of a lawyer would not be allowed to ruin his business. Not her. He would see her rot in hell first before he allowed her to strike down the finest thing he had ever built, and for what? A couple of pieces of paper?

Without missing a beat, he dialed again.

"Tess, I need you to go after all the directors and get them to hand in those information statements on the inside of 30 minutes. No excuses. Anybody is too lazy or too stupid to do it, they can leave the board right now, do you understand?"

"Well—yes, what..."

"No questions. Phone them, now. Do it."

"OK, fine, consider it done."

"Then dig out the subscription agreement for that ass McDowell and put it on my desk. I'm going to be there in less than 20 minutes."

"Connor, I don't quite understand...."

He had already hung up the phone again and weaved in and out of lanes, leaving furious honks and frustrated motorists in his wake. Did he really have to do everything by himself—again? Really?

He could give McDowell's money back. Five grand, shit, he had that kicking around somewhere in the bedroom at Kayla's. But that was not the point any longer. The point was the man had tried to fuck with him, and nobody did that—nobody. You did not try to mess up Connor Beauregard's biggest deal of his life and get away with it. Period, end of story. So he would deal with it.

TWENTY-NINE

He stormed into his office without looking left or right and slammed his laptop backpack into the corner. Tessa was still on the phone, talking to Josh as far as he could gather. Good. The little whiner could finally get off his ass and send in his statement. One form to fill out—one—and he had to be a whiner about it. Really, what did they think Connor did all day?

"You finish mine?" he asked Tessa when she got off the phone, and she nodded.

"First one I did—it's long, but not complicated. Josh just..."

"Josh will just have to deal or get out of the company. It's that easy. You put my electronic signature in it?"

"Yes."

"Good." He stood there tearing McDowell's subscription agreement into individual pages. "Here, scan the last page and do the thing you do on Photoshop or something that leaves the signature."

"OK. Then?"

"Then we are going to sign his agreement to the amalgamation."

"Connor, I can't. You can't do that."

"Maybe you can't, but I can. This deal is going to make millions for each and every man and woman who has invested in it, do you understand that? It will make a small fortune for you and your boyfriend. It literally is the best thing that has ever happened to any of us, and he is going to ruin this—really? Because of $5,000 he put in when he should not have?"

"Connor, all the man wants is to sit down with you and have you explain things to him."

"I am the president and the CEO of this company. A $5,000 investor is not going to dictate to me what to do with my time. He does not run this business. I do, do you understand?"

"I do."

"And if he thinks he can ruin this whole thing—this whole thing—just because he is an ass who does not have the slightest clue what he is doing, then he is just plain wrong, and he will not get any of my time, or of your time, or of anything. Is that clear?"

"Yes."

"Good. Then scan the last page of this agreement he personally signed—cut it or slice it or dice it, or whatever it is you do—and put it onto the bottom of the amalgamation agreement vote. And if you cannot do it, just send the lot to me, and I will do it myself or find someone who can because, so help me God, it will be done, and this amalgamation is going through right this minute. No ifs, ands, buts or anything else in the world. Do we understand one another?"

"Yes, we do."

Her words were tight and clipped and he knew he had talked himself into a holy rage—the same kind his father used to get into when he stood up there on the pulpit and told the people below he would eradicate Satan.

Don't think about that right now, Connor—that part of your life is gone.

"Let me know when it's done."

He went back into his office and slammed the door behind him, far too hard, but what the hell did it still matter? In his chair again he brought up his computer, turned on his music for a minute, and let it drone into his ears until he had come down a bit again. Dammit, he had so much work to do, and here he was cleaning up after incompetent idiots.

He pulled up the real estate brochure for the building and stared at it with something akin to love in his eyes. This was where it would be—this was where he would build the biggest deal of his life. Oh yes, nothing could stand in his way. Nothing would be allowed to.

Real estate lawyer. He would need a real estate lawyer, preferably someone who had never done any kind of business with him, someone who was hungry and new, and who would sign the papers, nod, and walk away without causing a fuss. In short—his kind of person.

Somehow, he had to find a way to get this Mirko character a piece of the action. The shares he'd sign a piece of paper for, but the equity in the building... Al, at the very least, would wonder—he was just the kind of guy who would read each and every page of the agreement—but Al wasn't on the board, now was he?

Of course! Connor grinned. He counted on Josh, Simon, and Rafael to be just lazy enough to want the profits and none of the work. Why not? That's why they had Connor. His board would play ball—just as long as he told them how.

Rafael. He checked his phone for the tenth time, waiting for the confirmation that Rafa had wired 100,000, and cursed.

"Come on, Rafa? How long does it take you to type out a wire?" he said, feeling the need to hit something again. He was—he really was—surrounded by ineptitude and laziness.

Tessa knocked and on his word stepped in and put a contract on his desk, without saying anything. Her face did not give anything away whatsoever, but there was none of the usual 'here you go, Connor, anything else you need, is everything OK'—none of that.

Well, he'd paid her enough money to sit here, file shit, go to the bank, and talk to that shark, Catherine Egan, so for once, she would have to put up with playing the big boys' game, if she wanted to stay.

He said nothing, knowing full well that she expected some sort of reassurance. *It's going to be all right? Well, of course it's going to be all right—and don't even fucking question every single thing I am doing. Then you will find out how all right I can make things.*

He leafed idly through a binder with real estate brochures and jumped onto the confirmation she had dropped on his desk, the moment the door closed behind her.

"Beautiful—fucking perfect," he muttered and squinted at the piece of paper in his hand every which way.

You couldn't tell—you simply could not tell that she had somehow copied the weasel McDowell's signature into the thing. Beautiful. Fucking-A, as Rafa would say...

He put the agreement into his printer and scanned it.

"Take this, Catherine, another one down the drain."

She'd find something else—sure and enough, she would—but now he was on fire. Now he had a building, he had put his foot into the sand where his biggest victory would stand, and nothing was going to stop him ever again.

On final thought, he sent a text to Kayla, asking her for dinner at La Cosa later, and could she please order a few more of those vitamins? They were making him feel just so much better when he was under stress.

He had barely finished, when Tessa knocked at the door again, peeking around the frame.

"Some weirdo dropped this off for you—said to just hand you the piece of paper, and you would know what it was."

"Thanks—leave it there." He nodded toward the edge of his desk and studied his email sign-on screen.

When she had left, he snatched up the paper and unfolded it. It was a copy of a wire, from some oddball account into his local business account. A million dollars, dated today. Even the account numbers were correct down to the last digit. Damn.

A handwritten note at the bottom said, 'Ready to send in.' And more wiring instructions—these for an account and bank combination he had never heard of. Mirko was not a man of many words. Just do it.

He checked his phone one more time, found that Rafa's short-term loan had finally hit his own account, and started to write out a wire. Worst day of his life, officially turned around into one of the best. And why? Because people were doing what he told them to do—that's why.

THIRTY

"Josh, Simon—glad you could make it. Sorry it's such a miserable day out there."

He shook their hands and smiled, every inch the brilliant, powerful professional, the shining star they all expected Connor Beauregard to be.

"This is a historic day in the history of our small company, gentlemen. This is the day when we lay the foundation for our combined wealth."

"Foundations better had be there and be solid," Josh muttered, a little peeved.

"This building is perfectly sound and safe, right down to the foundations, Josh. I know you wanted to be the one spearheading that end of the business, but the moment Al showed us that building—well, it was tailor-made for us. There was hardly any time or need to look for anything else."

"I might have had a few similar objects," Josh said brusquely.

"No doubt you would have, Josh, no doubt. But considering who Al is, and considering how perfect this building was—we just decided to quit looking."

Josh pointedly checked his watch for the fifth time. They had been sitting in this real estate lawyer's office for half an hour, and he needed everybody to know how much of his time was being wasted.

Connor leaned forward and smiled.

"You know, Al is a great guy, and he has done a lot for us," he said in a voice low enough so Rafael couldn't hear it. "But there are moments when I look at him, and the man just gives me the willies."

"The willies?" Josh asked, raising an eyebrow.

"Sure, I mean, he knows everybody in this town—everybody—and everybody knows him, or thinks they know him. There isn't a business around here he does not have his fingers into, and if anything is for sale, he is involved. Even if it's not for sale—yet—because if he wants it, it soon will be, if you know what I mean."

"Not entirely," Josh said. "What you are describing is like a character out of the underworld somewhere."

"I wouldn't be so sure about that. I wouldn't be so sure about anything. Not with Al involved."

"And you brought this man into the company? You trust him with our business? Connor, I have to say..."

"Rafael introduced him to us if you recall. Still, I am a cautious man, Josh. Look around. Do you see him on the board of directors? No, of course not. I took his money, and I took his deal, even if I took a chance it would—offend you. But in the end..."

"In the end it is better to offend me than Al—whatever his name is?"

"That's another thing. Nobody knows what his real name is. But no, I know you are a businessman, a respected businessman, and you deal straight, so I know I can trust you. I also know that a businessman of your experience knows that sometimes one has to make a deal that leaves a slightly bitter taste in your mouth, just to get to the end result we are all hoping for. You understand that, I'm sure—Al would not. I'm equally sure of that."

"Well..." Josh was only a little mollified. "As it turns out, I would have had to put a lot of work into finding something comparable, and it would not have been this fast, that is true. It would have been nice to have been asked, at least, but when you put it this way."

"I knew you would understand."

Connor smiled his most brilliant 500-watt Beauregard charmer and checked his watch. "Now where are these lawyers? You would think we had all the time in the world to sit here and have tea. Sure and enough, that will end up on our bill."

"Interesting choice of law office," Rafael said and sidled up to him. "Not someone we've ever dealt with? What's going on?"

"Time for a change." Connor shrugged. "You keep giving all of your business to one guy or one group of people, pretty soon they think they can dictate to you what to do and when. Better to keep 'em lean and on their toes, right?"

"Is that right?" Rafa's eyes narrowed, and he shook his head just the tiniest bit. "Something tells me that's a load of bull and not all there is to it, but whatever. Everything OK with this deal?"

"Everything peachy. Why shouldn't it?"

"'Cause just a couple of days ago, you were frantic trying to raise money and getting the amalgamation done. All of a sudden, it's like somebody waved a magic wand. Money troubles, gone, amalgamation gone through—everything is peachy... What's your secret?"

Couple of nights at the office, Tessa's magic software skills, Kayla's vitamins. Got things done, didn't it?

"Just hard work, Rafael, nothing else. Just plain old hard work."

Just then, their new lawyer stepped in. Luke Stone. What a joke. A tiny little middle-aged Jewish man. Which was precisely why Connor had picked him. This deal had to be the biggest thing he'd ever done, so yes, he did send Connor draft upon draft and accepted all of his changes on Connor's say-so that everybody would sign. Of course he did. He was just hungry enough for it. And stupid. God, Connor hated stupid people—even when they had their uses.

"Well, are you gentlemen all ready then?" he said and wheeled in a trolley, covered in paperwork—literally covered.

Josh and Simon paled a little. Connor had known exactly what was coming.

"Luke," he said gently, "my partners are wasting a lot of their valuable time, so as speedy as we can make this for them, the better it is. I am sure you understand."

"I understand perfectly—but everything still has to have its process and procedure."

"I couldn't agree with you more, Luke—I am glad you are as thorough as you are. I've checked over every single word in this contract, and everything is utterly perfect."

Luke smiled, and Connor moved in for the kill.

"I've had securities lawyers draw up documents where I had to correct each and every page. You, sir, are a rarity in your profession. Now, if we can get on with these signatures, so my partners can get back to their business, and PerCan can acquire its new home?"

"Thank you." Luke beamed. "Now should I start reviewing..."

"I really need to get back to the office," Josh said impatiently. "So, if you don't mind—Connor just said he had looked over everything already. Can we get this show on the road? Some of us still have to make a living."

"Well—if you are sure..."

"I am sure. Simon?"

Simon shrugged. "Can't even tell you if I have anything to contribute here, except my signature. I know we need the building, I know it is the right property for us—so I'd say let's go. I'd rather get back to work too."

The simple act of checking their ID documents made Josh snarly again, and Connor smiled. He deliberately drew the procedure out a bit, just to make sure everybody was good and rushed.

The trolley was literally piled with documents. Everything appeared to be there in triplicate, everything needed to be passed around, signed, countersigned, initialed... He could almost see Josh shuffling, raring to go.

Luke droned on, explaining what they were signing each and every time, and after a while none of them listened—just the way Connor had hoped. Josh took a phone call holding the phone with one hand, signing papers with the other, pointedly ignoring Luke Stone's pique. He wanted to get out of there—they all did.

Half an hour later, it was all done. Documents signed, the building his. And none of them had made the slightest little comment about Mirko—not that they would have noticed. Connor basically bounced out of the real estate lawyer's office.

Everything was going his way once again. Now all he had to do was sign up a few more investors, and life was good again.

On his way out of the lawyer's office, he felt a little tired and sluggish and stopped off in the washroom quickly to take a few more of Kayla's vitamins. Damn if those things did not make him feel invincible every time he got down on himself.

Right now, he just wanted to feel good. He had finally achieved what he had been dreaming about since starting this company—they were going public; they had purchased their building. Soon, so very soon, they would be the biggest cannabis producer in the country. Hell, the world if he had anything to do with it. That was what he wanted to feel right now—that power, that invincibility—and those vitamins were what did it for him at the moment.

Kayla had the champagne ready when he got in that afternoon, and he chuckled.

"Three in the afternoon—a bit early, is it not?"

"That depends—if you've struck the deal of your life, it is never too early. How did it go?"

Connor shrugged. "Fine, I guess. If you can call signing your name 500 times fine. God, these lawyers, each and every little fart needs to be documented and signed five times, you know? And then they have the nerve to charge you for it. Unbelievable."

"Well then." She handed him a glass. "This ought to take your mind off things. I've been thinking how to celebrate."

"Celebrate?"

"Of course celebrate—silly. You've just laid the foundation for the biggest company in the country..."

"Well..."

"Well nothing. Soon enough it will be. So, we ought to celebrate. I'm thinking about this huge party and reception—first class all the way, catered, with live music and a few bars and fireworks and..."

"Jesus—Kayla..."

"What? You've got this enormous building now. Somehow, we are going to have to celebrate and christen the thing now, don't we?"

"You christen a ship, not a building," he said. "Besides, the lot is ugly and full of garbage—no way to have a celebration there."

"All right, all right. Let's reserve La Cosa then, or The Lighthouse, one of the better restaurants in town, and let's just invite the core people, and our biggest investors perhaps, and their friends so they too can invest, and..."

Sounding better already.

"OK, let's—you got a deal." Connor threw his hands up and laughed. "Fine, let's go and have a party. You are right. We have plenty of good to celebrate. It'll bring everybody back together. We've all been so busy with our respective things."

"Right. And I do want to get to know them all better. And my reporters will be there, of course, so it will all be in the magazine, and people are going to read about your success and all the good things you've done. It will be fabulous. You'll see."

Connor was not paying attention any longer. If Kayla wanted to have an enormous party, so be it. He would show up and shake some hands and pose for the press. Sure. He was more worried about the text Dan had just sent him.

Things were not going so well with the license to grow marijuana. Hundreds of small-time producers had applied by now, and the licensing process had come to a complete halt while they tried to catch up. Damn. If they could not get a license, they might as well dump all the money they had just spent on a building down the drain. There would be no more investors and no construction loans from the bank unless they had at least good prospects for the license.

He tuned out Kayla's chatter and stood by the picture window. Now that they were riding a wave of success, everybody would naturally ask—how about the license? How far are you in the process? How does that compare to others? Damned questions.

Every single new investor would want to know, and he had no answers to give. Damn—he should have worried about the whole process earlier. Of course, he had been busy raising money, finding a building, and putting the dream team together.

Who the heck was working on this licensing process anyway? There had to be somebody he could sit down with, a man who would be reasonable, who would understand.

Kayla's voice penetrated his thoughts again, and suddenly, he turned as an idea started to take shape in his mind.

"Say, love, this party…"

"Yes—oh, God, Connor, I am so excited. I don't think I can wait."

"I can see that." He chuckled and put his arms around her. "How about you make it a little bigger than that?"

"Bigger? I thought you said…"

"Forget what I said a few minutes ago. I want this thing to be the biggest celebration this town has ever seen."

"Yes." She lit up like a Christmas tree. "I was hoping you would say that. See, I have so many ideas…"

"And you will be able to work on them all. One thing, though…"

"And that is?"

"Politicians. I need to bring a few politicians in and show them who we are and what we can do, and it needs to be good."

"Politicians?" Kayla made a face. "I was hoping for something a little more fun, you know… But—oh…" Understanding dawned, and she nodded. "You're concerned about the license? I read that in the paper this morning. They can't even handle the applications they have, never mind anything that isn't in the pipeline yet."

"I think we might be at the end of the line here." Connor nodded. "And I don't like it. So I want to make sure we—move ahead a little bit."

"By entertaining the right people..."

"Entertaining the right people, showing them we know what we are doing, and making sure they know it won't be to their disadvantage if they look kindly upon us and our application."

"Careful. If any of them even get the slightest whiff that you are trying to influence them..."

"Which I am not and which they won't, OK? We are just entertaining, showing off, if you will. Showing Perfect Cannabis from its most advantageous side. And you, my love, you know better than anyone else how that works."

"That I do," Kayla said, smiling. "Spinning a story is what I do after all. OK, tell me who you want to have there and what they need to hear at this party, what they need to see. Consider it done."

"I knew you and I could move the world," Connor said and kissed her. "I'm going to find out who is the guy with his hands on the big wheel, and I am counting on you."

He let go of Kayla and grabbed his jacket in one fluid move. "I'm going out to see TC and Dan. They probably know who is in charge. I also need you to go to your list and invite a few of the other politicians who like to be seen at these things. Just so nobody thinks..."

"I know what I'm doing. Ta—don't be late."

She was already flipping through her notebook, likely planning the party of the century. Somewhere in the back of his mind, he wondered how much that would run him, but what the heck. It was necessary for the license, right?

THIRTY-ONE

"TC, get serious. I'm not planning to bribe a politician. I just want to have a party to celebrate how far we have come, and I want to make sure the proper people see how much work has gone into everything. I don't see how that could be considered a bribe."

"You're planning one hell of a shindig, though, aren't you?"

"Kayla is." Connor made a dismissive gesture. "She has a horde of people cleaning up a section of the property and the building just now to have this party in. It's a women's thing, you know? They always want to have these—things. But she is right. It's time to show the public who we are, what we can do, and, most of all, the good we are going to do. Why hide in the shadows like real drug dealers?"

"I'm sure Dan won't see it that way. And since he's in California right now, sourcing lighting..."

"Dan has an opinion on everything, TC, and he usually takes the time to tell me about it. I'm asking you, as the person in charge, do you know who, at a government decision-making level, is working on our license?"

"Well, I might have an idea, although they don't actually broadcast those facts—just in case somebody gets an idea."

"Good, then tell me, and I'm going to make sure he or she gets invited to Kayla's party—only to see what we are doing. Not to be approached with anything as crass as an envelope full of money, is that understood?"

"Well—OK."

TC said it slowly, and Connor could feel the man's concern. More and more, it irritated him to be surrounded by people with small minds. Why, oh why could they not see that he knew what was best for the company and for them, and just go ahead and do it? Why did everybody always ask him to explain himself and his actions, as if they were five years old and needed somebody to hold their hand?

"Just do it, TC. I know you have a concern, but I actually do know what I'm doing, OK? I'm the person who got the company to where it is today. I'm the person who founded it and raised all of the funds—all of them. So, it's not too much to ask that my employees just simply do as they are told, is it?"

"No, of course not. You got it."

"Good. Then get to it and give my best to Dan."

Connor stalked out of their small office and drove back to his own, weary all of a sudden. The suspicions, the demands, the sheer weight of his position as president and CEO started to weigh on him harder and harder with every day that passed.

He stopped to take a few more vitamins and immediately felt better. On the way home, he stopped at The Lighthouse and washed the day down with a few glasses of wine—only to realize an hour later that a few glasses had turned into the entire bottle, but he chalked it up to stress and exhaustion.

Kayla did not even notice how long he had been gone. By the time he reached the penthouse again, she was still on the phone, surrounded by a small mountain of notebooks and papers, talking a mile a minute. She waved briefly at him, blew him a kiss, and went back to talking.

"Cheri, we simply need the best caterer in town—you don't understand. This is going to be the event of the year. Anybody who is involved won't have to worry about extra business for the longest time."

Connor tuned her out, his mind working a mile a minute again.

This party of hers—she was going to host it one way or another, and it was actually a decent idea. So how could he use it to the best of his advantage? How could he make himself and his company appear in the best light?

There's where he wanted to put the focus of this thing—celebrating his achievements—and that was good, but he needed something else, a kicker, a good cause... Something irresistible, that drew them in, that made people go *aw* and want to be part of his little company. Something that turned the drug-dealing villain into a hero.

"Kayla," he said suddenly, interrupting her phone call. "Find me a charitable institution, one of those compassion networks or some such thing, for people who can't afford their cannabis treatments. Then let's donate a sum of money to them and trot out a few unfortunate souls for the party. Find somebody who is suffering a lot and let's go have them there."

"You want to invite sick patients? To my party?"

"I want everybody to see how much good we are doing. I want it in the press, and I want it on TV. I want people to be crying because we are helping the unfortunate and those in pain—got it? The more tears, the better."

"Got it." She smiled. "You are playing the game. You're going to be Jesus standing there healing the sick."

"Somebody has to. Somebody has to make things look the way they should look. And nobody else is doing it. Lord love us, but if I ever hear TC saying this is not right one more time, I am going to have to strangle the man."

"Don't strangle anybody just yet. You need TC, if only to play the honest bloke for the theater. That kind of genius simply cannot be faked, I am afraid—you either have it, or you don't, and he has it."

"I do pretty well myself, you know."

"I know that, and I'm not saying it's not sickening, but that kind of person can turn things around for you, especially in the public eye. Because he would never do anything wrong because you can count on him. He inspires the kind of trust we need."

"Well, he is still an idiot who has no idea what he's doing and spends his entire day with his nose buried in some kind of plan."

Kayla laughed and walked away, waggling her fingers, and Connor relaxed into his chair. All right, good—he felt pretty good about things again, now that he knew where he was headed.

Now he had to make his financial situation look the way he wanted it to look because make no mistake, Mirko was not the nice guy from next door who would lend him a helping hand because he thought Connor was a good man who helped people and needed to get past a tough spot—not by a long shot.

He needed funds badly to pay the little weasel back, and quickly, so he would not have a chance to cause trouble for Connor. So think, think, think.

Connor pulled out his phone and flipped through the most recent list of emails. People who wanted money—mostly, people who wanted to get paid, always... But suddenly, after this first rush, there were no more investors lining up the way they had been a little while ago. Could be there were too many news reports about cannabis manufacturers going under, about double-dealing in the business, and shady, fly-by-night operators. Could be there were just too many of them around. Another reason to put PerCan in the media spotlight—just keep them in the public eye.

Irritated, he turned his phone off and back on again. How could there be nobody? For weeks, people had lined up, clamored to get an appointment with him, just to get in on the action—and now, nobody?

He dialed Rafa's number and tapped his toes while he waited for the phone to connect.

"Rafa, what's going on? You got anybody I should talk to—anybody with money burning in their pocket? Don't hold out on me now."

"Me? Am I not speaking to the hottest promoter in town? Did you dial a wrong number?"

"This is not a contest, Rafa. Me versus you—that's just stupid. I'm only trying to make sure I don't miss anybody who might want to invest big, you know? This might be the last moment in time for a big strike, and I don't want people to come whining—why didn't you tell me, I would have invested."

"Heard it before, Connor—save the bullshit. Won't work on me, remember?"

"OK, OK." Connor paused for a moment. "We were running hot, till just a little while ago. All of a sudden, it's the great wasteland out there—nothing."

"Too many news stories—and bad news stories at that. Crooks taking investors' money, doing no more than necessary, and taking off with it. Deals going sour, licenses being rejected. Especially in the cannabis sector. Investors are running scared. Everybody is taking a wait-and-see attitude."

"Mmmh." Connor toyed with a frilly couch pillow. Nothing he had not thought of on his own, really, no real insights here, but it still felt like a punch to the gut to hear someone else say it. Cannabis was cooling just a little. Easy money was getting harder to come by. All the more reason they needed Kayla's party. The woman was worth every one of the more expensive gifts he gave her on a regular basis.

"I can hear the gears turning over the phone—what are you thinking, Connor?"

"Give me a minute. Kayla is brilliant. She is planning this huge shindig out at the new building. Clean the damn thing up a bit, have a party, that sort of thing. Originally, I was only going to invite a few media people, our investors, and a couple of politicians in the license-giving sector. And yes, before you even tell me to be careful—I know not to be crass."

"Good, because I have seen you do crass, and it is not pretty."

"You're an ass. But the more I think about it, the more we are going to need this thing for our public image, you know? We need to show people where all of their money is going. The good we are doing—capital G good."

"Right now, if I might remind you, there's nothing to show yet."

"Exactly. That's why I need a few of your construction people out there. Knock down a few walls, I don't know, put in new ones, do something to the floors, anything that makes it look like a good and busy construction site. I don't know—you're the expert. Do something without actually—doing anything. And don't let it cost anything either."

"Well." Rafael thought for a minute. "We could knock out that one wall with all of the delivery bays in it. Not going to be any use later on anyway. Renovate what used to be the office area, which looks like shit."

"Good. Talk to Kayla. She can tell you how much space she needs and what she is going to be doing, but when people come there and take pictures, I want to have something I can point to, if you know what I mean."

"I do, indeed I do." Rafael sighed, and Connor heard him shuffle some papers in the background. "All right, I'll send a few crews out there to see what they can work up without doing too much damage, running up an enormous bill, or interfering with what we are going to do in the future."

"'K—thanks."

Connor hung up. This was only a temporary bottleneck, he told himself. Once the good news stories got out, especially the one with the donation for some less-fortunate patients.

The Come-to-Jesus story. He grinned and congratulated himself on his own brilliance. Nothing—but really nothing—got people right in the heart like doing the right thing, helping somebody... And if you could not do it yourself, at least you could give money to those who did. Open wallet, come on up, investor. This was going to work; this was going to work better than he had expected.

It had better because over the next few days, he fielded a constant stream of phone calls that had one common subject—*where is my damn money?*

Even Al—Al of all people—came by his office more than once, wanting to know where they stood financially, what Connor had done with the funds provided to him, and what his going-forward plan looked like. Exactly. Concretely. Damn!

"Look, Al," Connor said, trying not to let his annoyance show too much. "We are a startup company. You have to think on your feet most of the time. There is really no such thing as a concrete plan, you know? It's like survival training—you deal with what is directly in front of you, take care of it, and move on to the next thing. Plans rarely survive contact with the real world."

Al did not look like survival training made much of an impression on him.

"I'm glad you see it that way, Connor, but well over a million dollars has been taken in and spent again. It is not really too much to ask of you to show me where it went and why, is it?"

"Not at all, Al." Connor smiled and unrolled the plans he had picked up from Dan and TC just a little while ago, with a plan to have them laminated and framed for everyone at the party to see. "This is what your brother and TC came up with. As you can see, there's a lot of work that has gone into this, a lot of consultants who need to be paid, a lot of effort that—well—costs money."

Al studied the plans briefly and nodded. "Dan has showed these to me—more than once. I am quite familiar with the work he has done as a matter of fact. I am also familiar with the fact that he himself is footing the bill for the office space he shares with TC and much of the expenses..."

"The building, Al, the building. It takes a lot of resources. Consulting fees for a lot of people who work on this project, besides your brother. Really—if I had known you wanted somebody to explain our books to you, I would have made sure our accountant was here. He could have given you a much better overview. "

"I don't need an accountant, Connor—I just want an understanding of what is happening right at the moment. I want to know that everything is being done right, the way it ought to be done, and that everything is aboveboard."

Yeah, like you and your family are—right, Connor thought and forced himself to smile.

"Well as you should, Al, but let me assure you, everything—absolutely everything—is perfectly correct and aboveboard. And if you like, I will most certainly have the company's accountant confirm this to you."

"No need. I can just look at the company's public filings with the SEC very shortly. And I do hope we won't run into any kind of trouble with those filings. That's just on the side. But really—all that is is paper, Connor, and paper is incredibly patient. It will not care what you put down on it. No. I am interested in looking into a man's eyes when he tells me everything is aboveboard and the deal is straight."

Connor smiled gently and put his hands together. A benevolent gesture—a benediction, almost. He'd seen his father do it a thousand times.

"Yes, Al," he finally said when he had his emotions and facial expressions under complete control. "Everything about this deal is completely aboveboard and clean. This deal is completely straight."

Al searched his eyes for a long moment, but Connor knew enough to concentrate and keep his hands together, not revealing one single thing.

"OK," Al finally said. "You have convinced me."

He rose and shook Connor's hand. "I don't have to tell you that my father is quite worried about this project and the money he has already put into it, so he will be looking for updates on a regular basis."

"I don't have a problem with that at all." Connor smiled and returned the firm handshake. "I know how it is when you are not involved day to day. But I give you my word that there is nothing at all going on behind the scenes that would threaten his investment."

"He will be happy to hear this."

Al took the small briefcase he seemed to be carrying around with him everywhere and nodded.

"Thank you for taking the time to reassure him—and me. I will be in touch again shortly."

"Not a problem at all, Al. Just step in anytime if you would like an update. I am always available to you and your father."

He watched Al disappear though the glass office doors, nod quickly at Tessa, and then walk out into the main hall. Slowly, he counted to ten, not moving, then to ten again.

"God-triple-dammit, I hate that man." He grabbed all of the pens in the chic pencil holder on his desk and threw them at the wall in his office with enough force to lodge some of them in the wall, point first. The rest clattered harmlessly to the floor, and Connor roared again.

"Christ, Connor, is everything…"

He stared at Tessa, who had run in through the open door and stared at him, open-mouthed, as he stood there in the middle of his office, fists clenched tightly, rage pulsing in every one of his veins.

"Tessa, I can't deal right now, OK? Leave it."

"But is everything…"

"I said leave it."

She almost ran out of there, and Connor punched the door closed behind her with his fist.

"Dammit."

Not only did the door tremble, his knuckles sent a stab of pain down so deep into his gut he wanted to scream again.

"Goddammit."

Don't punch anything again. Last he needed to do was look like a beaten prize-fighter when he stepped into an investor's office, but goddammit, the rage was almost impossible to hold back.

He shook his fists hard and pulled out his desk drawer, dumping the contents on the polished glass desk. His vitamins—they had to be in here somewhere. Kayla had given him a few just days ago, right? They were there.

Trembling, he fished the vial out from between all the detritus on the desk and shook three of them into his palm, washing them down with cold coffee from this morning's cup. Did not matter—nothing mattered right this minute but getting himself under control again. *Get a hold of yourself, Connor.* Nothing happened.

Nothing happened.

The nosy bugger had just come around asking stupid questions—but darn it if he had not sent him away happy. This was what he did, telling the story. This was how it worked, convincing people. *Hang on, Connor.* He could almost see the famous Reverend Marty standing there and with his hands open and a smile on his face. *And may all of your generous gifts from the heart be a blessing to the poor and the downtrodden.*

Yeah, right.

But they bought it. And Al had bought it. Hook, line, and goddamn sinker. He had bought it with a smile.

"Take that, my dear Original Chef, just take that," Connor whispered hoarsely as his vitamins kicked in, and he could feel the calm spreading throughout his body. "Take that and stick it on your fucking hat. Everything about this deal is absolutely aboveboard."

He sat down and logged into a private new email server not even Rafa knew about. There it was: the confirmation from Dominik that he had purchased a million shares for him into the Swiss holding company. He'd read that particular email a good dozen times already, and it never failed to comfort him. He owned this thing, and he owned them all—small-minded criminals they were. They had neither the smarts nor the guts to start something like this, and they tried to come in and check up on him? They dared to ask if he was dealing straight? Really?

He owned this—and he owned them all. Soon enough, he would find a way to get rid of Al and his family. This much he swore to himself.

A little while later, his heartbeat had normalized, the rage had all but died down inside him again, and he stepped out of the office, where Tessa sat at her computer, barely daring to raise her eyes to him.

"Just a brief disagreement with someone over funds," he said dismissively. "You know how I get. I get angry. And people who are stupid and can't be bothered to look beyond the end of their noses make me angry every single time. It's all good."

She nodded without saying a word, and he knew she still had the scene in his office in her mind—pens sticking out of the wall like knives.

"Today's mail come in already?" he asked jovially and smiled as broadly as he could. "I'm waiting for a few subscription agreements, and I thought they might be in there. Keep us all in vittles for a little while longer."

"Over on the printer," she said and nodded in that direction. But she still refused to look at him straight.

So be it. Even Tessa was not irreplaceable.

THIRTY-TWO

Over the next few days, Connor felt as if he were a man on the run. If it wasn't Mirko he was trying to avoid, it was Rafa, or Al, or David, who had taken to calling him three times a day because of the 'error' on his check.

Connor refused to give in to the panic, put on his very own personal blinders, and plowed straight ahead with his plans. Nothing would stop him—nothing.

TC had finally come around with the name of the person in charge of their license at a government level, and he had fought down desperation and managed to pry a few more investments out of a few of his friends. OK, so the terms had been horrible. He had to give away the store to put a new lock on the front door, but beggars could not be choosers any longer. He took money where he could find it. Sometimes, you had to do what it took.

Kayla, sensing that all was not perfect in Cannabis Land, became his savior and helped out anywhere she could, thank God. He did not dare ask her for more money right out, but by sheer magic, it appeared. Kayla sent some of her friends his way, even though they had invested already, and, with 50,000 here and there, he kept them afloat.

"Just make sure these people don't get screwed," she would say, and Connor laughed. Of course not—they got the once-in-a-lifetime chance to be part of the next biggest thing, did they not?

Catherine tried to nag him on a daily basis as well, having run up her damned bill to close to $100,000. 100,000! Who had ever heard of such an amount in legal fees? And had he not called it a few weeks ago, had he not warned everybody that woman would turn into a serial biller if you let her? But no—*things need to be done, and they need to be done right.*

Now look at it. $83,000 worth of right and counting... He wanted to get sick when he looked at her bills, knowing full well she did not deserve outrageous amounts as those for shuffling a few papers back and forth—most certainly not. But his time was coming, and the thought gave him peace. He still had the last word when she would get paid—if ever.

If ever. That one little thought made him smile and gave him great comfort when he shuffled her bills to the bottom of the pile every single time.

Contracts he could damn well download off the internet if he wanted to. And Tessa—Jesus, Tessa could get you stuff you did not even want to know... No, no, no. No way was he going to pay her pumped-up fees. If you were going to play a game on Connor Beauregard, you had better get up very early and dress very warm. He had just as many tricks in his bag as the next guy.

His phone rang again, and with a sigh, he picked it up.

"David, what's the latest crisis now? I thought Tessa gave you a new check and apologized grandly for making an error on the original one. You want the girl to put ashes on her head? Can you cut her a break just once? What is wrong now?"

"Connor, wrong does not even begin to describe the state your financial records are in. You know that, don't you?"

"I'm not really a paper shuffler, never have been. We've already been there. I do the best I can."

"Paper shuffler? Connor, after the mess at the oil company, I thought you had learned a few basics at least. The best you can is—mildly speaking—a giant mess."

"I run the company, David, and I run it the way I see fit. I would appreciate it if you did not speak to me as if I were the summer intern, is that clear?"

He had spoken sharply without noticing, but once he thought about it, David and Catherine should really open an office space together. They would happily make each other unhappy with their insistence on records, paperwork, verifications, and signatures and leave the rest of the world to run their business in peace.

"No offense."

As if.

"I understand your position in the company only too well, Connor, but there are items on your company's books that defy any kind of explanation, and we don't have a hope in hell filing official financial statements as is."

"All perfectly explainable, I am sure. All you need to do is ask."

"Let's just start with a recent one. $15,000 to the condominium board where Kayla lives?"

"Oh, that—that's easily explained."

A slight miscalculation on his part, thinking he could make a few minor adjustments to the shower off the main bathroom. Something had gone wrong, probably because the idiots who installed the thing in the first place had no idea what they were doing and done it wrong. Consequently, he had ended up flooding the corner units three floors down. Contractors could not be trusted either.

"Meeting space, David. I needed a private meeting space away from the main office for investors who put a lot of money into this thing. Not all of them are comfortable or available seeing me at the office, so I paid a small fee for private space."

"A small... OK, what about 120,000 for your new car?"

"I needed to travel, especially now with the building—I spend most of my days in that car."

"120,000? It's still a private vehicle—and you can't just…"

"And it is still a startup company. One of these days, we'll be able to afford a clean separation between private and business. Until then, this is the best we can do. I need to get around to see people, and surely, nobody wants me to show up on a bicycle. You would have no investors."

"Bills from La Cosa, The Lighthouse, not to forget about an outfit called Señor Paul's?"

"Entertainment. Surely if a man puts half a million dollars into the company, you have to give him a little more than water."

"I don't see any investments that big."

"Doesn't always work out. You go up to bat, but there's no guarantee you'll actually score. David." Connor sighed and leaned back in his chair. "Give me a break. How often are we going to have this very same conversation? Have we had this conversation before, remind me?"

"We will have it as often as we need to. You think I can squeeze all of this past an official auditor for your SEC filings? Not without backup documentation. I could barely make a case for all of this—barely—if you kept proper records, and I told you this during EC Oil days. And every single time, you said you would definitely do so."

Yada, yada, yada... Connor put his phone on the speaker setting and checked his email in the meantime.

"I will, David..."

"I can't tell you how much this will trip you up when the time comes."

"Yes, I know I get carried away—a lot—because I focus on building the company. I appreciate you reminding me now and then to keep my shit together."

He needed something on Byron Cartwright, the Minister of Health, to expedite their licensing application. Nothing big, nothing crass. He was hoping he knew a guy who played golf with him or was otherwise connected to the man. Something that would give him a hook to connect, something that would allow him to approach him—friend to friend.

Hey—how are you doing? Oh, by the way, did you know we have a common acquaintance...

Nothing as obvious as a check. For a minute, he wondered if he should ask his friend Señor Paul if there was anything interesting his girls had on the minister, but that kind of thing usually came back at you and kicked you in the teeth. Too crass—no blackmail, just a friendly chat between businessmen. Perhaps a sailing trip together, or a game at a private golf course. A very exclusive, private golf course, something like that.

"Connor, I'm completely serious. We will not be able to file if you don't..."

"I will do my best, David, really. Like I said, thank you for reminding me."

Interesting—he had just found a picture of the minister with a small sailboat. Thank goodness for Facebook, no? Now there was something he could sink his teeth into. Kayla knew people in the local yacht club. Easy breezy. The dinky little thing he was trying to sail out really did not befit a minister.

"I will do my best, David—I promise. But I have to go right now, I'll talk to you later."

"Connor..."

Connor hung up and dialed Kayla's friend, the one with the enormous sailboat, down in the good section of the private yacht club. If the minister liked to sail, they'd show him the best time—period. Just making friends, nothing else.

For the first time in a while, Connor smiled again. Wasn't it great when things worked out in your favor?

No point in sitting in his office and letting people drag him down into doom and gloom, he decided, so he took a drive out to their new building.

Turning the corner, his enthusiasm left him a little as the thing still looked like just what it was—an enormous dump—but at least Rafael had managed to make a couple of construction trailers appear. Oh, and look, an enormous sign with a completely unrealistic drawing of a completely unrealistic building on it…. Connor roared with laughter. As if. But he had to admit, Rafael was good—really good.

He parked his car and dashed inside, skirting puddles and small piles of indefinable rubbish, where he found Rafael and a couple of construction workers deep in discussion over removing a wall and the potential consequences of this action.

Rafael shook his hand and cocked a thumb out to the general direction of the lot.

"Yo, Connor, you see our new project sign out there? Nice, is it not? Hope it works for you."

"Seen it, laughed my ass off. Who does shit like this for you?"

"Got a guy who makes these by the dozen—takes less than 24 hours, makes every construction site dump look good. Like we actually know what we are doing, you know?"

"We do actually know what we're doing. Just not yet—we need time. And we need to have a party. But I have to tell you, this already looks great."

"Got two dumpsters arriving tomorrow, carting most of the crap off the lot. That's going to help a lot. Grade it a bit, put in a few bushes…."

"Bushes? You going green on me now? I hope they are the harmless kind of bushes if you know what I'm talking about."

"Greenery always looks good—like you're environmentally conscious or some such bullshit. The people can pose in front of the signs."

"With the shrubbery."

"With the shrubbery," Rafael grinned. "You know any politician or businessman who wants to have his picture taken in front of a pile of garbage? Not me."

"You are genius, my friend. What else?"

"Taking out this wall—which seems kind of useless and has to go at some point in the future anyway, at least if this is going to be warehouse space."

"It is."

"Good. Then we are going to knock it out now. Jose is just going to check the plans one last time. God forbid the damn thing is load-bearing."

"Didn't think anything in these industrial spaces was load-bearing—but who knows."

"Exactly, who knows? And you don't want it coming down around your ears the night of the party, do you?"

"I do not. Awesome. Kayla has got the media all interested in what we are doing here, Tessa is doing research on unemployment rates, just to show how many jobs we are planning to create."

"Really? Did not think staffing needs were all that big, at least not for a few years anyway."

"They're not, but it's like your shrubbery out there—give 'em something good to write about, give people a reason to welcome us into their neighborhood."

"And then wonder why you've got triple fences, cameras, and 24-hour security guards with dogs."

"Has Simon been here?"

"He's looked at the plans. And he's picking up the guidelines from the ministry, what we are going to have to do. Considering we are actually going to be growing drugs in here, it won't be easy or cheap to comply. But your license depends on it."

"Well, the license depends on a lot of things—amongst others," Connor said smugly, and Rafael narrowed his eyes.

"Please tell me you have not gone and done something stupid."

"Stupid—Rafael." Connor spread his arms in a good old-fashioned Reverend Marty gesture. "Really, would I do something stupid? Is that what you think of me?"

"Of you? In a damn second. So tell me—what's your plan?"

"Byron Cartwright—Minister of Health."

"Yes?"

"He will be invited to the party."

"Good—and?"

"And so will Charlie Weaver."

"Pray tell, who is Charlie Weaver?"

"Charlie Weaver just happens to own several of the biggest sailing yachts out in the harbor club."

"Several?"

"Several. Plus, he has a smaller thing that he actually races."

"A thing?"

"Well, yes—God, I will brush up on the proper terminology, Rafael," Connor said, a little irritated. "I will just arrange for the two to meet and talk sailing, since that is what our dear Minister of Health seems to be into. Then—perhaps—the three of us can head out onto the lake for little sailing turn later. Show our minister a good time. Just some friends following their common hobby, getting a little better acquainted on a personal basis, you know? Then, when the time comes to issue licenses..."

"You don't sail."

"I do now. And you know me—when I put my mind to something...."

"You utterly excel at it. I have heard it many times." Rafael nodded. "I don't know how you do it, but all the best to you, my friend. Just don't..."

"Don't be crass. You've told me before, and I remember."

"No, I was going to say don't screw it up. I just recently read how many licenses are out there being applied for. Shit, it's like winning the lottery. There's a better-than-fair chance we may never get one. That frightens me if you want to know the truth."

"I do. But I never play a game that's not fixed, and I never play at anything I can't win."

Rafael shook his head and snapped the plans in his hands.

"Of all the badass promoters I have ever met," he muttered and went back to looking at the wall he was planning to take down.

"What, Rafa—what were you going to say?"

"I was going to say watch where the line is, between cutting a couple of corners just to make things happen, and actually dropping off into illegal territory, but for some reason, I don't think you much care at the moment, do you?"

"Not really."

Connor bounced on the balls of his feet, watching some workers carrying garbage outside to an enormous pile, waiting for the arrival of the bins Rafael had ordered.

"Kayla's big shindig is in a couple of weeks. By then..."

"By then all the trash will have disappeared from the lot in case you were going to ask—yes."

"I'd like to bring Dan and TC out here—get them some confidence, show them what we are doing. I think Dan has the potential, at least, to go rogue on me."

"What do you mean, 'go rogue?'"

"I don't know, Rafa. Every now and then, I don't like the way the man looks at me—like he doesn't think I know what I'm doing, like he's figuring out how to put somebody else in charge, one of his family, perhaps."

"You're getting paranoid." Rafael cocked an eyebrow. "I guess that's true of all the famous leaders... Getting paranoid that some of his officers are trying to do away with him."

"I don't think I like that analogy. Dan is not an officer. He's a plain old employee of the company, no matter who his father is. Half his family is sitting in jail for one thing or another, and without me, there would not be a company in the first place. Without me, those yahoos would be nothing but crooks, scheming for their next crooked deal, trying to stay one step ahead of the law. So if he thinks..."

"Hey, hey, hey...Connor."

Rafael raised his hands and made soft *calm down* gestures. "Slow down. I wasn't suggesting anything of the sort, all right? I was only suggesting..."

"You were suggesting that Dan and his stupid family might actually want to do away with me, and I will not have it."

"No, you were suggesting that you thought Dan was scheming. I simply made a military reference, and I'm sorry I did. Look—you're kind of getting in the way here, and if this were a real construction site I would have to ask you to wear a hard hat and some other fine protective gear. So why don't you drive back to the city, grab a drink at The Lighthouse, calm down, and call me when you are over being paranoid?"

"I am not being paranoid. I'm being careful. Al, Dan, their strange father... All of them are wild cards. I don't know what they're planning, and they're getting in the way of running this thing. And you had better remember that it was you who brought them in here in the first place."

"I made the connection, nothing else. Now go on, go back to the city—you are really getting in my way..."

Connor narrowed his eyes at the man in front of him, considering Rafa's place in the company. They'd been friends for too many years and too many miserable years to count, but even Rafa—even Rafa could probably not be trusted entirely at the end of the day.

Give it a rest, he scolded himself. Rafa? Turn on him? Not in 100 years. The man could not put a deal together if his life depended on it. He needed Connor. Not in a lifetime would he betray him, the man who brought the best deals around. Shit, he really was getting paranoid.

"There are people I need to see anyway," he said curtly and made a sweeping gesture around the room.

"Make sure all the trash is gone from here. I want people to see a glaring difference when they come around for Kayla's party—the nice, clean, ready-to-go part of the building and the old, messy, and disgusting side. Use a lot of white paint and stainless steel—make it look clean. Like a hospital."

"Yes, sir—now on with you."

Just for a moment, he wondered whether he actually liked Rafael—the man with a head full of curly dark hair and the sunny, happy-go-lucky attitude that always got him through when it shouldn't have. Just for a minute, he wondered—but Rafael needed him. He needed Connor more than the other way around. And that was good.

He drove back to town feeling tired and exhausted all of a sudden and took a few more of Kayla's vitamins. This wasn't the time to go slacking off; there were things to be done, and, as always, he was the only one doing them.

He ignored a bunch of voicemail messages from Catherine—really, voicemail, was there anyone left on the planet who still used voicemail?—and called up Kayla. She had found the perfect caterers, and the perfect jazz trio—when had a jazz trio entered the picture?—and now hunted for a decorator...

"You have this guy you know, love, the dude who sails."

"Charlie Weaver, yes—what about him? I have not spoken to him in a while, but if you're thinking he might invest..."

"No, I don't need him to invest. I need him to sail."

"I'm listening."

"Don't worry about it—all you need to do is invite this man to our little party and let me do the rest, OK?"

"Shouldn't I know..."

"No, you don't need to know, Kayla. Christ, is everybody asking me to explain today—and explain and explain and explain? Can't one of you just simply say, 'OK, Connor, if you're telling me that's a good idea, then it probably is,' and end of story. Just one of you? Jesus H. Christ, what is going on..."

"How many of those—vitamins—have you taken today, Connor?"

"Why?"

"Because you are getting a little paranoid, and that's one of the signs you might be taking these just a bit too freely. It's not candy—it is actually..."

"Jesus Christ, Kayla, just a couple, OK? And you are the second person today who tells me not to get paranoid. Is it any wonder? All

I need people to do is follow my lead, that's all. Realize that I know exactly what I am doing and what is best for the company and simply follow. It just should not be that hard."

He waited a moment, but Kayla said nothing.

"All right, if you must know. I'm inviting the Minister of Health, who happens to be a sailing nut, and I want to make a little bit of—nice weather with him, pardon the pun. Perhaps invite him out onto the lake for a good time so he will remember us fondly and think of us in a good light when it comes to signing off on licenses. And to do that, I need your friend Charlie and his yacht."

"Now that wasn't too hard, was it?" Kayla asked, and she clearly was irritated with him, but you know what? Connor just did not give a shit at the moment.

"Kayla, just tell me if you can invite the man, OK? Because if it is too much or it is too hard, I can go and look for somebody else. I just can't spend my entire day convincing people that I'm the one in charge around here. Neither should I have to."

"You don't. You should, however, clue in the people around you what's happening and what you are doing, so they can follow your lead in a sensible manner."

And have to explain myself the live-long day, Connor thought, and fought down his irritation hard. No matter what—he still needed Kayla and her contacts and her media savvy. *For now. Always remember for now, dearest Kayla.*

"You know how I get when I get excited," he said, putting as much charm into it as he could. Dammit, this was just way too annoying. "Now about this fellow, Charlie Weaver."

Weaver—what kind of name was that anyway? Weaver the Beaver. He chuckled at his own enormous wit, and Kayla took it as an apology.

"I will invite him. He and his wife are actually quite active in the charity sector, so they will respond well to your giving a lot of money to a compassion network."

"Some money—don't give away the store. We still have bills to pay, and we haven't started on the construction yet."

"I will be good, I promise. But making a statement simply does not come under 10, 15,000, you know. Small stuff does not get anybody's attention; it just makes you look like a poser."

A poser—more irritation. Connor swallowed hard and counted to 10, then again. It did not go away, but he had his reaction under control. Somehow, he would make all of this happen. Because he had to, and he wanted to. He was this close to showing them all, and finally, everybody would have to admit that he simply had the superior skills and intelligence. The hell with them admitting it. Even if they did not, it would be obvious, out there, for everybody to see.

"Yes, of course, I completely trust your judgment, Kayla."

He hung up the phone and headed for The Lighthouse. A drink—a drink was what he needed just now to wash down this day. It was early, but people like him just did not fit into the conventional molds. That was for others.

THIRTY-THREE

The weeks to Kayla's party started to fly. Connor knew in the back of his mind that the one person he should be most worried about was Mirko. Mirko Whatshisname. He had seen it on the share issuance; he had written it down carefully, made up the treasury order, and then thrown the paper away, not wanting to be reminded on a constant basis of that little transaction.

So he owed the man money—big deal. He owed Rafael money too, and a host of other people. Once Perfect Cannabis took off, none of this would even matter to anyone any longer. Big effing deal.

David continued to be a pain in the ass, as he had known he would, but man, what choice did he have? He needed an accountant. Actually, he probably needed one on staff. He just couldn't get himself to face that little fact. Accountants were as useless as tits on a—well, they were just useless.

Now, suddenly, they were facing the second quarter financial statements to be filed with the SEC. First quarter had been easy-breezy—no transactions, nothing material to be filed really. Now... David called him every hour on the hour, Tessa generated lists for him that grew by the moment and bored the daylights out of him... Christ, could the paper pushers figure this out amongst themselves and leave him to do his job? Which happened to be making this company grow and become successful.

He needed institutional investors—big guns, large amounts—but in order to attract those, he had to have his filings complete and signed off on. Blue Bayou had jumped ship already because of those damned filings.

But in order to get the filings signed off on, he needed David to sort things out quickly and stop asking stupid questions. Shit. Some days it was enough to make him tired of holding all those strings in his hands. Some days. Such was the life of a dealmaker.

He worked at it, not letting himself get too down because of all of those little things, but it wasn't an easy job. He built himself up—every day, when he went to see investors, he spent half an hour mentally building himself up, getting into winner mode, and going out there to slay the dragons. All of this irritation was starting to mess with his game. He hadn't managed to land anything but small-time investors in weeks. Little stuff that was gone by the time he paid Tessa and himself and a couple of utilities, depending on his mood. It had to be the irritation that was causing it, because if there was one thing he knew how to do, then it was sell.

And then there was Kayla. Her party had become a rock-star event by now. If he heard her one more time nattering on about the famous names she had invited, the money people, the stars, the entertainers...

Normally, he would have been happy to indulge her, but this time, it was costing him big-time. Christ, did she have to bring movie stars in by helicopter? Wasn't that, like, just a teeny-tiny bit over the top? If they'd had at least been people he had heard of—but, no, she had to pick some over-the-hill B-listers who would hang around, drink his booze, and generally contribute nothing to the effort.

If he had done this himself... For the hundredth time, if he had done this himself, things would have progressed a lot better and a lot faster—but no, he was surrounded by ineptitude.

His phone rang, and Connor looked at the screen. Where a couple of weeks ago he would have been excited to take the call—any call—he did not go near anything right now that did not look 'safe.' Any unknown number might be someone wanting money from him or, God forbid, Mirko.

Mirko had been quiet for the last while, and while he counted that as a blessing, Connor also knew it would not last. Eventually, the man would want his money back, or... Or. That particular word made him sweat. Or...

He'd had to go borrow ten grand from his mother to keep Mirko happy just recently, and if his father found out... Never mind. He would simply make sure it did not happen again, his father wouldn't find out, and all would be good. Soon enough, all would be good anyway. If only those paper pushers got off their asses...

"Connor, I have two questions for you."

"Two—that's a new record, Catherine. Don't you usually fire them at me by the six-pack?"

"Funny. You promised me some payments last week—your bill has run up a lot, as you well know."

"As I well know, and you will be paid, Catherine—you will be paid. I am just waiting on an investment that should hit the bank probably Friday, and you will be among the first ones to get a check."

"I hope you mean it this time. I have heard this before."

"This one is already committed, Catherine. He wants to be part of it. The man just has not got around to wiring the money, that's all. Things are progressing very nicely. There are a lot of investors lining up."

"Save it. Just make sure I get paid."

"You said you had another question?"

"I do—McDowell. The name mean anything to you?"

"McDowell—not really."

Connor stared off into the harbor beyond his office window and chewed on his fingernail, when it finally hit him. McDowell! $5,000 guy. Shit!

"Well, apparently, he is a shareholder, and I am not sure what his deal is because I have in my hands his vote in the amalgamation vote—but he clearly does not recall having signed it."

"Weird," Connor said, making a tight fist with his right hand. "Maybe he is just old and forgetful. If you have his vote in your hand, he must have signed it, don't you think?"

"The rest of his memory seems pretty sharp, Connor. I don't know. Would you please look into it? Just talk to him—I'm sure you can straighten it out."

"I don't know why you bother me with minutiae like this, Catherine," he countered. "I am the CEO of the company. Small stuff like a shareholder being forgetful surely can be handled by my assistant, don't you think?"

"No doubt, but when I asked Tessa, she said..."

"Just discuss it with her, will you please? I don't have time for this kind of nonsense. I have other things in the life of this company that need my attention—my full attention—and really can't devote any more than that to it."

He hung up on her and flung his phone onto the desk. Stupid idiot! What was he trying to do—make the amalgamation invalid and ruin the whole deal? Not like he could—but lesson learned. Never, never, ever, deal with people who were too stupid to understand how the investment game was being played.

Connor got up and paced his office like a caged animal. Progress, he needed progress. He needed things to be moving to start making money. Once his shares hit ten bucks a piece, even idiots like McDowell would have to admit that Connor had done the right thing. If he just did not have so many Goddamn idiots standing in his way.

"Tess?"

"Yes, Connor—did you need something?"

"Any word from David on the filing?"

"It's with the auditors—that's what he told me the last seven times you asked."

"And I'm going to ask as often as I damn well please, you got that?" Connor struck his desk with the palm of his hand. "What are they doing, for Christ's sake? Are they playing Monopoly or auditing financial statements? It's a straightforward issue...I just don't understand what their problem is."

"There are some transactions they don't understand and need clarification on. David has been going crazy trying to explain."

"Well, obviously, he's not doing a good enough job at it, or this would be done already, wouldn't it? And who picked these auditors anyway? They're completely incompetent."

"Simon recommended them, remember? He said they had done a good job on another company he knew, and they were the only firm who would touch a cannabis issue."

"Well, Simon does not have to sit here and deal with them," Connor snapped and rolled his eyes. "This should have been done weeks ago. Fucking incompetence. Let me call him. He had better put pressure on those morons... Why the hell do I have do everything myself around here?"

Tess lingered in the doorway, and for a moment, Connor spread his hands, as in what, do you want anything else? Then it dawned on him.

"You too, Tess? You're going to stand there with your hand out like every other idiot I've had to talk to today? Really? Is that what you are telling me? We've been working together for, what, five years now? And you are going to stand there, 'Connor, when am I gonna get paid...' You know how this thing works."

"Well—I know—and you've always come through..."

"And I will this time. Goddammit, Tess, don't go whiny on me now, please."

"I'm not going whiny, Connor—I just have rent that needs to be paid and food that needs to go on the table."

"Well so do I, Tess, so do I."

He paused for a moment and ran his fingers through his hair, making a frustrated sound deep down in his throat.

"Forget it. Sure, I'll get you something at the beginning of next week. Is that going to work?"

"Yes, of course, and thank you."

"No problem."

He already spun through the contacts on his phone.

"Connor, is everything OK? I mean, you've been—tense—lately and preoccupied. I just wanted to make sure...."

"Everything is fine, Tess. Don't worry about it. Don't go seeing ghosts where there are none. All I am is tired of putting up with people of lacking intelligence who have to be led by the hand to see what's good for them."

When she was gone, he slumped back in his seat and cursed softly. He really could not afford to lose Tessa; she held all the strings together back here at the office. Without her, he wouldn't even know where one single piece of paper was located. Except that he knew she had some sort of online space she organized, and she had shown him a dozen times how to use it—but, fuck, he couldn't be bothered with that kind of thing on top of running the company, right?

Except even Tess had to realize that she was working for a startup, a company that was going to be huge and invincible—one day. For now... for now, it might be a good idea if she cut back a few days a week and made some money with her—computer stuff, whatever that was.

Mentally, he composed a memo and cursed her for not thinking of it herself. Christ, the woman was young, but she had a good head on her shoulders. Should she not have seen that she needed another income in this type of situation? Well, shouldn't she have? Damn straight she should have. Once again, who had to do all the thinking around here? Connor Beauregard, that's who. And he was getting damn tired of having to do it all the time and for everybody.

His phone vibrated in his hand, and he looked down to see Mirko's phone number. Carefully, as if it might break it, he silenced the phone and put it down on his desk. This—he really did not need right now.

THIRTY-FOUR

By the time the morning of Kayla's party rolled around, Connor felt as if he had gone 10 rounds with some heavyweight boxer whose name no one remembered. He vaguely recalled having gone to The Lighthouse the night before, just to relax a little and not have anyone ask him for money.

Rafael had been there, of course—mercifully not asking for money—and picking up the tab when Connor's credit card was declined. He'd shrugged it off as one of those things, but in the privacy of the men's room, he punched the wall until his knuckles turned crimson.

He knew how to do this. He knew how to run a company properly, grow it and make it successful, so why—why on God's green earth did he always run into these snags, incompetent people and investors who just could not, for the life of them, understand what he was doing? Why? Somebody answer this question to him.

Rafael had said some nonsense about wanting things to work too fast too easy and too smoothly, but somewhere along the line, he must have got seriously drunk because Rafa called him the specialist on 'getting 'er done.' So that did not even make any sense—but what the hell.

Then the real drinking had started...

Mercifully, the rest of the evening was a blur. Kayla had actually sent him away to 'go have fun with the boys,' so she'd never even missed him, buried as she was in some sort of last minute lists and minutiae for her big shindig. Shindig. He was starting to hate that phrase.

Realistically speaking, though, it was him who would have to stand there in front of all of her guests and speak intelligently about the cannabis business. He'd have to get it together before then; he'd have to get himself into sales mode, make an effort to be positive. Right at the moment, he just wanted to throw up. What he really wanted was to get up, walk out that door, and just keep walking. Except this deal was too good. A business like this one only came along once in a lifetime. He could feel it.

If he screwed this one up—well, if he screwed this one up, he wouldn't have to worry about things any longer. He'd be dead, he knew that for sure.

If he wasn't dead anyway. Mirko had made some not-so-subtle hints last time they'd spoken on the phone. Mirko...

He'd caught a break a couple of days ago. A minor investor had given him a check, and he'd posted it and pulled the money right out and given it to Mirko. Tessa, of course, had noticed and wasn't speaking to him. David wanted to know about irregular postings to the accounts, and those damned auditors, those damned auditors would want an explanation.

Which he would find.

Connor dragged himself out of bed, washed three little white vitamins down with a huge glass of tomato juice, and stood under the rain head shower for a good 20 minutes. Then he felt almost human again.

Almost. He played with the vitamins in his pocket and decided otherwise. For once, he would have to wait. He really would have to kill at that presentation later. No need for slimy headlines—"Cannabis CEO Makes Presentation Stoned."

Yeah—that would go over.

Another half hour in the gym running on the treadmill with his iPod blasting techno into his ears, and he really was human again. OK—now the presentation really could get started. Now he was ready.

He would sell week-old newspapers if you needed him to. Connor Beauregard was back and back with a vengeance.

Again, he stood under the shower and dressed with utmost care. Kayla usually advised his fashion choices—and most of the time, it was easier to let her choose what he should wear, rather than listening to a litany on how a particular shirt or tie made him look more respectable, trustworthy, and honest. Today, however, he rejected one white shirt in favor of another and chose a different tie.

Kayla cocked an eyebrow and nodded approvingly. "Not bad either. A little more pushy, a little more forceful, but not bad either."

"I'm not here to be laidback and agreeable. I'm here to sell, to convince people to give me their money. And what, pray tell, is pushy about a Brioni tie?"

"You'll get it eventually," she said and ran her hand over his cheek. "At least your fashion choices are more conscious now rather than haphazardly wearing whatever they show in *GQ*."

Get real. These were the moments where he wanted to throw back his head and laugh—but not yet. Not quite yet. Over the last month, Kayla had been paying all of the bills, including the Brioni ties and the Cole Hahn loafers that were supposed to make him look successful, honest, and respectable. He had only sold a bare minimum of his Swiss shares to keep afloat. No point in getting rid of them now when the value was about to hit the roof.

After today's party...

After today's party, things would start to move into high gear. Politicians, movie stars, businessmen—all of them would soon be investors in his little company. All of them. He would make sure of that.

He downed a little more orange juice, his little nod to healthy living, and withdrew into his so-called office. He'd really just dragged a large table and chair into an empty guestroom at Kayla's, put down his briefcase, and called it an office. Here, people really could not find him. The doorman had strict instructions, and the elevator required a privacy key. If Connor did not want to see you, you did not get in. Sad that it had come to this, but sometimes, the road to success required a few sacrifices.

He opened his email to a handful of messages from Tessa, all relatively terse and depressive. That girl would have to find herself another job if she didn't change her attitude. Yes, he'd get her money—soon—but right now there simply wasn't any.

Catherine still went on at length about McDowell, who had forgotten to sign one thing or another, and David... David got most of his attention. If he would just finally push those financial statements past his idiot auditors.

He flew over the email and ground his teeth in frustration. "Missing backup documentation, unclear explanations, lack of proper authorization..."

He dialed on the fly before he had even finished reading the entire thing.

"David, what is this latest bullshit you've sent me? What on earth does lack of proper authorization mean—you want to tell me that? I am the CEO of this company..."

"Connor, Christ, you sound as if you're ready to shoot somebody. Cool it for a minute and let me explain."

"Explain, David, please do—these people had this file now for the last few weeks, and what have they done? Nothing! Just like everybody else, they're dragging their feet in order to run up a bill, and I will not have it. I need those filings complete so I can get on with the business of raising money. The one and only reason I'm in this mess is because of them. Now tell me what they want now."

"Share issuances. You've written out treasury orders for which there are no subscriptions or incoming money."

"So? I do that sometimes. I give shares to a guy who's done me a favor, shares to a guy who's been patient about his bill—what? It's normal. It's my company. Why the fuck would they care who I am giving shares to?"

"It's not your company, Connor. It's a public company. And you can't hand out shares like candy. I've shown you the rules. There is a specific set of circumstances..."

"Fuck the circumstances and the rules, David. If I need somebody on my side, I am going to write out an order to the transfer agent to get them some shares. Live with it. It's fine—they are all non-dilutive share issuances, so why would anybody care in the first place? If you need a piece of paper to make it so, tell me what it is, and I will make it up, but don't hold me up from doing business. You're killing me."

"No, you are killing this deal, Connor. You want to go to jail, that's fine, but you are not taking me with you. This time, I am not signing shit on your behalf that I damn well know is wrong, do you hear me?"

Connor did not answer for a moment at David's outbreak. The little accountant had never spoken to him like this; he had not dared. And all of a sudden, he treated him like a messenger boy? What the...

"Connor," David said, a lot softer this time, "I'm trying to keep you out of trouble, believe me. And making up documents at will and firing in electronic signatures is not cutting it. How long do you think before somebody notices and says something, really? Then what's going to happen? Do you want everything you've worked for going down the crapper because of something like this? I need you to lay low, do what I tell you to do, and stay out of trouble, just for a little bit while I straighten out this mess. Can you do that?"

"Kayla's party is tonight," Connor answered, which made just about as much sense as anything else, because he and David both knew he had no intention of changing his ways. "But I will give you until tomorrow. Hell, I'll even throw in the day after if need be, but then I'm coming down on these people like a ton of bricks, you got that?"

"I am going to try my best, Connor, really, I will."

"I'm not going to work with people who hold me up, stop me from doing business or act like I don't know what I'm doing, and that includes you, David, understood?"

He didn't wait for an answer, but hung up the phone and flung it onto the table. Accountants. Fortunately, they were a dime a dozen, and there was always somebody out there looking for work. OK, it had been a mistake to bring David back in, whining paper-pusher he was. After EC Oil—after EC Oil, they had all sworn they would never make another mess like this again, but you just couldn't cook a ten-course dinner and keep the kitchen clean at the same time, now could you?

Incompetence—nothing but incompetence all around him.

No matter what David and Catherine and the rest of them might think, there was a good reason he was running things and not them. They really wouldn't be able to grasp all the details anyway.

At the foot of that thought, he decided to rest for a couple of hours, since this shitty day wasn't going anywhere anyways, and he wanted to be fresh and in the best possible mood when the party started. What the hell.

THIRTY-FIVE

Connor had had his car washed and polished so you could shave in the reflection and pulled up to the building in the early afternoon.

Rafa, he realized with satisfaction, had outdone himself. The erstwhile scruffy, dirty, and smelly lot had been completely cleaned up, all the garbage dumped—somewhere legal, he hoped—and a crimson-red carpet rolled from the center of the lot to what would once be the front entrance. A legion of young men in dark suits waited by an enormous sign that read, 'Valet parking,' and Connor jumped out of the car.

"Good afternoon, sir—oh, Mr. Beauregard, it is you. Let me take the car for you, please."

"Do I know you?" he asked the young man who took his key, and the kid eagerly shook his head.

"No, but you don't have to—look..."

He nodded toward another sign, closer to the entrance, and Connor roared with laughter.

There it was, in man's high glory—a photo of Connor Beauregard in his best power suit, smiling for the camera. 'Building a Better Future,' the lettering read, and the way his arm was cocked in the photo, it looked as if he were inviting the guest to come strolling on into said 'better future.'

Rafael must have seen him coming because he stepped out through the double-wing glass doors and came toward him, grinning from ear to ear.

"Well, what do you think?"

"Cheeky bastard you are—but I like it. Where did you get the photo from?"

"Me, nowhere. Kayla, I have no idea, but she wanted to surprise you. Connor Beauregard—step right up into a better tomorrow."

"Surprise complete," Connor said and touched the four-foot-high cedars interspersed with white blooming orchids.

"Nice touch on the greenery and flowers—one would think… Oh."

He had reached the front door, and another waiter in a black suit approached him with a tray of champagne.

"Welcome to the grand opening, Mr., Beauregard. Would you care for some champagne?"

"Don't mind if I do. Dom, if I know my Kayla?"

"Yes it is, Mr. Beauregard, sir…"

"Jesus, I'm already impressed, and I'm not even inside yet," he said to Rafael. "What did you guys do, work around the clock?"

"And then some, my friend. I've had four complete crews working overtime to put all of this in, with Kayla supervising and cracking the whip. I tell you—that woman knows what she wants and how to get it."

"Don't I know it, Rafa, don't I know it."

He drained his champagne in one deep sip, put the glass back onto the waiter's tray, and finally put his hand on the glass door

"Here goes…"

The inside had been gray and dingy and, for a moment, it was tempting to think he might have ended up in the wrong place. Floors and walls shone in a bright white with a color-coded guidance system painted on the walls. "Administrative" in blue, "Grow Areas" in green, "Laboratories—restricted access" in yellow, "Storage—restricted access" in light grey, and so on and so on…

"Almost like we know what we are doing," Connor said and studied the layout map encased in Plexiglas on a pedestal. "Who did all of this?"

"Well, Dan and TC provided the plans, and I just played a little pretend. Beyond the big hall back there—where it says restricted access—that's really where everything still looks like what you saw a week ago, dingy and trashy."

"And if somebody wants the grand tour?"

"Not happening. Hard hats and protective shoes required... Besides, we have a virtual tour running on all the monitors."

"A virtual tour. Pray tell..."

Rafa shrugged and grinned broadly. "Spliced together images from the places we visited when we went to Denver and Oregon, together with a lot of informative slides from your very own investor presentation, construction photos, which I can drown you in, and a lot of stock photography of smiling young people in lab coats. Welcome to Perfect Cannabis Corporation time..."

"Christ, Rafa, you are the original gangster. Even I would buy this."

"Well, as you should, my friend—this is all your idea. Go ahead, enjoy it. Make it memorable."

Connor stepped forward hesitantly. He kind of felt as if he were visiting someone else's office. A very successful someone else, as a matter of fact. A large reception area had been erected on the right-hand side of the front hall, and given actual phone lines and employed staff—it could be in operation tomorrow. Where Rafa and his people had found the polished mahogany reception counter, the monitors, chairs and workstations, he didn't know—didn't want to know either, since it probably had not been a standard purchase—but it looked perfect.

A smiling young woman, complete with pillbox hat and scarf, greeted him cheerfully and chirped that he was at the head of her invited guest list.

"That is my accustomed place," Connor said and took another glass of champagne from a passing waiter.

"What does she do, work for an airline?" he asked Rafa in hushed tones. "Skirt and jacket, scarf, hat...?"

"Kayla's idea." Rafael shrugged. "Said we wanted to give the impression of uniforms. Everyone is a professional, everyone is just smiling, happy, happy. Voila, the pièce de résistance."

Another set of double doors opened, and Connor stepped into a former factory hall and put his hands together as if in prayer.

"I have come home," he said reverently.

The big hall shone in white and chrome splendor, just like the reception area. But here, enough greenery had been installed around the perimeter to give the impression of being inside a greenhouse. Red runners pointed a road around the place, and Connor could see the logical progression here. Bar number one, food and catering area, bandstand, bar number two. Along the left-hand side, a number of small tables had been arranged to allow for casual chatting areas. White tablecloth and silver ribbons carrying on the impression of clinical, squeaky clean. For the ladies in high heels, large white leather sofas had been brought in and placed amongst the greenery. In the center of it all, a wooden dance floor beckoned.

A beam of light crossed his path, and Connor stepped back, startled, but it happened to be merely an LED projector, hidden in the ceiling somewhere, projecting the lettering PerCan Corporation in bright green onto the pristine white floor. Matter of fact, there had to be a lot of these, since the wording randomly appeared on the floors and walls here, there, and everywhere.

Connor stepped up to one of the conversation areas and leaned against the table.

"Nice, private, and yet part of the whole thing."

"Just what you need to strike deal after deal."

"Two bars?"

"Stocked with the best my friend. $25,000 worth of liquor—some of it imported through channels only Kayla knows. Through that set of cedars over there is the smoking room."

"The smoking room—really—you've procured some product? Where, how—wait, don't tell me. I probably shouldn't know as CEO..."

"What do I look like, Connor, a moron? Cuban cigars, of course, imported through whatever contacts Kayla has. Cannabis only in the company name, really. But Kayla blows me away—she gets it done."

"She does at that," Connor murmured, his mind still stuck on $25,000 worth of liquor. And that was only the bar bill?

All of a sudden, he threw back his head and laughed, spreading his arms wide.

"25,000 bar bill—I am the king of the fucking world," he roared and laughed hard. "Yeah."

He hugged Rafael hard and grabbed another glass of champagne.

"Fuck, Rafa, this is it. We are here—we made it!"

Downing his glass in one huge gulp, he spun around, encompassing the room, the building, the lot, hell, the whole world in his arms. They had made it—they had truly, truly made it—and the entire world belonged to them. From here on in, it would be downhill all the way. People would be begging them to be part of this thing—begging. They would line up just to get a glimpse of how Connor Beauregard had changed the face of business, singlehandedly.

"Um, better pipe it down a bit, bro..."

Rafa tapped him on the shoulder and nodded toward the door. There, at the beginning of the red carpet, a vision in blonde and white appeared. Kayla wore a floor-length white gown, that might have doubled as a wedding dress in any other setting. She carried a glittering little purse that reflected sparks of light every which way and strode toward him, head held high, smiling, confident.

"I see things meet with your approval," she said, smiling, "although perhaps the CEO of the biggest cannabis company in the country should show a tiny bit of restraint."

"Fuck restraint." He picked her up by the waist and spun her around so fast they both got dizzy and stumbled to a halt, giggling. "We made it. We built this thing from when it was just a wine-soaked idea at the bar of The Lighthouse, Kayla. Now look at it."

"It is a monument," she said in a hushed tone of voice. "To your entrepreneurial spirit, knowledge, and talent. Your monument."

"Our talent." He took her hand and stood there, the king and queen, ready to receive their subjects. "You think we are being crass?"

"Just a tad."

"Well, fuck restraint." He roared with laughter and grabbed another glass. "To us—to our achievements, to Perfect Cannabis Corporation. May generations after us remember how it was built and by whom."

"Easy on the champagne, my love. You still have a number of speeches and a presentation to get through."

"Don't you worry—I can show this presentation in my sleep, drunk, and on drugs. Come to think of it, I think I have, and still I have sold more investors than anybody else. I am the king!"

Rafael shook his head and walked away to speak to one of the waiters. They wore little patches on their breast pockets, with the PerCan logo and bright green lettering—Perfect Cannabis Corporation. Kayla had thought of absolutely every little detail. Connor squeezed her hand, proud of her, proud of his own achievements. This, he decided in his mind, would be the best day of his life. Yes, it would definitely be the damned best day of his entire life, bar none.

At the same time, that thought carried a bitter sting. If this was the best day of his life, and he was only 35 years old, where the hell was he going to go from here? No, fuck that. He pushed the feeling down and took another gulp of champagne instead. Nothing was allowed to mess with the most perfect day of his life.

"I better go take position by the door," he said to Kayla. "Say hello to people as they come in. Makes a good impression that way. Why don't you stand with me?"

Kayla waved him on, smiling. "Go—this is your day. It should be just you. Go and enjoy your moment."

Connor took up position just past the wide glass doors. It was almost time—almost—and they would come to see him and his achievements.

As if on cue, cars started rolling up to the valet parking area, and well-dressed gentlemen and women strode down the red carpet toward the door.

Connor put on his most cheerful, brightest smile and extended his hand.

"Good afternoon , welcome to Perfect Cannabis Corporation. I am so glad you could join us to celebrate this milestone in company history. I am Connor Beauregard, president and CEO of the corporation. Please enjoy... Good afternoon, welcome to Perfect Cannabis Corporation. Thank you for celebrating with us this milestone..."

After a while, the words became an echo in his mind, and he repeated them, smiling, shaking hands, welcoming guest after guest, telling them how proud he was of this corporation and the fine things it would accomplish in the coming years.

A milestone.

An enormous achievement.

A shining moment in corporate culture.

Connor knew he had been standing there for several hours. He should by all rights have been tired, dead on his feet even, but he hardly felt the passing of time or the load on his body. The world was his, and he was opening the doors to show it to his people. Come and look at all the fine things Connor Beauregard had built, see the amazing structure he had built, from nothing, from nothing at all.

The smells from the main room behind him told him the caterers had begun creating their magic, soft strains of music from the jazz trio floated out to him, and the champagne just kept coming, along with the guests.

Press, media people, businesspeople, his own investors, celebrities— they all shook Connor Beauregard's hand as they entered the building and told him how fortunate the town was to have a trailblazer like him, a visionary, to build a corporation such as Perfect Cannabis and lead it to success. Connor could have gone on forever. This moment, this most perfect day of his life, could not end.

Kayla came up to him at a moment when the stream of guests had stopped for a minute and took his hand.

"Are you sure you're not getting tired? You've been at this for hours."

"I'm not even aware of it. I'm enjoying it. How is it inside?"

"Wonderful. The food, the music, the decorations—all perfect. People are enjoying themselves. They are getting ready for their speeches. As soon as the minister and Harvey Watson get here..."

"Harvey Watson—you invited Harvey Watson?" Connor asked of the movie star who had done a number of action style movies just recently. "Really? I didn't think he would do affairs such as this one."

"Well, I had to do a little—convincing. But he will give us tons of the most beautiful press, you know."

"Define *convincing*."

Kayla cocked her head and listened for something, then all of sudden smiled.

"I don't think I have to."

"What do you mean?"

Kayla put a finger across her lips and cocked her head. "Listen," she said quietly. "There he is."

Connor listened, but all he could hear was the clatter of a far-off engine—getting closer. Rat-a-tat...

"Oh my god. No..."

Kayla smiled. "Yes, I did."

The clatter got louder and closer, and Connor looked up. There in the sky it was—getting closer and sinking slowly. A bright green helicopter with silver lettering: 'Perfect Cannabis Corporation.'

"You bought a fucking helicopter?"

"Well—leased it for a little while. You like it?"

"Wow."

For the first time in his life, Connor found he couldn't speak. The best damned day of his life just had gotten about 20 times better. His own fucking helicopter.

A searchlight traced out from somewhere behind the building, found the helicopter, and traced out the Perfect Cannabis Logo, making it sparkle.

"Fucking awesome," he finally said and strode down the red carpet to stand where the helicopter would finally land.

He forced himself to stand still and look up toward the landing aircraft, even though everything inside him screamed to bounce around, wheel his arms, and scream, "My helicopter—is everybody seeing this thing? My own fucking helicopter. Beauty."

The sleek, long aircraft descended slowly, the retractable landing gear appeared, and Connor recognized the model—the famed Sikorsky s-76, same one Donald Trump bounced around in somewhere over New York City...

Beauty—sleek, white, and shining with the bright green logo. He'd be able to invite at least 10 of his investors to come along no matter where they went. This thing had an incredible range, and it could fly into the nastiest conditions you could throw at it. Oh yeah, he had wanted one of those. He'd contemplated the jet after their first trip to Denver and Oregon, but this—this was even better than the jet.

A few other guests joined him outside, wanting to know what all the noise was about, and he heard them comment on 'his' new toy. Basically, everybody wanted one of those. Basically, nobody could afford them, and hell if Connor Beauregard did not do things right—just because he could.

That's right, fuckers. Take a good look. This is what I have built, he thought, and stood a little straighter, and finally walked up to his helicopter when it had settled on the ground. Shit, he'd never even noticed they had put in lights for the thing to land.

The door opened slowly, and flashlights started popping behind him. Connor broadened his smile a little and straightened his shoulders.

The wait became almost unbearable until the doors finally slid open as if by magic. A young man hopped out, took position beside the door—and

Harvey Watson appeared. Camera flashes unleashed a veritable light storm behind him. Harvey stepped out of the plane, bounced down the red carpet as if he did this every single day, and finally shook Connor's hand.

"Mr. Beauregard…"

"Welcome to our grand opening, Mr. Watson. Welcome to Perfect Cannabis Corporation."

"Call me, Harv, will you—and thank you for inviting me." He sniffed the air a little and grinned. "Don't smell anything about it out here, or is it because of the helicopter?"

"Well, of course, there is no actual cannabis…" Connor hurried to keep pace with the man. "We are not—er—in operation yet. But we are building one of the finest production facilities for medical cannabis…"

"No actual cannabis yet, eh?" Harv laughed and shrugged. "Well, fortunately, we came prepared, and we can change that."

"Yes, sir—Harv—but I just wanted to tell you…"

Whatever he wanted to tell Harvey drowned in the questions and the hail of flashbulbs the media people fired at Harvey, their star.

Connor fought down his irritation. After all, that's what he had wanted—media attention for Perfect Cannabis and their project, their building, their plans… He had just kind of assumed the attention would center around him. Never mind. He had yet to make his presentation and—and then there was the helicopter…

He turned around again, only to bump into Kayla.

"Like the surprise?"

"The helicopter or Harvey?"

"Harvey was a last-minute addition. All I had on the guest list were B-listers and has-beens. My girlfriend heard a rumor he could be hired."

"You hired him? We're giving him money to be here?"

"'Course." Kayla shrugged. "It's all publicity. You shaking his hand will be in all the papers by tomorrow—page one. With your helicopter."

"My helicopter." He walked up to it again, since Harvey Watson now had disappeared inside the building, followed by the phalanx of reporters and celebrity-hungry guests. The rotor had stopped turning, two pilots still fussed with one thing or another inside the cockpit, and the young assistant who had held the door for Harv collected a few things from the inside.

"Nice machine," he said to Connor. "Mr. Watson was going on and on about wanting one on the way over here. Jeez—you could live in here..."

"No doubt," Connor said shortly and took another step closer. The interior might have been a small meeting room or a luxury suite at the Hilton. Wood paneling gleamed with a sheen enough to see yourself in, and cream, deep leather upholstery just invited you to sink into it.

One deep sofa ran the entire length of the aircraft, with little mahogany panels popping out of the upholstery in convenient spaces to hold your drinks or notepads. Other seats were arranged in private little groups, with a small table in the center—perfect to hold little private meetings. In a damned helicopter—in the air!

Each one of the tables had the Perfect Cannabis logo inlaid in gold into the gleaming mahogany, and the wide, flatscreen TV at the end of the cabin, where the doors to the cockpit now stood wide open, displayed the same logo in 3D, now rotating slowly. Below the TV, glass panels protected the bar, vintage champagne, crystal glasses, and fine wine. Every dream he had ever had came to life in here.

"This gives me ideas," he said and squeezed the soft leather, winking at Kayla.

"I like your ideas."

"Presentation first. Need to get some money out of those suckers—investors, I mean—before we can think about fun. This baby needs to be paid for."

Lovingly, he patted the leather again, took one look at the polished little meeting table and the shiny gold fittings everywhere, and closed the door again.

"Work first. No—drink first. This waiting for a helicopter has made me thirsty."

They were the last people standing out on the lot, waiting to be allowed into the helicopter, while Harvey probably held court inside about his latest movie or some such nonsense. He would take his moment of glory away from him; that much was sure. Getting paid to party with you. That alone was ridiculous—although not a bad idea, considering the bar bill he would leave.

Connor would take control again; he just needed to gather himself for a minute. And get a drink and perhaps a couple of vitamins for pep and energy. Then he would be invincible.

"Go, entertain," he said to Kayla. "I just need a minute. I will be right back out."

"Are you OK? You are not going to..."

"I am fine. Jesus, all I need is a minute to prepare. It really irritates me when everything I do is being questioned."

"Fine."

She clicked away on her ridiculously high heels, and every movement of her body let him know just how pissed she was—but he could hardly worry about that right now.

The waiter at the door had replenished his champagne tray, and Connor took two of them with him. Somewhere around the corner, Rafa had put in a little extra room for his maps and plans and all of his other stuff—right. He opened a door, found a desk and leather chair, and fell into it. Five minutes, just five minutes...

Once the door had closed behind him, he closed his eyes and took a couple of deep breaths. *Winner mindset now. You are the master of the game. Oh yes, I am—I am the ruler. I have a goddamned helicopter out there waiting for me. I am invincible. I rule, I make the damn rules, and I am the master of the game...*

Eyes open, shoulders straight. I am the master. I rule.

He looked into the mirror, directly into his own eyes, and repeated it a few more times. *I am the master—I rule—I am invincible...*

Then he had the mindset. Just for good measure, he took a couple of his vitamins, washed them down with the champagne he had brought, and basked in the warmth and the sharp, edgy feeling spreading inside him.

Oh, yes, this was all his, his creation, his show—his.

The last of the champagne. Damn, it was all gone... Never mind, there was an endless supply of it out there—after all, he was Connor Beauregard, and he ruled the game, and he decided. He decided what would happen and when, he decided who lived and who died...

He opened the door and stepped out into the grand opening celebrations once again. Actually, he thought, for his presentation, he would ask Rafa to dim the lights just briefly and then bring them up to full brightness when he entered the room, just for effect. Yes—he liked that. The light would rise where Connor Beauregard walked. Indeed, he really liked that.

"Hello, Connor."

The voice—Connor froze in his tracks and turned around slowly. That voice...

And there he stood. Al's father—the Original Chef, Mr. Whatever His Name Was. The man who never left the dingy diner.

"Well hello there," he said, more cheerfully than he felt. "I was not aware you were coming to our grand opening—but welcome nonetheless."

"Perhaps because I was not invited," the man said mildly and smiled, leaving Connor to squirm. What the heck did he want here? What was he looking for—the helicopter? Had he seen the helicopter?

"That—must have been an oversight." He found himself groping for words. "I was certain Al would—I mean—we did not issue..."

"Don't worry about it, Connor," the man said softly. "I don't actually require an invitation. I go wherever I please. And tonight, I wanted to make a brief appearance here."

"Well, be sure to stay for the presentation," Connor said, straightening, physically and mentally. "I'm sure you will approve."

"Official presentations bore me. You should know that. I prefer to see behind the scenes, Connor, the things nobody else gets to see. That's where I want to be."

"Well, there is not really all that much to see—yet," Connor said, smiling, and spread his hands. "We are still working on developing this company and..."

"I don't need the press release, Connor." He patted Connor's arm softly like a benevolent grandfather and smiled. "I can see what you have been doing here—which is nothing at all."

"Yes, but we have started on the construction. I am sure Dan showed you the plans."

Connor hated the fact that he sounded defensive. He did not have to explain himself to this man, not at all. He was the president and CEO—he was the leader, for god's sake.

"You know there is a lot to building a production facility such as this one. There are rules—regulations—but we are making steady process. Pretty soon we will put in our first crop and then—then..."

"Then we will see, my dear Connor. I would say that you have everything at your disposal to make this the best darn company it can be—absolutely everything."

"Yes, thank you. I knew you would agree."

"All you have to do, Connor, is get out of your own way and let the people who really understand this business do what they do best. "

"Well, we—I—" Again, he groped for words and hated himself for it. What was wrong with him, dammit? This did not happen—this never happened to Connor Beauregard. "I have put an excellent team together," he finally said proudly. "And I have every confidence in the world that we will be successful and indeed build the best medical marijuana facility the world has ever seen." There. He had it again. "We are poised to achieve revenues..."

"My dear Connor—I told you I do not need the press release. But thank you anyway. I think I have seen everything I need to see."

The man smiled, nodded the merest hint of a greeting, and disappeared at the end of a long hall again. Even Connor did not know where this hall led, so how did he know?

"Oh," the man said, just as he opened a door to vanish, "nice helicopter by the way."

And he was gone.

Connor stood there, mouth agape, like a schoolboy who had been dismissed. The sheer anger made him clench his fists so hard he could barely think. *Jesus Christ, Connor, get a hold of yourself.* His fists shook with repressed rage, and he could hear his breath rasping hard. *Get a damned hold of yourself.*

Again, he straightened with an effort, pulled his jacket straight, and squared his shoulders. It was easy. This man obviously had no clue what he was talking about, or he would have seen the amazing progress Perfect Cannabis had made since the day he decided to become involved. Obviously.

"Everything OK?" Rafa appeared beside him like a shadow, and Connor shook his head.

"Al's damned father snuck in here somehow, and he just disappeared down that hall."

"Down that hall." Rafael frowned. "Nothing but empty warehousing space and construction debris down there. That's weird—want me to have a look?"

"No, don't." Connor took one last clearing breath and made an effort to smile, confident that he had himself under control again. "Never mind. It's all good. The man just wants to freak me out—why, I could not tell you. Perhaps he is planning to take over."

He laughed at that, but even to his own ears, it sounded hollow and made up. Did he? Were there people waiting in the wings to take this thing over, as soon as he had the license arranged and the building built out the way it needed to be? They couldn't—they wouldn't dare.

"He is just trying to mess with my head," he said again, reassuring himself. "And that's the last thing I need just before the presentation."

"OK then." Rafael took one last look down the corridor where Al's father had disappeared and shook his head. "Still weird, though..."

Connor took a few deep clearing breaths and nodded. "It's fine, Rafael, really. I can't afford to think about this kind of nonsense right now. I need to be concentrating on the presentation. I can't have any other mindset at the moment but successful, dynamic, and wealthy, or it will come through, understand?"

"If you say so." Rafael shrugged. "I'm good—but the moment I see anything else hinky going on, or if you do..."

"If I see anything, I will let you know."

Connor hoped to God he did not. The encounter with the 'Chef' had shaken him more than he wanted to admit, and this presentation he was about to give could turn into one of these make-or-break moments of his life.

Think success...

He made himself smile, gave Rafael a thumbs up, and walked back into the main area, head held high, steps measured, confident and sure. *Fake it till you make it, Connor.*

"That was more than five minutes—everything OK?" Kayla appeared beside him and took his arm, smiling and waving at acquaintances in the crowd.

"Fine. Tell you later."

"If you are sure..."

"If one more person... Yes, I am sure."

She raised her hands and smiled.

"Fine—I will introduce you in a few minutes then."

Connor opened his mouth to contradict her and stopped himself. No, let her. It would not hurt at all to be introduced by a beautiful, successful woman who was obviously smitten by him. Expectations—set up their expectations and follow through. Another one of his rules.

"Go do that—and thank you."

He bent down and kissed her lightly, making sure the media folks saw it. After all, they were the ones who knew Kayla Montecito to be a wealthy and extremely successful woman. Bingo.

Connor had the rare gift to simply blank out everything he did not wish to deal with, did not want to see, or did not believe in and make it vanish. If he decided something did not exist, it did not. Period—end of statement.

Every time he picked up the phone to call an investor or spoke to someone in their office, he could read his own press releases, put on mental blinders, and nothing but the 'truth' he had written in his business plan or forecast or financial model need exist. It didn't. It was not allowed to exist and therefore never made it to the front of his brain.

Oh, people might warn him, talk about risks, tell him to be cautious—but he could stand there and tell them, "There is absolutely no way a disaster like this will ever happen; it simply cannot. I have set things up in a way it cannot."

His own personal truth became whatever he decided it to be, and because it was, he spoke with such conviction, such wide-open honesty, that his words never failed to make the desired impact.

Connor Beauregard simply could not lie. Every time he had to make a statement, he convinced himself of the truth—his truth—and it became so. Who needed to lie? Rafael would joke with him that he could pass any lie detector test in the world because at that moment in time, he would be so convinced of the veracity of his own words, the concept of a lie would never even occur to him.

Right now, he needed to focus on the facts in his presentation: the money they were going to make, the revenue they would generate, the jobs they would create, and the patients they would help. Nothing else was allowed to exist in his world just then.

Not even Al's father and his sudden appearance and disappearance.

Especially not Al's father.

Connor felt good about it. He had made every preparation he needed, he had clued Rafael in on his plans for the lighting, he had primed his guests with the symbols of success—the champagne, the hostesses, and let's not forget the helicopter—and now he simply needed to open his arms, and they would come to him. Just like they used to come to his father.

He felt the lights dim and disappeared in the shadows at the far wall of the room. The thunderclaps and bells his father used might have been a nice touch, he thought and chuckled softly. No—too much over the top, too old-school. No, just a very subtle raising of the ambient light and an extra blast of wind from the air circ system. That was enough; that was all he needed. And a kickass sound system and presentation monitor that filled the entire wall, 15 feet by 30.

He had thought long and hard who should announce him to the assembled guests—and still, there was no one better that Kayla. A local celebrity, most of the guests would know her, or at least have heard of her, and those who had not were most certainly acquainted with at least one or two of her publications.

Usually, the gossip magazine which outsold every serious publication or newspaper, although no one would admit to reading it.

Connor grinned. Hell, he had taken a liking to the rag himself. Did it not make him feel better about his own problems and antics and remind him that heck, at least he wasn't as bad as 'those' people?

So, he had chosen Kayla, who had accepted the invitation with grace and delight. She had come a long way from the blonde airheaded widow of Hanson Montecito, the publisher he had met a long time ago. Connor had to admit once he passed the ball, she had caught it and run with it, without a lot of extra coaching from him. Although that coaching made all the difference in the world.

Cinderella had just been waiting for someone to come along to teach her what she needed to know—someone like Connor Beauregard. He had made her and make no mistake.

Now he watched her move through the crowd, shaking hands, making small talk here and there, making sure everyone felt as if they were getting her attention. She had grown, somehow. Connor felt a stab of pride at that, although affection it probably wasn't. Affection was for losers—made you go soft, made you vulnerable, and people like him could not be vulnerable. Kayla was useful; that was it. He felt the pride of a craftsman who had created a fine tool.

Now he waited and flipped through a printed version of the presentation he was about to give. They were everywhere. Little stacks of glossy brochures—nice job those. Al had arranged to have them printed, said he knew a guy... Al always knew a guy, Connor thought and fought down his irritation.

That moment earlier when he looked up and straight into Al's father's eyes still stuck in his mind and in his bones, and he would rather not think about it. It made a cold shiver go down his back, and as he had told Rafael—he could not afford to think about Al's father just now.

Carefully, he put the presentation down, took a deep breath, and listened to the jazz trio ending their performance. People clapped, and Kayla stepped out into the spotlight around a sleek black little podium. The floor-length white dress swirled around her, her long blonde hair danced around her shoulders, and she clapped with excitement and grace.

"Thank you so much. That was wonderful. Ladies and gentlemen, please give a hand to our wonderful musicians."

Again, applause, and Kayla joined in politely.

"Now, ladies and gentlemen, I have the honor of introducing an exceptional man to you. Most of you know him already. Some of you have the honor of calling this special, talented, and exceptionally gifted man a friend. Ladies and gentlemen, Mr. Connor Beauregard has singlehandedly taken an idea and built a public company from it. He is brilliant, charismatic, funny—he is one of the most inventive and creative businessmen I have ever met. Will you please help me welcome tonight—Mr. Connor Beauregard."

On cue the light became a little brighter, the fans stirred the breeze a bit more, and Connor stepped into the light with sure and determined strides, raising his hands in the manner of his father to quell the applause.

"Thank you, thank you so much. Thank you, Kayla, for the inspired and kind introduction. I am not sure I deserve it, but thank you. Let me just get started by clearing up an error—I did not build this company singlehandedly. No, I put together an amazing team of experts who blow me away on a regular basis with their commitment and their ideas. They humble me, with their knowledge and their dedication, even when times are tough; it is because of them that I work as hard as I do."

Always strive to be humble, his father would have said—*even in your humility, they will want to lift you up even higher. Only the truly humble deserve to be exalted.*

So Connor did humble. He did not particularly care for it, but he had been raised on the right moves and phrases—and they worked. Every. Single. Time.

"Ladies and gentlemen, welcome to Perfect Cannabis Corporation. I see a lot of familiar faces here, but for those of you who don't know or walked into this party by accident, looking for the Bus Driver's Association annual general meeting—Perfect Cannabis Corporation is a public company operating in the medical marijuana industry. We are trading on the OTCBB, the so-called pink sheets, under the symbol PRCN. Current share price $5.50."

Connor took a moment to let the success of his new share price sink in.

"We intend to manufacture and provide the highest-quality medical marijuana on the market; we will help patients who are suffering from a myriad of chronic conditions to obtain their medication in a simple, perfectly transparent way. At this very moment, there are thousands of patients with legal prescriptions for medical marijuana who simply have no legal way to obtain their prescriptions. If they want to find any relief, they are forced into an illegal underground network of suppliers, and Perfect Cannabis will change all of that."

Connor took a moment to let the roaring applause from the local compassion network rise and slowly subside again. They were sitting over to his right, and he was about to hand a substantial check to them. He smiled as brilliantly as he could at their president and leader and the applause rose again.

"You are standing here," he continued and paused again, because they insisted on clapping again, "you are standing here in our newly acquired building, which will serve not only as our worldwide headquarters but also house a 200,000-square-foot production facility—the most modern, advanced, indoor growing facility of its kind, bar none. Let those figures sink in for a moment, ladies and gentlemen. 200,000 feet of the most advanced technology and knowledge to grow marijuana and produce the medicine these people so desperately need. This is the very reason why we are here.

"I have assembled an unrivalled team of experts in their field, assisted by an experienced management team, and we will enter the market as the largest producer in the country. Our knowledge, expertise, and experience are unbeatable—I can guarantee you that.

"Along with production, we are committed to research and development of new technologies to continually improve our service to patients and to generate a constant global revenue stream. Our company will be in the league of the biggest in the country—in the world, given a bit of time, and tonight, I am inviting you to be part of this dream team, of this corporation that will one day be a household name."

Connor was in the zone now. He quoted facts and figures without even looking at his notes or at the slides on the walls behind him. He knew them by heart. He knew what he had planned and what he wanted to build. Hell, he might not know how to grow marijuana or how to clone a female plant, what color and temperature the light had to be and when—he knew nothing of the sort, admittedly—but he knew enough to put the experts in charge when he needed to.

He looked around and could see he had them spellbound. They hung on every word, and he soaked it in. The more he believed it, the more they did. Except for TC, Al, and Tessa. The three of them stood together loosely, off to the side of the group, and their body language told him they were neither impressed nor amused.

They stood rigid, arms folded in Tessa's case, their faces closed off. None of them smiled at his humble jokes or followed the spirit of his speech. Quickly, he looked away again. Some little problem perhaps—he'd deal with it later. Right now, he needed to keep the spell up.

"For thousands of patients, ladies and gentlemen, we will change the way they are able to live their lives and manage their pain, but I realize that it may be too late for some. Some of them may not be able to wait eight months for us to finish construction and another six to prepare for the first harvest. Therefore..."

He signaled, and Rafael came from the shadows carrying one of those enormous printed checks that measured four feet by six feet printed on soft gator board.

"Ladies and gentlemen, I would like to present the president of the local compassion network with a small donation, to ease the suffering of patients right now and to show just how committed we are to ending the pain and suffering."

The check read $500,000. Alexa Thompson, the president of the compassion network, a mousy little woman close to 60, rose and clearly could not find the words. Connor held the check and motioned for Rafa to help her up to the podium. The flashbulbs from the assembled press threatened to blind him. Connor waded into it like a warm bath. This was his element, his life.

On his signal, Kayla appeared beside him. The Minister of Health, who had been seated beside Alexa Thompson, rose and congratulated both of them, on a whim possibly, but just in time for all of the photographers in the room. Connor basked in the glaring sun of his success. He had achieved everything, he had made it come true, he had reached the top.

Kayla took his hand, and he kissed it and smiled.

"We've done it," he said softly. "We have finally done it."

In the next 10 minutes, at least four people approached him and told him they would call him the next week, just to get more information about investing.

Alexa Thompson, nice choice. He would have to remember Kayla for inviting her. Just could not stop talking about the patients their money would help, the suffering it would end, and the gratitude of the people who really needed a miracle. A miracle—Connor liked that. Connor Beauregard, the miracle maker.

"Well, Alexa," he said, putting more warmth and kindness into his voice than he had ever even seen his father use, "this is what we do here after, this is why I built this company, and this is why we are all here tonight—to end suffering, and to put a new face onto medicine and pain management, wouldn't you agree?"

The press ate it up. He could see a few of the younger reporters scribbling, filing their stories over their cell phones already. This would be in the paper tomorrow, along with his picture. Connor Beauregard, the man who made miracles possible. Oh, yes—he definitely liked this.

There, by the grace of his talent and his dedication, one of the biggest companies in the country—heck, the world, might as well call it what it was, because he was heading there—had started, and they were changing the face of medicine.

"Nice show." Connor looked up, directly into Al's unreadable dark eyes. "You almost have me convinced you are the savior instead of a stock promoter."

"You're a terrible cynic, Al," Connor said, still on a high from his presentation. "This is what I do. I show our investors all of the reasons why they should put their hard-earned money into our corporation—and, as you found out tonight, the stock price would tend to agree with me."

"The stock price is largely jumping around because of speculators and because there are only a handful of free trading shares on the market. You know that better than anyone."

Connor said nothing and smiled, twirling his champagne glass. Heck, he did not have to argue with this fool tonight—or ever. If Al wanted to piss on his leg like a little street cur, let him. Connor Beauregard was the real hero here, and nobody—nobody could change that.

"David called me earlier; he has a few concerns."

"David is an accountant," Connor said, irritated. "He always has a few concerns, and if he does not, he makes them up as he goes along. You should know that. He simply does not understand how business works on this side of the table. We, the trailblazers who make things happen, need—a fair amount of wiggle room."

"Wiggle room? Wiggle room, Connor? I call a Sikorsky helicopter a little more than wiggle room. Matter of fact, I don't know what I would call it other than perhaps a tad over the top."

"A tad." Connor grinned, thinking of the giant beautiful machine in the sky with his logo emblazoned on the side. "And by the way, it is only leased for a little while. I need to be able to travel, and if I am going to find investors to meet our capital needs, I am going to need to travel a lot. So what is your problem?"

"There are such things as commercial airlines."

"And I am on a tight schedule." Connor put his champagne glass down hard enough to make a disturbing noise among the genteel murmuring and the soft strains of the ambient music. Immediately, he lowered his voice and folded his hands to contain the rising anger within him.

"What is this all about, Al? You want to stand here quibbling over a few thousand dollars with me, is that what you want? Then I suggest you come to my office tomorrow, and I'll open the company's books to you. You can have a look at anything and everything you want. But tonight—the opening night of our brand-new production facility—is not exactly the time to start this argument, would you not agree?"

Al had not moved during Connor's outbreak. He merely nodded softly.

"Point taken, Connor. I'm interrupting an important day in the company's history, which is unforgivable. I must warn you, though, that certain—excesses on the company's books have not gone unnoticed."

"And I will explain them—all of them—but not here and not tonight. Christ, is that why you sent your father here? To check out what was going on, to total up how much money I was potentially spending? That's kind of low."

Even for you, he wanted to add, but bit it back at the very last moment. Even in his anger, he knew that kind of comment was just out of place as Al's spying, but dammit...

"My father was here?"

Al seemed genuinely surprised. For a minute, Connor considered if he was lying to him, just to get a rise out of him, or playing his usual kind of games, but even he could not fake that kind of surprise. It was like his eyebrows shot all the way off his face, where usually he couldn't even crack a smile.

"Yeah—don't you guys talk when you're going out at night? Saves a bit of money if you carpool, you know."

"I was not aware," Al said softly. "I'll check with my father, what moved him to come here tonight and to see you."

"You go do that, Al... And by the way, when you talk to him, you tell him I run this company, and I run it the way I see fit. I have the experience and the education, and not to forget the reputation, to make this the biggest and best medical marijuana producer in the world, and I will not have anybody interfere with my efforts, do you understand? Nobody."

"Hello, Al." Kayla appeared by his side, summoned by the tone of his harsh words, and took his elbow. "Nice to see you here tonight. Are you enjoying our little celebration?"

"Very much so, Mrs. Montecito." Al bowed slightly. "Now, if you will excuse me, I have some matters that need attending to. I simply did not wish to miss this wonderful party. Congratulations."

He shook Kayla's hand and Connor's, his eyes once again dark and unreadable, indicated another bow, and disappeared just like his father, almost as if they managed to vanish into the background. Connor hated these people from the depth of his soul.

He made an effort to unclench his jaws and forced a smile to appear on his face.

"Everything all right?"

"A minor disagreement, love, nothing else," he said, by way of convincing himself. "You know—running a large public company is just so completely different from running a number of second-rate, shady clubs and pubs..." He shook his head. "Al is a decent businessman; I sincerely believe that—as long as he stays in his league and does not try to interfere with our business."

"Is that what he is trying to do? I don't quite understand why he is giving you a hard time—over what?"

"Envy, hurt pride—who knows..." Connor took Kayla's hand and slowly walked toward the crowd again, smile firmly plastered in place and the feeling of being a king presiding over his people washing back over him and enveloping him with its gentle warmth.

"What I—what we—are doing here is magnificent. And—I hate to say it—there is an element of envy there because he knows he would never be able to do the same thing, not in a million years, not with all of the money his family has. So he has to lash out at me to make himself feel better. It's all right. I can handle it. I know who I am and what I have accomplished here. "

He squeezed her hand again and nodded greetings to a few guests.

"Now, let's go find your friend Charlie Weaver, and our wonderful Minister of Health. It ought to be a strange coincidence if we can't arrange a little sailing excursion, don't you think?"

"I have told Charlie we may need his expertise and equipment to entertain some very famous guests. He is positively giddy with excitement."

"Giddy is good, my love—giddy is something I can definitely use right now. Lead the way."

Charlie Weaver turned out to be a ruddy-faced man of close to 60 who had spent much of his spare time on one or the other of his sailboats. Apparently, he owned a number of them, and Connor still did not quite know what the exact differences were, but he was a master at nodding and saying, "I see—yes, that makes perfect sense," in the right places, so the man actually believed he was talking to another expert.

For the life of him, Connor could not see any purpose in spending several days every week racing boats around buoys in the lake just to see who could do it faster and better than the rest of the group, spending all of one's time and money on said pursuit of racing around little buoys. But, as long as it got him to where he needed to be, he would stand there and profess fascination with the intricacies of regatta racing. Kayla, thank his lucky stars, had spent a few hours coaching him on the proper terminology, phrasing, and famous names he needed to know. Piece of cake. That's why the good lord had equipped him with an eidetic memory.

Half an hour later, he had Charlie Weaver convinced the president and CEO of Perfect Cannabis Corporation was indeed a secret sailing aficionado, and they were deep in animated conversation that really made no sense to Connor whatsoever. He congratulated himself profusely on still being able to carry on said conversation, punctuating it here and there with a well-placed, "It is such a darn shame I have hardly any time or spare funds to be out on the lake myself..."

"But, Connor—I may call you Connor, may I not—why did you not mention this to Kayla earlier? My wife and I would be delighted to have both of you out for a few afternoons of sailing, as often as you would like. My goodness, for a man of your position not to have some time to recharge is simply a crime..."

Kayla's cue. He smiled at her, and she nodded almost imperceptibly. The queen of gossip would now manage to introduce the honorable Byron Cartwright, Minister of Health, to the group, the conversation, and the shared afternoon excursions. Game, set, and match. Connor adored the moment when he had managed to set up the game pieces in the exact configuration he needed them.

Charlie Weaver still droned on, and he tuned him out, letting his gaze wander around the room and the crowd. Him. The people had come to see him—not Al, not his father, not Dan, nobody but Connor Beauregard, and that was the way it should be.

It only took him another hour, and Byron Cartwright—Ronnie, as they were calling him by now—was convinced only a stroke of luck had led him to this wonderful group of sailing enthusiasts who not only shared his passion, but were generous and authentic enough to share their good fortunes, their equipment, and their talents with him. Being that he was still only a beginner, albeit an enthusiastic one, he glowed with the excitement and anticipation of their planned long weekend excursion. What a wonderful group of people he had stumbled into.

"Ronnie, I am so looking forward to this. I cannot tell you how long I have waited to carve out some time just for me and this wonderful sport. It will be my pleasure to share it with you."

"Connor, the pleasure is all mine. Had I but known—I'm a rank beginner, as I have said. I will have to make sure not to embarrass myself."

"Please, Ronnie! You remind us all of the sheer enthusiasm and joy of learning and beginning—anything. After all, what is life if not a journey of learning and new beginnings? You know," he chuckled and looked deep into his champagne glass as if there were answers to be found, "I think one becomes a bit of a philosopher spending so much time out on the water."

"Oh, most certainly. One simply cannot help it! I say—just recently..."

"Would you excuse me for a minute? I am so sorry; there is something I have to take care of."

Connor narrowed his eyes. Just there on the fringes of the party moving from the dance floor into one of the larger groups he had seen someone. Someone who was most certainly not an invited guest. Someone Connor wanted to see anywhere but in this room.

He quickly moved to the other end of the room, but people stopped him, wanted to shake his hand, congratulate him on his speech, and by the time he finally reached the spot where he had seen him, of course he was gone.

He stood there, looking around, trying to rise above the murmur and movement of the crowd. Where had he gone? More to the point, why on earth had he come? OK, the why was not really such a big mystery—but what was his plan? What was his damned plan after everything Connor had done? Why now? Why today?

"What's going on? You look like you've seen a ghost. Is the Chef back?"

Rafael had appeared beside him soundlessly like his own shadow, and he startled Connor.

"No—worse."

"Worse? How could it be worse?"

"Mirko. I've seen him move across the dance floor and disappear."

"Mirko? The loan..."

"Hush."

"Yeah, never mind, sorry. That Mirko?"

"That one. Do you know any others? Because, by God, this is the time to tell me."

"I assume you're sure it was him, or you wouldn't freak out on me. Christ—I hardly know what he looks like, or I would send a couple of my security guys after him."

"Short, slimy, Eastern European..."

Rafael shook his head. "That will get everybody arrested from the—well, best not to say. No go, brother. You're going to have to stay with me until we spot him again. I'll take a quick camera shot and get the guys to escort him out. Wonder what he wants."

"Wonder no more—money, what else?"

"Now? Here? At the grand opening?"

"What better way to try to blackmail me into giving him more? Dammit—I miscalculated the day I got involved with him. I thought he would be reasonable."

They moved through the room together, tensely looking around. Rafael had an odd, efficient pattern in checking the room, Connor noticed, wondering why he had never spotted it before. They moved in odd circles and zigzags, but it seemed to be the quickest way to get a bead on every single person in the great hall.

"Not in this room," he finally said.

"All right, outside bar, coat check, auxiliary rooms."

"Auxiliary?"

"Power, heat, lighting, air conditioning—that kind of thing. We had to put an enormous amount of new services in here, you know. It used to be just a warehouse."

"I'm not arguing, just wondering."

"For efficiency, I moved it all into one old office area. Later on, we can always... Damn."

"Damn? What do you mean damn, Rafael?" Suddenly, his friend sounded alarmed and moved just a little bit faster, just on the edge of panic.

"He could shut this party down on the inside of 10 seconds if he cuts the power—and we'd have a massive panic on our hands. All these people running, trying to get outside... Throw in the massive alarm horn we installed in case of fire... What do you think would happen?"

His black, elegant suit jacket flapped behind him, and he picked up the pace even more, not bothering to hide the sheer emergency of this mission any longer. People looked, saw a man basically running outside, Connor following him—but Kayla did a superb job of distracting them. Outside of the great hall, Rafael stopped and barked brief orders into his two-way. Then he swiveled his head left—right.

"This way." He pointed down a darkened hall. "Fastest way."

Connor still followed. Somewhere along the line, Rafael had taken charge, and right now, he could not even care less. Mirko—the loan shark—the dark figure who never said two words when one would do and showed up with fine regularity every two weeks.

He would simply smile, say good morning, hold his hand out for the wire transfer order Connor put into it, and leave again. Easy. Except he did not take no for an answer; he had made that quite clear from the very beginning. No was not an option—ever—and he had made Connor assure him that he was aware of it and of the consequences.

They were never mentioned, those consequences. By mutual agreement, they did not have to be. And Connor would not have dreamed of being late with even one payment. He knew where they lived; he knew where they worked. Rafa had cussed him out roundly when he found out about Mirko, but by then, it had been too late and the deal done.

"You had no choice," Rafael said now, as if he could read Connor's mind. "Just tell me you did not stiff him on a payment—please tell me at least that, or I swear I am turning around now."

"What, do I look like an idiot? Of course I didn't."

'Course he did not, right? Trouble was the last couple of weeks had been kind of a mess between chasing investors, trying to stay away from Catherine and David, juggling the constant demands for money from regular suppliers, and an endless round of pills to keep his mood up, to wake him up, to allow him to sleep, bringing him up, taking him back down—whatever he needed at the moment.

Maybe it was possible. Maybe he had missed a meeting, slept through an appointment, plumb forgotten he was supposed to be somewhere. Maybe.

"I think..."

"You think, Connor? What is it you think? Tell me."

Rafael stopped in front of a plain, dark-blue metal door, hand on the handle.

"I need to hear something better than 'I think' right now, before I open this door, or I swear to God..."

"Rafael, the past couple of weeks have been sheer hell—stress from one end to the other—I never got more than three hours of sleep any given night. You think maybe I might have forgotten something here or there? You think maybe that wouldn't be by design but a sheer accident?"

"An accident..." Rafael pressed the ball of his hand against his forehead, the other still hovering close to the door handle of the auxiliary room door. "I need something," he said slowly. "If that man is in there, I need something better than 'I might have forgotten; I've been busy.'"

"Didn't you bring a gun or something?"

"A gun? A gun, Connor? No, I did not bring a gun. Number one, I am not a criminal, and not in the habit of walking around with a gun—which, by the way is illegal. Number two, this is a grand opening of a corporate headquarters. Why the fuck would I bring a gun? Can you tell me that?"

"Well you're acting like some sort of special ops security."

"I'm acting like the guy who is trying to save your ass—again—and you're not making it easy—again."

"Well, do something."

"Something..."

Rafael rolled his eyes and looked down at his hand close to the door handle.

Because suddenly it moved—it moved, and the door swung inward.

"Well, something would be good, gentlemen, rather than standing out here in the hallway having a grand discussion, no?"

Rafael took a step back, and Connor fought the impulse to run. Running would do him no good, not here, not tonight.

"Mirko," he said. "Welcome—welcome to our grand opening."

"Cut the bullshit." Mirko nodded at Rafael. "I'm glad to hear you did not bring a gun. What kind of man do you think I am?"

"Well..."

"I am a businessman, sir. I am here to make money. And I had an arrangement with this gentleman here only." He nodded toward Connor. "So, if you like, you may leave."

"S'all right." Rafael let his hands hang loose by his sides and another step toward Connor. "I think we are all businessmen in here, so I'm quite sure we can clear up any—misunderstanding—that might exist and move on to the business of the grand opening."

"A misunderstanding, is that right? How unfortunate. You always speak for your friend who has lost his considerable speaking power? Usually, he cannot shut up."

"Well just wait a minute here," Connor said, feeling his temper flare. "If you've listened to us from behind that door, then you've also heard that the last couple of weeks have been utter chaos. So, if I have forgotten anything—if—then it was an accident, for crying out loud. My PA should have reminded me and did not. I don't see where all of this is warranted."

"Ah—all of this." Mirko nodded sagely. "By that, you mean my coming here and hiding out in your utility room, threatening to kill your little party out there."

"I would probably feel better if you wouldn't use the word kill," Rafael said and slowly moved between Mirko and Connor. "It makes people think silly things, you know."

"Oh, I know," Mirko said, grinning again, a facial expression that transmitted everything but mirth and laughter.

He also did not correct his particular choice of words, and Connor shivered just a little.

"Look, Mirko, really, if I missed a payment, all that is is an accident. I wasn't trying to—skip out on you or anything."

"Not that you could, Connor. Not with this company and those investors out there who are so near and dear to you, or that wonderful woman by your side. But, you see, you and I have the same problem. We have a reputation to protect—a reputation as a businessman.

What do you think would happen if people thought, 'Oh, well, Mirko understands that accidents happen,' or, in your case, 'Connor cannot manage his money; he needs to borrow a ridiculous amount and can't even keep track of his payment schedules.' Now—neither one of those would be particularly good for our careers, do you not see?"

"I really don't see how ruining my grand opening is going to get you your funds any faster."

When in doubt, bluff your way out of it. Connor squared his shoulders and stood a little straighter.

"All it would accomplish is making people uncomfortable. I would blame it on shoddy construction, and there would be a couple of articles in the paper. Big deal. No such thing as bad publicity. Instead, if you come out to the car with me, I'll write a check for you..."

"A check." This time, Mirko actually laughed, a sound that was potentially more frightening than anything Connor had heard in a long time. "That is a good one, my friend—really." He slapped Connor on the back and then tightened the grip of his enormous hand around Connor's shoulder joint. "Really, is that the best you've got? You'll write me a check, and you think I am actually going to go through the trouble of taking it, going to the bank, depositing it, only to find out it is no good?"

The hand tightened a little more, and Connor winced.

"Mirko..."

"I am hurting you? Good, because I don't think you realize how serious all of this is. Let me remind you, only since you brought it up just now. We are still on a construction site. Accidents happen—all the time. Especially at a time like this one, when everybody runs around without protective equipment."

"Now really." Rafael stepped in a little and got right up into Mirko's face. "I don't think there's any need for this. We will make good on this, I guarantee you that. Message delivered. Now can we maybe shift down a gear?"

Mirko looked at Rafael for a long moment. They did seem to connect on some level Connor did not understand—something that excluded him in a way that he found deeply irritating.

"If it were just you, Rafael, I'd say no problem, give you a hard time about forgetting, and move on. And perhaps charge you 10 or 20,000, just to cover the trouble, time, and expense of showing up here tonight. But him..." A casual nod toward Connor. "Him I just don't trust. Do you understand that, one businessman to another?"

"I understand, Mirko. Truly, I do. But I am telling you, whatever the payment is Connor did not make—we are both good for it. Plus, your expenses, we don't even have to talk about it. And if you are interested in a few more shares..."

"Shares," Mirko almost spat. "Paper—nothing else. And if he runs the company into the ground..."

"I am not going to run the company into the ground, people!"

"Then it will be worthless paper. Do you not think I have been watching what he has been doing over the last few weeks? Nothing that would give me confidence—nothing. And yet he shows up here tonight with a giant helicopter, throwing a lavish event, all while not paying the direst of bills. That is the kind of businessman I am supposed to have faith in?"

"You know what, Mirko, you don't get to stand there and tell me..."

"Maybe he is not the type, but I am sure my name stands for something."

As one, the little group froze, and three heads slowly turned. There stood Al, backlit by the emergency light at the end of the corridor like some dark giant out of a cartoon movie. He moved slowly, casually, hands in his pockets until he stood with them.

"I am sure a man of your information sources, Mirko, is well aware that we own a large share of Perfect Cannabis Corporation, am I correct?"

"Well, yes, of course, Al. Forgive me—I did not see you out in the great hall earlier."

"No apologies necessary. Had I wanted you to see me, I am sure you would have. I'm sure you are also aware of the many and varied business interests our family has—indeed, several of the clubs you and your spies frequent belong to us."

"My spies... That is outrageous—I do not..."

Al made a dismissive gesture with his hand. "Do you think we are interested at all in the many little men and women you pay to drink at the better establishments, to listen in on conversations and find out who might be in some kind of financial trouble? That would be far too crass and obvious for us. Besides, you are in the money-lending business—not us."

Mirko said nothing, but his beady black eyes narrowed just a bit and fixed on Al with a deep and undisguised hatred.

"So, what do you want here?" he finally spat. "Plead for this fool so I leave his party alone and go home with a few shares and a check?"

"Oh, the way you say the word *check*," Al chuckled and shook his head. "Almost as if it were something dirty. But I understand—I have come here to offer you something much better."

"I'd really like to see that."

"I am sure you would," Al said, reaching into the inner pocket of his sports jacket.

Mirko visibly tensed, and his hands went to his sides.

"Oh, relax. Do you think I would be so foolish as to bring a weapon in here, shoot you with all those people out there, and think this could some-how end well? My God—there are surely better solutions than violence."

"If you say so."

Mirko, Connor thought, suddenly bore an uncanny resemblance to an exotic snake he had seen somewhere—coiled tightly and yet ready to strike, lethal, silent and just as deadly. He forced himself to suppress the sudden chill that made him shiver.

Al pulled a small brown envelope out of his jacket, convenient, palm-sized, just about the size of a pile of bills. Connor recognized an envelope full of cash when he saw one. And not just full—stuffed, ladies and gentlemen. The kind of stuffed that made you dream about taking off to a Caribbean island somewhere and living in peace and quiet.

He must have gasped involuntarily because Al cocked his head just a little and smiled.

"If you would like to count it, Mirko, it is all there, I assure you, but since we are both cautious businessmen, I will give you the choice."

"You would not dare stiff me," Mirko snapped and snatched the envelope out of Al's hands so quickly it almost dropped.

"You know my family quite well. Isn't it fun in this business we are in? There are only a few really big players, and they all know one another. Time to meet somebody new, my father always says, but then he never does."

Al smiled in that lopsided silly way Connor hated so much and folded his hands.

"Now that your demands have all been met, and you hold your money in your hands, what do you say we proceed to the enjoyable part of the evening? I hear Kayla ordered the most delicious champagne, and those hors d'oeuvres—I tell you, scrumptious, simply scrumptious."

"Stick it up to somewhere, Al—I'm not here to drink with this fool."

"Your loss, Mirko, I can truly tell you—but one simply cannot stop travelers or fools, so if you must go, you must. But you are missing something."

"I'm gonna pretend I did not hear you call me a fool, Al."

"Me? You misunderstand. I simply wouldn't. Now, let's all get out of this uncomfortable area of the building. I dare say it is hotter than Hades back here. Connor—lead the way."

The tension suddenly all but dissipated. Rafael rolled his shoulders and shook out his arms, the only sign that he'd been as tense as a broomstick.

"Thanks, Al," he said quietly, once Mirko had disappeared down through the door at the end of the hall. "No idea what that idiot would have done, but I'd really rather not find out."

"Oh, I don't think he was serious in any case. He backed off quicker than a jackrabbit when he saw who he was dealing with. His type is like the little Chihuahua dogs my mother used to have—noisy and annoying, but not seriously dangerous."

"Well, I'm so glad all of you think there was no real danger," Connor said, furious because his heart and his brain simply could not decide between relief and wild anger with Al for stepping in and solving everything in one stroke, and with one envelope full of cash.

And what an envelope! Connor shivered at the memory.

"I will pay you back, of course," he said weakly, and Al chuckled.

"No doubt, my friend, no doubt. I wish you had asked me before you borrowed money from this fellow. He is unpredictable and stupid—which in my book is one of the more dangerous combinations."

"I really…"

"We really did not have much of a choice, Al," Rafael said. "And we had come to your father often enough that it was a matter of respect to solve our own problems."

"A noble sentiment, Rafael," Al said and gave Connor a little sideways look, "but perhaps not the most brilliant thing in this kind of situation. Mirko's kind of people—they really can make a mess out of things because they are brutes. And they lack the intelligence to control that brutishness."

"Well, thank you anyway for solving this for us," Connor said a little stiffly. The look Al had given him when he said *noble sentiment, Rafael*—what, like he, Connor, did not have such nobility in him? Bullshit. "On behalf of this company and all of the people who are here tonight, I want to thank you for averting a crisis and an—unpleasant moment."

"Most unpleasant," Al said and opened the door at the end of the hall to let them back into the great room and the celebration. This was what it must feel like to step out of the space capsule, Connor thought all of a sudden. After the tension, heat, and darkness of the back hallway, the glamour, excess, and sparkle felt like a dream.

A good dream. Come on, it was still his party—the best day of his life.

He frowned to see Kayla standing with that two-bit actor Harvey and rushed over to take her arm.

"There you are, my love, is this man keeping you entertained?"

"Connor, I was starting to get a little worried—is anything wrong? All of a sudden, you were nowhere to be found, and people were starting to ask questions."

"Nothing—it was nothing at all love," he said quickly, deftly steering her away from that dumb action-hero boy and his unbuttoned shirt. "A small situation out back in the building. Fortunately, between Rafael and Al, they had it all under control within moments. No harm done."

"No harm—really, Connor, what you need to do is hire more people. You are the head of this company. It simply will not do to have you running around in back hallways dealing with small problems, the kind your staff should be able to handle without even involving you." She slapped him lightly on the arm. "I see I have a lot to teach you—you simply aren't used to not doing everything yourself."

"I just want it done right."

"And so you will, Connor—so you will. Now come with me. There are a few people I want to introduce you to."

The hell with it. Delegation, letting people do what they were good at and giving them the space to do it... Wasn't that what a good leader was all about?

All right then—let Rafael deal with Al, and whatever criticism he felt like dishing out because they had hired a loser like Mirko. Perfect. Rafael could listen to him, calm him down, and make sure he did not make any unreasonable demands.

No, he was really not happy owing Al's family more money than he already did, but in this case, there was no doubt—it had to be done. There had not been another way. Everybody would agree with this one. End of story. Move on to the next topic.

He squared his shoulders again and put his mind back into the winner's mode he practiced so often. He was, after all, the head of this company, the boss, the master of this particular domain.

"Connor, I want you to meet Markus Lanz. He owns Micro Parts."

"The computer company—I am well aware of your corporation. I've been following you," Connor said and shook the man's hand. "Thank you for coming to our little celebration tonight. I hope you are enjoying yourself."

"I am, thank you very much. That is quite a corporation you have put together here—from nothing. Just like I did, just like our fathers did."

"Trailblazers." Connor nodded sagely. "There are only a handful of us left. Tell me, are you interested in investing in something—other than chips and computers, then?"

And so it went. Kayla helped him work the room. Introduced him, fed him tidbits of information about each and every prospect he was about to talk to. It made him look like an enormous storehouse of knowledge, and Connor loved it. They made the perfect team, he and Kayla. How come he couldn't see this before? They really were an all-star team when it came to speaking in investors. He took her hand and squeezed it gently.

"We are a rock-star team," he said softly.

"Did you expect anything else? You put two brilliant people like us together and give us a project, and the magic is bound to happen, Connor. There is not even a question."

"We really are amazing."

This was where he excelled; this was his field—raising money. And none of them, not one, did it as well as he did. One of these days, they would all be surprised if Connor decided to apply his talents elsewhere. Where would they be then—just exactly where?

"Nowhere," he muttered to himself, and Kayla raised an eyebrow. "What's that?"

"Oh nothing... Wait—yes. Rafael, Al, David, Catherine, all of them. They insist on trying to make me do things their way. Meanwhile, I get things done. I bring in the money, and I run this company. With-out me, they would be absolutely nowhere. That's what I am talking about. And yet…"

"And yet they are simply jealous, Connor, don't you see it? You have built all this, when none of them could do it. That's all."

She laughed and put her hand on his arm. "And that bothers you? Please—you only need to remember that. And that it drives them crazy with jealousy. So naturally, they need to make it your fault. By now, you should be used to it."

"You have a point."

"Of course I have a point, Connor. I know you call these people friends…"

"Rafael—maybe. The rest of them…"

"Even Rafael. He runs a decent construction company, and he comes from a moneyed family—but other than that. Please. Just look at how he is dressed tonight. That suit looks like something he might have picked up at the Walmart, and the tie is horrid."

"I've tried."

"Don't, Connor, don't even try. It's about time that you let all of these people from your prior lives go and realize you have moved on. You have grown into another period of your life. There's nothing wrong letting people and things go if they do not serve you any longer."

"Thank you, Oprah."

"Don't mock me. You know that I'm right. You are the president and CEO of what will be the biggest company in the country. I run the biggest entertainment magazine in the country. Our friends and acquaintances should reflect that."

"You are right, as always," Connor said and took another glass of champagne from a passing waiter.

Nothing he had not thought about himself earlier. Nothing he had not realized over the last few weeks. He and Rafael had been friends for a very long time, true, but Rafa—Rafa was more at home in the auxiliary room or boiler room than out here, in the great hall, drinking champagne.

"You are right," he said and smiled. "Charlie, I apologize for abandoning you and Byron so suddenly earlier. A minor emergency my staff did not manage to deal with."

"Capable staff is the cornerstone of running a successful business," Charlie said sagely as if lecturing before a school class. "Unfortunately, it is also the downfall of many a successful man."

"How right you are. This business has grown so quickly that our staffing needs are incredibly pressing at the moment. And what are you going to do…" He shrugged his shoulders. "If I don't look after things—who will?"

"I admire dedication." Byron nodded. "Really—a true leader will be right there in the trenches with his people, and you, Connor, you have all the hallmarks of a true leader."

"I really don't want to brag," Connor said. "Neither do I need to. Everybody in here knows how hard I have worked to get this company where we are today. But—hypothetically," he grinned, "hypothetically, I would say you are so right."

The three men moved into the direction of one of the bars at the far wall of the hall, chatting amicably about good and bad staff, and Kayla left them to their male talk.

Connor did not know if hours had passed or merely a few minutes. Too many intense conversations, too many questions answered, business cards handed out, tentative meetings arranged—the king was back. The temporary ebb gone as soon as it had appeared. With every person he spoke, his mood improved, and he almost bounced back to the bar finding Kayla.

"I cannot thank you enough." He enveloped her in a great big bear hug. "This evening is the grandest success of this entire company. I cannot thank you enough for arranging it and arranging it so perfectly."

"Woah, Connor, let me down. Thank you is enough. Easy on the champagne."

"I don't have to take it easy on the champagne. Nothing can get me down today—nothing. You know that. The world is mine, Kayla, yours and mine. We rule."

"Easy."

The jazz trio had left, and another was taking its place. Connor relaxed and looked around. His world, his building, his company. Things were awesome again. Suddenly, the party had loosened up considerably, and, he suspected, the quantity of consumed booze had something to do with it, but who the heck cared?

Ties had been loosened up, jackets taken off, people were dancing, and the waiters had to hustle to keep up to the demand of fresh glasses. He took Kayla's hand, indicating a gallant kiss, and nodded toward the dance floor.

"Shall we, my lady?"

"You are on your way to being completely and hopelessly drunk."

"I most certainly am—if not there already."

"You ought to...."

"I really don't care what I ought to, Kayla. We have done something great tonight. The next weeks are going to be filled with seeing investors and taking money off them. Enough—now I want to dance."

"Connor...."

Her protests were weak at best, and Connor managed to drag her out onto the dance floor, where they seamlessly slipped in among the other couples. Connor relaxed and let the music flow over him, swaying softly. Shit, he was drunker than a sailor already. Who cared—as long as he did not make a fool of himself. There were a lot of guys around who'd been steadier on their feet when the evening started.

Even the stuck-up little Minister of Health, Byron Cartwright, had taken off his suit jacket and danced with a gorgeous blonde. Wait, wait, wait.... Connor spun Kayla around so hard she almost tripped, so he could see the couple better. The blonde, the curvy one Byron danced with. He recognized her—seen the woman before and even...

"Shit."

"Watch it, Connor. I have no intention of landing on my rear in the middle of the dance floor."

"The woman…"

The woman Byron was dancing with—of course he recognized her. He'd had—some fun with her. It was one of Señor Paul's girls.

"What woman—what are you looking at?"

"Who brought the professionals?"

"I was hoping nobody would notice." Kayla stiffened a little in his arms and shook her head, eyes blazing anger. "I think either Rafael or that brute Harvey brought them. Prostitutes—at my party. I am going to…"

"Hush, it's not a big deal, Kayla."

"Not a big deal? Prostitutes?"

"The talent. That's all. I'd like to know which one of the guys walked in with them. Don't think it was Rafa, did not see them on the chopper with Harvey."

"Well, when you find out, I expect you to speak to the man. It is an outrage. This was supposed to be a classy event—not an orgy."

"Relax—it's late enough most of the media people have gone home. Nobody will notice anything."

"Well I noticed, and I am offended. And I really want to know— how did you know there were prostitutes in the room?"

Busted. Connor could have kicked his big mouth into next week. Shit—this exact moment was why getting this drunk was never a good idea.

"Sorry, I didn't tell you. I was seriously hoping you wouldn't notice. Rafa told me earlier, when we were looking at the utility room. One of the men had brought five girls. He was laughing about it—couldn't actually believe it."

"That's not what it sounded like a minute ago, Connor—are you sure?"

"Yeah, I was hoping they'd gone home, or somebody had just hired himself a cheap date."

"Not that cheap from what I understand."

Trap alert! Step careful, Connor!

"I wouldn't really know. But perhaps cheaper on the ego than showing up solo. Some guys are—funny that way."

Kayla made a huffy sound and kept dancing. Crisis avoided. A few glasses of champagne less and she would have spotted his flimsy excuse. He had to—simply had to—stop doing this kind of shit. OK, so who was he kidding, he knew he wasn't going to, right? Not now anyway, when everything was moving in his favor.

"You know I would never stoop that low, Kayla. Although on occasion, when things are tough, I have been known to—perhaps—drink a bit too much."

"An understatement, Connor. And you better had get yourself over to the bar and have them make a strong espresso for you—or two or three. I don't want to read in the paper that the CEO of Perfect Cannabis was loaded at his own party."

Connor tuned her out. Yes, Kayla had helped tremendously, but for crying out loud, did women always have to start messing around in your life the moment they thought they could? He'd drink however much he wanted to drink and hang out with any prostitutes he wanted to, for three good reasons.

Number one, he could handle it, number two, he was the master of his domain and he had worked for it, and number three, he could pay for it. What else did a man need? Nothing.

"I'll turn it down a notch," he said softly, planning nothing of the sort, and let his eyes wander around the room.

Some of the less hardy characters had gone home when the press disappeared. Losers. That's when things could get interesting! And Al—Al still hung around the fringes of this party, annoyingly enough. Suit still perfectly unruffled as if they hadn't just gone through a major event, faced down a loan shark, been threatened a time or two—and all in the last hour. Not to forget, that he, Connor, had not even invited the man.

"You know who that is standing over there chatting with Al?" he asked and turned Kayla so she could see the two men, deep in animated conversation.

"Never seen him before now that you mention it. One of the staff? No—too well dressed. He does kind of look like Al. How many brothers does the man have, for crying out loud?"

Dan? No, Dan was still out of the country, wasn't he? He had made sure to send him on an extended fact-finding trip to Colorado. Did not want him and his superior attitude around during the party.

No—Dan was out. Then who? Al's family appeared to be large; it was possible... Then again, what did he want here?

Al did not seem to be too happy with the man either; he kept shaking his head and gesturing wildly.

"Something is not right there," Connor muttered to himself and put down his champagne glass. "I'm going to go see."

"Just—no more scenes tonight, OK?"

"Scenes? Of course not—there have been scenes?"

"You know what I mean. People showing up who were not invited, prostitutes at my event, you disappearing for the better part of an hour... I don't know what it was all about, Connor, but I highly doubt it was simply a building maintenance issue."

Connor sighed and took his eyes off Al and the new visitor.

"Kayla, it was nothing important, OK? Just something I had to deal with and deal with personally."

"Then there are the prostitutes."

"And likely Rafa is the culprit here—I told you. I will speak to him, make sure it does not happen again. Now if you will please excuse me, I really have to deal with..."

He turned around again, but as if erased by magic, Al and the new visitor suddenly had disappeared, and Connor cursed softly.

"Dammit, I wanted to know..."

"I don't know why I bothered to put together a guest list, if people were just allowed to wander in at will. Is this not why I hired a doorman? And gave him a guest list to be checked off? But no—somewhere, we have to leave a door open for anybody and their brother to walk in and make themselves."

"Kayla, you are perfectly right! The guest list—there is a guest list at the door. Somebody must have met him at the main door and invited him in, or he wouldn't have. I made sure the back door was closed after... after that incident."

"The one you don't want to talk about. Connor, I have to say..."

"You are brilliant, Kayla—brilliant. I will be right back, OK?"

He kissed her on the cheek quickly and disappeared before she could go on about the 'incident' and about the prostitutes. Jesus—that was all he needed just now, Kayla getting paranoid. She likely thought he had brought the women in through the back door while she herself held court at the party. Nonsense. Rafa, probably not, far too straitlaced. That left any number of guys here who wanted to show up with a treat on their arm—or more than one. Jesus, for a businesswoman, Kayla was still kind of dumb.

On the other hand, she likely had a lot of experience from the time before she met her late husband and became a respectable publisher.

At the entrance, so beautifully lit and decorated when he had arrived, he found a tangle of noisy chaos. Harvey Watson, two-bit actor and notorious drunk, apparently had decided to consume all of the liquor in the house, all at once, since it was free. A joint dangled from his lips, and if his speech had not been way too slurred to make any sense at all, he would have made advances to the mayor's wife.

Damned models and movie stars, Connor cursed silently. They had their uses as decorations and to attract the press, but if they could not hold their liquor, they were better off at home. Where was the man's personal assistant anyway, the one who had liked the chopper so damn much, and why was he not paying attention and taking this loser out of the range of the press?

"Hey, Harvey, what happened to your briefcase-carrier?"

"Dunno—where's the plane?"

"The helicopter. It is still out back, but I think we had better call you a cab and get you back to your hotel. I don't think you ought to be flying in your—well—if you are not feeling well."

"I'm fine."

"I can see that, Harvey. Where's—that young man you brought, your assistant?"

"Dunno..."

Harvey made another beeline for the nearest bar, and Connor double-stepped to catch up with him before another disaster happened. "Wait—Harv..."

"Mr. Beauregard, I just wanted to thank you once again..."

Connor shuddered and balled his hands to fists instinctively so he would not shrink back. A skeletal, bony hand landed on his arm and squeezed ever so lightly.

"What you did for us tonight—it will not be forgotten. You are making miracles happen."

The bony hand belonged to a man who would have to cross the street twice if he wanted to cast one shadow. Christ in heaven—a skeleton looked plump against him. Connor could see every single bone and vein through the translucent skin, and the eyes were sunk deeply in hollow sockets. The man was not long for this earth, but he smiled and shook Connor's hand.

"Thank you so much for your donation."

One of Alexa's sick people. Yes—he had wanted to make an impact with that donation, but did they have to touch him? Come up to him, breathe the same air as he did? What if the guy had something contagious? No, silly, they would not do that, would they? People just needed to get a sense of personal space again. Christ, he was going to have to hire somebody who liked to beat up assholes just to keep people away from him from now on!

"Oh, you are most welcome," he managed to say, forcing his mind away from sickness and disease and trying to keep an eye on Harvey Watson all at the same time. "At Perfect Cannabis Corporation, our main focus is on improving lives, on making things better for those who have suffered so much already."

"You are doing such a wonderful job at it already, too. If I look at this facility, and I know all the good it will be doing one day, I am just so filled with gratitude."

Not that you'll be around to see it, Connor thought and fought the urge to pull his arm away. Somewhere in the crowd, a few press people might still be hanging around. It wouldn't do—it just wouldn't do.

"That is our mission as I see it, sir, and I wish you all the best. I hope once we are producing and selling, we will be able to help you with more than just a donation."

The man smiled sadly, confirming Connor's suspicion that he wouldn't be around, and dropped his hand.

"Well..."

"Thank you so much for coming out tonight. I know it must be an effort to you. Would you please excuse me—I must seem terribly rude, but I see someone I absolutely must say goodbye to..."

The man nodded, and Connor followed the path of destruction to where Harvey stood leaning against a bar arguing with the bartender whether or not he should pour him another drink or cut the procedure short and hand over the bottle. Rafael and two of the valet parking fellows finally came to his aid and took Harvey between them, leading him away.

Christ—what a moron! His stomach turned when he thought of the money they gave him, just to be here tonight.

Connor straightened up an overturned vase, if only not to trip over it, and finally made his way to the front door, where the guest book lay unattended. Idly, he flipped through it. 'Wonderful building, great accomplishment, all the best, wonderful wishes...' Yeah, yeah, yeah—all he needed to know was...

"It is wonderful how many people wrote encouraging words for you, is it not, Mr. Connor?"

"Indeed." He looked up at the man in a butler's uniform, whom he vaguely remembered as having been on duty at the door. "Perhaps you can help me. Were you here for the end of the evening?"

"By the door, as I was hired to do."

"Splendid. My business partner Al, he met a man here tonight, and for the life of me, I cannot remember his name. Rather than embarrass myself, I'd like to look it up if you don't mind?"

"Mr. Al?" The young man cocked his head and appeared to be deep in thought. "No—I don't think Mr. Al met anyone tonight. I would have remembered because by some dreadful mistake..." The man put his hand on Connor's forearm, and this time Connor did pull back. Not another touchy-feely asshole. "By some terribly embarrassing mistake, Mr. Al himself was not on the guest list, but he convinced me that he is part of the management at this company. I hope that was all right."

Kayla indeed had invited Al, but he had not really wanted him at this party tonight, that was for sure. He'd been kind of hoping that entire family would stay away. So much for that, so he had sneakily dropped him off the guest list, hoping for a convenient 'mistake.'

"Probably he just goes by Al," Connor muttered and kept flipping through the guest list, "I mean he would either be at the top of the list because of the A, or at the bottom because he does not have a last name listed. It's not that hard, is it?"

The young man blushed, and Connor put the book down again.

"Never mind—so you are sure he did not meet anyone at the door tonight?"

"Positive, sir. I was paying attention."

"Good."

Connor rolled his eyes and walked away. OK, mystery on. He knew he had locked the back door after Mirko had managed to sneak in.

Not that way, so how the hell did the mystery man get in? How? Not on the guest list, not with Al—how in blazes?

Connor took a deep breath and let it out again. For a moment, the room spun around him, and his knees wanted to buckle. No surprise here—he'd been up all day running on 100 percent adrenaline and a host of chemicals he had dumped into his body. Basically, he was done, and his body tried to tell him to pack it in and let somebody else worry about things for a little while.

No way.

He straightened with an effort and forced a huge lungful of air in and out again slowly. If there was one thing Connor Beauregard did not do, it was quit. He was in charge—always would be. He was in charge now, and this would not change.

The boss, for god's sake, how would it look if the boss all of a sudden sat down and said, "I am tired—I don't want to do this anymore?"

So again, how had the stranger got in, and who was he?

Al and his father had snuck in through the side; so had Mirko.

"Way to go, Simon Graff of Graff Security," he muttered and grabbed an open bottle of champagne from a sideboard. Yuck, it was warm, but better than nothing, right?

So he sat in a spindly chair at the far wall that did not seem to have any purpose other than decorative and took a deep swig straight from the bottle. At the other end of the room, people took their coats off the attendants, shook hands, hugged, left in a rush of noise and laughter. Kayla made sure everyone felt taken care of in one way shape or matter. Where he sat, here between a potted palm and the now-abandoned pedestal, no one really saw him, so he could think for a moment in peace and quiet.

And drink.

Down went another swig of champagne. God, if you bought the good stuff, it didn't taste half bad, even warm. He stretched his legs out and put his head into his neck. Back to his problem.

Who was the damned stranger, and how had he got into the building after he, Connor, locked the side entrance?

"There's a man with the weight of the world on his shoulders."

He looked up at Rafael standing beside him, a bottle of beer in his hand.

"Beer—that's all you could hunt up at this time of day?"

Rafael shrugged. "Had enough of all the fancy stuff. There comes a moment when the simple things are what you are after."

"Never."

"Not for you my friend, I get that. So what's got you sitting here looking like you are trying to figure out the mysteries of the world?"

"Somebody else got in here—somebody who wasn't invited."

"I thought you locked the door after—Mirko, you know."

"I did—didn't want strangers coming and going like this was the mission or something. And still."

"Well, if you locked the side door, nobody could get in or out except by going through the doormen. How do you know he was a stranger?"

"How." Connor rolled his eyes. "How, Rafael? I didn't recognize him, that's how. Kayla did not recognize him. But she said he looked like Al—made me think…"

"Or maybe it was just somebody you invited and don't remember clearly—it happens, you know? Especially…" He nodded at the champagne bottle in Connor's hand.

"No—even drunk out of my gourd, I remember everybody. If all you want to do is stand there and tell me I am too drunk to recognize my own guests…."

"All right, all right." Rafael raised his hands. "Look, buddy, it's been a long day. I gotta get home. I suggest you take Kayla and do the same, and tomorrow—tomorrow we will come back here and figure out the mysteries of the world."

"Maybe."

He did not like it—did not like the thought that somehow there was still a way into his building, a way he couldn't control, but Rafael was right in one point—he was too far gone to have an intelligent thought tonight.

Not that he would admit it to anyone.

"Yeah," he said and grinned broadly. "It's been one hell of an evening, and I am back, man—I am so back. I am going to raise money so hard nobody's ever seen anything like it."

"Starting tomorrow." Kayla appeared on his other side and took the bottle out of his hand. "Tonight has come and gone. It is actually tomorrow already—so let's just do what everybody else is doing and go."

Connor rose and took one last look around.

"What about…."

"I've hired a caretaker. He will go around and pick up and clean up, lock the building and make sure everything is secure. The pilot is taking the helicopter back to the pad at the airport, the last of the guests have left, and I have a car waiting outside. Everything has been taken care of."

"You are awesome."

Connor staggered to his feet, realizing now that Rafa was indeed right and he was not only drunk—he was absolutely shitfaced. He leaned on Kayla and let her lead him outside to the waiting limousine.

"My night," he said unsteadily. "My fucking night. My building, my company, my helicopter, and my fucking night."

He was the king of the world. And nobody—nobody would ever take it from him, no matter what happened.

THIRTY-SIX

It took a few days for Connor to recover from that night. For the next day, he was content to lie in bed with the curtains drawn and a steady supply of pills by his side while Kayla told people he had caught a cold.

If he opened his eyes for more than 10 minutes at a time or tried to do more than wobble to the bathroom, he got violently sick and quickly headed back to bed.

In his mind, though, it had all been worth it. It had been more than worth it, and this was a small price to pay.

As he lay in bed, he tried to figure out what to do with the small fortune he was about to make. He would need a new house, that was a given. Kayla's condo was nice and all—but he needed something of his own. Something big, something people could point to and know, that castle over there—that's where Connor Beauregard lived, the founder of Perfect Cannabis.

They could always keep the condo here in town—for late nights at the restaurants in town, or for guests who should stay on their own.

Another problem solved. Connor grinned and reached for the drink by his bedside. Soda. He frowned and sat up. Kayla must be on her health kick again—Jesus. He'd have to get that out of her. He despised soda and would not drink anything without at least a little kick to it. One had to have standards.

In his track pants and t-shirt, he padded to the kitchen and raided the refrigerator for something edible and at least a glass of beer. Then he heard his phone ring, sitting on the kitchen counter. Connor picked it up, a chicken leg in his mouth, and checked the screen. 37 missed calls—no wonder he'd had such an enjoyable morning. He'd left his phone in the kitchen, and for the past few hours, it had rung itself hoarse with no response.

Finishing his snack, he thumbed through the calls. Catherine, David, Tessa…. Same old, same old.

David had called seven times, though. This could not be good. He had been trying desperately to get their latest financial statements filed with the SEC, and it wasn't going the way he had hoped. Damned bean counters got their way again. And David—the man he had specifically hired to deal with them, solve the problems, and get it done—did nothing but sit there and complain that he, Connor, was making his job too hard. Too hard, like taking his pay home every month was not too hard for him, right?

Connor finished his snack, downed half of his beer, and decided to call back David. He would at least try, if only so nobody could accuse him of avoiding the issues.

"David, tell me you're all done filing this shit with the SEC, please."

"Connor, when you say shit—well, let's just say you are completely correct. What have you done with the books once again?"

"Aw, come on, a couple of expenses here and there—I know some of this stuff may or may not be private. Everybody is doing it. You are not going to tell me I have to account for every sandwich and bottle of water I buy when I am out seeing potential investors, are you?"

"My dear Connor, sandwiches and water are not at all what I am talking about, be assured. I have just had an argument with our dear auditors over payments to a man called…" Connor heard him shuffle some papers in the background. "Mirko Jankowich, I think—I don't know how to pronounce it…."

Shit—Mirko. Yes. He had not meant to, but he had run some of his payments through the company account because his private was short… shit, shit!

"That's easily explained, David. We needed some quick cash to get the building in shape. Mirko was the guy willing to lend it—that's all."

"His terms are a little—aggressive, so to speak. There's no decent contract to be found anywhere either."

"It had to be done, David, you know it. Next."

"And from what I see, you gave shares to the man as well. Although I am guessing—there is no agreement here either."

"All part of the deal. He was willing to lend, at a price. And those shares were part of the price. He provided a service—this is perfectly legit, David, so what is the problem?"

"It would be, if there were a director's resolution okaying all of this, Connor. But there is not. You know you need a resolution to borrow money on that scale. You're running this company like your own private little kingdom. Again. Yet last time I explained to you that you need to play by the rules if you want to stay out of trouble. There are directors, shareholders—you cannot just…"

"I have the director's resolution, somewhere—here…. I just haven't got around to giving it to Tessa yet for filing. I told you. I have not been well."

"Do you now, really?"

How much sarcasm the little man could manage in that one short sentence was impressive. Without a doubt, David knew Connor was just going to make up any old document he damn well pleased and copy signatures into it.

"I do, David—you sound like you have doubts."

"Let's just say…."

"Let's just say, David, that I run this company, OK? And I run it the way I see fit. If you run a public company at some point, you can do it any way you please. This is my way. So now—I will get the director's resolution regarding borrowing money to you in the next few hours. I have it here on my phone. Is there anything else?"

"We are having a lot of problems with this filing," David managed to get out.

His words were clipped, and if he had been sitting across from Connor, he was sure the man's eyes would have blazed with anger. As it was, he could hear the irritation all the way through the phone. So David did not like to be reminded that he was just an employee, did he? Connor grinned. Good to know.

"That is why you are here—to solve these problems, David. By all means, send me a list of deficiencies, and I will get you all the documentation you need. Just get this filed, please."

"There is—a lot of documentation on the deficiencies list."

"Likely all on my phone or here in my home office. I'm not one to go and file every flipping piece of paper. Just ask me—do not sit out there assuming I simply do not have something. I need this filing to happen, and I need it to happen soon, do you understand?"

"Some of these expenses are...."

"Out of line from where you are sitting—I know. It often looks that way if you don't have the entire overview of what's going on, David. Don't worry about it. If anybody has a problem with something, I will be more than happy to explain it."

Fortunately, I know what I am doing—even if you don't.

He barely stopped himself before that last sentence slipped out, although he wanted to say it so badly he could taste it.

"Please work with Tessa and send me a list of what you need—understood?"

"Understood, Connor."

"If, for whatever reason, you feel this is all too much for you, please let me know. I will do something about it."

As if. If there was one thing Connor remembered about David, it was that the little man always chronically needed money. He did not have any vices to speak of, but somehow, the little accountant never did seem to be able to look after his own finances the way he did with others. First rule—always work with people who need you more than you them.

"It's not easy, David, but it does not have to be agony. You can tell me to go F off any time, you understand?"

"I am fine—never mind."

Fine, my ass. Connor hung up and dug through the fridge for more of the beer he had found. He knew damned well David would sit down later badmouthing him and his way of running a company… But he would not quit—oh, no, he would never quit. Connor held out just enough promise for the big payday to keep him in line and interested.

He found another chicken leg and more beer and sat down to thumb through his messages again. Catherine had finally stopped bugging him. Good. He had not needed her all that much in the first place, and lately, she had become nothing but an annoyance, just like all lawyers.

But Tessa—Tessa needed some attention. He actually did need her, and he needed her to be in a good mood, or she would walk away and leave him with a mess he barely understood now, never mind without her.

What a stroke of genius! He pulled out Kayla's kitchen laptop and quickly wrote out treasury orders issuing a bundle of shares to Tessa and to David. It would keep both of them interested, in a good mood, and working harder than they had planned to. And it did not cost him a single dime. Genius—sheer genius!

Having done his job, he decided to go up to the sundeck and fall asleep in one of the patio loungers up there. For today, he had done enough work, and tomorrow—tomorrow, he would be back to being the rainmaker, raising funds.

Still, even on the sundeck of the condo building, right up on the forty-second floor, surrounded by nothing but air, sun, and expensively maintained planters, the image of the stranger at the grand opening did not leave him.

Connor lay down in one of the loungers, ordered something to drink from the attendant, who came by to bring him some towels, and closed his eyes. He could see the man, standing there, talking to Al, gesticulating wildly, a fierce expression on his face.

He had asked Al, quite casually, if he had spoken to a new person, a potential investor Connor should approach... All easy and casual, "Hey, I saw someone I didn't recognize—anyone I should hit up for funds?" But no, Al had simply shaken his head and said no, he did not recall anyone like that.

He couldn't well argue the point, now could he? Al would get suspicious, ask questions. That would never do. He had asked the other doormen, and none of them remembered a man who fit the description. Finally, he was out of ideas. He knew he should just give up and say the hell with it, but in his gut he knew—some unknown person had snuck into his grand opening party, spoken to Al, and then disappeared like a puff of smoke.

That alone was something to worry about, and that alone would haunt him. Damn. With an effort, he pushed the thought away and tried to focus on David and their problems with the auditors instead.

Like every public company, they had to publicize their financial statements every single quarter. In order to do that, they had to be signed off by an official auditor. This process never failed to be a pain in his ass. Every. Single. Time.

Auditors did not get it either. Auditors did not appear to understand that a big company like this one could not be run like a widget store. There were things you had to do—unconventional things—to attract the big investors, compliment them and entertain them.

Connor opened his eyes again and slowly peeled an orange from the fruit basket the attendant had left by his side. Nice—one of the advantages to living in one of the most luxurious condo buildings in town. He would get attendants at his house when he built it, his castle.

"Well, judging by the smile on your face, you're thinking of something pleasant."

He opened his eyes to find Kayla there and grinned again.

"Feeling better?"

"Much."

"So you're going to share with me what has you smiling so sweetly?"

"Nothing, really—I was kind of annoyed. I was imagining what it would be like to tell everybody to fuck off."

"Not everybody, I hope."

Kayla ran her finger up his arm, and Connor smiled again.

"Not everybody—you got that right. Just the imbeciles I have to work with."

"That bad?"

"Worse. I simply do not understand why nobody can see my vision. I have it right here, right in front of me." He extended his hands as if he held a ball in front of his face. "Right here, Kayla. I can see how it's supposed to work. And I can do it—I know I can do it. I am the best at what I do."

"You are a true visionary."

"Right. But then I run into people like David, or the official auditors, or Catherine."

"Tell them to fuck off—and go do it anyway."

"That's what I am doing, my love."

Connor smiled again and took her hand. "I'm fortunate to have you."

Kayla squeezed his hand tightly and kissed his forehead.

"Hey, we'll get through this—I promise you that. Right now, what is the worst we have to get through?"

"This audit."

"They can't drag this out forever."

"Right now—unfortunately—it feels like they can."

"What about this guy who did not remember signing the name change agreement—that ever get solved? I remember Catherine calling dozens of times."

Connor frowned and shook his head. "He must have remembered or something, the idiot. I haven't heard any more."

He sat up, chewing on the corner of his thumbnail. "Weird, actually, considering before that the man would not leave me alone. He kept coming around and calling until I damn near gave him his money back."

"One fellow who finally saw the light. 100 to go. Maybe he found his documentation again and realized—hey, I did sign this. I'm an idiot."

"Maybe...."

"Of course, he could have called you and apologized. Then again, that's how people are when you are successful and at the top of your game. Jealous, mean-spirited, nasty."

"Is that experience speaking?"

"Honey, when you are a woman and head of a large publishing house, you get the worst of all of these characters, trust me."

"Well thank God I'm not a woman then."

Connor grinned and lay back on the lounger. She was probably right. McDowell had remembered, and life was good. Good—except for a bit of niggling doubt somewhere, a little voice that kept screaming at him that he might be wrong. The hell with it, Connor decided, that man had invested $5,000—$5,000—*if one day he decides to make a fuss again, so help me God, I will give him his money back and personally kick him in the ass while I am at it.*

The thought gave him pleasure, and he grinned up at Kayla.

"Now, why don't you tell me what brings you home so early in the afternoon? Other than a sudden need to see me, of course. Which is always understandable."

"Oh my." Kayla sat down on the lounger with him, ignoring its ominous creaking.

"Actually—I wanted to tell you not to make any plans for this weekend."

"OK.... What are we doing instead?"

"We are taking the helicopter out to Martha's Vineyard."

"You had me at helicopter, my dear. Tell me more."

"Charlie Weaver is participating in a race or regatta or some such thing down there—I have to read up on it first—but he invited us and Byron Cartwright there to join in the party."

"Martha's Vineyard…" he said and let the name melt on his tongue like fine candy.

This had possibilities. Never mind an ordinary sailing trip here on the lake somewhere.

"Yes. Think of all the contacts you're going to be able to make out there. People who have real money and real power. I can't wait to go, show these people all the wonderful things we have done with Perfect Cannabis."

"Investors—future business partners…"

"That's right. And Byron—Byron is not going to know what hit him. He is going to remember that trip for a very, very long time."

"Kayla, have I told you something lately?"

"I am sure you have, my love—but I'm always ready to hear it again…."

"You are absolutely brilliant!"

THIRTY-SEVEN

"I guess I don't have to ask you how your weekend was, Connor my pal. I can just open the paper and read all about it. Either that or look at your face."

"Rafa—what do you want?"

Connor groaned and opened his eyes to glance at the clock on the nightstand. He would complain that the ringer of his phone had woken him up, except that he hadn't been sleeping so much as been unconscious. The last 12 hours truly did not exist. Quick—what was the last thing he remembered?

"Martha's Vineyard."

"Martha's Vineyard, indeed, my friend—and you must have drunk the entire vineyard's worth all by yourself."

"That bad?"

"Worse, if the story in the paper is to be believed."

"Oh come on—it wasn't that bad. We were…" He held his head, took a few deep breaths, and tried his best to remember. "Charlie Weaver won his race—I think. I'm not actually sure."

"You're not sure? And I can see why. According to the papers, you proceeded to party with the best of them, got completely shit-faced drunk, ended up offering drugs to a few high-ranking government officials."

"Drugs? I don't remember that."

"Probably better if you don't. After you all got thrown out at the yacht club, you took the party down the road a bit to a bar."

"Don't tell me."

"Trust me—if I were you, I would not want to remember either. Bro—you are like the CEO of a big-time corporation now. You think you would learn a few things, you know."

"I swear to you I don't know what happened, Rafa."

"What happened is that your entire party or whatever you want to call it really got into things at said bar. You couldn't pay the bar bill and almost got thrown out of there, got into an argument with the owner…"

"Jesus Christ."

"Yeah—for some reason, I don't think he was there Connor. I mean, the episode is in the paper this morning."

"That's going a bit far. So we got drunk."

"Fall-down drunk is more like it. And I have not even got to the underage prostitutes yet…"

"Shit." Connor sat up, alarmed all of a sudden. Kayla! If there had been prostitutes… She'd be pissed off as hell. Shit, shit….

"What happened? Did I…?"

"For crying out loud, Connor—you really don't remember, do you?"

"How often do I have to tell you? I don't, Rafa. Now tell me what the fuck happened so I can prepare and head off the firestorm. Jesus—do I have to drag every single word out of you or what?"

"Be easier if you just read it in the paper—but I'm assuming you are beyond reading at this point. The way the story reads, you were drunk as sailors, which is rather fitting, I guess. I don't know where Kayla was at this point—I'd guess not with you."

He vaguely remembered an argument—a cab—a slamming door… Christ. He'd really sunk it this time, hadn't he?

"Then you, my friend, must have got sick and passed out. Next thing you know, Byron Cartwright is being arrested in the company of a couple of underage prostitutes and one unconscious CEO."

Plausible deniability. Not as bad as it could be. He could blame it all on Ronnie… Yeah—Ronnie had probably hired them.

"Ron must have...."

"Ron—as you call him—is facing his own problems this morning. Let's just say he may not be Minister of Health for very much longer..."

"It can't be that bad, Rafa."

"Not that bad, Connor? Not that bad? What did you think would happen to your license application when you got arrested, drunk, trying to skip out on your bar tab? What did you think would happen—realistically? Is there a brain in that head of yours, or is it all just shit up there?"

"Rafa—don't give me a hard time here, OK? This is not what I meant to happen."

"Oh, I am absolutely convinced that is the exact opposite of what you wanted to happen, my friend," Rafael said, the sarcasm practically pouring out of the phone. "Absolutely. But the way it looks from where I am sitting, and from where all the readers of this paper are sitting, is you took a minister to Martha's Vineyard to influence him in some way and on the occasion got drunk and with a few prostitutes. That's what it looks like. Feel free to come up with a statement to refute."

"Damage control, Rafa."

"I don't think there is such a thing any longer. Best you can do is own up to the fuckup and hope you don't get crucified."

"I can't do that—you know very well I can't. I'm trying to run a serious medical marijuana company here."

"Well, maybe you should have thought of this before you went on a bender."

"Maybe—I need to think. I need to figure this out, Rafa. I'll call you later."

Suddenly in panic mode, Connor hung up the phone and jumped out of bed, racing under a hot shower to erase a drinking binge of gargantuan proportions. How could he have been so stupid? Never mind—asking that question now would not help him either. The only thing that would help was damage control.

He'd been a victim. He couldn't help it. Unfortunate circumstances —anything—anything?

By the time he stepped out of the shower and stepped into a new set of clothes, he had three more messages on his phone. Everybody and their brother wanted a statement, no doubt.

He had no idea where Kayla was. All he could hope was that he wouldn't find a couple of packed suitcases by the front door—his. To his relief, no suitcases, no note to get the hell out, nothing. Time. At least he had a bit more time.

Tessa hadn't bothered to come to the office this morning—probably all the better. Instead, he found a note from Al taped to his office door. 'Get in touch with me immediately.' Nothing else. Just 'get in touch with me.'

And if irony wasn't enough of a bitch, he thought as he ripped the note off the door and disappeared into his own office, Al probably was the only one who could help him right now. As often as he had cursed Al, he probably had navigated out of worse than this before. Even though he wouldn't be happy with him. And his father—well, his father would be worse. Still, they could not run PerCan without him, period.

They needed him more than he needed them. Rule one. Screw the rules—right now, he needed somebody to get him out of this shit pile he had navigated himself into. One of these days, he would really have to quit drinking.

He ripped up Al's note and drove to the family restaurant where he had met Al and his father for the very first time what seemed like a lifetime ago. This time, he drove like a saint, sticking to the speed limits, making sure to come to a complete stop at every stop sign. Last thing he needed was being picked up for some minor traffic violation with enough alcohol and drugs left in his system to make him glow at night.

Dinah, the bored waitress, didn't even bother with a menu when she saw him come in, merely nodded toward the back and let him trot down there.

Al and his father sat in the same room where they had met last time, going over a large handwritten book. Probably a ledger book of some type. He could not really tell. He puffed out his chest, put on his best *fake it* grin, and closed the door behind him.

"Hey, guys—your note said to get in touch with you."

Al said nothing, and his father sat back in his chair, took off his reading glasses slowly, and folded them carefully, earpiece over earpiece in front of him.

"Have a good weekend, Connor?" he finally asked in a voice so low you had to strain to hear him. "I only ask because—according to the papers—it was actually quite stressful."

"Well—you know—it did not actually go the way I had it planned, no."

"And what did you have planned, Connor? Do you mind sharing that with me? Because I can see where a weekend bender of alcohol, drugs, and prostitutes would not be a very good plan at all—we are all in agreement there."

"All I wanted to do was befriend Byron Cartwright a bit, believe me."

Why the hell was he sounding defensive all of a sudden? If the dear good Minister of Health could not hold his liquor and hired prostitutes while he, Connor, was passed out, was any of this his fault? No—of course it was not. If he lost his wallet and could not pay for their bar tab that was unfortunate, but certainly not his fault either. Nothing to be crucified over—right?

"The idea was to take him to a sailing weekend with one of our very good friends. The fact that he should get so out of hand was just—entirely unexpected."

"I see."

Al's father folded his hands in front of his face and nodded. Drove him crazy. If the man had yelled at him or made a scene or anything at all but sit there....

"Look—I wanted to get him into a good mood because of our license. I thought a weekend away might..."

"Might what, Connor? Influence him our way? Because that is the question he is having to answer to his government this morning, and if he survives the day as a minister, there's a good chance you can kiss that license goodbye."

Shit!

"All I can tell you is that I had no idea Byron Cartwright would act so recklessly once we were there. Maybe he has a problem—had I known that…"

"Had you known that, what?"

"Well, for one thing, I would not have taken him anywhere where he was bound to be confronted by this much alcohol, right? I mean— you know what these regatta parties are like. It's like a giant frat house in their clubhouse after the race. Jesus, all of a sudden Cartwright just went crazy on me. I mean, I tried to rein him in, but he would not listen to me. Before I know it, some yahoo steals my wallet, and the whole evening just went down the crapper. The rest you can read in the paper."

"In living color," Al added. "The problem is what does this mean for our company now?"

"Al, I am telling you—I was neither trying to take advantage of our good minister's position, nor was I trying to compromise him to blackmail him."

"Had not even thought of that," Al's father chuckled. "Not bad."

"Well, I was not. It was a weekend outing to which he was invited which got out of hand due to no fault of mine."

"OK." Al nodded. "If that's what you are trying to stick with."

"Not trying at all, Al. That's what happened—period."

"So, what happens if he stands up and says it was all your fault? You brought the drugs, hired the prostitutes, and tried to influence him?"

"He won't."

"Well, you better hope he does not. Or, if he does, that there is no proof, Connor. Because if there is only the slightest shred, you are absolutely fucked. Done with being CEO—is that clear?"

"Perfectly."

The door had opened again. If there were the slightest shred of evidence—if—Rafa, Rafa was the one man who could make sure there was not. Connor wanted to jump to his feet and go talk to his friend, but he could tell Al's father was not done with him. Not even close.

"I need some type of assurance from you that this type of thing will never happen again, Connor."

"It won't, believe me."

"Those are just words—words, Connor." His hand slammed down onto the table, and Connor flinched. "Do you think that I put money into this company to watch you take it down? To watch you drink and whore and take drugs and have a freaking good time—all on my dime?"

"No, of course not, but...."

"No, of course not! We are trying to build a business here—a serious business—and you are fucking it up."

Just the way he pronounced the word 'fucking' and the way Al flinched, Connor knew to keep his mouth shut. The man was dangerously close to a line that should never be crossed—never, ever. Even his hands shook with the effort of keeping them still on the tabletop in front of him. Connor found himself staring down at those hands, wondering what they had done, how they had solved problems before, and his mouth went suddenly very, very dry.

"I need you to make a serious commitment to quit drinking and quit drugs. Is that clear?"

"Yes, sir."

"I need you to clean up and live the life of a saint, while we wait to see what this latest episode does to our company, is that clear?"

"Yes, sir."

"Good. Then you better get out of my sight while I have enough self-control to not strangle you. Go—and pray that this company is not done."

Connor nodded and jumped to his feet.

"And Beauregard?"

"Yes?"

"Don't forget it—I always have eyes on you, OK?"

"Yes, sir."

I always have eyes on you—fuck. He basically ran out of the back room, past the lunch counter, past the bored waitress, and out into the parking lot, where he stopped to drag in huge gulps of air. *I always have eyes on you.* His hands shook from remaining alcohol as much as from fear. Dammit, when he got his hands on Rafa, he would strangle him personally for getting him involved with a criminal like this one.

If you would tell him right now that Al's father was capable of killing a man with those hands, he would probably say, 'I can believe that.' The moment had been that intense. Connor pushed his hands into his thighs and stood there, breathing heavily for a few minutes. At that point, he did not even care how odd this might look from inside the restaurant, or to anyone who happened to drive by. He was ready to get sick right there in the parking lot.

Damn Rafa—except he needed Rafa right now. Rafael needed to find a way to make sure there would not be any evidence found anywhere, anywhere at all. Then Byron could take the hit. Damn the little nerd anyway—why did he have to get out of hand like this? Why?

Time to get to business.

He straightened up, pulled down his sports jacket, and looked around to make sure no one was staring. Nothing had really happened, right? He had taken the Minister of Health to a friendly sailing weekend away, unaware of the fact that the man could neither hold his liquor nor keep his pants closed. Not his fault.

He sat in his car and dialed Rafael.

"Thanks anyway, bro," he said by way of greeting. "Al's father..."

Rafael whistled. "You went to talk to him. I figured it was only a matter of time."

"What the hell were you thinking bringing those people to the table?"

"Hey, hey, you cool it. We needed money, and we needed it badly remember? I was not the one..."

"Just save it, all right?" Connor dragged his fingers through his hair, tired all of a sudden. "No point in arguing about it right this minute. I need you to get busy."

"OK—what?"

"I need you to make sure Byron Cartwright takes the hit for this one."

"Minister of Health?"

"Listen, I have no idea what he was up to while I was admittedly passed out. Suddenly, there are underage prostitutes? Drugs? Really? You going to stand there and point a finger at me?"

"Well—I wouldn't..."

"No, you wouldn't, Rafa. Don't say anything else now. What I need you to do is send some of your people down to Martha's Vineyard and make sure there are—no hard feelings at that bar where we all ended up late that night."

"OK."

"And if there are any—make sure they go away. Same goes if there is any—lingering evidence of some kind."

"Understood."

"You had better. If Al or any one of his family goes down there to have a look around, I want the only thing these people remember to be that I passed out drunk in a corner, could not find my credit card or wallet, and then got—trapped in an unfortunate situation."

"Unfortunate situation—understood."

"You don't have to sound so sarcastic about it, Rafa. Damage control—that's what the name of the game is right now, OK?"

"OK. What is Kayla's take on all of this?"

"I don't know—yet."

He did not exactly relish finding out either. This time a trip to Switzerland, some fine jewelry, or a damn bunch of flowers would not make up for it—if she was truly and honestly mad at him. If...

He had not seen her, spoken to her, or figured out how much of the entire goddamn nightmare she was involved in—and that frightened him almost as much as talking to Al's father did.

"I gotta find her first."

Rafael whistled again. "Don't envy you there, man."

"Yeah, well, you let that be my problem, OK? Go and deal with what I gave you and make sure there are no loose ends, all right?"

He hung up on Rafael and looked down on himself.

Presentable. For waking up out of a stupor this morning, he actually looked presentable. Better than he deserved likely for drinking and god-knows-what all weekend, but he could not worry about that right now. Best defense—charge forward.

He had never been there, but he knew where the headquarters for Kayla's magazine were—in a chic section of the older downtown, a converted warehouse. He'd head over there.

He cast one look back at the family restaurant, scanning the empty parking lot, and shook his head.

THIRTY-EIGHT

It took him a bit of convincing at Kayla's office to be admitted into the inner sanctum. With a mildly guilty conscience, he realized that he had never really worried about this part of her life. Kayla had just appeared on the scene one day and stayed there as far as he was concerned. There had never been any functions where he would have met her staff or been introduced to anyone.

In any case, once he had found out she was in-house for the day, he worked every bit of the Beauregard charm and persuasion and finally found himself knocking at her office door. Knocking—really? If it had not been for the security guard who insisted on accompanying him, he would have... Never mind!

Kayla looked up from a desk covered in manuscripts and took off her tiny silver reading glasses.

"It's fine, Harry—you can go back downstairs. I will call if I need anything."

The security guard left, and Connor plunked himself into one of the visitor's chairs.

"Nice office, love—I just realized I've never been here."

"No, you have not," she said coolly and stood to take a bottle of water out of her little fridge. "Here, you probably need this."

"Desperately—thanks. Listen..."

"Don't try and spin a story for me, Connor. Please at least spare me this."

"What? I was going to say what a disaster of a weekend. No need for a story there."

Kayla sat back down behind her desk and eyed him cautiously.

"If I had known Byron could not hold his liquor—heck, I would never have agreed to take him on the trip, you know that. Who would have guessed?"

"You were not far behind him if I recall correctly."

"Trying to keep the worst from happening, that's for sure. I have to admit—I lost track of you while trying to herd our boy away from the worst messes."

"Unsuccessfully."

"Unsuccessfully." Connor did his best to look rueful and downcast. "I tried, Kayla, but once he let loose—it was like trying to shove a storm back out to sea."

"Interesting analogy for a sailing weekend."

"As much of a repressed little nerd as he is in this country, once we got him out there—Jesus."

Kayla flicked the stack of manuscripts on her desk with a finger. "Yes— you've provided quite a bit of fodder for the gossip magazine industry."

"Must be a slow news day... It was far from the bar brawl with attached orgy they make it look like. The guy got a little out of hand, I could not stop him, and the whole thing went downhill from there. I was telling Al and his father earlier..."

"You went to speak to them?"

"Of course I did. What was I going to do—wait for them to read some nonsense in a paper? No offense, but at least I know what really happened."

"I am amazed, to tell you the truth. When I went back to the hotel to get cash, you were in no shape."

Connor made a dismissive gesture. "Sure, it looked worse than it was. But the damage is done now, and our license for PerCan..."

"Your license will be under review for quite a bit longer I would think. Especially now that you will have to start all over again, making friends in the ministry."

"What do you mean?"

Another flick of her finger, another news story. Connor whistled. "They are considering taking the minister post away from Byron—that's a bit harsh, don't you think?"

"According to the official statements, they are unwilling to stand there in front of the media comparing who-did-what stories with the other people involved in the incident."

"That would be me."

"That would be you."

"I'm sure he simply does not remember what went on either, Kayla. I mean, you should have seen him. He was..."

"I did see, Connor, and I really do not have any desire to rehash the entire distasteful event again. I've had quite enough of it. On top of everything else, I've had to take numerous phone calls asking about my involvement in it."

"I am sorry."

"And I really wish I had never planned this weekend away. I think what you need to do is seriously buckle down for a little while, lay low, solve your problems with the company, with your drinking."

"I don't really..."

Kayla lifted a finger and shook her head. "And with other substances. You've done amazing work getting this company off the ground. Don't risk it all now."

He nodded, knowing better when a good time was to shut up and look to be in agreement.

"Get yourself straightened out. Ask for Rafa's help if you need it."

"And yours, I would assume," he said, eyes downcast, hands folded in his lap.

"And mine—of course I will help you. As long as this kind of thing..."

"Never happens again. I got it. Al's father basically said the same thing to me just a few hours ago."

"Connor." She sat back in her chair and folded her arms in front of her body. Closed off—to him. "I don't know what happened to you over the last few months."

"Nothing, I swear to you. There were just a lot of—things going on. Incompetent people doing incompetent things. And I will admit that I did not always deal well with them. I did not lead them the way they should have been. Instead, I let everybody do their little share of what is, as you know, a humongous task. Then, when I looked back..."

"Connor?"

"When I looked back to see if everybody was following me, I realized how many screwups along the way I hadn't even noticed. Things that went wrong, people who were doing what they thought was right."

"Really—you are going to tell me all of this only happened because you did not pay enough attention?"

"Had I been more involved with every step of the development of the company, I don't think it would have happened. That's right."

She looked past him, at a series of framed first-edition covers of the magazine, and finally shook her head.

"OK. If you really think that's why..."

"Trust me a little here. I do know what I'm doing—I studied this shit in university."

"And I did not—I get it."

"No, that's not what I am saying at all. You misunderstand. It's— you see—nowadays, the old-style boss who was involved in everything does not exist any longer. They teach you to start little focus groups who all have their individual tasks and report to the overall leader on a regular basis."

"OK." Kayla nodded. "Works like that around here. And it works fine. But?"

"But, apparently, that's not how it works in our company. I try to give people tasks and leave them to do their thing, and they fail to get me results. I thought Al's brother Dan had the licensing process well in hand—turns out I have to go out and make friends with a minister to make it happen. Turns out the minister is a drunkard and into underage prostitutes... I also thought Al and Rafael had the entire retrofit process of the building in hand."

"But..."

"But look at what happened! I had to chase around half the night dealing with emergencies during the party."

"That was annoying—true. You should not have had to deal with that."

"Right. I thought David and Tessa had the SEC reporting and accounting firmly in hand. Never expected a problem from that side. Instead, I've been trying to file with the SEC for months now—not happening. Hence, we are having finance problems. Hence we are having all sorts of problems. Sometimes, I don't know why I do it any longer."

He signed and dragged his hand through his hair, all the while watching carefully for her reaction. His instinct did not fail him. She smiled and came around from behind her desk.

"You do it because you believe in it, Connor—we both believe in it. This is just a temporary setback."

She wrapped her arms around him, and Connor leaned heavily against her.

"I wish I could believe that. Sometimes it's enough that I just want to walk away—do something else, you know. Something where not every single step is a battle."

"Don't you dare give up on this now. Connor Beauregard, you are not a quitter, and I am not going to let you quit, you understand?"

"You are far stronger than I am, Kayla."

"Bullshit—don't go maudlin on me on top of everything else. This is where it is a bit of an advantage not to have all of your education."

"How come?"

"Because I am a street fighter. I've always had to fight for what I want. I did not have the luxury to sit in a university lecture and learn about all of this. So, if it is not working, I figure out a way to make it work."

Connor said nothing. He'd never heard her talk like this, and it disturbed him a little. 'Whatever it takes' suddenly took on an entirely new meaning, and he had no doubt whatsoever she would get what she wanted. With or without him—that was the problem.

He smiled and took her hands into his, pressing his lips into her palms.

"I'm not giving up. Don't you worry about it. I just needed to hear that you are still standing behind me 100 percent. That's all. I am—under a lot of fire these days, as you might imagine."

"Life of a leader, my love—been there many a time too. Don't apologize and don't explain. Just do what you think is best, and it will all work out."

"Thank you—thank you for standing with me. I really mean that."

He shook his wrist to turn the big gold watch Kayla had given him a few month ago and checked the time.

"I think this kind of calls for a drink, do you not?"

"Three in the afternoon?"

"Not all that early, is it?"

Kayla smiled. "Right—OK—let me just finish a couple of things here, and I will meet you. The Lighthouse?"

Connor hesitated for just a moment. Almost everybody who hung out at The Lighthouse at this time of day was bound to know him. Then again, there was no good reason to hide out from anyone. There was no point in wondering if anyone might bring up the article that had been in almost every major paper this morning. Somebody was bound to bring it up within half an hour of Connor walking through the door. It only qualified as bad publicity if they spelled your name wrong. So, people would talk, and there he would be, front and center, telling the whole story—the real story.

"Yeah, might as well. Face the firing squad and all that."

"Don't apologize—don't explain, remember?"

"Yes, ma'am." He indicated a fake salute and jumped to his feet. "Thanks. Really. It means the world to me. Now hurry up—I'll be waiting."

THIRTY-NINE

He'd been right—he hadn't quite made it all the way to the bar before somebody asked him if he'd met any good underage prostitutes lately.

"I have to admit I have not," Connor said after a moment of pretend thinking. "But, then, I was lucky enough to take our wonderful Minister of Health out for a few drinks, and what do you know? They showed up! By the droves no less."

Raucous laughter—excellent. He had their attention at least.

"I am sure you partook, my dear Connor. You are not usually one who—questions something that is offered, no?"

"Well, considering I was with the Minister of Health, I could at least be sure we were talking about a clean house."

More laughter. He had walked into the perfect crowd for this type of off-color joke. And he enjoyed it. Why not? Let loose, have fun, joke around... Everybody in this bar—or nearly everybody—was the kind always chasing after the next big deal. They were alike, pushing deals back and forth, arguing, quibbling, financing each other's projects, secretly calling each other an ass behind the other's back. And it was all good at the end of day.

"So, what's that do to your license?"

"I don't know yet," he said, frowning. "We will have to see how this whole thing plays out. I really wish I had known Byron was such a..."

"Sissy?"

"Dirtbag! If I had known, do you think I would have placed the fate of my company into his hands? Of course not! I would have avoided the man and his prostitutes like the plague. C'est la vie!"

He raised a glass in a mock toast. "Next round—never give up."

"There are those who steadfastly claim the minister is actually an upstanding citizen—and this was more your fault than his."

Connor shrugged and grinned. "Yeah—that's what I would say too if I had a ministerial post to lose. Fortunately..."

"Yeah—fortunately, we already know you are a dirtbag. No secrets there."

More laughter, more jokes, and Connor ate it up. He knew they would pipe down when Kayla appeared. He also knew most of them suspected he was not entirely as innocent as he made it sound—but they were his kind of people, which meant it did not count.

"Did you not hear?" somebody finally said. "Byron Cartwright just stepped down as minister. Personal reasons, he says."

Connor could not keep the grin off his face. "Well, then, I am sure what he wants is to avoid a long, drawn-out scandal. Too bad for the man. He wasn't all bad. Made a few mistakes..."

"Hung out with you—that was one."

"Hey, hey, guys—let's keep it clean here. I'm not the one with the teenage girls here."

"Well—I'm not so sure. I think Señor Paul would..."

Someone hushed the speaker, just in time for Kayla to walk in and right up to stand beside Connor.

"Cartwright resigned," she said by way of greeting.

"I know. I heard. That's—good news, I guess."

"Not if you're him, I'm sure. And we don't know who is going to follow him."

"But by the time we do," Connor said and generously indicated a round for himself and all of his friends, "by the time we do, nobody will know, remember, or care what the heck happened in Martha's Vineyard."

"Teflon Beauregard," a voice somewhere in the crowd said, only to be drowned out by laughter, and Connor laughed right along. Yeah—he liked that one. He really did like that one.

Teflon Beauregard had every intention of reforming—or if not reforming, at least trying to do a little bit better going forward. The episode with Byron Cartwright had cut just a tiny bit too close to disaster for even his comfort. What if, indeed, he himself had been caught out the way the minister had? End of sweet life here at Kayla's hilltop condo with the never-ending supply of booze and vitamins and other pretty luxuries. End of being president and CEO of a hot-and-coming medical marijuana manufacturer. End of being the hero and golden boy of all the business magazines. Yesterday, they had called him the wizard of weed. *Tomorrow, well, you are only as good as your last press release, Connor*, he reminded himself. He did not even want to think about having to scrape about trying to find a new project again and starting over. No, sir, he'd been there, and he was not going back!

He'd tasted the good life, and he liked it. Therefore, he decided to pull himself together and be very, very good—for a little while. It wasn't that hard; he'd done it before. And it was not forever.

For a few days, he worked out every day, drank in moderation only, and actually went to the office every single morning at nine o'clock to do—something. The 'something' tripped him up now and then because, while Tessa remained buried behind a wall of papers, stoically not speaking to him unless it was utterly unavoidable, he really felt kind of useless and lost most of the time.

Obsessively checking his phone every three minutes, hoping some potential investor had called and his ringer was dead for some reason, he flipped open his laptop, staring at the screen, looking busy. Mostly, he cruised idly around the internet, trying to locate more stories about Byron's demise. It was not pretty; that much he realized.

He knew he needed to generate some kind of documentation for David, and he tried his best. But every time he did, suddenly, David would come back to him and complain the date was wrong, or the signatures not complete, or the wording ambiguous. Damn that man anyway.

Fortunately, he had been able to skirt the issue of the trip to Zurich. That one David could not investigate or check out. Not the Zurich trip.

Having all those shares safely tucked away with a couple of nameless corporations in Switzerland gave him a marginal feeling of safety. If the worst ever happened—if the worst happened, he could transfer those shares a few at a time and still make some money. As long as Perfect Cannabis remained a viable entity, nothing could happen to Connor Beauregard. But all of that depended on the fact that no one knew who really owned those shares.

No one—not even Kayla, not even Rafa.

Rafa would have given him the lecture on insider trading and the dangers of said operation, and Kayla would have been pissed off at him for not sharing. He owned more shares at the moment than he should anyway. He'd have to be very, very careful and not rock the boat with Al and his family members. Always look out for number one; always have a little bit of insurance up a sleeve somewhere. Always. Rules his father taught him a long time ago—not exactly in this very format and not on this subject, but even the good old Reverend Marty had lived by those rules.

In his heyday, the good reverend certainly would not have been above insider trading or hiding shares away in dummy corporations for future use. That kind of stuff just went under 'having a plan.'

Forget the old man. If he had said it once, he'd said it a dozen times—he did not have a son any longer. Connor rested his hands on the armrests of his chair and stared beyond the screen of his laptop out at the busyness of the harbor. Say what you would about Al's family, but at least they seemed to stick together and closed ranks against strangers.

That particular thought reminded him about the guy at the grand opening again. Weeks had gone by now, and still, he could not figure out who the man had been. He had tried to forget the incident, and still, it would not leave him alone. Persistently nagging at his gut, he needed to answer the question, who had walked in without his knowledge, spoken to Al, and disappeared again. Period, end of story—he just needed to know.

Connor looked up when Tessa said goodbye for the day and wished her a pleasant evening. Since he had given those shares to her, she had at least stopped whining about money every single day. *Oh, how easily ye of small minds are blinded.*

If he played his cards right, he would get a few more months of decent work out of her before she started up complaining again.

David, on the other hand, knew how the game was played. He had taken his shares and muttered something about this would do—for now.

Before everyone's patience ran out, the damned SEC filings would just have to be done, one way or another, so he could raise a little more money and be the hometown hero to all again.

In the meantime—in the meantime Connor felt like one of those wild animals you saw on TV that had been stuck into a cage. He wanted to move forward, wanted to run, to get going. He just did not know what direction yet.

The shadows outside his office window lengthened, and he realized he had spent one entire goddamned day inside an office. That had never happened before. Never in as long a history as he could remember. One entire day. Jesus, if it wasn't such a sad damned thing, he would have congratulated himself on his business and goodness. Damn—he needed to do something. Anything!

He would have gone to La Cosa or The Lighthouse for a celebratory drink, except that his closest friends, led by Rafa and Kayla, were keeping an exceedingly close eye on him since the Martha's Vineyard incident.

He paced back and forth for a while and, on the spur of the moment, decided to take a drive down to the building. He had not been there since the night of the grand opening, and he really wanted to see what Rafa had done in the meantime.

If he had to take a guess, probably nothing. Or maybe torn out a few more walls and put up a couple of new ones. He had a strong suspicion his friend could create work for himself until the end of all time without actually accomplishing anything.

"Not much point complaining, old friend," he said to himself, pocketing his car keys.

Thanks to Kayla's generosity, the monster SUV had escaped repossession—this time. It was really high time things got back to normal. Starting with David getting that goddamned filing out of the way, so the people he spoke to could have some confidence in him and in the company again, instead of seeing a holy mess when they attempted to look.

FORTY

Behind the building, he could still see the outline of the great big white square Kayla had had painted on the ground for the helicopter—his helicopter—the night of the grand opening, and he became a little melancholy looking at it.

Again, since the ill-fated trip to Martha's Vineyard, he had followed the advice of his friends and laid low for a while, parking the helicopter instead of taking that beautiful machine here, there, and everywhere. He just burned to take it out and get some mileage out of it.

Rafael's people actually had been busy, he discovered, sprucing up the outside of the building so it did not look like the giant rectangular trash heap it really was. The rented greenery from the grand opening had disappeared, but there was decent outside lighting, a paved parking lot, and a newly painted loading dock at the far end.

Which, come to think of it, was just typical of Rafael again, now was it not? Look at it—a loading dock? What the fuck would they need a loading dock for now of all times? Production was still months ahead—if not longer, given the delays in licensing—and another six months on top of that before they finally shipped the first harvest. Had no one but Connor himself read the capital expenditures plans? No one?

It took him several tries to find the right key for the giant security glass front doors and once he stood in their impressive entrance hall, he smiled again. Yes—this was still what he had built. This was the confirmation that he had done it right.

He stood there and for a minute allowed himself to imagine what it would be like, with receptionists and front desk people, a switchboard and a couple of security guards right there. Had to have security guards, given the kind of product they were manufacturing. And right over there, past those grey steel doors, if he remembered correctly, would be the grow areas.

If he closed his eyes, he could see Dan's plans. The man really had done an amazing job for someone who had never grown marijuana before. Or maybe he had—you never knew.

And somewhere above the first floor, he would install a glass cube that was his office, so he could look down at everything that was going on. Yeah—he would definitely do that!

Connor opened his eyes again. His company. Yes, it would be amazing. He kind of imagined that was how a father would feel, looking around at his brood of children. And children kind of just happened. This—this he had had to work for, hard.

He took a deep breath and tried to take it all in—his company. It did not fail him. The pride raised him up and healed the bruises of the past few weeks. Now he was complete again.

People coming and going. Signs, brochures, posters. All proclaiming the good they were doing here. He would have to tell Rafael to do something about the awful transformer hum that echoed in the front hall, though. It was enough to drive you crazy if you listened to it for more than a few minutes, and nowadays, there was no good reason for that kind of annoying hum any longer.

That thought made him stop and turn back into the middle of the entry hall. Two things: One, if the building was empty and not much happening, what the heck was that noisy transformer powering anyway? And two, if the building was empty and nothing happening, could he finally give into his curiosity and find out where that mystery stranger from the grand opening had gained entry?

Connor took a step toward what looked like newer doors, feeling oddly like an intruder in his own building.

He straightened his shoulders and tried to ignore the pit in his stomach, and one minor push on the doors and he flicked the lights on in the great hall. It was all as he remembered it—minus the pomp and circumstance, the bandstands, the buffet tables and the bars, the red carpet, the lighting, the glitter and glam. Too bad, really. Now it looked like what it really was: an enormous warehouse building with metal pillars spaced at regular intervals, conical industrial light fixtures every ten feet, and a few dirty skylights that would have to go.

Connor stood under one of the skylights and looked up. They really would have to go.

A sound made him twitch, and he turned one complete circle to try to see where it might have come from. Just a short, sharp thwack. The kind you got when you slammed a door or dropped a giant box of some sort.

"Beauregard, you are starting to hallucinate," he said out loud, laughing at the way his voice echoed.

Man, he really was losing it. Maybe he had been drinking too much over the last few months, and the drugs—well, the drugs could not help either, now could they? *OK, you, me, and the fencepost, Beauregard,* he thought. *You have been overdoing it big time. So cut back a little. Just a tiny bit, that's all... No need to go overboard.*

Another thunk.

"Go home," he said out loud to himself. "Go home. Take Kayla out for a nice dinner."

But, there it was again—metal clanging, maybe. Muffled but still definitely there. He stood facing the wall and put his hands into his sides.

He moved toward the north wall of his building, slowly, stealthily as if he expected someone to jump out of the shadows.

"Get fucking real," he muttered and stopped, scrutinizing the wall before him. It was just that, a goddamned white-painted gypsum wall. The end of the building.

Fuck, what was he doing here—what was he even looking for? This was the outside wall of the building, was it not?

Connor took a step closer and put both of his hands against the wall. He could feel warmth. More so than he had expected from an outside wall.

Connor dropped his hands again and looked around. The left- and right-hand walls, though at least 50 to 100 feet away in either case, were rough, unpainted, cinder block walls.

Outside walls: plain, unpainted cinder block, probably cool to the touch, reflecting the outside chill.

He turned to the wall in front of him again.

Smooth, white-painted gypsum board, warm to the touch.

Meaning... Meaning there was something beyond it radiating heat. Meaning there was a part of the building he did not even know—yet.

Another utility room? A part that did not show up on Dante's plans for the manufacturing area or Rafael's construction plans either. He was sure about it. More powerful than his initial curiosity, righteous anger now drove him to get to the bottom of this, and he strode all the way to the northwest corner of the building. He put one hand on either side of himself. Cinder block cool roughness at one end; smooth, painted gypsum on the other. Warmth on one side; chill on the other. He turned perpendicular to the smooth, painted wall and began to pace it off one step at a time, his hand trailing along the painted wall.

One, two, three, four, five. Counting did not serve any useful purpose whatsoever, but it helped him focus and concentrate. 15, 16, 17. Nothing. He could neither see a door, a hatch or any other opening in that goddamn wall, and yet he knew there had to be one. If something lay behind that wall, there was a way to get to it—some way—and he would find it. Now. Then he would go home.

347, 348, 349—still nothing. Connor wanted to scream. Nothing. The goddamn white wall mocked him, solid and still. All the while, he knew something lay beyond and had no way to get there.

Stoically, he turned around again and began pacing the same way back, slower this time. Right about halfway down, a pillar blocked his path, about a foot away from the gypsum wall. Last time, he had stepped around it. This time, he kept his fingers trailing along the smooth wall, picking up dust, dirt, and paint, and squeezed between the pillar and the wall. Damned thing. It got in the way right where it was; it would have to go.

And then he felt it—the slightest bit of an irregularity, a seam in the smooth wallboards. Just sanded and finished finely enough so you could not feel it unless you squeezed your body right between the pillar and the smooth wall.

Connor stopped closed his eyes and let his fingertips feel the seam in the wallboard. It went all the way up from the floor to about a six-foot height. Then it turned 45 degrees perpendicular.

Like a door.

Damn, he needed a flashlight. When he closed his eyes, he found it—the tiniest gap between wallboards, hidden carefully by the meager lighting in the hall and the awkward placement of the pillar behind him—but there it was. He followed the gap a little and finally found that it gave to a more energetic push: a more-or-less hidden, but almost invisibly installed, swinging door.

When he had pushed it open perhaps an inch or so, he stopped, heart pounding violently, palms sweating, convinced that in some way he had been or was doing something wrong. Which was absurd, of course. Here he was standing in his own building, a building he had purchased while getting into bed with a loan shark, had protected, celebrated, and cursed at times, and still, he worried about going through a door he knew nothing about?

Absurd.

He took out his cellphone to call Rafael, his closest friend in the entire world, who would most certainly know what to do about it, and had just punched in the area code when he put the phone away again.

The swinging door was installed so perfectly, so seamlessly and well hidden—who but an experienced contractor could do a thing like that? Who but someone like that would be smart enough to hide the doorway behind an inconvenient pillar like this?

The realization and instant feeling of betrayal made his stomach sink again, while at the same time, his hands tightened to angry fists, and his jaw set. Dammit.

He and Rafael had thought of this company together. They had stood there, shoulder to shoulder, while he raised the first timid funds, sold a few shares, fought through the acquisition of the shell company and the amalgamation. They had drunk together, celebrating every little step of the way, gone through hell and back together to get it done, and now—now Rafa would betray him? After all of it?

Never. Rafael would never in his life betray him.

Connor repeated the thought in his mind, more to taste its flavor than to convince himself.

Connor smiled when he remembered the way they had stood outside the auxiliary room door, arguing about what to do about Mirko, looking like utter, complete fools, he was certain. Rafael had not even hesitated to stand there with him; he had not left either when Mirko told him he was free to do so.

Everybody else—but not Rafael, of that he was certain.

And if he needed yet another reason to find out what was located behind this wall, then that was it. Resolutely, he pushed against the swinging panel, opened it just a little further, and stuck his head through the gap. No need to announce himself in grand fashion if anyone were really there.

Not that he need have worried.

Beyond the swinging wall panel, a tall and narrow room opened to his view. Someone had simply cut a good 30 feet off the end of the building in an area no one was likely to look closely at.

This part of the building was brightly lit by a row of closely spaced overhead lights, and it was hot in here—hot enough to make the sweat bead on his forehead almost instantly. This, he thought, was why the wall had been warmer than the actual outside wall, which, of course, was what had led him here.

Connor slipped into the open space and stood close to the open panel door for a moment until his eyes had adjusted to the bright lights. He wiped his face with the sleeve of his shirt and loosened his collar. Squinting upwards to the ceiling almost blinded him, and he quit trying. These, he knew, were no ordinary warehouse lighting fixtures. The stuff you bought at Home Depot emitted neither this kind of heat nor the intense brightness. No. The reason the sweat now poured profusely from his brow and back was most certainly due to the fact that he stood below rows and rows of hydroponic grow lights.

He'd seen them during his trip to Colorado and recognized the shape: large, square, super-bright. Lights with silvery, wing-like reflectors behind them, focusing the brightness downward, down to where it could be used for its intended purpose:

To grow enormous amounts of cannabis.

Connor felt as if he would pass out from the hammering of his own heart in his ears. The only time he'd seen the stuff other than in bags as a college boy had also been during his trip to Colorado, but who was he kidding? Before him stretched rows upon rows of healthy, five-fingered, lush greenery, each plant nestled not in dirt, but in deep trays of gel-like growing medium. He could almost hear Dan's voice in his ear.

What we need to do with these plants is to play God, Connor, and the only way we get to play God is to provide a controlled amount of everything these plants need—light, nutrients, water, and support.

He had read about all of this in Dan's reports and plans. The pale white grow medium, releasing exact amounts of nutrients; the lights turning on and off at prescribed intervals, changing colors; regulating the temperature via integrated exhaust and air conditioning units behind every single lamp.

Connor knew the function of each and every piece of equipment in here. He had seen it before, read about it, explained it to investors, and, without taking another step closer, he knew what he had come upon: An extremely efficient and sophisticated marijuana-growing operation, right under everyone's very nose.

He heard the thumping noise again—the very one that had alerted him earlier that all was not right in his own building, and he turned toward it. One of the lights, he realized, was failing. Perhaps the air conditioning device had broken or something in the light itself was broken, but all of a sudden, it had started to vibrate violently and in doing so struck the metal strut beside it at regular intervals. Clank—clank. If it had not been for this broken light, he would never have found this room.

A little distance away, he saw a few computer monitors and a control panel glowing in the dark and an emergency light flashing at 20-second intervals, and immediately, he realized a couple of things:

One, someone amongst his closest friends was betraying him, and two, whoever it was had put the most sophisticated operation he had ever seen together. This was an expert. And since said expert could not be here personally at all times, he would have a installed a way to monitor and control this operation remotely.

He would be aware of this alarm—and he might be on his way into the building at this very moment.

Connor wiped his hands on his pants and stood undecided for a moment.

Rage at having been betrayed by someone made him want to take a convenient crowbar and smash everything in sight until nothing but a trash heap was left, curiosity made him want to wait to see who might be showing up to fix the problem, and self-preservation told him that his car stood out there in the parking lot, broad and visible under the bright security lights, and anyone driving up to the building would know he was in it.

Get out of here—in a damned hurry, he thought.

Good plan! Connor took a step closer to the marijuana plants in front of him and touched the leaves of the closest plants almost lovingly. The spiky texture of the leaves felt rough and unforgiving to the touch, fighting back where he wanted to reach out and grab them.

Healthy little buggers they were. If nothing else, it was good to see their planned operation indeed worked in real life as well as on paper.

Whoever had put this little operation behind that wall stood to earn a good chunk of money, and, if Connor had anything to do with it, he would get his just share. There was just no way—no absolute bloody way in hell—anything about this little extension was even remotely legal. No way at all. Period, end of statement.

But it did have potential. Potential and possibilities that bore thinking about. What he was standing here and staring at so open-mouthed was the end to all of their money troubles.

Why not, he thought? Why not use all of the money, clout, and opportunities the legitimate company would afford him, to support a little sideline? Just a tiny little operation, to produce recreational-use marijuana in quantity and quality acceptable to a moneyed and discerning end user? In a way, when he and Rafa had been sitting there, drinking and joking, that's what they had said—*let's go be drug dealers.*

There had to be a legitimate side to things—naturally.

The sharp clunk from the broken light brought him sharply back to reality. Indeed, it was time to split. This was neither the time nor the place to negotiate with the brilliant mind that had cooked this operation up. His time would come—most definitely—but this was not it.

Connor left through the panel in the wall, making sure to close it up as carefully and tightly fit as he had found it, and stood in the shadows again for a moment until his eyes had adjusted once again to the sparsely lit warehouse hall.

The remainder of the building lay in silence. Connor did not dare move and listened into the dark for anything out of the ordinary. There was the odd clanging sound from behind this wall, the hum from an overhead light fixture, and the much louder one from the mysterious transformer he had noticed earlier. It must have provided a steady power supply for all of those lights in there, Connor thought, and wondered how anyone had got away running up a hydro bill as much as they must, without being noticed.

When he was finally convinced he was still the only person in the building, he left.

FORTY-ONE

Outside, he dashed to his car. Without looking back, he put the vehicle into gear and fought the impulse to peel out of the lot.

He hit the highway and drove like a saint, skirting the speed limit right at the proper edge. He needed to think right now, and neither Kayla nor Rafael could help him.

Rafael...

His hands clenched tighter on the steering wheel when he thought about his friend. How long had they known each other now? 15 years? 20? How many deals had they done together, how many triumphs and failures celebrated holding up the rails of some seedy bar together, hoisting a drink to one more time, to a better tomorrow, to a rosier future? How many?

Let's face it, Connor thought. Who but a skilled contractor could build a hidden room such as the one he had just investigated?

When he had left the outskirts of town behind, he decided to pull off the highway and coasted into the parking lot of the nearest bar he could find. The hell with being good tonight. His life had just received a major blow to the kidneys, so to speak, so his liver would simply have to deal.

He picked a simple, nondescript bar in a strip mall just off the highway, plopped himself behind the bar, and ordered a large beer. That one down, he ordered another.

Facts, Beauregard, just facts.

Fact. Somebody was growing marijuana in his building, in his company, working into their own pocket.

Fact. This person might—would have to be—one of his closest friends and insiders to pull the entire thing off right under his nose, using knowledge and information Connor had probably paid for.

Fact. Connor was not getting anything out of this deal but trouble. Trouble with hydro bills, trouble with regulators, trouble with the licensing board… the list did not even bother to narrow down there, never mind end.

Connor brought his hands together and put them up to his nose. Something had to be done about it—the question was what. Coincidentally, it was a brilliant idea. Growing marijuana in a marijuana-manufacturing facility. How absolutely perfect, brilliant, and simple. How amazingly genius!

Hiding in plain sight, where nobody would bother to look, or know what they were looking at if it slapped them in the face.

Dammit, why had he not thought of it himself? The possibilities were endless, and if done right—if done right, endlessly profitable. His mouth began to water thinking of all the money he could make.

The solution to every problem he had faced in the past few weeks was right in front of him. Now he could go and hire the most brilliant and gifted growers to be found in the country and offer them all the money in the world. Suddenly, he could expand and hurry the project up the way he wanted to… damn!

Connor Beauregard, the builder of companies, would be the hero once again, while everybody else tried to figure out how the heck he had done it. It was perfection on wheels once you thought of it.

So, who had thought of it first? Who was it who had got there before him and stolen the best idea? Whoever it was, he would have to be eliminated because Connor Beauregard did not share.

"You look like a man with the weight of the world on his shoulders."

He looked up into the bright blue eyes of a young man of maybe 20, standing behind the bar, waggling Connor's empty glass.

"Another one?"

"Sure." Connor nodded. "Need it today."

"Trouble at home?"

"Depends on how you define at home," Connor said, taking a deep drink from the fresh beer. "At the very least—royal betrayal."

"Betrayal. Sounds like it sucks big time."

"When I get my hands on him," Connor said, letting his fantasy run wild, "when I get my hands on him, he'll pay. Friend or not."

"Wouldn't blame you. Your friends are supposed to have your back—always, no matter what. Are you sure?"

"Yes—maybe—pretty sure." Connor took another drink and stared at the amber liquid in his glass. Was he sure? No. Not 100 percent, but realistically—who could be behind it?

Rafael fit all the criteria. At the very least, he would have to know about it, have come across it, being as personally involved in the construction as he was. But then there was Al. How about Al? He'd have the knowledge, the underworld connection, the personality... everything. He also fit the profile. Together? Would they pull it off together? Al had come and gone through the building like he owned it—through that space, perhaps? Did it have another entrance? Was the mysterious stranger Al's personal grower and gardener? And how and where did Rafael fit into their scheme?

"No, I am not sure," he finally said. "Don't have all the facts—yet. But I just can't see a way he could not know....And why, why would he do it?"

"It's amazing how fast betrayal becomes a viable option, given the right set of circumstances," the young bartender said and moved down the bar to serve a beer to another patron.

Given the right set of circumstances... But Rafael really had no reason to betray him, did he? Al, on the other hand...

"So why would Al want to betray me?" he said to himself and folded his hands in front of his face, thinking.

"Friend? Business partner?" his young bartender asked, and Connor nodded.

"Business partner. Makes no difference, does it?"

"It could."

"You know," Connor said, "for a person who knows nothing about this at all, you have an amazing wealth of knowledge to impart. Perhaps he wants to take over—that is a definite possibility."

"Glad to help."

The young man shuffled off, and Connor looked back into his beer glass again. What would he do if he were Al and wanted to take over Perfect Cannabis? How would he do it?

Of course. Easy. He would discredit Connor in one way or another, buy up a large majority of outstanding shares while the share price took a momentous tumble, and then vote him out with a majority shareholder vote. It could work like that. Why a secret little grow op in the back of the building, though? What purpose did it serve?

Come to think of it, there had been more than enough chances to discredit him, and no one had tried. So why now, and why like this?

Follow the money, then. Grow ops generated cash—large amounts of cash. Perhaps that was all this was about—cash. Enough to buy up those shares? Except he was still missing something. Some tiny little detail he could not put his hands on.

Damn, what was he missing? Money, cash… did Al's family not have enough money to do what they wanted? Why did they need extra? Greed, perhaps? They just wanted it? No—that did not feel right either. There still had to be one element he was missing. Damn.

Connor put down his money on the table and finished his beer. He needed someone to talk this through with. Somebody—anybody. Rafael? For as long as he could remember, Rafael had been the one man he could go to when he needed to work something out in his mind.

He stepped into his car and sat there for a moment.

How big was the chance Rafael was involved in any of this? Pretty big. He had to deal with that. Pretty goddamned big. He was out there—every single day almost. How did he not see that false wall? How did an experienced construction manager not see that there was a whole end of the building cut off? How?

Slowly, he took his phone out and dialed Rafael's number. When his friend answered, he took a moment.

"Connor, is that you?"

"Yes—yes, Rafael, I am here."

"What's up? It is bloody late."

Do or die, Beauregard, ask the right question. Did you or did you not put an illegal grow op into the back of my building without involving me in any way?

"Have you been out to the building lately?"

"I try to drop by—look in on things…."

"I don't want to know if you drop by, Rafael. I want to know if you've been there, checking on the construction, doing what needs to be done, working on the build out."

"I—shit—Connor, I haven't been at the building since the grand opening, OK? It's not like we did any real work there. Rip out a couple of walls, put on a show, put in some offices, not like you needed me there for anything."

"So, you did not supervise the process yourself? Answer my question. Have you spent any kind of time there?"

"Jesus, Connor—what is this? An accounting of how much I do for you? There was no need to be there on a regular basis. We weren't doing any serious construction."

"Did you or did you not supervise the construction perfectly every single step of the way? Just answer me. A simple yes or no will do."

"I…."

"Rafa—fuck—just answer, OK?"

"Fine, fine, Connor. OK. I did not, all right? You can crucify me over it later if you want—but there's a big downtown strip mall I have to work on, so I let Jesse take the brunt of the supervising."

"Jesse?"

"Construction supervisor I hired for my company. He's new, but he's pretty good. Does his job. Look—he knew all he had to do were a few cosmetic things, and he did them. I checked on him now and then, and he seemed just fine. Now what is this all about? Did some damned wall fall down or what? Because I can't see...."

"No, Rafael, don't worry about it," Connor said, feeling the pit in his stomach open up with a huge sigh of relief. "No—it's perfectly fine. It is absolutely fine."

"You gonna tell me what this is all about?"

"I—might...." Connor said, unwilling to open everything up just then. "I will, at some point. For now—for now—this is enough. "

"I don't get it."

"Neither should you, Rafa. This is good. I will talk to you later."

He hung up without another word and rested his face in his hands. Not Rafael then. Not his friend. Rafael could not lie worth shit, and he would have known if he tried. Not Rafa. For a moment he was happy—unreasonably happy—and at the same time angry with himself because it made a difference. Hell, Connor Beauregard was a lone wolf, but every man needed someone he could talk to without judgement and without filtering and editing every word said, and Rafael had always been that man.

He did not want to need anybody, but still, he was happy to have a decent assumption that the betrayal did not originate with Rafael. And the fact that he was happy about it bothered him even more than the possibility of betrayal had in the first place.

He drove back into town slowly, trying to assess his options. If he took Rafael out of the equation, he was left with Al and his miserable damned family, except for the one fact that he could not figure out. Why would he do it? Why?

Not for the money. It just did not feel right. He did not know how he knew, but that was not it.

It struck him when he least expected it, pondering the grow op in the building: Kayla's voice. *He looks a little like Al.*

Of course. What if he were another one of Al's family—a brother, a cousin, someone Connor had never seen? The storybook crime family—and he had come around to make sure that his secret stayed safe?

"God-triple-damn it," Connor said and started the engine.

He floored the accelerator, letting his anger have free rein.

Tonight, he would take his company back from Al and his goddamned family once and for all—repeat—no matter what he had to do to get it. It all ended right here and right now.

Connor drove by Rafael's office building and saw the light still on in the corner office he knew to be Rafa's. Leaving the car stopped where he was, right there at the curb, he stepped out and ran up two floors, taking the stairs two at a time.

He stormed into Rafael's office without knocking and found his friend staring at the bluish screen of his little laptop.

"Connor, what the…"

"Al—when you need to get him, how do you do it?"

"What do you mean?"

"When you want to call him or talk to him or meet him—how do you do it?"

Rafael took off his reading glasses and leaned back in his chair.

"Tell me what's going on, bro. You look like—well, you look like shit. That's what you look like. First, you call me with a stupid question. Now this…"

"Not now, Rafa. Al—how do I get in touch with him?"

"There's—a way. But I'm not going to tell you while you stand in front of me acting like an asshole."

"Rafa…"

"If you meet Al or one of his family acting like this, you're more likely to end up behind the dumpster of one of his bars with a few extra bruises, OK? So bring it down a notch or two and tell me what the fuck this is all about."

Connor blinked. Rafa really did not swear all that often—at least not in a serious tone the way he did right now. Which made you pay attention when he did. And he had a point, after all.

Connor dropped his body into the visitor's chair across from Rafa and tried to do just that—come down a notch. There was still a chance, a chance, that Rafa was involved somehow.

"Something—happened out at the building."

"Something? Something serious? Something wrong with the construction we did? Problems?"

"Nothing like that, no. I just—have to talk to Al, that's all. And I have to do it now. I would not ask you if it were not important."

"Better. I still don't like it."

"I know you don't, but you're the only one who can get me in touch. I can drive out to that stupid hole-in-the-wall diner where his father hangs out..."

"I would not suggest it."

"And I don't think they would let me into the back or ever admit they were back there in the first place. What the hell are they into, Rafa, and why did you get me involved with them in the first place?"

"If I might remind you—you needed money for this project, badly. And your experience with Mirko ought to have shown you..."

"No more loan sharks. That might have been a little ill-advised, I admit it, but, hell—Al and his family? How much worse are they? 100 times."

"Possible. They have their hands in a lot of cookie jars, but Al has always been upfront with me. No bullshit, no hiding anything."

"That's why you end up behind a dumpster getting the crap beat out of you. That's real straightforward," he said, shaking his head.

Rafael shrugged. "Al has a few lines he won't cross. His father, who knows?"

"So get me in touch with them. There is something I need to know, and it can't wait."

"You won't tell me?"

Connor shook his head and forced himself to ignore the look on his friend's face, the hard line of his jaw and the narrowed eyes.

"OK then—wait here."

"But…"

"Wait here, Connor." Rafael all but pointed at the chair in which he sat, and Connor felt his hands clench again with anger, but he said nothing.

Five minutes and the door opened again, and Rafael stepped back into his office.

"Done playing hide-and-seek?" he asked, not even caring that he sounded more like a spoiled brat, instead of the finely honed sarcasm he had been trying for.

"Half an hour," Rafael said simply and sat back down. "At the diner—go in like usual. Don't ask too many questions."

"That's it?"

"That's it… Oh, and—what the fuck?"

What the fuck? *Same thing I want to ask*, Connor thought, but he was not going to hang around and discuss it with Rafael. He picked up his keys and left the office with a curt nod. Once it played all out, once he knew who had done what, and why—he could always come back here and sort things out with Rafa. Now he had a few questions to ask of his odd business partners.

FORTY-TWO

By now, the drive had become rather familiar. The diner set back in the humongous parking lot, lit up like a Christmas tree but mostly deserted. *Be hard to sneak up on somebody right here, wouldn't it,* he thought as he parked, and put that thought away again right quick. Not now.

This time, he actually found a couple of patrons sitting in a corner booth, eating some type of deep-fried substance that made his skin crawl, loudly discussing a ballgame he was not familiar with.

Instinct made him sit down at a table first and wait for his familiar bored waitress.

So he sat down, picked up one of the menus, and pretended to read with his head down until a red-and-white checked apron appeared in his field of vision.

"What'll you have?"

"Mineral water—and a conversation."

He looked up, and Dinah put her pen away again, cocking a thumb over her shoulder. "Back there, and hurry up about it, will you?"

Hurry up about it. Connor bit the angry answer back and rose. Past the familiar dim hallway and the noise and smells from the kitchen, he finally stopped at the plain door at the end and knocked. *Not too timid now, Beauregard.* He straightened his shoulders and knocked again, until the door finally opened as if by magic.

There they all sat at the long end of the plain gray table he remembered—Al, Dan, and the Original Chef. Al rested his chin in his hands, Dan fidgeted, and their father sat as always, straight-backed with his hands in his lap.

"Hello, Al, Dan—sir," he said, forcing as much calm into his voice as he could manage.

The three of them sitting there… something—his survival instinct again, perhaps—told him to tread very, very carefully.

Al and Dan merely nodded.

"Hello, Connor," their father said almost pleasantly. "Well now—the second time in just a few days. This is indeed unusual. I assume you have come here because there is a problem you need my help with."

Straight to the point then. If that was the way he wanted to play it, Connor was game. He pulled out a chair and sat without being asked to. A flicker of irritation crossed the Original Chef's otherwise bland face, and Connor enjoyed it.

"You bet there is," he said and looked at Al and Dan in turn. "You bet. I was out at the building tonight checking on a few things, and you would not believe what I found."

"It is pretty hard to impress me these days, Connor, so why don't you just tell me without a lot of drama?"

Connor locked eyes with Al and Dan in turn, challenging them, and only Al would meet his gaze. Dan looked down at the piece of string he'd been fingering all along, and Connor almost smiled. Bingo. Something going on there.

"Why don't you, Dan?" he asked sweetly. "I'm sure you know what I am talking about."

"Nope." Still not meeting his eyes.

"How about you, Al? There's another piece of the puzzle here anyway. The unexpected visitor at the grand opening."

Al blinked as if Connor had reached out and slapped him.

"The—visitor…? What do you mean?"

"I mean the man I saw you with at the grand opening. No one seems to know him, no one had heard of him, he was not on the guest list. But—imagine that—Kayla felt that he looked a lot like you. Or your brother Dan here."

At this point Al's father raised both of his hands, index fingers extended. He looked from Al to Dan and hissed something Connor didn't catch. What he did get was the man was not happy—not at all.

Al answered in the same language, confusion spreading on his face.

"What's going on?" Connor asked, considerably annoyed. "Did no one ever teach you that it is impolite to speak in a foreign language when not everybody is familiar with that language?"

"I do not believe I have asked for your opinion," the Chef said, narrowing his eyes at Connor. "I am having a conversation with my sons, and believe me, they understand every word I tell them—better than you do, perhaps."

"Oh, this is bullshit." Connor rose and snapped the cuffs of his sports jacket. "If you need me to spell it out, sir—somebody put an illegal grow op into the back of the building, and I am pretty sure one or both of your sons are involved here, and I have no intentions..."

The blow came so fast Connor had no chance to react or prepare himself. All it had taken was one single gesture from the Original Chef, and the doors behind Connor had opened. As far as he could tell, two men had entered, grabbed his shoulders, kneed him in the back, and forced him to sit back down in his chair.

They stood left and right of the door now, like statues, while Connor fought to take his next breath.

"Fuck..." he coughed, pushing his hand into his lower back.

"Perhaps you need to remember your manners as well, Mr. Beauregard." Without missing a beat, their father turned to Al and Dan again and rapidly fired questions at them. It could have been Spanish; Connor thought it sounded a bit like it, but he was no expert. His chest became tight, and he felt as if he might black out.

"Fuck..."

It earned him another stern look, but he really did not care at that moment. The rapid exchange between the three men grew in volume and speed, and he would have given money to know what they were talking about. Dan gestured wildly, the string he'd been fidgeting with flying around the air. Al kept shrugging his shoulders and waving his hands. He did not know, Connor realized. He really did not know anything. Interesting father-son dynamic. He'd always assumed Al and his father were close.

Yeah, just about as close as Marty and he were.

He rose from his chair just a little, and the two goons behind him moved in about a foot each.

"Oh, relax," he said. "What do you think—I'm going to attack him in here, with all of you standing there? I might be crazy, but I am not an idiot."

"Perhaps it is better you leave now," Al's father said, and the two goons came to stand to the left and right of him, ready to grab hold.

"Look—all I want to know is what happened out there at my building. It is my company."

"Perhaps, Mr. Beauregard, perhaps—although I think the last time I checked, it was a public company, and our family owned quite a few shares."

"You can't do this. I don't care who you are—but you can't just have an illegal grow op in the middle of town, no matter how many shares you own."

The goons came a little closer, each one of them now taking one of Connor's elbows, and he shook them off rudely.

"Dan—you are the one who read all the licensing requirements. Come on. Tell him this is not happening. It can't happen. This will ruin the entire company."

"He's right, Connor. Just let us sort this out, OK? Trust me—it will be straightened out without your intervention."

His two guards took hold of his elbows again, and Connor reached out to slap one of them away. Bad move. Really bad move. He realized it as soon as his feet left the floor and he felt a crushing blow to the back of his head.

He was getting rid of them—this time he was really getting rid of them, he swore to himself, even as the blackness took hold of him.

FORTY-THREE

The parking lot lay entirely empty, and all the lights in the diner had been extinguished by the time he came to again. His dashboard clock read well past midnight, so he had been unconscious for the better part of a couple of hours.

"Fuck."

He rubbed a goose-egg-sized bruise at the back of his skull and swore again. Never—never in the most desperate moments of his life should he have taken these assholes' money and given them a part of his company. His company! By now, he was almost certain they had something to do with the grow op in the back, although what, he still could not figure out.

He felt in his pockets for his wallet and phone, relieved to find both. Why he thought they might have robbed him, he did not know either, but the thought of being stranded without money or his phone in the middle of the night in a bad part of town sounded like something they might enjoy.

He had missed a couple of calls from Kayla, which he would return later. Hell, if they took his company, nothing much would matter anymore anyway, now would it? He was just about to slide the phone back into his pocket when it occurred to him. Rafael—this most likely meant Rafael had nothing to do with the whole thing.

"Rafa, it's me."

"Connor, shit—what the heck did you do this time?"

"Nothing. I need you."

"No shit—you got any idea how late it is?"

"12:49," Connor said, glancing at his dashboard clock. "I need you to meet me at the building right now."

"Whatever it is, it will have to wait until tomorrow."

"It will not. Rafael, if I've ever asked you for a goddamned fucking favor in my entire life, this is it. I need you to meet me at the building right this minute. This is important."

Something, perhaps the desperate tone of his voice, made Rafael pause for a moment.

"Connor—you're OK, aren't you? You sound..."

"If I were OK, would I call you at 12:49 in the middle of the night? No, I am not. Now I'm leaving the other side of town, and I will meet you there in 20 minutes."

He hung up the phone and turned it off completely this time. One last glance at the darkened diner, and he suppressed a shudder.

Rafael had to help him get rid of these people. He had brought them in; he would know how to get rid of them. Sometimes when you were afraid of someone, you just had to take up with the people they were afraid of.

Wasn't that what Rafa had said about Al's family and the motorcycle gangs they'd been so concerned about, half a lifetime ago? And who was Al's family afraid of?

No one, the little voice in his head said, and he silenced it.

Everybody had something, and there was always a way. Always. He put his car into gear and drove as carefully as he could past the dingy old diner up onto the beltway toward the other side of town, thoughts racing around his head.

Everything would be fine, once he had gotten rid of them.

It became his mantra until he finally pulled up in front of his building. HIS building—capital letters. Make sure of that.

Rafael's pickup truck stood parked closer to the main entrance, and Connor jumped out, squared his shoulders, and strode up to the truck.

Nobody else here, no alarms clanging anywhere, nobody asking any questions—good. At least it looked like they had not been found out yet.

"Hey…" he said, pretending not to notice his friend's sleepy, annoyed facial expression or the equally rumpled jeans and stained t-shirt. "What—did you fall into a laundry hamper on your way over here?"

"Sorry if I don't get dressed up fancy because you have a brainfart emergency in the middle of the night."

"This is serious."

"I am hoping so—for both of our sakes. My wife does not take lightly to interrupted sleep. I really don't feel like joking around just now, Connor. What the heck is all of this about?"

"Come along." Connor nodded toward the building and walked ahead, not really looking behind him to see if Rafael followed or not.

He unlocked the building and stood in the great front hall for a moment, listening carefully. He had been right; the clanging sound that had alerted him to all the trouble was gone now, and the building lay once again in perfect silence.

He did not even want to think about what might have happened if whoever came in to fix the problem had found him here, or worse, back there amongst all of the marijuana plants…

Rafael finally arrived behind him, huffing and puffing as he scrambled to keep up with Connor and flipped on the lights. Blazing brightness filled the entrance hall, glinting off sharp surfaces and metal corners.

"It's your building, you know, might as well have light."

"How opportune of you to mention it," Connor said dryly. "My building and all that—about time somebody notices."

"I assume there's some insider joke here I am not party to because really—I don't get it, bro. Right now, you're acting plain crazy. You're not drunk, and I don't think you're high, so whatever is going on with you, it's got to be big."

Connor nodded and moved past the entrance through the big metal doors into the warehouse space.

"Man, I feel old," Rafa said as if he could read his mind. "Slow down before you kill me, will you?"

"Interesting thought, that."

Rafael bungled through the warehouse after him, a little too out of shape, a little too overweight to keep up with Connor, who was driven by pure fury and the intense desire to reclaim what was his, to put his mark on it for all to see.

Pretending to look elsewhere, he still tried to keep an eye on Rafael. Did he look in the general direction of the hidden doorway? Did he avoid the far wall? Did he betray himself in any way whatsoever?

He did not. Rafael simply struggled to keep up with Connor and checked his watch now and then, plainly betraying his annoyance at the late hour. Again, Connor had to put aside the relief.

After a few cursory circles through the warehouse, he finally stopped close to the structural pillar that hid the doorway.

"What do you see?"

"Um—the warehouse? Is this a trick question?"

"What else?"

"Nothing. I don't know, Connor—shit. Some overhead lights, a dirty floor, a couple of pillars. The boys took all of the trash and the remnants from the previous tenants out before the grand opening. Took three dumpster loads. So? Don't tell me something's missing."

"Not missing, no."

He took Rafael's elbow and guided him closer to the wall.

"That—wall…"

"Yes—it's a wall… Again, so?"

"Why is it here?"

"Because—that's where the building ends?"

He grabbed Rafael's hand by the wrist, even though the other man wanted to draw back from his intense and rough touch, and put it flat against the wall.

"This what an 'end of the building' type wall feels like?"

"Connor.... Shit."

Rafael stepped a little closer and this time put both palms flat against the wall.

"Shit—what's going on here? This should not be...."

"This should not be warm to the touch. This should not even be here, Rafa. If you look at the plans, you'll realize the building still goes on for an extra 20 feet or so."

"I... That's why you called me earlier, isn't it? That's why you are watching me like I'm the guy who is going to pinch your wallet—to find out if I know anything about this? Well, why didn't you say something? What the heck is behind this...?"

He looked left and right, up and down the apparently solid wall, did so again, and frowned.

"OK, I give up. This is definitely not normal. What the heck...?"

Connor still watched him. Was he playing him? Heck no. Rafa was no kind of actor. He really did not know.

Without speaking, he guided his friend behind the structural beam and took his hand again. He had to feel around the minute gap again—it was definitely well done.

"Shit..."

"You said that before," Connor said dryly and finally pushed open the hidden door.

"Welcome. Sorry I can't offer you any refreshments. I didn't know any of this existed until a few hours ago."

"You think I did? I can't even begin to guess.... Wait—wait—you are not suggesting... Connor, you are not suggesting whatever is going on back there, I had anything to do with it? Because I am telling you right now, I have never...."

"Keep going before you run out of excuses. Go on—see the rest of it. I promise you. It is good."

Rafael stepped through the opening—careful, as if something might jump out at him at any moment, Connor close at his heels.

The realization came just as quickly as it had for Connor, and the rapid-fire line of swear words would have been funny and impressive, if they'd been sitting there joking around.

"Unreal. Connor, who the fuck—wait, wait, first, tell me you don't think I had anything to do with this. Because I swear to you as I am standing here before you, I did not. I've never seen this before in my entire life. I don't even know how to grow weed. Even when I was in college..."

"Relax, I believe you," Connor said and encompassed the entire area with a sweep of his arm. "Impressive, though, isn't it? Maximum yield on minimum space. Everything top-quality, top design and engineering—just the way we had hoped it would be. I knew it would be when we got to this point. The money that is going to come out of here is astronomical..."

"C—you're not telling me this is yours, are you? Because I don't have to tell you the kind of trouble you are inviting doing this..."

"No, sorry." Connor shook his head. "Not mine, although once you get past the first shock, you have to realize it is one heck of a good idea. I mean—look at it.... Perfect cash crop, hard to find right under everybody's nose... how much better could it get?"

"It could get a little more legal so neither one of us goes to jail for it. That would be pretty good, don't you think?"

"No doubt. Perfect Cannabis will always be a legal operation and decent profits growing marijuana for medical purposes—of course. We have shareholders, after all. But then there's you and me. Why shouldn't we get a little extra for all the trouble we've gone through, you know?"

"No, no, no, Connor. A dozen times no. You can't just...."

"Shh—don't argue about it right now. Everything will come together in time. First things first. Who the fuck put this into my building?"

"You don't know?"

"I have no idea. And when I find out—well, let's just say when I find out who it is, it's not going to be pretty. What the hell were they thinking putting this into my building?"

"Had to be somebody who knew—everything. Basically… This is verbatim what we were planning. Just on a smaller footprint and not legal."

"Trust me, I've gone there. It has to be somebody who knows everything about the operation, somebody who has an in…. One of us, Rafa. It's one of us—betraying the rest."

"No, come on. One of the guys on the board? Not on your life. Simon is too straitlaced with his security business and all, and Josh…. Well, Josh is a weasel, but he is not creative enough. You can't think Kayla…"

"Not on the board then. Who else is there who is devious and crooked enough to pull this off and has a lot of experience in shady dealings? It's not that hard a question, Rafael."

"You're thinking Al—I know you are thinking Al—but I am telling you no."

"Why? They are all crooks—the whole damn family."

"I realize you don't like his family much."

"Much? I would get rid of them today—on the inside of five minutes, if I could."

"Hear me out. They are secretive, and they do things in an unorthodox way, correct. They own every seedy bar and strip joint between here and the next town over. That's the way they operate. But Al—Al is kind of… decent in his own way. He tries to do the right thing at least. Even if he is not always successful. No, I am telling you he wouldn't do this."

"You're wrong. Dead wrong, Rafael. I went to see them—confronted them, even…."

"Shit—you did not blaze in there and accuse them of running an illegal grow op right off the top, did you?"

"Not right off the top, no—but it did come up in conversation."
"And?"

"And everybody pretended not to know anything about it—especially their father—and when I asked too many questions…" He rubbed the back of his head where his bruise had settled in nicely. "Let's just say they gave me a little souvenir to remind me not to ask too many questions."

"Connor, you are lucky you walked out of there in one piece and a nasty bruise is all you brought with you."

"It is my company, Rafael, my company. Mine. Has that sunk into anyone's head yet? I started it. I run it. It is my goddamn company, so don't come around doing shit like this and expect me to be OK with it."

His arm encompassed the entire growing area again, and just for good measure, he kicked at a convenient metal trash bin.

"They are not taking what I have worked to build up—not while I am alive and have anything to say about it."

The kick at the trash bin echoed eerily, and Rafael shrugged.

"I don't know what to say—except be more careful. How did you find all of this anyway? It's not like anybody even suspected this was here. It's not like that doorway is visible even when you know where it is."

"Came down here to think," Connor said, straightened the trash bin, and nodded toward the doorway. "Let's get out of here before somebody comes back. One of the lights malfunctioned and made some noise. Look up—they all look fine to you?"

"Far as I can tell."

"Well, then somebody was here while I was talking to Al and his family—fixed it up again. They are monitoring this area. I am not sure how, but I'd rather not have them show up again while we are standing here chitchatting."

"There is your answer—could not have been Al, then."

"Come now—even for you, that's weak, Rafael. Of course Al does not do the heavy lifting—he has people. Jesus. You got anything better?"

"Let's just pretend for one minute—just for one minute—you are right, and it is Al."

"I don't have to pretend."

"Hear me out—why? Why the hell would he do it?"

"Money?"

"Al has access to more money than he will ever be able to spend in his entire life—more money than you can name without counting the zeroes off on your fingers. This much I know, Connor. He does not do anything 'just' for money. He does things for a reason. It has to be a good reason."

"Fine, then—you make a suggestion. And while you are at it, tell me why they all went nuts when I mentioned the guy from the grand opening?"

"What guy?"

"The one who walked in without an invitation—the one Kayla thought looked like Al."

"You're still going on about that one?"

"Yes I am—because he has something to do with them, OK? A pretty big something, or they wouldn't have reacted the way they did."

"Another son," Rafael said slowly. "Sure—I hadn't thought about it."

"What are we talking about, another son?"

"I heard somebody say once there was another son, besides Al and Dan… One who had broken with the family. Some falling-out over an issue… "

"'K. So what does he do? Who is he? Could he have been the man at the grand opening? Could he be behind this?"

"I don't know. They don't talk about him. It's like a rule or something, like he does not exist. I overheard Al say something once that made me think maybe the third brother was in jail—but I really do not know…"

"Let's just assume it was him then," Connor said slowly, turning his keys around and around in his fingers as he thought. "Just for a moment—if it were, would it make sense then?"

"Dunno—if he had been in jail, he might know a thing or two about drugs."

"Correct. Not that wild an assumption. And if he had broken with his family over some issue, he would not want to do anything with his family. He would not care if he screwed them."

"Or you. He doesn't even know you."

"Which means, Rafael, which only means that I should get to know him," Connor said, tossed his keys into the air, caught them again, and looked at his friend.

The excitement came back to him now, the familiar rush when he was figuring out a deal, when he was that close and the ideas just kept coming hard and heavy. All he had to do was ride them. Yes—that was the right trail....

"My enemy's enemy is my friend—is that not some famous quote from somewhere?"

"*Art of War.*"

"Right, whatever. If I want to get rid of Al and his family, and this man has the kind of knowledge that made this possible," Connor cocked a thumb back at the building in the shadows behind them, "then he is automatically my best shot at doing so."

"I don't know, Connor. Talk about going to bed with a snake. This is not war. This is not survival of the sneakiest. You are trying to build a good, decent company here, are you not? So what on earth is this infighting going to accomplish? I agree—the illegal grow op has to go, and my guys can take care of it in a couple hours flat. But what is the purpose of a confrontation with Al and Dan and their father?"

"I don't like them. I want them gone, and while we are at it, I am going to take all of their shares from them."

"Why?"

"Because I can. That's why. Because I don't like them. Because I want them gone. Now let's go. Tomorrow, we will make a plan. You're going to do some research for me on this third brother. I need to know who he is, what his weak spot is, what he wants, and how to get in touch with him. Me—I will figure out how to use that," he pointed toward the end of the building again, "to my advantage. If they thought they could mess with me, they are going to have to get up one hell of a lot earlier than this. I can tell you that."

"Let's just get out of here."

Rafael turned away and began walking, his shoulders set in a rigid line, his head upright and straight. He'd run into Connor's stubborn and determined streak before, and he would do as asked.

Connor turned off the lights and fitted the hatch door precisely back into its spot.

"Wait, Rafa."

"What?"

"This can't be the way they get in and out on a regular basis. Think about it. You would have to see it, don't you think?"

"See what, Connor?"

"The coming and going—it's too awkward to come through the warehouse space all the time. I think there's another door on the other side. I bet you that is how they got all of their equipment in too."

"Well, can we check it out tomorrow? Tell you the truth, I am completely done in. I for one am going back home, going to bed while I still have a couple of good hours left."

"Wimp."

Connor stood there for a minute looking back at the warehouse space. It couldn't. It really couldn't be the way they got in, but in some ways—even if he didn't tell him—he had to agree with Rafa. Enough for one night. He would come back. He wanted to know every tiny little detail: how they got in, who had given them the knowledge they needed, who 'they were' in the first place, how they planned to distribute all of the product.

The list continued to grow, but Connor did not mind. If he wanted to make contact and, more importantly, make use of Al's mysterious third brother, he'd have to wait for Rafa to make the connection anyway. He could wait—for a little while.

FORTY-FOUR

The next day found him wired on his natural enthusiasm almost as much as Kayla's vitamins. The more he thought about it, the more he liked his initial idea. This man, this third brother—he would have to give him a name, or it would drive him insane—this man was basically the answer to all of his problems.

They could run a nice little secret operation together, making money for everyone. They could take away the shares and company positions he had been forced to give to Dan and Al. They could remove anyone from the board who did not think along the same lines and run a great little operation together. They would hold all the power.

Magic—sheer magic.

And the best part: nobody would ever know. A nice legal operation in front—and the real deal out back.

This was how the circle rounded out then: Connor provided the space and the company that became the cover and his new partner the know-how and the distribution network. Done. All they had to do was wait for the money to come rolling in.

As much as he could see it, right there in front of him, he forced himself to be patient. He still needed Rafael to make the introductions, to make sure everyone was comfortable. If dealing with Al and the rest of his family had taught him one thing, these were not people you could casually get to know and do business with. He needed Rafael for the moment.

"Later on, who knows?" he said softly and held his wineglass up to the setting sun streaming in through the tall windows.

"Who knows what?" Kayla asked. "I've hardly seen you these past few days. Are you sure you still live here? Because…"

"Kayla, my love, don't you worry about it. I've had a lot of problems with the company—and I mean a lot."

"Anything you can't handle?"

"I thought so. As it turns out, the solution to everything was just handed to me—on a silver platter, if you wish—and right now, I am simply… savoring."

"Anything you care to share with me?"

She came over and draped herself over the armrest of his club chair, putting one arm around his neck.

Slowly, he shook his head. "Not quite yet. There are a few things I have on the go, but until at least one of them crystallizes, I don't want to say anything." He knocked on the wooden table in front of him. "Superstition, you know."

"I've never known you to be superstitious."

"All innovators and trailblazers are. Some just hide it better than others."

She raised an eyebrow and said nothing. Had he annoyed her just a touch with his secrecy? Give just a little bit. He still needed her too—at least for the moment.

"You'll see soon enough, love—really. You'll be the first one."

It took about a week. He was sitting in his corner office, idly shuffling through papers, when his phone rang, and he recognized Rafa's caller ID.

"Rafa, tell me you got good news."

"I got news, bro. I won't vouch for its quality or authenticity, but…."

"But?"

"Roberto Ivers. Third son of the man commonly known as the Original Chef…."

"Ivers—their last name."

"Likely was changed somewhere along the line. Haven't come across it anywhere else either."

"'K—carry on."

"Our friend Roberto broke with the family a few years back. Seems he was highly involved in—oh, surprise—drug dealing. Crystal meth, weed, uppers, downers. You name it, he either made it, grew it, sold it, or both."

I knew it, Connor's heart sang. *I knew it—the man is going to have a distribution network just ready for us. This is where it gets good.*

"Sounds like an enterprising man. So how did he end up on the outs with the clan?"

"Basically, he got greedy, and he got caught. Long story short. Got picked up, went up to court—nobody would testify for him."

"Ouch."

"Yeah. Al's people usually pull together around their own. Always somebody providing an alibi, testifying on somebody's behalf, coming up with evidence, making evidence disappear or appear or just making it useless, but not this time. Rumor has it, the Chef finally wanted to go legal, wanted to protect his youngest son."

"Al?"

"The very one. He wanted to protect Al from everything the other two had done. Al needed to be clean. He needed to be the one who had never spent a single night in jail or even heard about it. It became an obsession, they say. So he told Roberto to quit drug dealing or be out of the family."

"And Roberto did not quit."

"He did not."

Connor sat back and let the harbor landscape beyond his window work its magic on his mood once again. This man—Roberto, now that he finally had a name—Roberto sounded like the perfect business partner. Experience, no scruples when they got in the way, and what had to be a deep-seated hatred when it came to Al and his father....

"And what's more," Rafael said, "it looks like everything Dan knew about growing marijuana and setting up an operation came from Roberto. People tell me he literally wrote the book on it."

"Shit," Connor laughed. "Sounds like we've been dealing with the wrong brothers all along. Bring on Roberto—I want to meet him."

"Not so fast, Connor. I don't know if he is the kind of guy you want in our business. From what I hear, he has a mean streak on him that's a mile wide."

"So do I."

"You do, my friend, but from what I've heard—you don't kill people when they get in your way. Roberto… let's just say there are rumors, except nobody wants to own up to knowing anything. Too dangerous."

"Oh, here comes the drama, Rafa. Isn't that what they say about every criminal? 'Oh, he's killed a few people.' The ones who talk about it are usually just that—all talk. Am I right or am I right?"

"See it whichever way you want to, Connor. I'm standing here telling you it is far too dangerous to pull someone like that into the boat. You think you were having a hard time with Al and his father? Try dealing with someone even they don't want to have in their business."

"That is exactly what you told me when you brought in Al—you need somebody who is going to put the fear of God into the motorcycle gangs—so now I need somebody who is going to put the fear of God into Al. Done deal. How much worse could it get?"

"A lot. You don't know."

"And at the moment, Rafael, at the moment I don't want to know. Right now, I want to make a deal. The man has put a grow op into my building—my building. Good manners, if nothing else, demand that we at least get introduced and speak to one another. After that, we will see."

"Don't say I did not warn you."

"You did, and I won't say it. So now, bring it on—how do I meet this mysterious man? When and where?"

The excitement was coming back. Connor could feel it—the excitement like a keen predator instinct that always rose inside him when he smelled his prey, a good deal that would make him a lot of money.

"So?"

"He is coming to see you."

"OK—guess that runs in the family too, huh? Don't call me, I'll call you? Fine, I'll be ready."

"I don't have a good feeling about this, Connor. I really don't. I know you don't want to believe me right now. I know you are sitting there thinking I'm a coward or something…"

"Didn't say that."

"Stay on the straight and narrow, Connor. Do the right thing. This business, if done right, has everything you need to be the biggest deal you and I have ever pulled off. Don't fuck it up now by bringing in an element…."

"I won't, OK—I won't. I'm just talking here, you know me," Connor said and leaned against the picture window as he talked. Somewhere out there was the man who could really make this business huge. And he was about to meet him. It did not get any better… "I wouldn't mess up what we built—you know that, Rafael."

"I thought I did."

Still not convinced. He would have to pull him in a little because right there, about five minutes ago, Connor had decided that Rafael would have no part of this new branch of the company he was planning. Rafael would not even know about it. This was his and his alone. His and Roberto Ivers's.

Rafael? Too straitlaced for this kind of deal—too honest, too open, and yes, too cowardly. He'd never pull this off. But—but, Connor thought—he was still the perfect face for Perfect Cannabis, the medical marijuana producer. Sure! Just listen to the man! Do the right thing, don't get involved in anything illegal or dangerous, stay on the straight and narrow… Yada, yada. You needed that kind of person—needed them badly! Mr. Poster Boy!

"Look, Rafa, how many deals have we done together? Dozens, right? You know what I am good at, and that's talking. That's what I'm doing here—talking. Throw 17 things onto the wall, see what sticks and looks good up there. And you know what, you're right. I don't have the guts to be a drug dealer either. Fact remains, Roberto is kind of squatting in my building there, so I'm going to give him an opportunity to pack his bags before I have to involve his father."

"I know you want to meet him and give him a piece of your mind—I can hear it in your voice. But hear my words. I'm convinced you would be better off letting Al and his father handle this. After all, they are shareholders, they are involved in the business, they have an interest here. Let them do the heavy lifting."

"You think?"

"I think, Connor. From what I heard out there about Roberto, I really did not much care to meet him, never mind having him involved in this business—our business."

Almost involuntarily, Connor's right hand closed to a fist. *Our business, is it,* he thought. *So all of a sudden it's our business? You run into something you can handle, and it becomes ours? Asshole. Cowardly, whining asshole.*

He forced his hand to open and the fingers to relax and pasted a fake smile on. People could hear it on the phone when you smiled. He'd read it somewhere.

"I trust your judgment, Rafa. You know I always have."

"Good. I have to go now. That downtown mall project is turning into a nightmare."

"Don't say another word. I'll get Al involved—tell him to get the grow op out of the building by the end of the week. Don't know what they will do with it, don't really care either. Just get it out of my face. You available for a drink later—at The Lighthouse?"

"Always."

"You got it."

Connor hung up the phone and stared out the window at the busy anthill of the harbor. *So, to recap*, he thought, *we are definitely going to have to move that grow op—which is a damned shame because the setup was perfect back there. Shame. But I need Rafa, and by extension everybody else, to believe I am still the white-hat grower over here.*

Fuck—I can only hope Roberto is reasonable and won't give me any grief about this.

On the other hand, perhaps he could liquidate some of the Swiss stock and cut Roberto in for a share, just to show some good faith. With the waters smoothed, so to speak, they could set up another hidey-hole somewhere in the building and this time keep it a secret from all prying eyes. Expenses he need not have gone through if he had kept his own mouth shut in time.

"Damn, Beauregard, you fucked up again," he said softly to himself, "Fucked up by telling Rafael. You're going soft in the head."

Damn, he wished he could talk to this guy—now—to see what he was thinking. Yet all he could do was wait once again. Wait for Roberto to get in touch with him, wait for Al, wait to see if he could talk Roberto into this deal, wait to see how much it was going to cost him, wait for a whole lot of things. And he hated waiting!

He sat back down at his desk to deal with David's latest requests for the financial audit—would that little man ever get tired of asking Connor to hunt down elusive pieces of paper?—but his mind wandered.

The possibilities! The beautiful, endless possibilities—and the money that would come rolling in, from the legal medical marijuana department, and from his and Roberto's little private enterprise.

They would have to figure out some way to launder it, of course, and bring it back into the realm of legality. Perhaps Roberto had some experience there, too. No perhaps about it. A guy like Roberto? Sure, he would know about cleaning up suspect funds. But he would need someone else—no use giving Roberto all of the power. He would need his own people there.

Then he would have to figure out about Kayla. Dare he tell her about the good news, their new source of income, or was it better to keep it to himself? Was Kayla even still going to be part of—things— when it became an issue?

He finally got up again and paced the length of his office, back and forth.

He couldn't afford to fuck it up a second time. From now on, only a select number of people could know what he was up to. Kayla, who owned a gossip magazine? Definite no. Rafael, also no. Not as easy as Kayla, but definitely no.

"Sorry, old friend," Connor muttered, making the turn at the end of the office and pacing back. Exactly 10 steps—damn, he would finally get a bigger space. And Rafael, Rafael would be just fine. What was he, after all? A contractor at heart and by trade. He'd never be happy running things the way he and Roberto would run them.

Check. That meant Rafael was out.

Sorry.

The others? Why, hell, the others could stay with Perfect Cannabis, the official producer—and they could be quite happy there, having a little seat on the board, doing what they thought was the right thing, worrying about nothing, helping the sick and suffering and generally feeling like the hypocritical bunch they were. Heck, he would even help them out and become Connor Beauregard, fine upstanding citizen. For official public purposes anyway.

End of the room again, turn again. He had it all laid out in his head now. But....

But—he stopped and listened. His entire office had fallen completely and unnaturally quiet, he realized all of a sudden. Where he usually heard Tessa move around, click on her keyboard, slam the file cabinet doors or chat on the phone… suddenly, there was nothing.

She might have stepped out for a minute, he thought, but she usually told him when she did, so he would know the reception area was empty.

These are not the kind of people you want to mess with.

Excitement and fear warred within him for a moment.

He straightened up, squared his shoulders, and stepped out into the reception area, all in one movement, carefully orchestrated to look carefree and relaxed.

Tessa indeed was gone.

Instead, a young man sat in the reception area in one of the old, beat-up chairs, legs crossed casually at the knee, reading a magazine.

"Brought your mail for you," he said without looking up and turned a page in his magazine.

A white envelope lay in front of him, the kind that carried a solicitor's logo and a dozen official stamps. The kind that was never any good news, no matter who brought it in.

"Where's my secretary?" Connor asked dumbly. As if he had nothing else to worry about, but the guy's casual manners threw him off his game.

"Gave her a little break—grab a coffee, stretch her legs. You don't mind, do you?"

Finally, he looked up, and Connor instantly recognized him from the night of the grand opening. He also realized what Kayla had meant when she said 'he looked kind of like Al.' You would have to be dumb and blind to miss the resemblance. Except for a 10-year difference, he and Al could have been twin brothers.

"Roberto Ivers, I presume," he said stiffly. "You have the same manners your brother has—show up unannounced."

"It's a talent. Keeps everybody else on their toes. You never know what you might find when people aren't really expecting you."

He lifted the white envelope and dropped it on the coffee table in front of him again.

"Like this here. You've been a bad boy, Connor Beauregard."

Connor looked from the envelope to Roberto's face and back again.

"I don't get it. You brought in the mail?"

"Not just any mail. Important mail. A court summons."

"Court summons?"

He sounded like a goddamn parrot repeating everything the man said with a question mark at the end. *Goddammit, pull yourself together, Beauregard.* How were they ever going to have a proper business relationship if he acted like a dimwit who had not had an original thought in the last 15 years?

"Forgive me, Roberto—you really do catch me off guard. I've been on the phone most of the morning, so if I appear a little out of touch and unfocused, it is only because...."

"Creditors?"

"What?"

"Been on the phone with creditors most of the day? Because this little court summons here is going to add to your problems. Lady by the name of Catherine Egan—and she is suing you over an unpaid bill."

"Shit. Bloodsucking lawyer is what she is—not a lady—and all she did is waste everybody's time. If anybody does not deserve to get paid...."

He stopped himself and forced a smile. No need to let his anger with Catherine ruin this meeting.

"What I mean to say is there is a disagreement over the actual work done...."

"Except she is not the only one, is she? And not paying your people—that's just really, really bad manners. At least in my kind of business. Stirs up all kinds of trouble and attention you don't need. Creates unhappy people, and unhappy people create problems."

Connor felt the sweat roll down his back and forced his hands to still. Dammit—what was wrong with him? This fellow had put an illegal grow op into his building, and while he was about to suggest they pool their resources and abilities, he did not know that. For all he knew, Connor was about to threaten him for taking over his building.

"And just what is your kind of business, Roberto? The drug-dealing business? Because from what I saw back at my building, you are really good at that."

Roberto shrugged.

"Some. A little of this, a little of that. You know how it goes. Still, I know that not paying your own people just makes you enemies you don't need. You have your hands full with the enemies you do need to have and keep in check."

"Overcharging for nothing is not really the Miss Manners style either," Connor said, a little impatient. "And that's just exactly what she was doing. I am not entirely sure why we are talking about this woman anyway." He picked up the envelope and flung it in the direction of Tessa's desk.

His excitement at meeting this man Roberto had all but disappeared, along with his nice image of how they would get along, like brothers, and run their little empire together. And why? Why? Because of Catherine once again. As if the woman had not caused him enough trouble.

Roberto leaned back and spread his arms wide and grinned.

"No reason, just like to see what kind of people the folks I am dealing with are. Don't let it bother you."

"The lawyer and her unreasonable bills bother me, not you. Now why don't we go into my office?"

"Perfectly fine out here, Connor. Now I am told you want to see me. I bet I can guess why that is."

"Your little illegal grow op in my building perhaps," Connor said and awkwardly pulled out Tessa's chair, since he did not have another handy in the reception area and was not about to stand in front of this man like some sort of damned messenger. "I bought the place to grow marijuana, true, but I kind of meant for our own people to do it."

Roberto laughed.

"Just making a bit of use of all that empty space that's just sitting there. You know, you bought that building quite a bit oversized… Not that there's anything wrong with that."

"Well, we are planning to expand," Connor snapped. "Besides, growing cannabis takes a lot more room like you might initially expect. I mean—just for starters…"

He stopped, remembering that Rafael had told him this man had all but written the book on growing cannabis.

"Yes?"

"Nothing you wouldn't know already, I hear," Connor said and forced the charm back slowly. "Matter of fact—it looks like I've been dealing with the wrong set of brothers all along."

"Your information network at least is half decent. Go on."

"Dan and Al—how should I put this—they are not exactly the kind of people I was going to hire, but your father insisted I do."

"Al is decent," Roberto said in a way that shut every discussion down right there.

Al is decent. You did not argue with that short sentence or even offer another option. Not if you wanted to stay on the good side of Roberto.

"Dan, on the other hand—he is a snake."

"His knowledge appears extensive."

"His knowledge," Roberto huffed, and Connor did not miss the instant flash in his eyes. "His knowledge, what there is of it, he stole off me. I am the one who wrote the book on growing cannabis. Is that what they told you?"

"Yes."

"Well, they are right. And I mean I wrote a book about it. The little backyard growers still pass it around like the bible. If it is not in my book, you don't need it to grow marijuana."

"And Dan…."

"Dan stole the thing when I—when the damned family betrayed me and sent me away for a while. Then the little shit comes around to you, pretending he knows all there is about growing weed. Meantime, he knows nothing but what I put down on paper."

Anger he could work with, Connor thought, anger actually worked in his favor. *So keep being angry, Roberto, keep on railing about your brother.*

Roberto caught himself again and smiled.

"Well, at least I hear he got a nice little position in your company with all of the—knowledge he has. That's kind of nice for him."

"Your father invested," Connor said. "Actually made me hire those two… Not that I did not have my own team in place."

"That's Dad to you, looking after his own."

Roberto smiled and folded his hands behind his head as if they were just idly sitting in a bar having a few beverages together, and Connor felt his temper returning.

"As to the reason for your visit—mind telling me why you would put an illegal grow op into the building? You must have known that it could jeopardize the entire operation. You must have known that the entire licensing process could grind to a halt if anybody were to find out…."

"That is, if the licensing process was not disturbed already by the fact that you got the minister drunk and out with whores, you mean."

"That was not my—well—he did not know how to hold his liquor, let's just say, OK? Not like there was a plan behind this or anything. You, on the other hand…."

"I put a lot of work into my little operation. I'm actually surprised you found it. Surprised and a little disappointed. I thought it was better hidden."

"Why Roberto?"

Roberto shrugged and relaxed a little more in his chair.

"Money—why does anybody do a thing like that? Plain, old-fashioned money. Now you are going to get all snobby and superior and tell me to get my stuff out of there, and I am going to tell you—you are far too greedy for that."

Connor said nothing and stared unblinking at Roberto, who seemed just as at home in his front reception room as he would have at home at his own—desk or whatever he used.

"I'm serious," Roberto repeated. "I can see it in your face. You've already calculated through how much money you could make off my little operation, and you want it. You have a penthouse downtown to pay for…."

"My girlfriend's."

"An expensive girlfriend, a private helicopter, and you want that money. Correction—you need that money, or some pretty bad things are going to happen."

He nodded toward the white envelope at Tessa's workstation.

"Not like they aren't already. So now you tell me, Connor, why?"

"Why what?"

"Why should I work with you? Why should I waste my time and my knowledge on somebody who knows shit about the drug business?"

"You know about drugs—I know about business."

"Not a good enough reason, Connor. Try again. Besides—look at how you are running things." Another nod toward the envelope. "Does that look like you are running this business properly and the way it should be?"

"I told you," Connor said and jumped to his feet. "I told you this was a disagreement about billing. This has absolutely nothing to do with the way I run business."

Roberto remained in his chair, completely undisturbed by Connor's temper.

"And you have a temper, Connor Beauregard. You don't have yourself under control. Another bad thing in our business."

'Our business.' Connor barely managed to keep himself from smiling. 'Our business…' He still could make it happen. Dammit, but he resented being on display like this, like he was at a job interview or something… 'Tell me about your greatest weaknesses and how you are planning to handle them…' He'd sworn he would never go in for that kind of nonsense, ever again.

They needed one another, they would be good together, and one way or another, he would make it happen. What did Connor Beauregard know best? He knew how to spin a story. Slowly, he pulled out Tessa's chair again and sat. He put his hands together before him like he had seen his father do many, many years ago and smiled slowly.

"This," he began, "was the greatest idea since the invention of the wheel. Hiding an illegal grow op right in the middle of a legal facility for medical marijuana. That alone is a stroke of genius. None of the red flags that usually point in the direction of an illegal facility are ever going to go up. Ever—end of story."

Roberto nodded, smiled, and Connor knew it had been his idea.

"Two perfect parts to the perfect deal. The legal company—out there for everyone to see, to visit, and to inspect—and the department that is going to make more goddamned money than anybody could ever spend in a lifetime. Two..." He held two fingers up on each hands. "Two parts that come together to make one perfect whole."

His hands came together in a perfect circle.

"You and I, Roberto—you and I are going to have the most perfect symbiosis ever. There's no end to how far we can take this."

The storyteller took over then, weaving in the air the picture of the perfect business setup for both him and Roberto Ivers. Painting in glorious brilliant color the kind of money they would make, the places this would take them, and, most of all, how easy and how much fun it would all be.

By the end of his speech, he saw that Roberto sat a little straighter now. The cocky grin had disappeared from his face, and he looked a little more serious now.

Oh, I've got you now, don't I, Connor thought, but he wouldn't allow himself to grin.

Rafael, in a very strange way, was actually right. This was not a competition. Nobody would walk out of here a winner or a loser. That was the entire point, dammit. They needed each other, and when they cooperated, magic. All he had to do was make sure Roberto actually got it.

The man rose now, slowly, but deliberately.

"Do you see now what I am talking about?" Connor asked. He had one more bullet in his gun, and he wasn't about to quit yet.

"Basically, yes. It's not that hard to understand." Roberto stood and brushed an imagined speck of dust off himself. "I'll get back to you."

"Don't—not yet, Roberto. There is one more thing."

"Really?" Roberto cocked his head, grin firmly in place again. "You've been talking for a straight hour, man—you ever get tired, or you just go on and on and on, like the battery bunny?"

"I'm serious here. One last argument. Then you can go and think about how much perfect sense this makes."

"OK—one last argument—other than the 15 you've already fired at me in the last hour. Go."

"Your family."

The look in Roberto's eyes suddenly became dark, and Connor knew that he had hit dead center. Direct hit. Now he had him.

"Your family. They abandoned you and let you go to jail."

"You know a lot about my family."

"I hear things."

Roberto grinned again and winked this time.

"It's my company, my idea, my hard work. I don't want to let them walk in and take over everything—including your research. With the money we are making from our little deal, we can finally stick it to them. Both of us."

Roberto nodded.

"That your last argument?"

"That was it."

A little disappointing. He had expected more smoke, fire, and brimstone from a man who had gone to jail because his family abandoned him—but whatever. He had played his hand.

"I look forward to talking to you again."

He offered his hand, and Roberto looked at him for one long moment before taking it and shaking.

"Like I said, I will get back to you. I have a few things to do just now."

"Like finding a new place for the operation?"

Roberto shrugged. "Not that hard, you know. That whole building is full of little hidey holes you don't even know about—and likely never will. There's a really old part to it on the other side of the lot… Never mind. You're better off not knowing."

"Right you are. But I have to go to my other partners and tell them I've got rid of the problem—that's important."

"And you will. I shook on that. By tomorrow, no one will even be able to tell it was ever there."

Roberto inclined his head and took the door. "See ya, little man. And pay that lady lawyer—we don't need that kind of trouble around us. The less people are looking at us, the better it is."

He disappeared down the hall, and Connor let out a breath he did not know he had been holding. Shit. He could have just saved himself and made the biggest deal of his entire life. Shit—shit—shit—and there was nobody he could tell about it.

He picked up the phone to call Rafael and remembered that Rafa was not in this deal any longer. Then he wanted to call Kayla and remembered that she, too, couldn't know anything about it. Tessa— out. Simon and Josh—get real. Nobody.

The less people are looking at us. He had used the word 'us.'

Connor smiled and put his phone back into his pocket. OK, so he'd have to keep this one to himself. A shame really, since it was his biggest accomplishment—ever. But that was one tiny little tradeoff he would have to live with.

Think about it, he encouraged himself. With all of the money he stood to make, he could do great and wonderful things for Perfect Cannabis. He'd still get to be the hero; he'd still get to be Connor Beauregard, President and CEO. And he could rightfully point to it and tell them he had put all of his own money into this project, just to make sure it was successful.

Oh—it would work out.

And just like any goddamn deal he had ever worked on, the moment you needed it, had to have it, were jonesing for the thing to take off, it just would not. But turn away from it and look at something else for a little while and watch the damn thing blossom like you had poured pure fertilizer on it...

Strange the way these damn things worked...

He picked up his laptop and slowly made his way down to The Lighthouse. Some things would never change, and this was one of them.

FORTY-FIVE

"You're looking chipper today after all," Rafael said, checking him out top to bottom. "You took my advice—I hope?"

"It's all handled, Rafa. Don't worry about it any more."

He slipped into the bar stool and leaned back, folding his hands before his face.

"Aw, man, it's been a tough couple of months, but I think we have finally turned the corner my friend. Finally—it is all coming together."

"That sounds like awesome news for a change. Let's hear it—you finally finished that damned audit and got it signed off on, ready for the SEC."

"Not quite, but we are closing in on the thing."

"You've been closing in on it for a number of months now, and every time, it's more like circling the drain."

"Every time these damned auditors say they're going to sign off on it, they find another stupid little reason not to. Tell me about it, Rafa—tell me about it. And David..."

He shook his head and took a deep drink. "David is just about the slowest guy on the planet. There are days I just want to shake him and kick him in the ass until he flies across the room. "

"If it were not for good manners."

"If it were not for good manners," Connor repeated and took another drink. "No, we've had to apply for two extensions with the SEC now—two of them. Makes me look bad is what it does."

"These are the moments," Rafael said, "that I am glad to be running a little construction company and not a publicly traded outfit. But getting back to the reason for your excessive good mood—especially given what happened out at the building."

It burned in him—it really did burn in him to tell Rafael, to lay the entire plan out there for him to look at. But no, it could not happen.

"Oh, you know what," he said and shrugged. "I just turn it to my advantage... Old salesman's trick—take a disadvantage and turn it around to your advantage. Use it. You would not believe how many of my investors feel badly for me, empathize with me, just because this is happening. Still put their money in. They understand, you know, especially the ones who have been here before."

"I guess. Shared suffering and all that. I had not expected it, but hey—take whatever help we can get. You line up any big ones recently?"

Careful now—don't give too much away. Tell him just enough.

"Got enough big fish on the hook that one of them is going to bite for sure. At least a mil, maybe two. That ought to be nice, don't you think?"

"Get a few people paid and off our backs—that would really be nice." Rafael nodded. "And get down to some of the real construction on the building. You know, there are a couple of things Dan showed me..."

He stopped and cocked his head at Connor. "You're still not too happy with Dan, now are you? Tell me, what did Al say—are they going to take care of it?"

"Yup, not to even worry about it—it will be taken care of, and nobody will ever know this little grow op had even been in there. Damn shame in one way, but..."

"But you know you are better off without it."

"Amen to that." Connor raised his glass. "Can you imagine what would have happened to our license, all the money that's gone into the building, into business development, all of our shareholders—shit."

Rafael smiled and put his hand on Connor's back. "Thank God. For a while there, I thought you were actually in favor of this illegal growing. Scared the crap out of me as a matter of fact. Can't tell you how happy I am you've come around. And anyway, something is really not right with that brother of Al and Dan's. Can't tell you what it is, but everybody I talk to kind of tells me the same thing—stay away from him, and you will sleep at night."

"I am sleeping just fine, my friend."

Connor lifted his glass again and smiled, although not for the reasons Rafael thought.

"Better this way," he said and drained his glass. "Really—it's better this way, Rafael."

He worked with David for a few days, although it annoyed him to the point of wanting to scream. Keeping up appearances—instinctively, he knew that he could not do anything out of the ordinary if he wanted to keep Roberto and his secret safe. He still needed to work on their triple-damned audit, go see people and raise funds, talk cheerfully to Kayla at night, as if nothing had happened at all.

Three days later, he finally drove out to the building again. Even on the way out there, he had a hard time keeping his mind on the driving and kept looking in his rearview mirror. What if nothing had happened out there? What if everything still looked the same? What if Roberto just ignored what he had said?

He had come alone and parked in the same spot he had previously. If Roberto had someone monitoring the building, surely they knew by now who he was and what kind of car he drove. He parked and stood there looking at his building. His building.

You really couldn't tell that anything was wrong at all. It just—sat there. Dark, quiet, unassuming, a large gray rectangle with hungry-maw loading bays on a large, messy lot. That was it.

After a few minutes of sitting there, staring, he finally got up his nerve, found the right key from an enormous bunch, and confidently unlocked his building.

His building.

He kept having to remind himself of his fact. This was his. He had raised the money for it, purchased it, tricked his board members into signing off on Mirko's equity position on it. It was all his.

The thought of Mirko came back to him momentarily—he hadn't heard from the filthy loan shark since the night of the grand opening—but he pushed the thought away and let the door fall shut behind him.

There was time enough to worry about Mirko later on. Right now, he really did have other things to think about.

Much as he wanted to rush right over into the great warehouse hall to check on the fake wall, he stood still in the entrance for a while—simply listening.

Nothing.

Nothing was good. Nothing meant that the noisy transformer (had it been Roberto's all along?) had been either fixed or removed. Nothing meant there was no malfunctioning grow light fixture making hell's own racket, drawing attention to the fact of its existence.

"Nothing," he said out loud and listened to the sound of his voice fading away.

He did a preliminary sweep of the entrance hall, and indeed, if he hadn't known something happened here, he wouldn't have. Every little thing looked exactly the way it had a few weeks ago, and at the time of the grand opening. If they had moved their grow op out through here, they had done an amazing job.

He moved on into the great warehouse and at this point decided the hell with caution. Without looking left or right, he rushed over to the east wall and put his hands against it. Chilly, rough, painted, white cinder block walls. Beautiful, ugly, cinder block walls.

Thank God, Roberto had come through.

Although, Connor thought, he would like to know where he had ultimately moved the new grow op to. He really would like to know.

He listened again, but only confirmed what he already knew. The building lay in total and complete silence. All was good—and still he wanted to know. For a good 15 minutes, he roamed around the perimeter of the hall, checking the walls, pointing a little pen flashlight into dark corners and hidden cubbyholes, but the warehouse remained just as empty as it rightfully should be.

Damn—what had Roberto done with the grow op?

Connor stood right where he thought the operation had been, but even the floors and those ugly skylights looked exactly the same way as they did in the remainder of the warehouse. Exactly. Yet he was sure the skylights at least had been covered in Roberto's operation.

He had to hand it to Roberto—even in cleaning up, he was good. Not as much as a shred of a leaf remained on the ground.

Satisfied, Connor did another sweep of the remainder of the building. He realized he knew precious little about the thing he called his and his alone, and he would have to change this pretty soon. But, so he reasoned, if he didn't know anything about it, then that meant that most likely, no one else did either.

Time to get out of there.

Over the past few weeks, he had spent way too much time on his own, and it really started to get on his nerves. He was talking to himself, for God's sakes! If that wasn't a sign of impending madness!

He locked up the building again and jumped into his truck, as fast as he could, cranked up the radio, and hit the highway for the way home, flooring the accelerator all the way.

Even speeding did not drive away his irritation the way it usually did, as if he could leave everything behind by racing away, forward. What the hell else could he want, pray tell? His cash problems were all but gone, the company he had started was all over the news, and he, Connor Beauregard, was being touted as the new savior, the man with the magic.

The little donation they had made during the grand opening was working wonders. Sick people everywhere were all but donating money to make sure his company would continue to grow.

David had not bothered him with any of his usual audit-related nonsense for an entire day, so either he or the official auditors had finally run out of stupid questions to ask him and documentation to demand, as hard as that was to comprehend. Perhaps they finally started to understand what he was doing and decided to quit interfering with the magic.

Kayla, too, was doing exactly what he expected her to do: using her influence in the media to ensure continued positive coverage of Perfect Cannabis and its meteoric rise. So once again—what else could he possibly want, and why did he feel a restless urge driving him on?

For once in his life, everything was going perfect, and all he'd had to do was discover an illegal grow op in his own building.

The mere absurdity of the thought finally did make him laugh out loud. OK, so right at the beginning, he had been just a touch concerned when he first stumbled upon it. No, to be precise, he had been freaked out, but hey—he had had it straightened out on the inside of a couple of days. It really did not get any better, right?

FORTY-SIX

"Kayla, my dear," he said, walking into their downtown condominium. "Kayla, I have an excellent idea."

"Excellent sounds good. Pray tell, what have you come up with now?"

"Let's take a brief timeout."

"Timeout—now? Right this minute? I thought you were in the middle of this audit, and we were having all sorts of problems."

"Well, as it so happens, I have solved all of our problems in the past couple of days. For once, everybody is happy and doing what they are supposed to be doing, so it is time for us to think of nothing but ourselves right now."

"Not that I am arguing, Connor, but shouldn't you…"

"There are a dozen things I should right now—none of them I want to worry about at this moment."

Connor wrapped his arms around Kayla and spun her around for one turn.

"Life is good right now. I've solved all of our problems—didn't you hear? All of them. Everything is done. The solution I was working on? It came through. All we have to do right now is wait for David to finish this idiotic audit, and I can go on the road and raise more funds."

"And the money?"

"Coming in—very shortly. I am telling you I have it all covered."

"You are sure this time? No more loan sharks, no more borrowing from…?"

"I am absolutely sure, Kayla. I have it in hand. But if you don't want to go with me on a brief vacation, just say so. I can go by myself. It's not a problem."

"That's not what I was saying, Connor. It's just—very sudden, that's all."

"These things are always very sudden when they finally happen. You should know that from being around me this long. So are you up for a vacation or not?"

"I—yes, I guess—I mean, of course I am."

Kayla smiled and came back closer to him.

"Yes, of course. What did you have in mind?"

"I don't even know yet myself." Connor shrugged and went over to the sideboard to pour himself a large vodka and soda—easy on the soda. "South Pacific maybe—somewhere sunny and warm. Somewhere nobody is going to get a hold of me for the next week and a half, so I can finally reset my brain and start fresh."

Kayla looked at the glass in his hand, but wisely, she said nothing.

"South Pacific—sounds delicious and I have never been. Not any place we can take the helicopter, though."

"No, the helicopter is staying put for a while. I have taken enough grief over the thing that we are going to fly plain old commercial this time."

"Commercial?"

"Well, first class of course."

"Of course." Kayla smiled again. "I'm going to research something and get back to you, OK? Oh, this is exciting."

"Well, don't take too long. I want to be out of here and on a hot, sunny, deserted beach with a stiff drink in my hand by the end of the week. Think you can handle that?"

"Yes, sir, I can handle it."

Kayla mock-saluted him and disappeared into the next room, presumably to consult her computer about the 'in spot' in the South Pacific right now. Whatever it was, he would gladly go to get away for a week. It did not matter to him whatsoever where the fuck they went, as long as nobody could get to him until he and Roberto had hammered out a few details.

Not that there was even a shred of doubt it would all happen according to plan, his plan, he reminded himself. He was merely tired of people hitting him up for money and questioning his way of running things.

South Pacific was fine—far away enough, though he wondered what had made him think about it in the first place.

In any case, it took a few days for Kayla to finish hammering out a travel schedule. Wouldn't you know it—it involved just a tiny bit of helicopter travel?

Connor grinned when he knew she was not looking; he really could not blame her the slightest bit. He loved that beautiful machine himself—he'd just gotten tired of taking artillery for having it. And he did not even own it.

According to Kayla's schedule, they were to take the helicopter to New York City and from there catch a flight. Australia, New Zealand, Tahiti, Mo'orea—his head spun just from reading her itinerary—but when Kayla did something, she did it right, whether it was running a magazine or planning a quick getaway for the stressed and overworked executive. Perfect.

The pictures attached to her plans all showed blue oceans, brilliant white sand beaches, and brilliantly colored flowers. Connor could not have been more satisfied.

Tessa, on the other hand, did not exactly take the news of his impending vacation in the same spirit of excitement as it was offered.

"You're going away—now of all times?" she asked when he told her in the office the next morning not to count on him for anything but the direst of emergencies for a week or so.

"You of all people know what the past few months have been like, Tess. I seriously need to get away if I want to keep up this pace and grow the company. For my own health and that of everybody else."

"Yes, but there are a ton of things to do."

"Nothing you can't handle."

"People come in and call almost every day about outstanding bills, and I myself…"

"I have it solved, Tess—just a little bit more patience and everything will be paid off. I have investors coming in with large amounts, and then we can all breathe a little easier. But I need you to be patient for just a little bit longer. Can you do that?"

"Of course, but…"

"Tessa!"

"Connor!" She knew him well enough to get right into his face and bully back when she needed to, one of the things he hated and loved about her at the same time. Tessa did not take crap from anyone—not even Connor Beauregard himself.

"There are people suing us—Catherine Egan, for one, and a couple of others. I neither want to nor can I deal with that. This is shit you need to handle."

"Then just leave it. When I get back, everybody will get their money, and life will be good again. Nobody needs to deal with anything."

An overstatement, he thought. Even if everything went just as he had envisioned it for him and Roberto, it would take a bit of time for the first crop to be finished, sold, and the profits divided—but there was no reason to let anybody in on that little fact. How much time did it take, anyway, for cannabis to ripen, or whatever it did while it was just standing there under those grow lights?

Shit, he would really have to read up on this stuff or risk Roberto taking him for a ride. Nobody was taking anything that was his— ever again. And if he had to study how to grow drugs to make sure, then that's what he would do. Period. He would learn how the entire operation worked—from one end to the other. Only then could he keep Roberto in check.

His new partner might be different—in every single way that mattered—but he was still one of Al's family, and therefore not to be trusted.

Time to hit the books, Beauregard, he thought. *Study this shit and study it well, or you might as well tattoo* loser *on your forehead.*

His work was just simply never done, he thought, shaking his head, and realized Tess was still standing there, frowning, waiting for a good answer.

"It won't be long now," he said and put on his most brilliant 'I am the hero' smile for her. "I thank you for your patience, and believe me—I have suffered just as much as everyone else, so I know what you are talking about."

"As long as you do."

Just as he took a breath to respond to her somewhat hostile remark, she turned on her heel and left him sitting there, and he grinned and shook his head.

Damned woman—if she did not know her stuff and were not absolutely 100 percent devoted to him, he would fire her.

Somehow, he hoped, Roberto would get in touch with him before he and Kayla left for the South Pacific, if only to put his mind at ease. It would make everything else just a bit easier.

Damn Rafael for being so bloody straitlaced, right at the moment when he needed somebody to help him talk this thing through. He did not need a babysitter, he didn't need somebody to point out right from wrong—he just needed somebody to listen while he worked this out in his mind.

FORTY-SEVEN

Everything was working out just fine.

He thought it as he gathered just a few things for the trip, and he thought it when the helicopter dropped them off in New York City. No news from Roberto—yet.

"I thought you wanted to get away," Kayla complained as he shoved his cell phone back into his pocket. "That just is not going to work if you keep staring at that thing every five minutes."

"Just some last-minute—stuff I need to check on, love. Nothing serious."

"Then let it be. We are in New York City, for crying out loud, one of my all-time favorite places in the world to shop and enjoy, and you keep staring..."

"Just a deal I was working on as we left, and I want to know it's all in place."

"OK. Now stop thinking about it and put that damn thing away. You're the one who wanted this vacation."

His temper flared, but at the last moment, he shoved it down. Not now—really not now. She was right; everything would work out fine.

"You are right. Just being obsessive. I don't want to spoil this trip."

"You better not." Kayla smiled again. "Let's go hit Fifth Avenue before we catch the flight to Auckland."

"Why not? Lead the way! Armani Exchange for starters. I think I'm going to grab a few things for our trip."

In the end, they left behind everything they had brought with them and loaded three new suitcases filled with new purchases on the flight to New Zealand. Connor had not checked his phone even once during their intense shopping marathon, and he did not even care any longer.

Gleefully, Connor handed their old suitcases to the porter at the Trump Tower hotel.

"Get rid of these, will you?"

"Pardon, sir?"

"You heard me—not needed any longer."

He and Kayla collapsed into their cab, hurting with laughter. Life was good.

FORTY-EIGHT

Auckland, New Zealand. Connor lifted an expensive glass of wine and toasted life being good. Sydney, Brisbane, Papua, New Guinea—more drinks and toasts to life being perfect.

Destinations flitted by them in brilliant blue-green and white. Food and drink arrived and was consumed. Inevitably, someone would hand him a slip of paper to sign, and Connor did without so much as glancing at it. Life was good, he had it all figured out, and he had it by the neck and squeezed it for as much as it was worth.

Vaomar Island, the tiniest of islands somewhere out in the Coral Sea—a private yacht charter that had brought them there.

Beautiful Polynesian people in bright cotton clothing who greeted them, smiling, and brought them more food and drink. Intense drinks served in hollowed-out fruits and coconut—likely made with mostly rum. Connor downed them all and asked for more.

He could have everything now, absolutely everything.

Vaguely, he became aware of Kayla beside him telling him to slow down, and he threw back his head and roared with laughter.

"Connor, slow down, please—you've been drunk for the past five days."

"Not drunk—absolutely shitfaced from ten o'clock in the morning on, and I love it, you hear me? I love it."

He downed another drink and threw his hands into the air.

"I fucking own the world, everybody."

And with that, he simply jumped over the side of the yacht into the deep blue ocean, laughing all the way.

They told him the next day the captain had had to send three men to fish him out, and he was never welcome on that particular yacht again.

Who gave a fuck anyway? The guy who owned the yacht was likely on the run from the law anyway, spending his days and his money on Vaomar, safe from extradition to US authorities and from his enemies.

Kayla gave him some sort of lecture about his liver, but he barely heard more than the sound of her voice. He was too busy planning another getaway to this little island in the middle of nowhere. Sunshine, beaches, friendly people, and all the rum one could handle. No legal or regulatory bodies he could discern, no extradition treaties, no jails, no cops. Basically, no rules at all. Connor Beauregard needed his very own getaway place here—just to have somewhere to run to if he ever got sick of everything back home.

He sobered up long enough to have an interesting chat with a Portuguese man who owned a fishing boat and a ramshackle hut on the other side of the island. Not that the sobriety lasted long—one way or another, every Western person on this island seemed to be in a constant state of drunkenness—but he very much enjoyed the company and the information he received.

They shared a common thread, he thought: Allan, the man who owned the yacht he was no longer welcome on; Cristos, the Portuguese man with the fishing boat; and finally, Connor himself. Interesting that—then another drink arrived, and the remainder of the thought was lost to the glorious feeling of not giving a shit any longer.

Kayla managed to flip through the in-flight magazine without looking at him or speaking to him and at the same time convey her intense displeasure with him. Talent that—not a word needed to be spoken.

"Go too fast, these getaways, don't they?"

No answer.

"I coulda used a couple of extra weeks."

No answer.

"Not like you need to tell me—I know you're pissed at me. But you know this is how I relax."

A sideways look—and still no answer.

"This is who I am. I work hard, and I relax by playing 10 times as hard as this. You knew all along this was who I was—so live with it."

Still no answer but a blazing look from the airplane seat beside him.

There was still not even a single message from Roberto, and again, it began to worry him. Roberto had his ways of getting at information, so he likely knew what was going on; he would know Connor had gone away for a few days. Maybe that was why he hadn't bothered, but a brief note would have been nothing more than good manners. 'All good—our deal is on,' something along those lines.

Connor sighed and checked his phone yet again. Dozens of messages: from the office; from Simon, who all of a sudden wanted out of the deal; from Rafael, who gave intricate and boring status reports. Nothing from Roberto.

"Right, OK, so it's the safe thing to do," he muttered to himself. "But just one little acknowledgment—would that have been too much to ask?"

"What's going on?"

He looked up at Kayla silhouetted against the huge window at La Guardia Airport and made a face.

"So, you're talking to me again, are you?"

"Maybe. OK—you have to admit..."

"Admit what?"

"You went just a little far on this vacation. Even you have to realize that. If you strung together two hours of not being drunk in the entire ten days, it was a lot. And the entire pouch of pills seems to be empty."

She looked around cautiously, but the true New Yorkers couldn't give a hoot what somebody in the middle of the air terminal might be talking about.

"You have to admit," she said and shrugged. "You went too far."

"Depends on how you define 'too far.' I don't think so, but, hey—be my guest."

He looked back down on his phone and stubbornly pushed buttons.

He'd had their suitcases shipped separately, only to find out that it would take forever to load them into the Sikorsky, so he decided to leave the luggage where it was, have it shipped back home—or not—and just simply fly back.

Kayla whined and complained all the way about the souvenirs she had to leave behind that might never make it home, but it was his turn to give her the silent treatment and impersonate the phrase 'tough shit—deal with it.' He quite simply could not care less, and he cared even less who knew about it. Souvenirs, for God's sake!

He cared about getting hold of Roberto. Did they have a deal now or not?

Breathe, he reminded himself and purposely relaxed his stranglehold on the armrest in the helicopter

"What's going on with you?" Kayla finally asked.

"I just want to get there, that's all. This is taking forever. Damned vacation was far too long."

"You're the one who wanted to get away, Connor. You insisted on it."

"Maybe I did. But a couple of days would have been more than enough. I've been out of touch. I don't know what's going on. For all I know…"

He stopped and got up from his seat, peering out the side window. Nothing—of course there was nothing. They were flying through thick clouds, as their pilot had predicted.

"For all you know what, Connor? Is something going on back home that I do not know about?"

"There are—developments—in the company that I need to keep an eye on, OK? I just need to get back."

"What does that even mean? Developments in the company? Can you give me a straight answer?"

Connor did not answer, paced to the front of the helicopter, looked at the pilots and chose not to say anything, went back to his seat—got back up again…

"Connor!"

"I don't want to talk right now."

He found a ballpoint pen in his pocket and mangled it, twisting and untwisting it until nothing more than a handful of broken pieces remained. Now—he had to get back now.

FORTY-NINE

He would have run off the helicopter and straight into his office when they finally got there after an interminable wait at the airport, save for the fact that Rafael stood there to pick him up.

"Rafa, what's up, bro? You got nothing else to do, so you are earning money as a chauffeur?"

"Hardly. Hey, Kayla." Rafael nodded, and Connor noticed lines of tension around his eyes, as if he had not slept well in days. Not a good sign. What the heck?

"No luggage, guys?"

"No," Kayla said pointedly. "Somebody was in too much of a hurry to get back home and to the office. Will you drop me at home please? Then he is all yours."

"What's going on, Rafa?" Connor chose to ignore her pointed looks and slipped into Rafael's car. "Anything I need to know?"

"Maybe—yes—no—fuck if I know. Sorry, Kayla."

"What, Rafael?"

"Everybody is acting—strangely—that's all."

"Define *strange*."

He could feel it—panic in his stomach, growing, taking over—and he fought it. No need yet; no reason to. Maybe Roberto planned it this way. Maybe he had done something, maybe…. Damn that man for not communicating.

"Rafa!"

"I told you I don't know," Rafael said, too loudly to be casual. He made a jerky left turn that barely missed a cyclist waiting for his turn and shook his head. "I don't know, Connor, but something is—hinky."

"First strange, now hinky. Thanks for the grammar lesson. And still no details."

"I dropped by the office a couple of times last week, like you asked me to."

"And?"

"And Tessa was not there both times. Whole place looked deserted."

"Oh." Connor relaxed a little. That was it? "She probably took the chance to work from home—you know how she is. That was it? That is why you are all worked up?"

"No." Rafael looked into the rearview mirror to check on Kayla, but she was busy thumbing through the messages on her phone. "I haven't heard from Al since you've gone away either. Usually, he checks in with me now and then, lets me know what's going on."

"I did not know that. All this time—he's been giving you regular updates on my company? Who does he think he is?"

"Our company, Connor—our company. And I was the one who brought him in, remember? So, he thought…"

"Never mind what Al thought, Rafael. I don't like it, but fine."

"I just don't know—that's the whole point. Before you went away, every day someone would bug me about something—unpaid bills, the fact that you're not doing things by the book."

"And they came to you with this? Now you're telling me? Who is 'someone,' anyway?"

Rafael raised his hands and slapped them back down on the steering wheel and let out a frustrated growl.

"Come on, Connor. You know who you are. You don't do things the straightaway manner. You need people to tidy up behind you—so they come to me."

"Who?"

"David, sometimes Tess, Simon, couple of folks at the auditor's office."

"Catherine?"

"Sometimes. She'd need the answer to a question and couldn't find you or couldn't get a straight answer out of you. But even she's quit calling me. Not that I mind at all. Woman is relentless."

Connor balled his hands and took in a deep breath, letting it out slowly. Traitors, his gut screamed, and if he could have, he would have asked Rafael to stop the car so he could get out and run back.

Rafa looked at him from the driver's seat and shook his head.

"You think I liked it, them coming to me? Man, of course I didn't, but I also knew they'd only cause trouble for you if I didn't give them something at least. A few crumbs to make them happy."

"So you fed information to my…"

He stopped and shrugged.

"Don't say enemies. These are the people helping you build this company."

"And they didn't trust me enough to do it—that it?"

"No, Connor, that's not it. They just knew that—your head is in the clouds sometimes, building a vision. So they came to me."

Connor said nothing, still fighting the urge to run from the car. After all, they had known all of this for years. Years they had spent running projects together—Connor the dreamer, visionary, and salesman, and Rafael, the guy who had his feet on the ground and usually could be relied upon to clean up after him.

Fuck. If he needed another reason why doing this deal with Roberto alone and nobody else, he'd just been handed that reason. Rafa—of all people.

"And that has you worried—nobody is coming to you any longer?"

"Well? Don't you think it's strange?"

"No, Rafael, I do not think it is strange," Connor said tightly. "I straightened things out before I left. I told you that, did I not?"

"Yes you did, but…"

SABINE FRISCH

"But, as always, you thought, hey, Connor needs me to come in and clean up?"

"I did not think that, Connor. I just meant that usually…."

"Usually—usually, they'd all come to you because you are the good guy, and I am…"

"Come on, Connor. You're mad at me now, fine, but let's just think for a minute…"

"Connor."

Kayla looked up from her phone and gave both of them her best schoolteacher look.

"Boys, if the two of you are done arguing, I would really like to go home, which is right around the corner, Rafael. And what about you, Connor? Are you going to come home with me and relax for the rest of the afternoon, or are you going to keep spinning like a little windup toy and argue with Rafa?"

Connor said nothing, and Rafael only shrugged.

"Sorry, Kayla, didn't mean to involve you here."

"That's OK. For whatever reason, Connor is a little tense today." She patted his shoulder and smiled. "Probably missed the office, as hard as that is to believe."

Connor wanted to strangle both of them—right here in the car. He pushed the nails of his fingers into his palms so hard the pain pulled him back and finally forced himself to breathe lightly and evenly.

"You are probably right," he said with as much casual warmth as he could muster. "I don't do well being idle for long stretches of time. So, I will check in at the office. You, my dear," he patted Kayla's arm lightly, "you go home and take a nap or whatever it is you need to shake off this long trip, and you," a nod at Rafael, "thank you for picking us up, and I will catch up at The Lighthouse with you later."

"Connor!"

"All right, in deference to Kayla, tomorrow then. I will catch up with you tomorrow. I am sure there are a few developments I might have missed."

"If you think so."

"I think so—please. As a matter of fact, I insist."

God—his mouth started to hurt from smiling at those two dimwits for so long. *Just let me get out of this car*, Connor thought, *and do what I need to do*. Which was get hold of Roberto, get things straightened out, and get a large drink. In that order.

Maybe he should even drive out to the building to check on things. Just to make sure the new location of the grow op was sufficiently hidden. Nah, Roberto probably had all of that in hand. Hadn't he told him there were places on his property he did not even know about yet? He looked forward to finding them.

Unable to contain his impatience waiting for the elevator, he took the stairs to his office two at a time and all but stormed in, only to stand in the middle of the room, staring around him.

Rafael had indeed been correct. Tessa shone with her absence—and from the looks of it, she hadn't been there for a couple of days.

For one, her workstation looked freshly tidied up, clean as he had never seen it before. For another, a leaf from the plant on her desk had fallen over her keyboard and simply lay there, crinkled and drying up. Tessa did not allow anything to touch her computer, not even the plant he had put there for her birthday.

She had not been here in a couple of days, all right, he thought and fought the sinking feeling in his stomach.

She'd work from home. Of course she would. She'd never pass up the chance not having to fight for space on the subway to get here and back home again. It was her biggest complaint about working downtown—the time it took to get here and the misery of the train trip... And he had told her not to deal with people who came around asking for money. Made sense that she would hide out at home, right?

But something did not feel right—something just did not.

The door—the door to his private office stood wide open. That definitely did not happen unless Connor Beauregard himself was in there and Tessa out here at her station. His office was his private sanctuary. It did not stay open. Ever.

Breathing slowly and deliberately, Connor took off his coat and hung it up on the coat rack, put down the little portfolio he carried everywhere, and straightened his shoulders.

His space had been violated. His personal, private space, the room from where he ran his world, had been left open for anyone to step in and sit down. Somebody was going to pay for this.

He could hardly imagine Tessa leaving the room open; she knew how he felt about it, knew how furious he got if he even thought someone would walk in and go through his stuff. Even at her most forgetful, she wouldn't do it—but who else?

Connor still stood there staring toward the open door to his office when he noticed the reflection from his desk lamp. It was an enormous crystal globe Kayla had given him, just after he moved in with her, and it cast mind-boggling shadows against the walls—especially if you were drunk or stoned. God, he remembered...

"You might as well come in all the way, Connor, instead of just standing out there like some sort of messenger."

That voice! That voice belonged to a man sitting at his very desk, just out of view from anyone who might be standing in the reception area. Connor bristled with anger, at the knowledge that someone sat in his very own chair, and at the sound of the voice—the voice of the man he hated most right now!

Two furious steps brought him to the doorway of his office, where he stood and glowered at the man who reclined comfortably in Connor's Jacobsen Egg chair.

"You know these things look horribly uncomfortable when you see them for the first time, but this is actually quite nice—I could get used to this."

"As long as you are comfortable—in my private office. How'd you get in here? I thought you never left the diner."

Connor forced the words past the fury that wanted to choke him and shoved his hands into his pockets so the tight fists would not give him away.

"Oh, relax, Connor. I just wanted to—welcome you back home. I hope you had a wonderful holiday this time. I don't even know where you went. It did not hit the news this time, you know."

"What do you want?"

"Oh, so aggressive, Connor. Is that any way to say hello to your business partner?"

"I would hardly call you my business partner—Mister Original Chef. Or should I call you Ivers instead?"

The man in his chair shrugged. "Whatever works for you. After all, names are just words."

"Why don't you cut the bullshit and tell me why you are here, Ivers? It couldn't be to look at my vacation photos."

"There are photos? Oh, good, I so love to look at other peoples' vacation shots. I don't get away much, you know. Business..."

He still made no move to vacate the seat behind the desk, and Connor had no choice but to stand or grab the visitor's chair. He chose the latter. Dammit if he stood before this man like a schoolboy being reprimanded. He plunked himself into the admittedly uncomfortable chair, stretching his legs far from him and resting his elbows on his knees.

"Well?"

Al's father put his palms together before his face and looked at him for a long time before he finally spoke again.

"As you wish, Connor. Right down to business then."

All the joviality had left his voice, leaving behind a hard, almost metallic sound that sent a little shiver down his back. This was not good—this was so not good at all!

He sat up a little straighter and put on his best poker face. Bluff—bluff like he'd never done before because whatever Ivers wanted here in his office, he was 100 percent not going to like it. This man never left his little dump of a restaurant from all Connor had heard. He ran an empire out of the back of that rathole. The fact that he had actually come out to see him—twice if you counted the night of the grand opening—that alone should have scared him.

Now, under the hard, white light from Kayla's pretentious globe, he could see the hardness in the other man's eyes. Black ice chips—that was what they reminded him of now, and almost automatically, he found himself wishing he had not come out here alone tonight.

"I am disappointed, Connor." The Original Chef, the man he now could call Ivers, relaxed in his chair and put his hands on the table before him. No weapons? The thought flashed through Connor's mind, and by the tiny little smile on Ivers's face he could tell the other man knew it. Knew it and it pleased him.

"I gave you money, Connor—a lot of money if you remember—to start a business that was nothing but an idea in your head. A good idea, mind you, but nothing but an idea."

"And I appreciate that very much. I have done everything to make sure…."

"You have done nothing I can see but spend money. You had in your hands everything to make this business huge. By God, growing marijuana… When you went out to sign up investors, I was not so sure, but it turns out you could not stop people from throwing money at you."

"It was a sound business decision—the stock…."

"The stock should be valued a lot higher than it is now, and it would be, if you were not so dreadfully delinquent in your filings with the SEC."

"We've had—problems with our auditors, I am sure you are aware of that. And David, the man I put in charge of finance, he lost control over the process. He ended up mired in unimportant details and did not manage the situation at all. I admit, I should have…"

Connor brought up his hands and shook his head. "I should have—checked on him, perhaps, made sure that he knew what he was doing, but there were a lot of moving parts to this thing."

"Uh-huh…" Al's father nodded and took off the slim, wire-framed glasses he wore, leaning back in Connor's chair and using the glasses in his hand as a pointer. "So help me understand this, Connor. You had everything you needed in hand, but the man in charge of your finances was horrendously incompetent? That's why things did not work the way they should have?"

"Don't worry about David at this point—he is gone anyway. He was incompetent, yes, but I wanted to give him a chance. Bad judgment. We will find someone else who can power this thing through. Once we are back on solid ground…"

"And all the procedural errors and paperwork deficiencies your auditors are questioning—David was in charge of those as well?"

Shit—the man was way more informed than he gave him credit for. Connor felt tiny beads of sweat forming on the back of his neck, crawling into his collar. He really should not have come in here tonight, alone, just off an intercontinental flight. He should have waited until he was a bit sharper….

Again, he shrugged. "You know auditors—they will always find something, even where there is nothing to find. Why don't you tell me why you came all the way out here tonight? I'm sure it was not personnel problems."

"Not your personnel problems, Connor, no."

Again that feeling in his stomach—*not your problems*? That emphasis on the word *your*?

"Oh, don't look at me like that, Connor. You did not think I would give you a great amount of money and just let you mismanage the company as you like, did you?"

"Mismanage—look, if you are talking about that damned helicopter, Kayla simply leased the thing to please me. I had no idea she was doing this at all. I know it does not look good for a startup company. I will—believe me—I will get rid of the thing at the earliest possible opportunity."

"OK. So your financial officer made a mess out of the audit, your girlfriend does not know about due process or managing expenses properly—anybody else involved here at your level I should worry about? Now that we are talking about it, I mean?"

Connor shrugged and said nothing. Anything he could have said would just dig a deeper hole than the one he was in. This man was pissing him off rather quickly.

"How about your lawyer, Connor, Catherine Egan—did she make mistakes as well? Is that why you would not pay her, and she is now suing you?"

"Catherine did not… Look—I don't know where this is leading, but I am not in the mood to sit here and defend myself. Yes, mistakes were made, and we will correct them. This is a startup company. Things happen. It is not always smooth sailing. You learn from what happened. You correct course and move on. That is the way it works."

"Mistakes were made. That is an interesting way of phrasing things, Connor. Yes, I guess they were. I wonder if you remember this man." He reached down, and, for a moment, Connor thought his heart might stop. Stupid idea. Of course he wouldn't bring a weapon in here. *Christ, get a hold of yourself,* he thought. It was just a slim manila folder the man pulled out of a plain white plastic bag and placed on the table before him. Awkwardly, he put his glasses back on and leafed through the papers inside, licking his fingers with every page he turned.

"McDowell—William McDowell. Interesting fellow that."

"$5,000 Guy," Connor groaned. "This man has been more trouble than all the other shareholders together."

"Oh, do tell."

"Ah." Connor waved his hand through the air as if he could wipe McDowell away with it. "The moron forgot he signed the consent to the amalgamation and name change. He is probably old enough he simply forgot. Never deal with these small-time guys—never, I tell you. They give you more headaches than a $500,000 investor sometimes."

He could see the little flash of annoyance on Ivers's face before the man caught it, but too late now.

"Really? When I met him, he seemed quite sharp to me."

Met him. Met him? All of the air seemed to have leaked out of the room suddenly, and Connor fought to take a breath. *When I met him?* Al's father had gone out of his way to meet up with unhappy shareholders? Small-time investors, people who might have a grudge against him? What did that mean—where was he going with this, and who else might he have gone to see?

"I went to see this man because, you see, he is still an investor in this company, our company, and no matter what—he worked for those $5,000, and you would not believe what he told me."

"What did he tell you?" Connor forced out, fighting the urge to get up and leave his office right at that moment. He needed—something, some way out, some escape.

"He told me that he just did not sign this consent form. He would have, if you had simply gone and spoken to him, explained things to him properly. That was all he wanted. Imagine that. But you would not do it. So he got stubborn and decided not to sign it until you spoke to him."

"Oh, come now, surely you don't believe that old codger. I am sure he is spinning a story. The amalgamation was the right thing to do at the time to get this company trading on a US stock exchange, and you want the CEO of the corporation to go out and sit down with a minor investor to explain the stock market to him? Surely not."

"I am not telling you how to run this business, Connor. What I am telling you," he carefully pulled a sheet of paper out of the file and placed it on the table between them, "what I am telling you that this here is a fake, and you know it."

Connor only had to glance down to see that it was the consent-to-amalgamation form—the very one he had signed with McDowell's signature. Catherine had been on his tail back then; time was running out. He really had not had the leisure of a free afternoon to go talk to this old man back then. Jesus, business moved in totally different ways nowadays. Did no one get that? No one?

"I know nothing of the sort," he said. "Nothing. You and I know the amalgamation had to be done, and just because some geezer does not remember—"

"He is barely 50 years old, Connor, and I would appreciate if you stopped calling him senile just because he challenged you."

"Fact remains he did sign it. You have it front of you."

"Well, somebody signed it." Al's father lifted the paper by the very edge. "And a graphologist tells me it was not Mr. McDowell."

Connor swallowed hard and said nothing. For once, all the bluster and verbiage he usually wrapped around himself failed him. He simply sat there, his throat closed up, his hands folded, staring at the piece of paper between them.

"You know who signed this, Connor—and, more to the point, so do I. Do you know what would happen if that man whom you call an old codger would go to the SEC and challenge this merger? The whole damn thing would be invalid."

He dropped the paper from his fingers as if it were on fire, and Connor watched it sail down onto the table top, mesmerized. All the more, he twitched in shock when Ivers's hand stuck the table, hard. The slap felt as if he had taken it to the face.

"Are you goddamn insane or just incompetent? You would do this knowing full well that it could endanger the entire company for years to come? Why would you take such a stupid risk?"

"It was just a piece of paper, goddamn it, and he has not even asked about it in months."

"You are right, Connor—he has not. And you know why? Because he is not a shareholder any longer."

Connor looked up and blinked. Once, twice, to let this latest bit of information sink in.

"Not a shareholder...?"

"That's right. Don't look so surprised. I made him an offer he would have been stupid to refuse, and you know what? The man is neither old, nor forgetful, nor stupid. He sold his shares to me. And so did a few other people who were a bit—shall we say unhappy—with the way you run things."

Connor swallowed hard. This was really not good. As a matter of fact, it was a giant disaster, and before it went any further, he needed to get out of here, get his head together, and figure a way out of this mess. Dammit, dammit, dammit—how could he have been so stupid?

What he needed to do now was think—and get in touch with Roberto. Shit, they would need their combined resources to fight what this man was up to. Roberto. He had to help him—had to.

"I would appreciate it if you resigned quietly, Connor. You can make up any reason you please, but please do so before the end of the month."

"You have got to be kidding me."

Connor got to his feet and stood before his own desk, arms loosely by his side. Finally, he cocked one finger toward the door.

"I will ask you to leave my office now, if you please."

"This is not going away, Connor—not until you resign."

"Really? You waltz into my office, sit in my private office on my chair, and presume to make me resign because of what is, at best, a minor procedural error? I am telling you right here that man did sign that agreement."

"And I have proof that he did not."

"And I am going to get proof that he did. You think this is hard? You think I know nothing about life? How much money are we going to spend on both sides, proving our points to one another? Hiring specialists to disagree with one another? Do you really want to do that? You think that is going to save the company?"

"No, of course not. What is going to save the company is someone who runs it properly and does the right things properly."

"And you are that person, really? Give your head a shake. The moment you make yourself CEO of Perfect Cannabis, the company is done with, and you know it, no matter how many shareholders you blinded into selling their holdings to you. So I suggest you leave my office—now."

"I don't think you are thinking this through."

"Out—right now," Connor thundered, pointing at the door, not caring that his temper suddenly got the best of him. Another two minutes and he would grab the man by the arm and throw him out physically, so help him God.

Who did he think he was anyway? Half a million dollars? Fine and good, it was a decent investment, it had been the start to this company, but that did not give him the right...

"Get the fuck out of my office, and stay out of my company," he hissed. "It is enough you saddled me with your sons. Neither one of them knows what he is doing. And you would come in here and presume to take over? I have shareholders. I have a board of directors that would vote with me—to a man. To a man. Now get out."

Al's father stood and inclined his head lightly.

"It is obvious you have to do a bit more thinking. I will be back."

"You will not. And take this shit with you."

This time, Connor did give him a push, none too gently, and threw the folder with McDowell's paperwork after him.

He only felt better when the door slammed into the lock, and he had turned the deadbolt, twice.

"Fuck," he muttered.

Ivers likely picked the lock, too. His hands shook as he dialed the number for an all-night locksmith company.

And Tessa—where the fuck was Tessa when he needed her? For starters, he needed to know how they had got their information, how they had come in here. And he needed to safeguard against such a thing happening again.

Shit, $5,000. Why had he not given the man his money back when he started to be a problem? He had run out of time of course, had been busy with other things, and the money was always needed elsewhere.

Dammit, Roberto—he needed to get hold of Roberto....

Rafa, what could Rafael do for him? Could he pull this cart out of the shit pile it had skidded into? Maybe—he knew these people. He had not wanted to involve Rafael again, but right now, he needed all hands on deck.

He barked orders at the locksmith and at the same time made notes on a pad of paper. Kayla had to get involved to save his company—her reporters needed to dig up some shit on Ivers and discredit him. If he wanted to take over this company, he would have one hell of a time being credible in this town.

After two hours he collapsed in his famous egg chair—the one he all but wanted to carry to the curb and leave for garbage pickup after tonight—and rested his forehead on his arms.

He had a plan. And it was a decent plan.

His plan depended on getting everybody on site with him. Rafael, Kayla, Simon, Josh... They had all been on the sidelines while Connor had fought this war at the fronts. Time for them to step up. With his board of directors solidly behind him, he would get rid of this damned family.

Then he would hire some decent outside consultants to bring everything that had been slacking internally up to speed. Ivers was right in one area—too much had been simply left to slide; too much was not done.

Next, he'd sacrifice some of his Swiss shares, finally, and buy out Al and his family. Thank God and all of his angels they did not know about those. He had the money to buy them out the same way they had bought out other shareholders. They would never know what hit them.

And then—together with Roberto—he would run the most charmed, efficient, and profitable marijuana grow op in the whole Western hemisphere. They would be unbeatable. Last item on the list.

Connor raised his head again and smiled this time.

That fucker had no idea who he was messing with, and he would unfortunately live to regret his error. Too bad Connor would not be there to see the look on his face when he finally realized that you did not take something away from Connor Beauregard. Too damned bad, wasn't it?

He and Roberto would lift a drink—or two or seven—to the unfortunate demise of Ivers Senior.

"Original Chef, my ass," he muttered. The man was a fool, nothing else.

FIFTY

Back to work. Connor did what he did best—he called the people around him.

Rafael, Simon, Josh, Kayla—everybody who had been there at the very beginning—he told them to be at his office the next morning, early. No objections, no excuses. This was an emergency, as big as they come.

To his surprise, nobody put up too much of a fuss. He had expected Josh, who never had more than 10 minutes to spare, to put up a fuss, and yet... His secretary said he would be there. Period.

Connor wondered, but he had no time to get into it. Still no sign of Tessa. She did not answer her phone at home or her cell phone, and that really worried him. Come to think of it, he had not heard from her at all, not since he left for this goddamn South Pacific vacation. Why now? What on earth could have happened? OK—he knew she was sore because he had not paid her in a while, but come on, she knew how things stood with the company. Tessa knew everything.

That particular thought kept nagging him. Tessa knew everything, and if she ever decided to screw him over...

She would not do it. She simply would. Not. Do. It. Dammit, she would not. They had worked together for years and years. There had been tight spots before—she would not come around now and stab him in the back.

Forget it. Maybe something had happened? Who would know? Her boyfriend... Connor realized he had no clue about her life at all.

He barely knew where she lived—barely. That was it. If something indeed had happened, he would never find out.

Connor stood and stared at his own reflection in the window glass.

"You're seeing ghosts," he finally told himself. "Nothing happened. She'll be there tomorrow morning, with her enormous coffee mug and a scowl on her face because she still wants money. You'll see."

The next morning, though, he stepped back into an empty office. It looked the same as he had left it—had it only been hours ago?—and again, he scolded himself. Of course, he'd had the locks changed the night before. If Tessa had come in early, she would not have been able to get in.

He flipped on all the lights and waited. And they arrived almost at the same time, just as he had called them.

Kayla had been sleeping already when he came home the night before, so she knew just as much as everybody else did and looked at him with curiosity in her eyes.

"What's going on, Connor?" This from Rafael, who refused to sit down, even though Connor had pulled enough chairs into the round.

"Sit, Rafa, this is going to take a while."

"It had better not. I have meetings."

"No doubt, Josh, but I need everybody's full attention."

Finally, when they all sat, he straightened his shoulders

"I'm not going to waste anybody's time here, folks, but we need to act because this company is under attack."

He saw the dismissive look on their faces and shook his head, pressing on.

"Please don't take this lightly, but it has come to my attention that Al's family—namely his father—has begun to buy up blocks of shares of Perfect Cannabis Corporation."

"OK, so?" Simon asked, checking his watch for the third time in less than 10 minutes.

"Are you listening to me? The man wants to take over, probably put one of his sons in as CEO? You cannot possibly stand there and tell me. Don't you know the potential consequences?"

"I know the consequences, Connor, believe me. I'm not exactly new at this game. You, on the other hand."

Josh's sentence trailed off, just so, and for a moment, Connor felt the pit in his stomach open up again.

"Just what are you talking about, Josh? You, on the other hand? Do you mind explaining?"

This was entirely not going the way he had planned for it to go. He looked around the room and realized that Josh and Simon would not meet his gaze, Kayla looked confused and not entirely awake, and Rafael—Rafael had not said one single word. If he wanted to describe how his friend looked at that moment, he would have to say… guilty. That was exactly what the man looked like. Guilty.

"We can't let this happen, people—we have worked for this company. We have put our money into it—our hard-earned money. We are the ones who thought of it, who sweated for it, who built it."

"Save your breath, Connor," Josh said. "You talk a good game. I will give you that. Any time you want to come over and sell in my agency, you are welcome to do so, but as a CEO—I don't know. I just don't think you cut it."

For the first time in his life, Connor understood the meaning of the phrase 'deafening silence.' No one in the room would meet his eyes. The blood thundered in his ears, and he blindly groped for the chair behind him, sitting down heavily.

Even Rafael—even Rafael looked down at a pad of paper before him, as if written there he could discover the answers to every question in life.

"Just what is that supposed to mean, Josh?"

Another long silence, and Josh looked around the room and finally spoke.

"I admit that none of us have been paying a lot of attention to the way you were running things, Connor, but it has come to our attention recently...."

"Has come to your attention? Just how has this come to your attention, Josh? You want to tell me that? How? Oh, don't speak, let me guess—our friend Al or his father, Ivers, whatever his first name is. Asshole, I presume... They come to you, they give you a song and dance, and you believe everything they say? Is that what you are telling me?"

"No, Connor, that is not what I'm telling you. What I am telling you is that there are accusations of you forging shareholders' signatures."

"Ridiculous! An old codger who invested no more than lunch money and now suddenly does not remember what he has done. Buyer's remorse, they call it."

"Then there was the issue with the Minister of Health."

"Who couldn't hold his liquor and hired underage whores to entertain himself, go on."

"Numerous issues with auditors, with the SEC. Irregular share issuances. There seems to be a lot of money and quite a few shares that have gone to—let's call them unknown parties, shall we?"

Connor quit listening and simply tried to stifle the panic, full-blown, regular, old-fashioned panic. This could not be happening. This could simply not be happening to him. His plan—the beautiful plan—would only work out if he were still CEO. Goddamn it, these people had to help him. They had to stand with him as one. Were they not the ones who owed everything to him? Was he not the one who had founded, built, and grown this company until all of them made money? Dammit!

"Josh, I refuse to be crucified via rumors and innuendo spread by the very parties who wish to take over this company. Give me a break, really. Are you falling for this—all of you?"

He looked around the room, and no one would meet his eyes. Not one. Not even Rafael. *Don't think about this—do not think about this right now.* Kayla, dammit—Kayla would stand with him.

"Kayla, do speak up. You have been with me from the very beginning. You know what's happening here. Say something."

"Connor, I really don't know what to say. There's been so much that has happened, and I don't understand—I just don't understand what these people are talking about."

No help there.

"I am telling you," he said slowly, his voice hard and clear, "I am telling you all that these charges are made up. Made up by Al, Dante, and their father. At no point in my running this company have I ever—I repeat, ever—done anything to harm it."

The silence stretched. Still, no one would meet his eyes, but that was OK. Now someone would have to speak up and say *I do not believe you,* and no one would dare. They just would not. They just...

"I wish I could believe you, Connor," Josh finally said. "I really do—if it were not for one tiny little fact."

Connor did not even ask. He looked down at Josh and spread his hands.

"When we signed the offer on the building, do you remember that day, Connor—do you?"

"Vaguely."

"Well, think carefully—because that was the day you tried to screw all of us."

"What are you talking about? No, of course not."

"Really?"

"On my life, Josh—as I am standing here before you—no, I did not try to screw you."

Rafael could only look down at his hands, and there in his fingers was an old ballpoint pen, so mangled and bent by the abuse it was taking it would not last another two minutes. *The Lighthouse*, Connor thought and wondered why he recognized the damn thing at a moment like this. It was one of the pens they were always stealing at The Lighthouse, promising to use it when they signed their one big deal.

"What?"

"Mirko Jankowich," Josh said, and his voice had lost all color. "Name ring a bell?"

A great big bell began tolling in his head. This was the moment—the one moment when he realized he had lost. It went on and on.

"Mirko…?"

"The loan shark, Connor. The man you borrowed money from, and you hid an equity position for him right in the sale documents of the building—without telling any of us about it. You built a clause into the purchase contract that gave him an equity position and a lot of shares, without telling us, discussing it with us, or even explaining it. That's what I am talking about."

"No."

He knew he had lost. Game over, cut your losses, run—but he just could not. He refused to do it.

"No, no. I was not trying to screw any of you. We needed this money to make the building deal happen, and I made the money happen. That's all. I made it happen. Jesus—I am not the bad guy here. I make stuff happen."

"Not the bad guy, Connor, no. But you are not the king and ruler either. You have a board of directors to make sure decisions do not get made by one man and one man alone."

"Thanks for the lesson, Josh."

"You're asking us for help now, when all along you ran this company as if it were your own personal property, as if you never had to answer to anyone before. How often have we all heard you say it—'my company?'"

"I founded this company," he said, and he hated the fact that he sounded like a loser. A whiner—the kind of person he hated the most.

"I founded this company, Josh. So yes, I made a lot of the decisions, and tell me—where were you?"

He looked around and stood to make himself rise above them. "All of you, you have your own little businesses, your own little concerns you run day by day, and you were quite happy to check in with me now and then and to make me run this thing and make money for you. You are busy. You don't need another thing to worry about. So all along, you've been quite happy to let me do it. And I did—every single goddamn day, I worked for this company, solving problems, making things happen—so don't you dare stand in here right now telling me, 'That's not the way we wanted it.'"

He stopped and let the silence drape over them all. Shit, he wanted it to swallow them and make them disappear for good. That's what he really wanted, but he still needed them—for now.

"Look," he finally said, "I will admit that I cut a few corners, just to make things happen. It's just what happens. Have you seen the list of regulations lately? Enough to make you sick. So I cut a few corners, yes, but I always did it with this group right here in mind." He moved his hand in a circle to include all of them. "I did it to make money for all of us, to make us successful as a business and as a group. That's why. Not for my own personal gain or my own personal glorification. If I wanted to do that, I would not have started a public company, people!"

Still, nobody looked up to meet his eyes or put up any more arguments against him. Good. There were not any. *Procedural errors—my ass.* Add Josh to the list of people who would soon be looking for a new project.

"Tell me what you want as a board," he finally said, not even bothering to hide the sarcasm. "Do you want a criminal running this company? Somebody like Al or one of his brothers? Because that is what you are going to get unless we all stand together now."

Rafael finally looked up from the wreck of a pen in his hands.

"It's not that, Connor," he said softly. "We all want this company to be successful, to earn money…"

"Hear, hear."

"But you have to admit that there are some things you are good at, like raising money."

"I'll say, Rafael—look at our shareholder list."

"And then there are some that are—maybe not quite in your wheelhouse."

"I never argued that point. Yes, I am going to need a decent COO and soon, too. I am going to need a financial officer who knows what he is doing. But for crying out loud, people, don't hand everything we've worked so hard for to a bunch of thugs. What did they do—make you an offer you can't refuse?"

"That's neither here nor there, Connor," Josh said, not willing to give up so easily. "Fact remains. You abused your power and our trust, faking signatures, committing us to a few things we may not want, all without as much as telling us, never mind asking. I for one am worried if any of this could come back to me. What happens if the SEC starts looking into all of this?"

That particular argument woke Simon too, who had said nothing right up to that point.

"What do you mean, come back to us, Josh? Are you serious? I have a reputation to protect. For God's sake—Graff Security—and then suddenly, I'm involved in something illegal? You can't be serious."

"Nothing illegal is happening here, Simon." Connor forked his hands through his hair, aware that he was losing them again. "Don't you see—this is all made-up stuff. Made up by the very people who want to take over this company. I have not done anything wrong."

"Except forge a few signatures."

"You admitted yourself you were cutting corners."

"Just how far were they cut, Connor?"

"And there's still money missing, or so they say."

"Shares issued to people who should not have any."

Everybody talked at once all of a sudden, and Kayla looked between the men, dazed and confused, as if she were at a tennis game, trying to follow where the ball had gone just now. Rafael, his former best friend turned traitor, looked down at his phone, following a message, frowning deeply.

Connor made a living talking to people, convincing them, making them give him money for the next big project. It was what his father had done before him, and if ever, god forbid, he had any children, it was most likely what they were going to do years from now. He had never been able to explain how it worked or put a blueprint of the process together—he just knew it worked.

It worked—and it worked well.

But he did not know how, and he did not know if one day, just out of the blue, it would fail him. It was the kind of stuff that made him wake up at night and worry—and drink to make it go away again.

Don't let this be the time, he prayed silently, looking around the room, at the people around him who held the key to his future right now. *Don't let this be the time when it fails me.*

He thought of his father and his drama and theatrics when he preached, the way he connected with his 'parishioners,' the way he took their money and called them suckers behind their backs. He had always criticized his father as being a hypocrite, condemned him as a liar, a cheat, and a fake, and here he stood.... Here he stood doing the same goddamn thing.

Don't let it fail me now.

"This company," he stubbornly insisted now. "This company has everything it needs to become truly big and successful and marvelous— the biggest thing ever. We are right on the brink, people, right on the brink of becoming the next big thing. That company they are going to be talking about 50 years from now. 'Yeah, I heard about PerCan. I wish I had invested then because everybody who did is now a millionaire.' It is right there in our hands."

He stretched out his hands as if he were holding a ball in front of them, just the way he had seen his father do. *Good Reverend Marty, you will never know.*

"Let us not stop now, people, just before we become the great company we were meant to be. Let us just stick together and defend our company from those who would take it away from us. Please—do not make a mistake now."

Rafael still stared at his phone. Something about the message he had just received bothered him to the point where he almost could not sit still, but Connor could not worry about it now. Connor had Simon and Josh to convince. They were the ones who held a huge portion of founder's shares. If they voted with him, he was good to go. He had Kayla and Rafael, of that he was certain—but he needed both Simon and Josh to stand against a vote by Al's family. Especially if they had been busy buying up shares from disgruntled shareholders.

Simon wobbled first. The next big thing, of course, Connor had had him at the next big thing.

"I have nothing against you, Connor. I hold you in the highest regard, and I know you just want this company to grow. All I am try-ing to do here is keep my name and my reputation clean so my own company does not suffer—and with everything that's been going on…"

"All just rumor, innuendo, and false accusations, Simon, I assure you. Nothing will ever touch you or Graff Security. I would not be able to rest if I did not know that for sure."

"Well—maybe then it is just…"

Suddenly, both Simon's and Josh's phones rang with a tiny but distinctive little sound. Messages received. Kayla's phone made itself known just a second later. Simon stopped mid-sentence, just because it was the kind of coincidence that might happen—but the odds were just so astronomical.

They all looked down, and Connor felt his own phone vibrate in his pocket. As if propelled by a force he could not explain, he pulled it out.

"What the hell is this?" Josh already asked, staring him down. "These shares for that Mirko—that loan shark? Something else? What else is going on here?"

"It was part of the finance arrangement, Josh. I told you—we needed the money to make this building of ours happen."

"But that's not everything, now is it," Simon said. "There's a directors' resolution attached here, okaying all of this, but strangely enough, I've never seen it."

"Apparently, you signed it, though," Josh piped up. "And so did I—and, oh, look, there is Rafael's signature." He turned on Rafa now. "Did you know anything about this? Are you working with him?"

"Come on, guys—working with him? Of course we are all working together. It is our…"

"That is not what I am asking, Rafael. Did you or did you not know anything about this, and did you sign this resolution? How much simpler do I have to make the question for you to understand?"

"Well…"

"Well what, Rafael? Yes or no."

"I really don't think…"

"Yes or no, Rafael—it is as easy as that."

"Save it," Connor said and waved his hand, sitting hard in his chair again. "Rafa did not know anything about it. It's like I told you. I needed the money to make the building purchase happen, and I cut a few corners. That's all."

"So you fake our signatures on a director's resolution. That's not a cut corner, Connor. That's fraud. Plain and simple."

Josh stood now, pointing his phone at Connor as if he could make the offending directors' resolution disappear from the screen that way. Connor felt tired all of a sudden. So overwhelmingly tired and exhausted, as if he had been running for weeks and finally stopped. And in a way, he had.

Was there still any way to make them get on side with him, to ask them to vote with him against Ivers's takeover? Maybe—but he needed a miracle to do it, and right now, he was fresh out of miracles. Oh, for the good old days, when his father used some genius audiovisual trickery to make miracles happen, right in his church… And he figured at this point he did not have to wonder about what had happened to Tessa anymore either.

There was only one way Ivers could have gotten the information he had just sent to all of them—only one single way—and that was if he gave Tessa enough money to betray him after years of working together.

Wonder how much it was worth to her, he thought and silently started to gather his papers and his tablet computer, shoving them into his little black bag, looking down at his hands as he did. Let them see the shaking in his hands, he thought, let them see that he was unsteady on his feet. Perhaps they would understand that he had worked himself into the ground for this—for them.

"Josh, I really don't think you ought to be bandying about words like 'fraud' when all we are talking about are a few procedural errors."

Rafael tried—he had to give him that. Too little, too late, but at least he tried.

"Procedural errors? Really? Putting my signature on something I've never seen? How far would he take this, Rafael? Can you tell me that? How far? Because I'd sure like to know what I am in for here."

"Can you honestly tell me you would not have signed this? No way, not under any circumstances? If it came down to 'lose out on the building' or 'sign a share issuance for a loan shark?'"

"I would have wanted details. I would have wanted to know. Christ, Rafa—maybe I would have or maybe not, but I sure would like to be the one to make that decision, don't you think? I mean, he is running this as if he were some goddam emperor."

Josh's voice trailed off behind him because Connor had at that point finished putting his paperwork, his tablet, and all of his pens away neatly. With a flare of drama, he took a couple of pills out of his suit jacket—plain aspirin, he thought, at least he hoped so—swallowed them down, and left the room with unsteady, sloppy strides. Let them see what they had done to him. Let them come back and apologize and beg him to come back and run the company. Beg him.

Connor walked down the street of his office with giant, ground-covering strides, not looking behind him, not caring if anyone followed him.

By the time he reached the corner, he felt the spring in his step again. "Learn this lesson well, assholes," he muttered and hailed a cab for himself. "Without me, you are fucked."

Sitting in the cab, he started grinning for no reason and even ignored the cab driver and the strange look he got in the rearview mirror.

Oh, he wanted to be there, when they talked about making him resign—making him, what a joke—and then realized that not a one of them had the cojones to run this business, never even mind the brains to do it.

Connor tapped the driver on the shoulder.

"Hey, I've changed my mind, buddy—let's head on out to the harbor district. The Lighthouse bar and café."

He could see the question on the man's face—at this time of the day?—and he almost answered it—yes, at this time of the day—but in the end, he did not bother.

Originally, he had planned to go home—Kayla's high-priced, over-decorated home, since he had given up his small little bachelor pad downtown—but suddenly, he did not feel like staring at her artwork and her fancy antiques and overpriced, designer light fixtures. He just felt like getting old-fashioned, rip-roaring drunk, forgetting anything had happened back there at his office, and starting over again tomorrow.

Kayla would go look for him at home. She would have endless questions and want explanations, which he did not feel like giving. Screw them—screw them all and wait for them to come to him. That was his strategy, he finally decided. They would never learn their lesson if he did not make them.

FIFTY-ONE

His second drink already neared the bottom of the glass when Connor looked up and saw him—just sitting there beside him, stirring sugar into a cup of coffee, looking as harmless as the bar goods salesman who had come and gone a few moments ago.

"Now you show up," Connor grumbled, downing the rest of his drink. "Now, after everything's gone down the crapper. Your sense of timing stinks."

"It's a talent. And if things went down the crapper, it sure wasn't my fault."

"Uh-huh." Connor looked around, annoyed that his bartender just decided to do something else, go elsewhere, at the precise moment he needed him.

"Maybe you want to take it easy for a bit." His neighbor pushed the coffee cup over to him. "Might need that, here."

"What are you, my mother now?"

"Naw. Your mother is too religious for my taste. Couldn't handle that much God-fearing hypocrisy all day, every day."

"You know a lot about me."

Another shrug. "Helps if you're going to do business."

"Oh, we're going to do business now, are we?" Connor turned around on his barstool to fully face Roberto, who had not bothered with a stool and casually leaned against the rail. "You've got some nerve, Roberto Ivers. You put a—an operation into my building, pretend we may do business together, and then disappear for a couple of weeks."

"You're the one who went on vacation, Connor."

"And not a word from you. I can't get a hold of you no matter how I try—and I have to tell you, it bothers the shit out of me. So from here on in, we are going to have to find some way to communicate on a daily basis. Some way that does not involve me wandering around town waiting for you to be ready to find me, you understand?"

Roberto shrugged. "Guess old habits die hard, you know."

"Old habits, Roberto? What are those, prison habits? Don't be offended now, but business runs a little different out here. Out here, we communicate openly."

He could not be sure, but he thought he saw just the slightest frisson of annoyance, of irritation, on Roberto's face, and he liked it. That was how he could get to the man; that was his key to Roberto.

"That's in my wheelhouse," he said gently. "Business—the way it runs, the way it speaks, smells, operates, and talks... You do your thing. The growing, the distribution—I take care of the business end of things."

Roberto nodded.

"That easy, huh?"

"That easy. I know. It looks like magic from where you are sitting, but once you get used to it?" He shrugged. "I guess I've been doing it for a very long time, you know. So—on to the part of communication."

"Communication?"

"Yes, Roberto—pay attention here. As in calling me on a daily basis, as in being in touch constantly, exchanging important information, making sure you and I are on the same page and know what is going on in our circle of influence."

"Circle of influence." Roberto nodded. "Got it. Tell me, wouldn't that alert the DEA to the fact that something is going on? I mean you, the medical marijuana guy, talking to an ex-con on a daily basis? That might raise a few red flags, don't you think?"

"Right, you are quite right." Connor frowned and nodded, wishing for a moment he hadn't already downed three drinks and were a bit sharper. "Right—some type of encrypted communication. Don't you know something about that kind of thing?"

"You mean—because I am a convict."

"Ex-convict," Connor said with a dismissive gesture. "No labels now—we don't need them. We are two business partners who are building something together. We are equals, so our history does not really matter."

Roberto thoughtfully stirred his coffee again and nodded, watching the liquid swirl around in his cup for a moment.

"You mean the way you and Rafael were partners—equal partners."

"Rafa—yes. We've done many a deal together, successfully. We did well too. We had different skill sets that came together well. Except now—never mind. Does not really matter now, does it?"

"I guess not."

Roberto stopped stirring and put his spoon down gently, almost lovingly, to avoid the harsh clatter of cutlery against china. He folded his hands and put his index fingers against his lips.

"Connor, tell me—you don't mind if I call you Connor, do you?"

"No, of course not—we're all friends here, are we not?"

Roberto nodded. "Connor, you sit there, on your best way to get absolutely shit-faced at 11 o'clock in the morning."

"It's been a tough morning, Roberto, as no doubt you would know."

"I am well aware of it—still." He sighed deeply and shook his head again. "So you sit there, giving me a pretentious, snobby lecture about how business is run, and how I—a mere little ex-con—would know nothing about this."

"Hey, hey, Rob, that's not what I was trying to say. Listen, I know I come off a little—well—bigmouthed sometimes, but that is so not…."

"Don't call me Rob—I hate it when people call me Rob, Connor. Now, you sit there, drunk, telling me how business ought to be run, telling me—me, your new partner, mind you—how well you and your previous partner did together, the one you are planning to screw royally."

"Hey, Roberto—sorry about the Rob—but really, I am not trying to screw Rafael. You've got it all wrong."

"Oh, good that I got it wrong. You see, I thought when you told me you and Rafael worked really successfully together, worked out really super well—and oh, by the way, this new deal here is just between you and me. Nobody else will have any part in it, do I have it right? I am just asking because I am a dumb shit ex-con, you see. I want to make sure I got it right."

"Roberto, like I said, that is not what I meant. I am sorry if you misunderstood. Rafael, Rafael really does not want to be part of this—this deal you and I are working on."

Roberto nodded again, sagely, and stared for a long moment down at his hands on the polished bar before him. Too long. Far too long. Connor fought the panic inside him. He just should not have tried to do anything today except go home, go to bed, and let it all be until tomorrow. He still could. He still could just say, "Let's leave it be and pick it all up again tomorrow."

"Look, you're right—I am upset and had a few drinks, so why don't we pick this up again tomorrow or the day after when we are a little sharper?"

"You know, that sounds like the most brilliant idea you've had in the last 24 hours, Connor Beauregard."

"Great." He thumbed through the entries on his phone, although he knew damn well there was nothing scheduled for the next day. "Let me see. I am pretty much available all afternoon—you want to meet right here again? Maybe late afternoon, chat a little, make some plans, kick around a few ideas. Does that work for you?"

Roberto sat almost motionless, his eyes unblinking on Connor's. Connor had to look away from the uncomfortable stare and checked his phone again. Dumb shit—did he think his stare was going to impress Connor? Not really…

"You really think I am still doing this—with you?"

The question, when it came, was so soft Connor almost did not hear, and the alarm bells started tolling in his head again.

"Well of course, Roberto—why wouldn't you? It's a fabulous proposition, and with my company and your talents…"

"Because I really don't need you, that's why."

"Don't need… Well…" Connor shrugged. "I guess you can stay a small-time dealer for the rest of your life if it makes you feel more comfortable. I'm just saying—if you are ready for the big time, if you really want to make this thing happen, then you and I working together is the only way."

"The only way—really?"

He still had not moved as much as a muscle, and Connor shifted uncomfortably in his bar stool. Was that what they taught you in prison? Stay perfectly still to unnerve your opponent? Not happening, and anyway—they were not opponents, right?

"Come on, Roberto—you can see the potential here. The possibilities. We can take this thing…"

"I can see you sitting there drinking, and I can see your mouth move, although you're not really saying anything of real value, so let me ask you again. After everything that happened, you still think I want to do this with you?"

"Everything what happened? What are you talking about?"

"You tried to screw your business partners, did you not?"

"No—I did not. I have no idea what this is all about, Roberto, but if it is poisoning our business relationship, you better get it out so I can tell you what is really going on."

Roberto waved his hand again.

"Talking, talking, talking, Connor—do you ever run out of steam at all, or do you just keep going until you pass out? Trust is the most important component in any business deal, would you not say?"

"Of course it is, and I trust you 100 percent."

"Maybe you should not. That ever occur to you? And Rafael—Rafael definitely should not trust you at all."

"Rafa—what the hell does he have to do with anything here?"

"He's your business partner, the one you started this with, the one you call brother when you are sitting here and drinking."

"Well yes, but…."

"And he trusts you. And yet you would drop him and your—what did you call it—years of successful cooperation and just do a backroom deal with me. And you would forge your board of directors' signatures on resolutions and just generally go ahead and do whatever pleases you or comes into your head at any particular moment in the name of getting it done. Would you say that is correct, Connor?"

This could not be happening, not today, not right now—it could not be allowed to happen. Connor felt as if the entire world suddenly became fuzzy and unreal, as if he were looking at it through the empty beer glass in his hand

No, you have to convince him, his mind screamed. *He's got to go along with it. You have to convince him. That's where all the money is coming from, dammit, convince the dumbass. He has to—no alternative.*

"No offense, Roberto," he forced out between stiff lips, "but you have it all wrong. Rafael—Rafael does not want to be in on our little deal here. He can't. It goes against his nature. He is too…"

"Honest?"

"Honest, naïve, whatever. He would hate knowing about it—that's all. So I thought it would be better if it were just you and me. The fewer people who know about it, the better."

Roberto chuckled. His coffee long finished, he leaned back and toyed with the spoon for a moment.

"You know, you sound good, Connor. You sound really good. When you talk, I bet it's easy for people to say, 'Yeah, all right, whatever he says.' But, you see, there's a difference between what you say and what you do. I hear you say that I should trust you, which is the first clue to me that I shouldn't. Sorry—no can do."

"You need me," Connor said, now fighting the righteous anger that made him want to jump up and strike the man beside him. "You need me—because your little operation sits in my building, don't forget that. You think for a moment I'm going to let you just carry on as if nothing had happened?"

"No, probably not. But it's not your building, Connor. From what I hear, you may not even be in charge of the company for very much longer."

"Your family," Connor scoffed, and this time he did signal the bartender for another drink. "Of course—your family. They are trying to take over. What makes you think you can trust them any more than you can trust me? They sent you to jail once from what I hear—you think they are just going to sit back and say whatever you want, Roberto? Get real."

"No, they are not. But you just let that be my problem, OK? You went down to the building and looked. Tell me—is there any trace of a grow op left?"

"No, but…"

"Good, Connor, very good. Then why don't you forget any of this ever happened and move on with your life, in whatever form pleases you? Because I, for one, do not want to do business with you—ever." He rose from his bar stool, put some money on the bar, and nodded to the bartender. "I wish I could say it has been a pleasure, Connor, but hey, I don't think we will meet again, so take care."

He disappeared as quickly as he had come in, and Connor sat there, staring dumbfounded at the door that had closed behind him.

What the fuck? This had to be the worst day in his life. This had to be definitely the worst day in his entire life—ever. What the fuck? *Think, quick,* his mind ordered. *Think—there has got to be a way out of this. There has got to be a way to save this entire mess. Damn Roberto— damn that entire Ivers family.*

OK, new plan, new plan. He pushed the beer away and reached for his wallet. Dammit, but he needed a clear head right now. This was not the first time he had to change horses in mid-battle. It had been done before. This was what he did after all—innovate, come up with creative solutions. *Think, Beauregard, think.*

He was just about to put his jacket back on when someone took the bar stool beside him again. Thinking Roberto had changed his mind and come back, he turned around with a grin that froze on his face.

"Rafa—it's you...."

"Well, don't look so crestfallen. Who'd you expect anyway?"

"Nothing—never mind. What's going on?"

"What's going on? You ask me what's going on, seriously? What the heck was that back at the office? You just up and walked out on everybody, after you called us in on an emergency? What the hell?"

"You expect me to sit there and have Josh rake me over the coals for nothing more than a couple of minor procedural shortcuts, really? This company is under attack, Rafael, and this is the time where we all need to stand together and defend it, not point fingers at one another over some minor shit. I thought it best to leave before I lost my temper entirely."

"Probably a good idea, but you have to admit, faking signatures..."

"I did not fake anything, Rafael. I took a few shortcuts to make stuff happen. I knew that given enough time to talk and talk and think and debate, they all would vote with me because it was the only way. So I took a shortcut. We did not have the time to sit around navel-gazing forever. That's not how business works."

"I understand that, Connor, but you have to understand Josh and Simon and where they are coming from. They feel that you made decisions that did not include them, for a company they own a piece of and have put their money in."

"I get it," Connor said meekly and sat back down.

Perhaps this was fixable after all. Rafa, now sitting there, by his side again. Perhaps, if done well, he could stand there, confess, take a few lumps, and do some penance, and all would be OK again. Step one—get Rafa on his side. He did appear to have everyone's ear, and the fools trusted him.

"I get it, OK? I got caught up in the deal and in the excitement. All I wanted was to make it happen, and yes, I took some—inadvisable—shortcuts. I will admit that, although I won't say I am sorry. What I did had to be done."

"Connor."

"Yes, OK, it was not entirely correct, that what you want to hear? Jesus. We need to defend our company, not quarrel amongst ourselves. Brilliant strategy on Ivers's part anyway—releasing all of this information to my board of directors, just as he is about to take over the company, brilliant. Did he tell them that his jailbird son wanted to put a grow op into my building, until I discovered it and made them remove it? Did he tell them that? Because I am sure if he had, they would not be crucifying me over minor stuff. They are playing right into his hands."

"This is not entirely about Al and his family, and you know it."

"Yes, I know it. Still. They put this entire scenario in motion for one reason and one reason only—to make me resign. That was their whole plan from the very beginning, and that is why I need all of you to stand with me right now. We need to make sure they don't succeed. Tell me, Rafael—can I at least count on you?"

"You even need to ask that question?"

"I need to hear the answer, that's all, so what's it going to be?"

"This is offensive."

"No doubt. So what is it going to be, Rafael—are you with me? Are you going to help me bring the board around and convince them to vote with me against Ivers?"

"Yes, Connor—dammit. As much as you can be annoying, I don't really think you have trickery or betrayal in you. I am sorry I brought these people on board, believe me. It seemed like a good idea at the time."

"No apology needed—and I thank you for standing with me."

"You think there is going to be a vote—really?"

Connor shrugged, and this time it was he who signaled the bartender for a couple of strong espressos. Now he needed a clear head, like never before. He had managed to bring Rafa back in. One down—now for the rest of his board.

He had done this before. He had the magic; he knew it. All he needed was a chance. Rafael would give him that chance.

"I can't tell you, my friend. It might. I mean—Ivers came to see me last night, trying to get me to resign. This morning, a whole bunch of nonsense information is being disseminated to my board of directors, all designed to discredit me. You think he is heading for a vote? It's a good guess. He bought up a pile of shares from weaker shareholders."

"Who—do you know?"

Connor waved dismissively. "Couple of small-time guys without the guts to stick it out when things don't go as planned. It's annoying, nothing more. But if he manages to force a shareholder vote, then I could be in trouble, because he will trot out every single minor mistake that ever happened and make it look bad. You can believe that. It's his game."

Rafael accepted the coffee graciously and sighed deeply.

"Man, what a mess. I hope you know that I am going to do everything I can to straighten it out again, Connor. I am so sorry for every time you warned me about Al and I told you he was a decent character."

"You assumed because you don't expect trickery the same way I do—it's fine. Just make sure you are on my side now."

"Of course. What I can't figure out is what the heck was that grow op all about? I mean—you told them to straighten it out, did you not?"

"Yes, of course, just like you told me to. Went straight to Al and his father and told them to get that thing out of there. I did not want to have anything to do with it. Next day, it was gone—good call."

"But I still don't get it. I mean, it makes sense to think it was Al and Dante's brother who put it there, but you said they didn't look like they knew about it? So what the hell?"

"We will never know," Connor said, desperate to move the conversation on. The one thing he could not let Rafael know now was that he knew Roberto, that he had tried to make a deal with him, that he had indeed done each and every single thing Al and Ivers tried to accuse him of.

No, that one had to stay a secret—forever. Fortunately, he was a lot better at expecting, fielding, and dealing with trickery and betrayal than Rafael here was.

"This is our project, Rafael. We were sitting right over there at this bar, having a few when we thought of it, when we put together a plan and then followed through. You and I—at the very beginning, now when we are under fire, and right to the very end, whatever that is going to look like."

"Don't even say that, Connor."

"I don't let anyone take what's mine. You know that better than anyone. This is our company, Rafael—ours. We dreamed it, worked for it, sweated over it. Now we are going to stand together and save it—I promise you that as I am standing here, by the very life inside me."

He rose and stood before Rafael for just one second, then slowly and deliberately offered his friend his right hand.

"This is my promise to you, Rafael."

Rafael swallowed hard and took Connor's hand, shaking it.

"Right back at you."

"Good." Connor finally exhaled, as much for personal relief as for dramatic effect. "That is a load off my mind, Rafael. Now I need to make sure the board is on our side as well. First, though—there's one other thing."

"Oh?"

"Tessa. There's only one person who could have given all of this information to my enemies."

"And that is Tessa?"

"Think about it, Rafa—who had access to all of the documentation, to the correspondence, to my personal emails and phone calls, for God's sakes? It could only have been her."

Or Kayla, he thought. No, this had the hallmark of someone very smart—smart and desperate.

"I wonder how much they paid her," he said bitterly. "How much is betrayal worth these days, you think?"

"I don't know. Guess it depends on how desperate she was and how much you owed her."

"A—a bit," Connor said, barely holding back the 'a lot.'

"It's been crazy, Rafa—you know it, I know it. Come on—she's worked with us for a lot of years. She should have known what it's like in a startup. There was no reason—none whatsoever—to go out and stab me into the back like this, and I just...."

He stopped and lowered his head for a moment. Just what?

"Just what?" Rafael asked, reading his mind. "What purpose do you think this will serve, Connor? You want to confront her, yell at her, scream at her, offer her more money—what?"

"I don't know. For starters, I just want to know why."

"You just said it—money."

"I gave her shares. A lot of shares."

"Shares she could not trade. Come on. You and I know what it's like working for paper—that girl has rent to pay and a tremendous Starbucks latte habit, from what I've seen. So she needed cash."

"And that's a good enough reason to fabricate classified documentation and then disseminate it?"

"They got her at a weak moment. You running after her and confronting her will serve no good purpose, Connor."

"I just want to know what else..."

"I say leave it. So what if she knows everything and gives everything to them? You've cut a few corners—big deal. If that is everything..."

"I just swore to you that it was."

"So let it go. Learn the lesson, let it go, move on. Just move on. I can't see anything good coming from this, OK?"

"What about my satisfaction—what about this bothering the shit out of me? This is personal, Rafael. This is the girl I trusted—with everything. She had the most sensitive information about me at her fingertips. What if she uses that, too?"

"If this is just about money, then I don't think she will. Now if you have pissed her off royally in some personal quarrel I don't know about..."

"Rafa, come on."

"Just saying. Don't get sidetracked making it personal right now. Don't worry about her for the moment. Make saving our company your first priority. When Al and his father are gone, then you and I can personally deal with Tessa—in the appropriate manner."

"Which includes?"

"Which does not include running to her house right now ranting, raving, and screaming, OK? We will figure it out. Right now..."

"You're right." Connor took another deep breath and let it out, slapping Rafael's shoulders. "You're totally right. Company first." He rose, silently vowing that no matter what happened, one day, he would get back at Tessa—one day.

He had to remember to exhale, so intense became the feeling of revenge. *Relax, Beauregard, relax. Your day is coming, and don't make any kind of mistake about it. Watch out, Tessa.*

Oh yeah, this time he did allow himself a little smile. Oh yeah— revenge would be so, so sweet and all his. *Watch out little, techno witch, Beauregard is gunning for you.*

He realized Rafael had said something and forced his mind back to the present.

"Pardon? Sorry—mind on something else. It's been crazy."

"You're allowed. I was asking if you wanted to call the board back to your office. You and I will stand together and speak, and together, we should be able to convince them. Unless you're wanting to stay here, while I do this by myself."

"You would do this for me? Face the board and argue on my behalf, when they've gone and told you what a loser I am?"

"Well, they are wrong."

"I know that, and you know that."

"And so will Kayla when she has a moment to get her head out of the clouds, and so will Josh and Simon. It's a matter of presenting the facts without everyone getting all upset by rhetoric and flying innuendo."

"Thanks."

Connor looked down at his hands, chastened for a moment. He did remember that moment of insanity just a few short hours ago, when he had told Roberto that Rafael was simply too naïve to run in big business.

"I'm a big boy, Rafa. I can handle it. I think I need to face them myself. Show them I have done nothing wrong and nothing to hide. But if you would speak for me, that would help a lot and mean the world to me."

"You don't even need to ask."

Rafael nodded at Connor's empty coffee cup. "Order yourself another one. You're going to need to be sharp and together for this. I'm going to call all of them back to your office, OK with you?"

Connor nodded and for once did as told and ordered himself a coffee. This was how he was getting his company back. A little humbling, a little humility would do no harm. All was good.

And then there would still be time to get back at all those who would have betrayed him and taken this great company away from him. Oh yes—that would be sweet.

He could humble himself before the board just in order to enjoy his revenge. He could tell them that 'mistakes had been made' and 'corners had been cut' and—oh, yes, even better—he had nursed a snake in their midst. Tessa. The very snake who had gone and sold information to the enemy, perhaps from the very beginning, and why not? If he could make them believe that, he could make them believe anything.

Nice! He would tell them he had suspected her from the very beginning of collaborating with Ivers and his sons. Had he not caught her several times turning her monitor away from him when he walked into the room, blanking her computer screen? Of course he had.

When Al had walked in for the first time, who had been the person to meet him at their offices? Of course. Who had brought in the check in a giant envelope? Who had always been in charge of receiving and delivering messages? Of course.

Connor smiled again.

Oh, she would pay all right. She would never know what hit her. And once he had his company back, Ivers and his miserable, lying pack would not want to have anything to do with her any longer either.

Too bad, so sad, Tessa—should not have gone to bed with dogs.

He enjoyed that coffee—strong, black, and sweet, just the way he liked it. It hit his brain and his heart just about the same time, making him alert, sharp, and dangerous. He was ready—ready for anything—when Rafael turned around and clapped a hand on his shoulder.

"One hour, in your office. Don't look so downcast. I think everybody is on side with us—just depends on the proper spin."

"And I have spin," Connor nodded, "do I ever."

"Connor!"

He chuckled. "Relax, Rafa, I am not going to do anything dramatic and stupid, OK? I just have a good feeling about this, now that you and I are on the same page again, now that we are good again—I know we are going to get the magic back. It's been lost far too long because of others, like Catherine and Tessa and David."

"David?"

"David. Bloody accountant holding up everything because of three pieces of paper he can't find. You know—it wouldn't surprise me at all if he were with Ivers as well."

"Doubt it. He's the most straightforward, honest guy I've ever met—a little too detailed for my taste...."

"A little," Connor scoffed. "A little—takes him a week and a half to dot all of his fucking i's, and then he goes back and checks them. Only to cause trouble for me. He is in on this all right."

"One enemy at a time, Connor, OK? Maybe that second espresso was a little strong. Now let's move."

Rafael paid the bill, Connor noticed with a certain amount of satisfaction, and led them both out to his car.

FIFTY-TWO

Focus—focus, focus, focus. He closed his eyes for a moment and concentrated. This was what he did—use his words to spin a story and convince people. *Showtime, Beauregard, showtime for the biggest event in your career. Connor Beauregard, starring in 'saving my company.'*

"At all times while we were building this company—every single minute of it—there was only one thing on my mind, Rafael, and that was making Perfect Cannabis the best new startup there ever was. Never once was it about the money or about enriching myself. I wanted to build this company for all of us and for the patients, who would ultimately be the real winners here."

"I know that." Rafa gave him a sideways glance. "No need to perform for me. But you do have a somewhat—unorthodox style at times, you have to admit that."

"I get things done, Rafa, that's all. I am not a bad guy. I am just good at getting things done. And after the energy deal—when all that went south, I have to tell you, for a little while there, I thought it was me. I thought I couldn't get it done. And then PerCan happened, and the money came in, and the people were happy, and I knew I had built it. I knew I still had it."

"Nobody says you don't. If you would now and then just listen for a minute."

"I do, Rafael, I really do. But I am a builder of dreams and a maker of chances. I simply can't waste my time on anything but the big magic. The story that holds it all together."

"Fine then. So once this is all over, and the company is back in smooth waters again, we will hire you a decent COO, and you do what you do best—talk, make the dream a reality...."

"Build empires out of thin air." Connor laughed and opened his eyes again. "Yeah—I guess that is what I am good at, isn't it?"

"The best—you just need a slew of people around you cleaning up and making sure you don't get into too big a mess."

"Mmh—that's what you guys are for."

Connor tried not to remember that he had called Rafa naïve and stupid before—but by then, they had arrived at his office. He could tell by the cars in the lot that everyone had already arrived. They had to be upstairs, in his boardroom, waiting.

Showtime.

He walked in slowly and without saying a word of greeting to anyone, did not even catch Kayla's eyes. Rafael took a seat beside him, but Connor remained standing, put his hands flat on the table before him, and exhaled slowly.

"Without a doubt, people," he said, his voice low and soft, "I have, in the name of getting things done, cut corners and taken shortcuts that were at times—unadvised."

"Hear, hear."

Simon. But Rafael hushed him again, very quickly. Connor refused to rise to the bait and still did not look at anyone, only down at his hands in front of him.

"I hope you know that at no time during my time as CEO of this company have I ever done anything, committed any acts, made any deals designed to enrich myself or my family. What I have done, right or wrong, was all in the name of Perfect Cannabis and to ensure the continued growth, viability, and success of this company."

He paused, and this time, no one felt the need to comment.

"If I became shortsighted at times, then I humbly ask forgiveness for getting caught up in the moment, in the success, and in the unstoppable, powerful drive to make this company the biggest thing the stock market has ever seen."

His hands rose now on either side of him, as if summoning an unknown deity to come to his aid.

"We have in our hands, right here, ladies and gentlemen, everything to make this happen. This is the moment where we change the future of this company, the future of alternative medicine—indeed, the very future of millions of sick and suffering patients. Right here in our hands is the power to make their tomorrows possible, to make their dreams come true, and I intend to do everything, to draw on every last ounce of strength and support I have, to make this happen."

His hands were beside his face now, shaking, and he took a moment, letting the raw power of his voice and his words sink in.

"That is the only thing on my mind when I get up in the morning right up to the very moment my eyes close again some 18 hours later. It is what I breathe, what I eat, what I drink. It is my very essence. Quite simply speaking, people—it is my life."

Now he looked up and met every person's eyes for a moment, each and every one, making sure he had them and making sure they were in his thrall.

"Nothing else."

Another dramatic pause. Rafael sat silently beside him, nodding in agreement. Simon and Josh looked down at their notepads in front of them. Was it a tiny bit of embarrassment in Josh's face—just a bit? Please? Connor forced himself to remain still. He was almost there. They had to come to him.

"We know that, Connor." Kayla. She still did not have a clue what he was trying to do here, but honestly, even she could not screw it up for him now.

"There is nothing else," he repeated softly, letting all the air go out of him so he shrank into himself a little.

"This company is it. And if you are standing up today and telling me that for the good of this company, it is necessary to step down, to let somebody else take the reins and lead this company to the glorious future I know it can have, then…. Well, then, ladies and gentlemen, I will have to accept that, for the good of PerCan."

He exhaled again and sat down, looking at his hands on the table, waiting… Waiting for them to come back.

Rafael sat a little straighter and nodded. "Simon, Josh, and, of course, you too, Kayla. You know who I am—we've been doing business for many years in some cases. Josh, you and I sit on a couple of boards together. We've done more deals than I can count on both my hands."

"Don't need to convince me, Rafael. I know you are a man of your word and of honesty and integrity."

"Thank you, Josh. Then I hope you will all believe me when I tell you, Connor—well—Connor can be a royal pain in the ass sometimes."

That one got a chuckle from Simon at least, and again, Connor forced himself not to smile. You just couldn't buy that kind of endorsement.

"He is. If he wants to get something done, he is worse than my wife's dog going after a bone. He just will not stop until it's done."

His hand struck the top of the table a couple of times, to emphasize his last words.

"He won't. That's what makes him so good at getting things done because Connor has a genetic problem. He can't hear the word no. He will just bash away at it until it gets done. Does that make him a pain in the ass sometimes? You bet it does, people. But you know what else?" Rafael looked around the table now, from one to the other. "It makes him the best damn guy to leave your company with. Because he will not give up, he will not take no for an answer, he will not settle for good enough. He is going to take this company to the very top—and no discussion about it."

"That's all very nice, Rafael," Josh said. "But you have to admit there have been—irregularities. Things that should not have been done, at the very least not have been done without the full support and consent of this board of directors. I'm really not interested if Connor is a pain in your ass or not. I am more concerned about him striking deals and doing things that could turn out to our disadvantage. That's what it really comes down to, wouldn't you agree, Simon?"

"Agree. I mean, you bought a goddamn helicopter."

"I leased the helicopter for him," Kayla piped up softly. "As—a present, as a thank you."

"And I still don't even care about the helicopter either—have it or don't. I don't give a damn as long as the money is here for it. It's the backroom deals and shady connections that worry me. Do you understand?"

"Josh, I hear you," Connor said and stood again. "And I will tell you this. As long as I have been in charge at Perfect Cannabis, there have never—I repeat, never, at any time, been any kind of backroom deals that could harm the company or any of you, that could bring bad press or legal problems to the company, or that would disadvantage you in way shape or manner. I will give you my word on this."

He took a step closer to Josh and offered his hand, silently counting. Josh let him stand there, his hand outstretched, his words in the air between them, for a good 20 seconds. Then he stood slowly, looked Connor straight in the eyes, and shook his hand, slapping his back with the other.

Bingo. Game, set, and match. They were back.

He was back.

Connor finally allowed himself that smile and sat back down, raking his hands through his hair.

"It—means the world to me, Josh, that you would trust me at this time, over the word of those who would discredit me without a shred of evidence. I cannot tell you how humbled I am by your continued confidence and trust in me."

"You damn well know we are going to keep an eye on you from now on."

"Bring it on. Josh, Simon—bring it on. Anything you need. I promise you that I will do anything to restore your faith. I will not let anything happen to this company that might make you look back one day and regret having put your trust in me."

He clapped Rafael on the shoulder and laughed. "And thank you, my friend, for standing with me, when nobody else would."

"For starters," Josh began, clearly uncomfortable with the emotion Connor let swirl around the room, "for starters, we are going to establish a regular communication protocol. You are right in one thing. We—all of us—have sat back long enough and let you take the brunt of things. We need to get more involved, all of us. Simon, Kayla, are you two OK with this, with taking a more active role in the company?"

"Well, sure, yes—if that is what is needed."

"Absolutely," Kayla breathed, looking adoringly into Connor's eyes. "I have just been waiting for the chance to help you build your company—our company."

"We will have regular meetings, and everyone—everyone—will be held accountable for completing the tasks they have been assigned. Kayla, I am afraid your first task will have to be to sort out the PR mess Ivers and his sons have gotten us into."

Connor allowed himself to lean back and relax. It wouldn't last long. For a while, it would be a pain in the ass, sure, and he would have to pull himself together and toe the line—for a bit. When real life intruded again and everyone got busy, that was when he would have the freedom again to run his company the way he knew he wanted to. *Be patient, Beauregard, be patient. Your day is at hand.*

He stood and spread his arms, smiling broadly, openly, so they all could see his joy and enthusiasm.

"I, for one, am deeply grateful today. I am grateful that we have all decided to band together and defend our company. I..." He let his voice trail off for a moment and brought his fingertips to his lips. "I am truly humbled by your trust and by your—unquestioning loyalty. For that alone, I promise you, I will double my efforts."

He stopped because Josh's phone started to ring with the most insistent, annoying sound. He barely suppressed his annoyance when Simon's started, and Kayla's, and Rafael's, and finally his own.

Just like a few hours ago. What did they have—cameras in his office?

Connor started to sweat. Not again, not this time. Not when he finally had them. It could not happen again. *Damn you, Ivers, what do you have this time?* He could not have anything else. Dammit, there was nothing else, was there?

No, there was nothing else. Of course not. Except for—no, there was nothing else. Period, end of statement. There just wasn't.

He straightened again, forced a smile, and looked down on his phone.

"Well, of all the coincidences, folks. Anyway, what I wanted to say—I am sure whoever is trying to interrupt..."

"Channel 6 News—now," Josh read off the display of his phone and looked up at him. "What—what the hell is this, Connor?"

"Nothing, some prankster, I am sure."

"I got the same message," Simon said.

"Me too—odd, that we all..."

Thanks, Kayla, thanks for nothing, most likely.

"Let's just carry on," he said, trying to keep his voice from shaking just a little. "What I meant to say..."

"There is a television in your office, Connor." Josh's voice suddenly had an edge he had never heard before, an edge that allowed no disagreement. "I think I want to see what this prankster is talking about. If it is all bullshit..."

He stood and opened the connecting door to Connor's private office, letting the light from the high windows flood into the conference room.

"Simon?"

"Behind you—I think I want to see this."

Connor trembled. He did not need to be psychic, did not need a degree in any kind of applied psychology to know that this was bad news, really, really bad news. Ivers had been alone in his office. Shit, they should have met elsewhere. Too late—too fucking late... Connor exchanged a glance with Rafael, who appeared dumbfounded at the moment.

"What the heck, Connor?" he asked softly, and Connor shook his head.

"Wish I knew."

"No idea?"

"None."

"Connor, I just stood there and told these people I trusted you with my life. If there is the slightest thing that I need to know before I step into that room and see what is going on, on that news channel, this is the time to tell me about it."

"And I am telling you I have no fucking clue what these people have come up with now."

"These people?" Simon asked, and Connor shook his head.

"Simon, it's obvious, at least to me, that Ivers and his crew are trying to discredit me as a CEO in hopes of not only taking over this company but also buying up large blocks of stock as the stock prices take an insane tumble in the wake of my demise... Who knows what kind of trickery they have manufactured this time?"

He could not help it. His voice shook, and even to himself, he sounded unsure—frightened, even. Dammit, Goddammit...

Josh had reached the television and turned it on, changed channels once, twice, until he hit the Channel Six newscast.

"Weather and a ten-car pileup on the highway," Connor said, allowing a bit of relief. "Looks like we all ran in here for nothing."

He smiled again—and then paled, when the picture of the highway carnage on the screen changed. The newscaster appeared again, and the bold PerCan logo appeared behind him.

Shit.

"In business news today, it appears that the charismatic CEO of this country's rising star, Perfect Cannabis Corporation, had a bit of a hard time waiting for his company to receive an official license from the Ministry of Health to grow and distribute marijuana."

The image of the logo behind the pleasant newscaster disappeared, and Connor thought he might get sick. There, in all his glory, stood he himself, Connor Beauregard, in Roberto's illegal grow op behind the south wall of his own building. Dammit, where did they get the picture? Surveillance cameras? Just as he opened his mouth to say something—anything—in his own defense, it got even worse. It was not a picture. It was full-fledged, high-def video. Connor Beauregard moved amongst the plants, touched the leaves, inspected them, and smiled.

Sure, he'd found the stuff. He had touched it, marveled at how wonderful his own plan had worked—except it wasn't his grow op. It wasn't his business. It was something he simply found.

"I found this installation," he said tonelessly. "Behind the wall there. I had nothing..."

"We have just received information," the newscaster continued, "that while the company was fighting recent allegations of attempted influence on a minister and still waiting for a decision on an official license, the company's CEO, Mr. Connor Beauregard, installed a full-fledged marijuana grow operation in a hidden portion of the building Perfect Cannabis just recently acquired for their main operation."

Kayla gasped, Josh cleared his throat and folded his hands before his face, and Rafael could only stare. He knew—dammit, he knew. Why did he not come to Connor's aid?

"We found this—this thing behind the wall, Josh. I swear to you, it was not like they are making it look like right now. This was put there by one of Ivers's sons, Roberto. The fellow just got out of prison. I swear to you, Josh. I had nothing to do with this."

He knew he sounded frantic. His words and sentences flip-flopped all over the place and one over the other, but right now, he could not even care how he sounded. Dammit, they were making him look like some sort of a criminal. He had not done this. He had nothing to do with it whatsoever. Come on, people. How could he make them see?

"According to our sources," the newscaster continued, "Beauregard quickly realized that he did not have the necessary knowledge and experience in the field of growing marijuana and solicited help from a rather dubious side."

Connor wanted to throw up. How the fuck had they gotten this? A perfect picture, a real family-album shot—he and Roberto Ivers, sitting in his office across from one another, shaking hands. *Damn you, Roberto*, he thought, *damn you. You already knew when I came back from the South Pacific we would never do a deal together. Damn you. You shook my hand, used me for my own purpose—worse, for your father's purpose.*

"You said you never met him," Rafael said beside him, and at the same time, Connor could feel him move away a bit. Ever so slightly putting distance between himself and Connor Beauregard, who consorted with criminals? "You said..."

"I had just got out of prison," Roberto said on the TV screen, giving the interview with the ease and comfort of a pro. "I was kind of surprised when Beauregard approached me to see if I wanted to work for him. I mean, with my history, working for a drug manufacturer is the last thing my parole officer wants to see—but anyway, my family owns a portion of the business, so I went to see him. Except working for the medical marijuana manufacturer was not what Beauregard had in mind for me."

"So you are saying he was looking for an illegal grow."

"I can't make a statement to what he had in mind, really," Roberto said and smiled broadly into the camera. "And in my position, I shouldn't make any statements. Suffice it to say he told me that hiding an illegal grow op in plain sight, right behind a federally licensed medical marijuana facility, was the most brilliant idea of the century."

"Investigations into the allegations continue," the newscaster said. "And according to our contacts at the police office, an illegal grow operation was indeed located in the facility slated to be a medical marijuana production facility. What this might mean for the hundreds of investors into this hot new startup is yet to be determined. What will happen to the industry's charismatic rising star, Mr. Connor Beauregard, is also undetermined. If accusations of criminal activity prove to be correct, Mr. Beauregard may indeed be looking at some serious jail time. He is at the moment a person of interest."

Connor felt the space around him. Everybody had moved away from him, as if the physical distance could keep them from harm. *You fucking morons*, he wanted to scream. *You morons, can't you see? Ivers is trying to set me up.*

"It's a setup," he said hoarsely, but nobody took any note of him because right there on the screen, the good Reverend Matthias Beauregard appeared, clad in regal black, his hands folded before him, a serious and pained expression on his face.

"I knew my son had financial problems," he said solemnly and sadly. "He came to me begging for money, telling me something serious might happen to him if I did not help him out. I just never imagined the devil had claimed his soul to the point where he would stoop to becoming a drug dealer. More than anything I wish..." Vintage Reverend Marty—his voice shook, and his eyes turned heavenward. "More than anything, I wish I could have helped him see the right way."

"Don't you see?" Connor finally exploded. "They are setting me up. Ivers and his goddamned sons—they are setting me up. I never did any of this."

"That was not you right there in that grow op?" Josh asked, and before Connor could answer, Rafael stepped in.

"You told me you found it. You showed it to me."

"You knew about this, Rafael?"

"He told me," Rafael said and moved to stand closer to Josh and Simon. "He told me it was there, showed it to me. All proud he was because everything we had had in mind for growing worked, just the way we had planned."

"Rafael, you were there," Connor screamed. "You were there—you know it was not me who put it there."

"Do I now, Connor? Do I really? I have to tell you right now, I can't tell. You were standing there, saying just those words to me—hiding a grow op behind a medical marijuana facility is bloody brilliant."

"I did not mean it, Rafael—it was all Roberto. You've got to believe me. He put it in there. I had nothing to do with him."

"I see. And that's why you shook hands on it then, right here." Rafael pointed at Connor's desk, now between them. "Right there—after you swore to me you had never met him and would not do business with him for anything in the world. Is that how it works now? You were trying to screw all of us. Including me?"

Connor looked from one to the other. Josh, Rafael, Simon, Kayla—not one sympathetic face among them. Not one who would be convinced to stand with him.

Dammit, Ivers, you have won, he thought. *Dammit, you defeated me in my own house.*

"Turn yourself in, Connor," Josh said softly. "Maybe there is some way you can—I don't know—explain. The financial difficulties, the problems you were having at the time. Maybe..."

Investigations are ongoing. Beauregard is considered a person of interest.

The sentence all of sudden hit him with the force of a crushing blow. Of course. If they had managed to manufacture all of this evidence, bringing forth the rest would be a piece of cake for Ivers and his Goddamned family. And then what? Then what, pray tell? He, Connor Beauregard, would spend years in jail for something he had never even committed.

God-triple-fucking-dammit.

There was no way he would allow it. Fool me once, shame on you. He wasn't going to let them play their game. Not if he could help it. Again, he looked around. No, none of these people would help him right now. He would have asked Kayla, but Kayla already texted away on her phone, wildly, without even looking in his direction. Probably trying to save her reputation, he thought. The gossip queen who had slept with the criminal. Comical almost, he thought. Really, almost comical.

And Rafael.

He did not dare look at Rafael. He knew what he would find. Betrayal of the worst kind. And there was nothing he could even say in his defense. He had tried to make a deal with the devil himself, called his best friend naïve and hapless, and got stabbed in the back in the process.

"Give me a minute," he said tonelessly. "I need to gather myself for a minute—I'll be right back."

He stepped back into his conference room and closed the door behind himself. No way was he letting this happen, not if he could help it. Right at the moment, he could not see a way out, but there had to be one. There was always a way out—but in order to find it, one needed time. Time Connor Beauregard would not have it if they locked him in jail and threw away the keys.

Let's be drug dealers. It's the best business going.

He and Rafael, sitting at The Lighthouse, getting plastered, joking about the drug business.

It wasn't me, he thought. *It wasn't me—goddammit, it was not me.* He struck his board room table and paced the room like a caged animal. *It wasn't me.* The mantra repeated in his head, on and on. Ivers—Ivers and his damned clan had cheated him. Cheated him out of his company, out of what was rightfully his, and now, they would cheerfully see him go to jail.

Nice move, Ivers, he thought. *Really nice move—using Roberto to lure me in, and then using all of it against me. Damn, that was well done.*

Somewhere in a corner of his brain, he could appreciate, even admire the kind of strategy that used his own moves right against him. In another world, he would have admired Ivers Senior, even tried to learn something from him.

Now...

Jail was not a place he wanted to think about. What if he were convicted now? What if, indeed, he had to go to jail?

He did not stand a chance. Who knew what other evidence Ivers would manufacture? He had already shown he was not above using anything and everything. He was the most dangerous kind of man at all, one without scruple or morals, one who would not hesitate to send his own son to jail and then use him again.

Jail was not an option—he could not go to jail. He would not. He needed time now, time to find evidence against Ivers, and a way to use it, but if he ended up going to jail... no, it simply could not be allowed to happen. He had to remain free, to figure out a way to get his company back.

And he would.

By God and everything that was sacred to his damned father and the people out there in his private office, he swore right here to get his company back. He would show them all. One day, when his day came, he would stand out there in the building again and say, "This is my company."

He had imagined it, he had seen it, built it, sweated over it, lost his best friend over it—he was not giving it up. Not while there was one breath left in his body.

Time. He needed time to plan his revenge against the fucking Original Chef and his family. He needed a place to lay low for a while, and he needed money.

Money. Money wasn't even his biggest problem, he realized with a start—because his Swiss shares, his beautiful little package of Swiss shares, were still safe in a deposit box at the airport in Zurich. Not super easy to get to but not out-of-this-world hard either. He would have to make some sacrifices, but he had money. Good thing he had not sold any of them when he was still trying to convince Roberto, the fucking snake.

Now he needed time, and indeed, he needed a place to disappear for a while. Dammit, was he really thinking that? He checked himself, stopped his pacing, and took a breath.

What's it going to be, Beauregard—stay or fight?

Damn, like that was even a choice. Fight, of course. He would fight. He had just promised he would fight to get his company back, and he couldn't do that if he waited desperately in some jail for a second-rate lawyer to get something—anything—on a man like Ivers.

If there even were such a lawyer willing to take it on.

So?

And Connor remembered.

Remembered the five minutes during his South Pacific getaway he had actually been something approaching to sober.

"We all have money," his new Portuguese friend on Vaomar Island had told him, "more money that we can ever spend. What we don't have are friends. So help me out there. Play a game of cards. Drink."

Vaomar Island. In his drunken stupor, still he had recognized that it might be useful someday. Vaomar Island.

His eyes darted around the room and back to the connecting door to his office. He did not have much time. What, a few minutes at the most? Then one of them—likely Josh—would stick his head in and ask him if he were ready to do the right thing, to turn himself in and wait for law and order to take its course.

Right. Law and order. As if.

As if anyone would doubt Ivers's story once they had seen the video. It was all too clear what they wanted to accuse him of... No—there was no waiting around for him. Was he making himself look guilty by running? Probably. But he did not really have one damned choice, now did he?

There were always his Swiss shares. There was always money to be made.

The hushed voices on the other side of the connecting door finally died down. He was down to a few minutes. *Now or never, Beauregard.*

The conference room had no windows, but it did have its own private washroom. And the washroom had another door into Tessa's little cubicle. Tessa—the original traitor. Somehow, he would think of a suitable punishment for her too. She would not get off easy; that much he swore to himself. He did not need anything else now, did he?

The carryon bag he had brought from his South Pacific holiday still stood where he had flung it in the corner of the room, so he picked it up again. Passport? Dare he travel with his own passport? Shit—if he stayed one step ahead of them, by the time they finally decided to search for him, he would have reached Vaomar, safe from extradition.

"Connor?"

Kayla this time. So he had been wrong about Josh. Go figure.

He stepped into the washroom and locked the door behind him, jimmying the door into Tessa's space at the same time.

See you later, losers. And don't make one single mistake. If you thought you could take my company away from me, you were wrong—you were dead wrong. Because I am going to be back.

EPILOGUE

By 10 o'clock in the morning, the sun had risen high enough, and collected enough firepower, that anyone standing out there in broad daylight, without the protection of a roof or at the very least an umbrella, was bound to perish on the inside of an hour.

The roughhewn timber walls of the little village church kept the heat outside, where it belonged, and although the good Reverend Bartholomew liked to remind his parishioners that it was God holding his sheltering hands around the little roadside church, the miniature air conditioner he had installed in his far office might have just had a little something to do with the cooling breezes he let float out into the main church off and on. Whenever it suited his purposes.

They would arrive soon, his little lambs, his flock of believers, and by then, the church had better be in decent shape. In this case, it meant evicting the drunk who slept in the last pew—the one with the comfortable cushioning—as he did rather often in the last little while.

He stood above the snoring Portuguese man for a moment and finally shoved him none too gently with the tip of his polished black boot.

"Cristos, lest you are staying for the 11 o'clock sermon, I have to insist you get your ass out of here. Not that I mind you staying, but you had better put something sizeable into the collection plate to make up for the smell and the noise coming off you."

"Fuck you, Beauregard."

"Bartholomew. If I have told you once, I have told you a thousand times."

The man and his loose tongue would be a problem one day—and one day fairly soon if he did not quit or at least curb his drinking—but the reverend didn't plan to hang around that long. By the time Cristos drank himself into a stupor and fell off the nearest cliff, he wanted to be back on the mainland, where he belonged.

For a moment, he allowed himself the pure vision of his life once he got it back, once he took his rightful seat again from those who had stolen it off him. Visualization, he called it, and he could visualize just fine. He could see himself standing there, speaking, and the crowd hanging on to his every word. If he listened really closely, he could even hear the far-off beat of helicopter blades. And he would smile and turn to the crowd listening to everything he had to offer.

Not this ragtag bunch of old and toothless natives, who brought him live chickens and eggs when they could not afford to leave a few pennies in the collection, nor the drunkard who lurked in the cool of his church—no, a real audience. Moneyed investors, and power brokers, millionaires, politicians, and movie stars. His kind of people. And when he was done—this part was his favorite—when he was done, he would wave and step back into his helicopter.

Cristos snored again.

"Yo, I told you—out of here... I still need to write today's sermon."

"Sermon—bullshit. You make it up as you go along. If you are a regular, honest-to-God priest, then I am the Virgin Mary."

"Hold your tongue, disbeliever."

Bartholomew used his best thundering voice of God and chuckled.

"Like my daddy was a preacher before me. Now get the fuck out of my church. And take your liquor with you. Sunday, my friend, Sunday is coming."

For a moment, he towered over the man crouched on the floor and raised his arms as if summoning a power greater than him. "It's Friday,

Jesus is praying, Judas is betraying, Cristos is drinking—but Sunday's coming." His voice trembled and hitched up just a notch, just enough to raise the gooseflesh on Cristo's arms. "The crowd is vilifying, but they don't even know—that Sunday is coming."

"Fuck—I'm going, I'm going, you don't have to beat me." Cristos grumbled and muttered, groped around under the pews for his right shoe and his earthen liquor bottle, the one that went with him anywhere, filled with anything from rum to moonshine to pure alcohol as far as Bartholomew knew.

"Sunday—Sunday is coming."

He finally found both, groaned, and complained while he put his shoe back on and tilted the bottle to his mouth, finishing the last available drop.

With a huge belch, he sat back, stretched his legs from him, and held out the bottle before him.

"I was with her when she died."

"That is disgusting, Cristos. Almost as disgusting as that bottle you carry with you everywhere. It's got to be crawling with germs by now. Get that thing out of my church before it…"

Cristos roared with laughter. "Ah, Reverend Bart, you are so entertaining when you get all self-righteous and stuck up, but you know what? You are the same as all the rest of us sorry white people on Vaomar—sad-looking bunch."

The bottle dropped from his fingers and clattered harmlessly to the ground, where he kicked it toward the reverend, roaring with laughter.

Reverend Bartholomew picked it up with two fingers and held it out to him again. Disgusting, not to imagine the trouble it would cause if one of his parishioners found it under the pew. Not that he had anything against a good rip-roaring drunk—but it had better be the good stuff, the imported stuff, not… He squinted at the inscription on the thing and tried to wrap his mouth around the words written there.

"What is this shit anyway, Cristos? Ladron—what the fuck…"

"Ah—but that's not what's inside, my good friend. Inside is pure scotch whisky imported straight from Scotland."

Now the reverend regretted not having asked for at least part of the brew the night before. But who could have known?

"It's still disgusting," he muttered and put it back into Cristos's hand.

"Used to be my mother's. No fucking idea where she got it from. Lord knows why I carry it with me all day long—x'cept I like it for some reason." He turned it around so he could read the inscription and declared in thundering words rivaling the reverend's, "Ladrão que rouba ladrão tem cem anos de perdão."

"He who guzzles this shit is not long for this earth," Bartholomew suggested and discreetly opened a window close to his friend.

"Bullshit. It's actually—well, it's, like, the thief who steals from another thief receives 100 years of pardon.... Like, it's not wrong to steal from a thief, you get it? No fucking idea why my mother had this. She was like more religious than your little flock of sheep here."

Bartholomew froze in mid-stride and stood still, listening to the tolling of a bell deep in his brain somewhere.

The thief who steals from a thief—like, it's not wrong to steal from a thief, you know?

His eyes lit up with a deep and passionate glow, and anyone standing close enough might have felt the shiver running through his body.

The thief who steals from a thief.

"Now, if you don't mind," he said with an effort. "If you don't mind, I still have today's sermon to write—so get."

He all but pushed his friend out the door and locked the church after him, running into his office and locking that door as well. When he had let the air conditioning calm him down for a good 10 minutes, he took a piece of paper and pen and wrote without looking up for the better part of an hour.

This one was good. This one would lure every last penny out of their pockets.

Now that he finally had his goal in front of him, he vowed to be more frugal with the money that came to him from Switzerland at far-too-infrequent intervals. Something about the last few hours had suddenly restored his determination and his energy to take back what was rightfully his.

Making sure one more time that the door to his little church office was indeed locked, he moved the carved file cabinet a parishioner had made for him aside by just a foot, enough to reveal a small gap between the floorboards beneath.

His hand slipped into the gap and pulled a sheaf of papers out of the little cubbyhole.

The notice at the top had been folded over and over and bore the creases and stains of a long journey made to the hands of the good Reverend Bartholomew, care of The Church of the Believer, Vaomar Island, South Pacific.

"Justice Department almost ready to give up," he read for the fifteenth time. "Major pieces of evidence disappeared—remainder hardly worth anything. Your day is coming. Send money now."

The little missives always ended with the same sentence—send money now—and if he could have, he would have been furious with the little shit, whoever he was, who'd been draining his financial reserves for the last few years. But if he wanted to keep those little notes coming, if he wanted to keep the hope and the faith, he had no other choice.

That note right there was all he needed to get his strength back and his spirits up. That and the writing on Cristos's goddamn liquor bottle. *The thief who steals from a thief...* Laughable. "It is not wrong to steal from a thief then, is it," he said softly and pulled the black robes of the priest over his shorts and Lacoste polo shirt. Look the part now.

They were packed in again today—his Sunday sermons always brought them out to the last parishioner. They clung to his words like they had 30 years ago, when it was still the Reverend Matthias.

"And Jesus," he said, raising his hands to the thatched roof above him, "Jesus was crucified between two thieves. And one of those thieves, he turns to him, and he says, 'Jesus,' he says, 'Jesus, remember me when you come into your kingdom! And Jesus said to the thief, truly I say to you, today you shall be with me in Paradise."

His hands rose a little higher, and his toe touched the hidden switch down by his pulpit, releasing a breeze of super-chilled air to sweep through the church. Some of the women shivered.

"You shall be with me," he said, softer now. "He forgave the thief. He pardoned him and promised him redemption. As he promises redemption to all of us."

Touch on the switch again—end of cold breeze.

"There is hope, and there is redemption for all of us," he said, smiling softly, and spread his arms. "A pardon for all of us."

His parishioners smiled broadly, and so did Bartholomew. Before his mind's eye, he could see it—the pardon. *The thief who steals from a thief receives 100 years of pardon.* What choice did he have, then, but to take back what was rightfully his and to set right again the wrong that had been done?

"Here is our redemption," he said and smiled.

For the thief that steals from another thief will receive 100 years of pardon, his own redemption.

ACKNOWLEDGEMENTS

Thanks to Scott K. for additional research, terminology and editing ("I can edit bad paragraphs, but I can't edit nothing").

Thanks to the team and staff at Paper Raven books—everybody did so much work in making this a better manuscript, and finally making my dream a reality, and to my K9 emotional support team for listening, for being there, and for getting me up and out of the chair when nothing was working at all. You all had a part in making this an amazing book. Get ready for the next ones, crew!

www.ingramcontent.com/pod-product-compliance
Lightning Source LLC
Chambersburg PA
CBHW070151120726
47909CB00001B/70